# SUMMONED

TOR TEEN BOOKS BY ANNE M. PILLSWORTH

**The Redemption's Heir Series**

*Summoned*

*Deeper* (forthcoming)

# SUMMONED

## ANNE M. PILLSWORTH

TOR°
TEEN

A Tom Doherty Associates Book
New York

SUMMONED

Copyright © 2014 by Anne M. Pillsworth

A Tor Teen Book
Published by Tom Doherty Associates, LLC
175 Fifth Avenue
New York, NY 10010

www.tor-forge.com

Tor® is a registered trademark of Tom Doherty Associates, LLC.

The Library of Congress Cataloging-in-Publication Data
is available upon request.

ISBN 978-0-7653-3589-0 (hardcover)
ISBN 978-1-4668-2657-1 (e-book)

Tor Teen books may be purchased for educational, business, or promotional use. For information on bulk purchases, please contact Macmillan Corporate and Premium Sales Department at 1-800-221-7945, extension 5442, or write specialmarkets@macmillan.com.

First Edition: June 2014

Printed in the United States of Am~

0  9  8  7  6  5  4

*To Deb, my wife and first and best beta reader,
without whom Sean would still be summoning monsters
only in my head. The page is a safer place for him.*

# SUMMONED

1

Every occult Web site agreed: For weird-ass books, Arkham was the center of the New England universe, and Horrocke's Bookstore was the black hole at the center's heart. Dad said that Sean had enough crazy stuff to read, since Uncle Gus had given him his Lovecraft collection. But Uncle Gus had also spilled that Cthulhu (aka Old Squid-Head) wasn't just a monster Lovecraft had invented, he was a god in a totally legitimate mythology way older than the Egyptian and Greek ones. Since then, Sean had been nuts to go to Horrocke's and get the real dope on Cthulhu, and so when Dad drove to Arkham to price a window restoration Sean and Eddy hitched a ride. Eddy insisted on sightseeing first, but once they hit the bookstore and found the weird-ass section even she had to admit the place lived up to its reputation. "Little Shoppe of Mysteries" was what TrueTomes.com called it. Hokey but accurate, because as Sean pulled a thick volume off the Cthulhu Mythos shelf a mystery ambushed him.

Like its neighbors, the book he pulled (*Infinity Unimaginable*) was glossy new. The book that dropped, that he just managed to catch, was old as hell; even at arm's length, it exuded the smell of an open tomb. Not a nasty mildewy rotting-flesh kind of tomb. More like a tomb in the desert, a Pharaoh's crib, all cloves and ginger and—what was that other spice thing, the bitter one?—yeah, myrrh.

Sean shifted *Infinity Unimaginable* under his arm so he could inspect the mummy-book. It was in decent shape, the black leather spine intact and the stamped gold title only a little rubbed out. *The Witch Panic in Arkham* by Ezekiel Greene Phillips. Sean and Eddy had probably seen the guy's grave in the Lich Street Burial Ground, where everyone was an Ezekiel or a Hepzibah or a Zacharias or some other Puritan name with a *z* in it.

He got a better armpit grip on *Infinity* and opened *The Witch Panic*. Paper fluttered to the floor, but thank you, Jesus, it wasn't a page from the book. The fallen bit was a newspaper clipping someone had used as a bookmark a hundred years ago, from the look of its brown and brittle edges. Sean parked both books and picked up the clipping. He'd been close on the hundred years. In fact, the clipping was older: At its top, he could make out *ham Advertiser, March 21, 1895.* "Ham" had to be Arkham. The city's newspaper was still the *Advertiser*; dumb name, made you think the paper was one big classified section. Speaking of which, a couple columns of classified ads was what he lifted closer to his face, squinting at the minuscule type. One ad was circled in faded red:

> Wanted, an apprentice in magic and in the service of its Masters. For particulars, apply to the Reverend Orne, redemption@RevOrne.com.

That "apprentice in magic" part was freaky enough. It took Sean a second reading before he got the true freakiness of the ad. You were supposed to apply to the Reverend Orne by *e-mail*? In 1895?

"Eddy!" he said. Okay, he kind of yelled.

Her voice came from the back of the store. "What? God, tell the world."

Sean grabbed his finds and threaded through stacks of new and used books to the locked cases that housed the really old stuff, the *tomes*. Eddy had been drooling over them since they'd arrived. She hadn't run out of saliva yet, judging from the way she crouched in front of the current case, fingertips to carpet, a sprinter ready to explode out of the starting blocks and right through the protective glass.

"Look," she said without turning to him. "This is like a wizard's library."

The case guarded books in Latin and German and French, in Greek and Arabic, in English rendered undecipherable by some kind of curly-swirly Gothic type, and the whole bunch of them were beat up with age. Sean would have been dripping spit, too, except what he had in his hands was even more exciting. "Eddy, check it—"

"Keep it down, will you?"

What, were they in church? He lowered his voice. "Check it out. I found this book."

"One we can afford?" Eddy tapped a discreet price list posted on the glass, and there was nothing under a thousand dollars. She stood up, sighing.

"This one about the Cthulhu Mythos." He glanced inside *Infinity Unimaginable*. "It's only twenty bucks."

"Let's see."

"Wait, here's something cooler." He had put the newspaper clipping back in *The Witch Panic* for safekeeping. He eased it out. "Read that ad."

"This is crazy old." Eddy handled the clipping gingerly. "'Gentleman recently graduated from Miskatonic University seeks position as tutor.'"

"No, the circled one."

"'Wanted, an apprentice in magic—'" Eddy shut up. Sean

watched her eyes dart over the rest of the ad, then dart to the top of the clipping. Back to the ad. Then she turned the clipping over, but all it showed was a woman in a dress with sleeves a mile wide and waist about an inch around. Finally Eddy looked up, her forehead corrugated. "Where'd you get this?"

"When I got down the Mythos book, another book fell off the shelf. The ad was inside."

Eddy relinquished the clipping and took *The Witch Panic in Arkham*. "This old book was with the new stuff?"

"Yeah. Only I didn't see it until it fell. I guess it was stuck behind the other one."

"Like someone hid it there?"

He shrugged. "Maybe."

She leafed through the pages. "This was published the same year as the newspaper. Except the clipping's got to be fake. Like a hoax. Or not even a hoax, because who'd believe in an e-mail address from 1895? Somebody made it for a joke."

"It's a damn good fake. It even smells old."

"That's because it's been sitting in this smelly book."

Leave it to Eddy to come up with a reasonable explanation. She had to be right, but Sean teased her a little. "I bet a time traveler went back to 1895 and put the ad in the newspaper, except he forgot how there wasn't any Internet yet."

Eddy kept leafing. "We better give *Witch Panic* to Mr. Horrocke. It probably belongs with the rare books."

"And then the time traveler was all, 'How come nobody's answering my ad?'"

"Shove it."

"And so he sends the ad into the future in *Witch Panic,* and it lands on the shelf behind *Infinity* just as I'm taking it down."

"No, because if that happened, the book and the ad would be new." Eddy had reached the index and was trailing her finger down the page. "There," she said. "That's what I thought."

"What?"

"The guy in the ad, redemption@RevOrne? Redemption Orne's mentioned in this book. He was married to Patience."

And Patience Orne was a total rock-star witch. Sean had been reading her name on historical markers all day. HERE'S WHERE PATIENCE ORNE LIVED. HERE'S THE COURTHOUSE WHERE PATIENCE ORNE WAS TRIED. HERE'S THE GALLOWS ON WHICH PATIENCE ORNE SWUNG. He shook his head. "But if Redemption's from Puritan times, how come he's advertising in 1895?"

Sean had walked into it, and Eddy pounced without mercy. "Because he's a time traveler?" she said.

"Ouch."

"Got another explanation?"

"No, but you do."

"Because some crazy Redemption Orne fan boy stuck a fake clipping in the book?" Eddy handed Sean *The Witch Panic*. "It's almost five. We've got to meet your dad. Are you buying *Infinity*?"

"I'm buying them both."

"You won't have enough money for the old one."

Probably not, but he was going to try. When a book jumped at you from a shelf, what else could you do?

～～

In the front room at Horrocke's, where a college girl stood behind the counter and the smell of hazelnut coffee filled the air, books wouldn't have the nerve to jump at customers. The back room was a whole different world. First off, you came in through a door with a brass plaque that read: QUISCUNQUE QUAERAT, IN-TRA. According to Eddy, who'd just aced her sophomore year of Latin, that meant "Whoever seeks, enter" or, in plain English, "Looking for something? Get your butt in here."

They had gotten their butts in, and they had been rewarded with row after row of enticingly labeled shelves. No SELF-HELP,

GENERAL FICTION, or COOKBOOKS here. It was ALCHEMY, AS-
TROLOGY, CABALISM, NECROMANCY, VOODOO, WICCA, and more.
Lots more, including the cases of tomes beyond which Mr. Horrocke sat, dwarfed by his mahogany desk, sipping espresso from
a tiny white cup.

Horrocke had been sipping from the cup when they'd first
ventured into the back room. For someone who put away so
much caffeine, he looked amazingly sleepy. He was a skinny old
guy to begin with, in a navy suit with a red silk handkerchief in
the breast pocket. The handkerchief looked like the tongue of a
smart-ass who'd been sucking a cherry Popsicle. Even creepier,
Horrocke's own tongue was Popsicle red. As Sean and Eddy approached, he touched it to his lower lip and set the tiny cup on a
tiny saucer. Under the desk, his jittering feet clicked on the floorboards as if he wore tap shoes. Maybe after they had gone, he
would dance it up around the stacks.

The idea of Horrocke getting down almost made Sean lose
it. Good thing Eddy started the talking. It sounded like she'd
already made friends with the old guy, probably while he was
mopping up her drool with the red handkerchief. "Hey, Mr. Horrocke. I think Sean's found a book he wants."

On cue, Sean put down *Infinity Unimaginable*.

"Ah," Horrocke said. "An excellent choice, Edna. I always recommend Professor Marvell's books. He's chief archivist at the
Miskatonic University Library, you know. One of the world's
foremost authorities on the Cthulhu cult. Indeed."

Would Eddy explode at Horrocke's use of her real name?
Though, duh, if Horrocke knew her real name, she must've given
it to him. Sean stopped holding his breath and said, "That's
great, Mr. Horrocke. There's this other book, though. I found it
behind *Infinity*. It kind of fell on me."

"Indeed? I hope it didn't hurt you."

"Ah, no," Sean managed. "I caught it all right. I don't think it
got hurt, either." He put *The Witch Panic* down next to *Infinity*.

Horrocke drew the old book toward himself using a pencil hooked over its top. Before he opened it, he put on white cotton gloves. Oh man, and here Sean and Eddy had been pawing it with their grubby hands. Delicately, Horrocke turned pages. "The Greene Phillips, 1895, first edition," he murmured.

First edition. Bad. Read: *expensive.*

"In good condition. Minimal foxing, sound text block."

Better. At least Horrocke couldn't accuse them of having *foxed* the crap out of the book, whatever that meant.

Horrocke had come upon the newspaper clipping and balanced it on his gloved fingertips. While he read, Sean again caught himself holding his breath. If anybody could explain the circled ad and how the clipping had been faked, it had to be Horrocke. You didn't throw around words like *foxing* and *text block* if you didn't know all about books and documents and forgeries.

Horrocke studied the clipping even longer than Eddy had. A couple times his Popsicle-red tongue touched his lower lip. A couple times he glanced toward the cases and the stacks, as if he expected to see someone there. Once he stared straight up at the ceiling, as if he followed the progress of something across it. Sean looked for a fly or spider. He saw nothing. Maybe the old guy had overdosed on espresso after all.

At last Horrocke gave up on the invisible bug. He tucked the clipping back into the book, closed it, and pushed it toward Sean. "Indeed," he said.

Indeed what? Sean and Eddy waited, but Horrocke seemed lost in contemplation of his gloved hands.

"So is that newspaper ad a crazy joke or what?" Eddy asked.

Horrocke started taking off the gloves, finger by finger. "I have no opinion of the advertisement, miss. However, I can tell you that I don't have a first edition of *The Witch Panic in Arkham* in stock at the moment, only modern reprints. I don't know how the book came to be on the shelf." He looked at Sean. "Since I don't own it, I believe the book is yours."

His? That easy? "That doesn't seem right, Mr. Horrocke."

"On the contrary, it's exactly right. The book came to you of its own accord." Horrocke's laugh sounded like somebody playing a botched scale on a flute. "I imagine it's your destiny."

*The Witch Panic in Arkham?* As destinies went, that didn't sound too hot. But who could argue with free? "Well, thanks, Mr. Horrocke, if you're sure."

"I'm quite sure." Horrocke had folded his gloves. He put them back in his desk and took out a notepad and pen. On the top sheet, he wrote: "NO CHARGE FOR THE GREENE PHILLIPS, N. Horrocke." He handed the sheet to Sean. "Give that to Miss Anglesea at the cash register when you pay for the other."

Sean grabbed both books off the desk. "Okay, thanks. I guess we better go now. We're supposed to meet somebody."

Horrocke's lips stretched in what he probably meant as a smile. "I imagine you are, Sean. Indeed. I hope you enjoy your books."

Sean couldn't get out of the bookstore fast enough. As soon as he and Eddy were through the door, he started laughing. It was part victory laughter—he'd scored a free first edition! Uncle Gus would flip when he heard about that.

It was also part freaked laughter. "That was insane," Sean said.

"What, Mr. Horrocke?"

"Him and getting this book for nothing. Got the fake ad for nothing, too!"

Eddy's cell phone rang. "Text from your dad. We're late."

She took off up High Lane, toward the old railroad station that had been converted into a boutiquey mall. The college-girl cashier had tucked Sean's books into a navy-blue plastic bag, and he shot a quick look inside to make sure *The Witch Panic* hadn't bailed now that it had seen him in the light of day.

Dad was parked outside the station Starbucks when Sean and Eddy ran up. "I was about to call you again, Sean," he said. "No, wait. I was about to call Eddy, since you forgot your phone."

Dad had griped about the AWOL phone the whole ride from Providence to Arkham. "We were at the bookstore," Sean said. He showed him the bag.

"Say no more. I know how Eddy is around books. You guys want anything here, or do we go to the pizza place in Kingsport?"

"I vote pizza," Eddy said. She and Sean piled into the backseat of the Civic. "How'd your consultation go, Mr. Wyndham? What was Ms. Arkwright like? Scary?"

The consultation must have gone well, because Dad only snorted at Eddy. "Why should Ms. Arkwright be scary?"

"Because her house is. We walked by it when we were doing the witch tour. How about that big old plaque? The Arkwright House. Anything that's the Blankety-Blank House has to be haunted."

"I didn't see any ghosts," Dad said. He had pulled out of the parking lot and turned onto Garrison Street. As they rattled over the bridge, Sean saw the tops of the ailanthus trees that choked Witch Island. "No ghosts, just plaster dust and ripped-out wiring. As for Helen Arkwright, she looks like she's about twenty years old and too nervous to say 'boo.'"

"Maybe she's nervous because of the ghosts," Sean said.

"More likely because she's trying to renovate that whole monster at once. She said the uncle who left her the house lived in the library and let the rest go." Dad shook his head. He didn't believe in letting stuff go. "That's where the stained-glass windows are, in the library. They're in rough shape, but they're spectacular. You'd like them, Sean. One of the panels has the Devil in it."

"What, like Satan?"

"Ms. Arkwright called him the Black Man. I guess that's

what the Puritans called him. He didn't look like a devil to me, though. He was in this Egyptian getup, no horns, no hooves, no tail."

Sean leaned in between the front seats. "So, are you going to restore the windows?"

"I think so. Big job. I'll have to take them out and do a full refabrication, new support system, the works."

"So you'll have to come back to Arkham?"

Dad grinned; Sean saw it in the rearview mirror. "Which would mean *you* can come back to Arkham. You have that good a time?"

"It was awesome. This place owns Salem for witches. We went to the Witch Museum, and the Witch House, and the courthouse where they had the witch trials, and Witch Island—"

"We only saw the Island off the bridge," Eddy cut in. "Sean wanted to swim out to it, but I wouldn't let him."

"No, I didn't. I wanted to rent a kayak and *paddle* out to it."

"Only there's like three waterfalls between the Island and the kayak rentals. Then we hung out on the University Green for a while. I so want to apply to Miskatonic now."

"I'm applying for sure," Sean said. "Then we went to the bookstore."

"I see you bought something."

"This book about mythology, that's all." And it *was* all that he'd bought. No need to mention the *Witch Panic* book and the newspaper clipping. It was too complicated, and Dad had just inched into the jam of cars on Main Street. Dad hated traffic. The only way he could deal with it was by turning on the classic rock station from Boston, which he did now. "Jumping Jack Flash" blared. Dad joined in without missing a snarl.

End of the interrogation, excellent. Eddy had already snagged *Infinity Unimaginable* and was slumped comfortably, reading. Sean pulled out *The Witch Panic* and let it fall open to the clipping. "Wanted, an apprentice in magic and in the service of its

Masters." If it only said "an apprentice in magic," that could mean it was hocus-pocus, saw-the-lady-in-half magic. Stage stuff. But it also said "and in the service of its Masters." With a capital *M*. That made the whole business sound more serious. Who were the Masters of magic, anyhow? And why did the guy who'd faked the ad call himself Reverend Orne? Sean checked the index. He found a listing for "ORNE, Redemption, husband of Patience, minister at the Third Congregational Church." The Reverend was a big enough deal to appear on a dozen pages.

"Hey, Eddy."

She kept reading. "This book is wicked. Can I borrow it?"

"Sure. But listen. Maybe I'll write to this Reverend dude."

That made Eddy look at him over the top of *Infinity*. "Why?"

"I don't know. He must be pretty cool, coming up with this ad and getting it to look so real. And I can ask him what the hell he's talking about, apprentices and Masters of magic and all."

"Yeah," Eddy said. She bugged her eyes out and got sarcastic-breathless. "You better do that right away. You know what Mr. Horrocke said. He said, 'It's your destiny, Luke.'"

Of course she did the Darth Vader imitation just as the Stones segued into a discount furniture ad and Dad dumped the radio volume. "What's whose destiny?" he asked.

Eddy knew better, but she was on a roll. "It's Sean's destiny to be an e-mail wizard's apprentice. See, he found this ad at the bookstore—"

She'd propped her feet up on the back of the passenger seat, so Sean couldn't kick her. *Shut up shut up shut up,* he willed in her direction.

Either his telepathy worked or Eddy came back to her senses. She knew how paranoid Dad was, especially about Internet freaks. Like they were after geek-boys, not the girls hanging their boobs out on Facebook.

"What ad?" Dad prompted. The traffic was so tight, the Civic might as well have been parked; Dad was able to turn around and look at them. Sean hustled the clipping into the book, the book into the map pocket on his door.

"This dumb joke ad," Eddy said. She'd switched voices from breathless to bored. "Apply to be a magic apprentice. Nothing much."

Dad's eyebrows vanished into the shock of hair that fell over his forehead. "You didn't really think about answering an ad like that, Sean."

"God, Dad. I was just kidding Eddy. I can't believe she took it seriously."

Eddy put her feet down and gave Sean a kick to the ankle, as if *he* were the one who deserved kicking. He stifled a yell.

"Because that would be stupid," Dad said. "You know how many scammers and predators there are on the Internet. I don't have to tell you."

Not more than ten times a day. "I know, Dad."

The cars ahead started moving. The cars behind started honking. Even so, Dad gazed at Sean for what felt like a whole minute before he faced forward and drove. "I would hope you know by now."

Sean had signed up for an online ghost-hunting course (with Dad's Visa) four years back, when he was twelve, a kid. Dad might forgive, but he never forgot. "I do know," Sean said. "Besides, I don't even have the ad. It's back at the bookstore."

He got his feet up before Eddy could kick him again. He kept them up until she glared, shrugged, and went back to reading her book.

Once off Main, the Civic cruised unimpeded toward Orange Point. Tour buses at the Hanging Ground Memorial slowed them down again. They'd checked out the Memorial that morning, or Sean would have asked to stop. The sun had dropped low enough to spill pale gold over the ocean and the cliff-top grasses and the tombstones of hanged witches. It looked like a movie scene the special-effects crew had colorized to make everything pop. Sean craned around to see the path that led to Patience Orne's grave. She'd been such a bad-ass witch that they'd planted her away from everyone else, in a little clearing surrounded by scrub blueberries and dune roses. The edge of the cliff was a few steps from her splintered stone. Sean pictured the stone new, and Redemption standing over it. Maybe he'd gotten so worked up mourning, he'd thrown himself over that convenient edge. Except he couldn't have. He'd lived long enough to put an ad in the 1895 *Advertiser.*

Sean laughed.

"What's up?" Dad asked.

"Nothing. Except I was thinking we should get double anchovies on the pizza. And pineapple."

Dad and Eddy went into bouts of bogus retching. As they began the descent into Kingsport, Sean slipped *The Witch Panic* from the map pocket and hid it under Dad's seat, where it and the newspaper clipping could stay safe until he got a chance to do something about them.

**2**

**Stupefied** by his pizza binge, Sean slept through the trip from Arkham to Providence. He woke up when they stopped at Eddy's house, but he was too late to keep her from jumping out with his Mythos book. It was after nine, and traffic was light; Dad made it home in five minutes and went straight over to his studio. His eagerness to get to work on the new commission was good luck for Sean—he recovered *The Witch Panic in Arkham* unseen and, after checking his recharged phone for messages, flopped on the back-porch glider. The scent of cloves and ginger and myrrh wafted off the pages as he flipped through them. Nice but weird. Most old books were sneezy with dust and mold. Maybe the last owner of this one had burned incense all the time, some kind of special preservative, the Crypt Freshener of the Pharaohs.

The newspaper clipping fell out on Sean's chest. He set it on the wicker table by the glider, well away from his sweating Coke can, and looked at the page it had marked. In ghost stories, people were always reading the future by picking a Bible passage at random. The passage in front of him was in an appendix of short biographies, and it was titled "The Unfortunate History of the Reverend Redemption Orne." Damn. Eddy would never believe it. She'd say Sean had marked that page on purpose, but he hadn't. The last time he'd shoved the clipping into the book had been in the car, when Dad was getting nosy and Sean was trying to get it out of sight quick. In an emergency like that, how could he have picked any particular page? Random, baby.

Sean started reading:

Redemption Orne was born in Cambridgeshire, England, in 1669, the only surviving child of nonconformist minister Jonathan Orne and his wife, Susan Cooke. In 1681, the Ornes emigrated to Boston. There Redemption attended the Boston Latin School and Harvard College and earned a reputation for scholarship, eloquence and piety that attracted the notice of such influential figures as John Eliot, in whose Algonquin Bible Redemption took much interest.

In 1690, Redemption graduated from Harvard and published several well-received tracts. His uncle Richard Orne, an early settler in Arkham and one of its most prosperous merchants, invited him to become teacher at the new Third Congregational Church. Redemption accepted and soon won the approbation of pastor Nicholas Brattle and the congregation.

Redemption also took on the spiritual guidance of a village of Christianized Nipmucs near Dunwich, where he boarded at the house of Enoch Bishop and his daughter Patience. From the Sachem, Peter Kokokoho, he learned the topography, flora and fauna of the wild interior. Of the Nipmucs, Redemption would privately write: "While during the day the Indians pray to our Lord Jesus Christ, at night, when the hills speak, I fear they turn to other gods."

Patience, too, knew other gods. Dunwich believed Enoch Bishop to be a wizard, but that lonely town knew better than to oppose him. Under Enoch, Patience had studied witchcraft since she'd been old enough to dance upon the stone-crowned hills. Though she used the craft to cure, hers remained a dark power.

It appears that Redemption was too smitten with Patience to perceive her true nature. In 1691, he married her. In 1692, following the sudden deaths of Richard Orne and his wife (deaths later ascribed to Patience's magic), Redemption became sole heir to his uncle's estate. During this prosperous period, Redemption's fame spread through the colonies, and he wrote his natural and spiritual history, *The New Wildernesse*. Soon after, their daughter, Constance, was born.

As the Witch Panic intensified and spread to Arkham, suspicion fell on Patience. As noted in trial records, the Black Man had favored her with a monstrous familiar and it had devoured many domestic beasts and several people. Many testified to seeing this daemon kill soldiers sent to arrest its mistress. Patience was hanged on Orange Point.

Redemption fell under suspicion when his secret journal revealed he had known of Patience's witchcraft. He was imprisoned but disappeared before trial. Some speculated that the Black Man had spirited him away. Others less fanciful believed he had escaped into the woods and there met some unknown but natural fate.

Much of Orne's printed work was destroyed after his fall from public grace. A few volumes and tracts may be found in the collection of seventeenth-century literature at the Arkham Historical Society, while Orne's journals have recently been removed to the Archives of Miskatonic University.

By the time Sean finished the mini-bio, the back of his neck was prickling, and not from heat rash. He had gotten the same prickle from H. P. Lovecraft's stories, the ones so loaded with details that they'd momentarily convinced Sean that in his fiction Lovecraft was telling truths the government didn't want told. The government couldn't let people know about Elder Things and transdimensional monsters and giant blobs of proto-plasm. Everyone would start jumping out windows. Well, *Sean* wouldn't jump out a window—he'd be cool with it. But that wasn't the point.

The point was, why should he get prickles from the Orne bio? It didn't give any details. Like, how did Patience kill old Richard and his wife? What did Patience's familiar look like? Did it swallow cows and passersby whole, or did it leave little bits behind, covered with slime to show how it wasn't wolves or bears that had done it? To be fair, that stuff was probably in the actual book. The bio was only an appendix.

Sean skimmed it again. Some lines popped out at him. Dunwich was afraid to mess with Enoch Bishop, a wizard. Patience knew other gods and used her magic to heal people, but it was still a dark power. All that sounded like the writer believed in witchcraft. But in the end, he poked fun at the people who thought Redemption was grabbed by the Black Man. The writer said the "less fanciful" believed that Redemption escaped and died of natural causes.

It sounded like they never found Redemption's body. What if it was because he didn't die? He was alive in 1895. He was alive right now, because he had an e-mail address. And a time machine, for traveling back to 1895.

Man, Sean was giving himself a headache, trying to come up with a logical explanation. Good thing it was fun. He glanced at the clipping, which trembled in the breeze from the ceiling fan. Then he glanced across the backyard to the carriage house.

All the second-floor windows were lit up, so Dad was still hard at it.

He carried book and clipping to the family-room computer and pulled up the e-mail account he used for online gaming. It would be safe to e-mail the Reverend from that, and, come on, it wasn't any lamer to go by *Lord Grayfalcon* than it was to go by *Redemption Orne*. Sean clicked for a new message. He read the circled ad once more. He typed: *Hey Rev, I found your want ad that says you're looking for an apprentice in magic. Me and my friend think it's way cool how you faked the old newspaper clipping. How did you do it anyway? The old guy at Horrockes didn't seem to know and if you can stump a guy like him you're good. So you're really into this Orne guy. I'm reading about him in the book where the ad was. Looks like he rocks.*

Sean paused. It was always tricky to joke on the Internet, especially if you didn't know the person. But he couldn't chicken out now. He typed again: *Anyhow I was wondering if you're still looking for an apprentice. I think I'd rock as one. Do you have to be out of high school or what? Lord G.*

No use typing more when the message would probably bounce anyway. Sean added a blind cc to Eddy and hit send.

Five minutes later, when he was deep in the latest flame war on his Warcraft forum (Orcpwner versus U_All_Sukk), he got an e-mail alert. That would be from Eddy, chewing him a new one. Except it wasn't. It was from "Reverend Orne," and the subject was "The apprentice position."

The prickles hit Sean's neck again, big-time. He stared at the new e-mail. Okay, here was what was going to happen: He was going to open it, and it was going to be a picture of some gross sex act (apprentice position, ha-ha), and under that would be a giant *LMAO noob, you fell for it.* Which would be fine; he could deal with that.

He opened the e-mail. There was no picture. There was one

scant paragraph: *Thank you for your interest in the position of apprentice in magic. I would enjoy discussing it with you. If you remain interested, chat with me tomorrow at four o'clock p.m. My ID is rorne. Cordially, Redemption Orne.*

While Sean was still cranking his jaw off the keyboard, Eddy texted him: *hey lord g get on NOW*

Sean texted back: *u got my cc huh?*

*i cant believe u did that ur so DEAD if ur dad finds out*

*omg he already answered*

*????*

*orne*

*shut UP*

*rly—he said ty 4 yr interest, chat tomorrow 4 pm.*

*u going to???*

*hell yeah*

*idk i still think ur crazy can i sit in?*

*sure ill come over yr house after work*

*good bc mom is making strwbry pies gag >_<*

Sean would get to eat Eddy's share, since she had a freakish hatred of strawberries. He was about to type *no problem* when the porch door opened, then smacked shut. A quick *gtg* was all he could get in. Eddy would understand. Luckily, Dad made a stop at the refrigerator—bottles rattled in the door. That gave Sean time to pocket his phone and tuck *The Witch Panic* and the clipping under a couch cushion.

A bottle gasped open in the kitchen. "Sean? You're not on the computer, are you?"

Sean shut it down. "No. Except to check my e-mail."

"That sounds more like a 'yes.'"

"I'm off now."

"It's almost eleven. Joe-Jack's picking you up for work at six, right?"

"Right," Sean said. Maybe it would rain. Hard. Joe-Jack

couldn't rebuild a porch in a downpour. That would give Sean a chance to hang out at Eddy's and prep for his interview with the Reverend by reading the book she'd cruised with.

"Sean? Bed."

"Right, Dad." Before Dad could come into the family room, Sean retrieved *The Witch Panic* and hit the stairs running.

3

**The** next morning was depressingly cloudless. Dad dragged Sean out of bed at five thirty, shoveled raisin bran down his throat, and packed him into the J-J REMODELING van five minutes short of six.

J-J stood for *Joe-Jack*, and Joe-Jack was Joseph Jackman Douglass, who back in his hippie days had dropped out of law school to learn carpentry. Since then, he'd been restoring old houses to their original splendor, only with all the modern conveniences. Joe-Jack was skinny, and his ponytail and beard were streaky gray, but if the working guys in his favorite working-guy bars tried anything, they'd find out that every ounce on him was knotty muscle. Not that working guys messed with Joe-Jack. He got along great with them, being all for the rights of labor except where his own employees were concerned.

For the summer, Sean and Joe-Jack's son, Beowulf, were his only employees. Beo was snoring in the back of the van, and he didn't wake up even when Hrothgar started drooling on his face and hammering his kneecaps with his hairy club of a tail. The van smelled like Hrothgar, who was always wet from jumping into the Pawtuxet River. It smelled, too, like oiled tools and raw wood and Coffee Exchange coffee, which was the only elitist thing Joe-Jack went in for. Joe-Jack poured Sean a cup from his working-guy thermos. "That's the Sumatra," he said. "They finally got some that was Fair Trade."

"Great," Sean said. At this time of day, he would have drunk it if it had been produced by child slaves in shackles. Joe-Jack brewed his coffee strong; after a few sips, Sean felt alive enough to call Hrothgar over to him. The chocolate Lab scrabbled up and stuck his head into the cab. Sean scratched him behind his damp ears. "We're on the East Side today, right?"

"Doyle Avenue. You have a good time in Arkham yesterday?"

"Yeah. I got this cool book about the witch trials."

Joe-Jack scowled. "Witch trials. That was some steaming heap of crap."

"Right. But it's interesting what people used to believe."

"The bosses never believed in witches," Joe-Jack said. "The politicians and ministers. They just used the superstitions of the uneducated to get rid of their enemies."

*Just like now.* Sean waited for it.

Joe-Jack drank off his Sumatra. "Like now," he said.

"Yeah. Hey, Joe. Will you drop me off at Eddy's later?"

"So you can read about witches?"

"I don't know. But she said her mom's making strawberry pies."

"Well, strawberry pies make sense. Save me a hunk."

Except for lunch, Sean and Beowulf and Joe-Jack worked nonstop ripping apart the porch of the house they were renovating on Doyle Avenue. Hrothgar squeezed through loose latticework and lay on the cool dirt under the decking. For a dog named after a Danish king, he was pretty democratic about how the stirred-up bugs swarmed over him. A ginormous centipede went up Joe-Jack's jeans. Sean and Beo about peed themselves when Joe-Jack hopped and dropped his pants and yelled, *Jesus-*

*H-fucking-Christ!*—which he never said around them even though it was a perfectly good working-guy expression. He didn't kill the centipede because of the oneness of being, and, shaken free, it went off to demonstrate oneness by exploring Hrothgar's orifices.

Between the heat and the grunt labor, Sean was a dripping mess when Joe-Jack dropped him off on Keene Street. Eddy lived right next door to Sean's aunt Celeste and uncle Gus; when he opened the arched gate between the houses, she vaulted like a maniac over her porch railing. "Where you going?" she demanded.

"Um, to take a shower?"

Eddy wrinkled up her nose. "I didn't know Joe-Jack did sewers. But hurry up! We have to meet the Reverend in ten minutes."

Damn, that was right. "Hold him," Sean said. Then he ran around the house to the back porch, where he pulled off his dirt-caked work shoes and socks. The screen door was unlatched. Sean let himself into the kitchen and yelled that it was him, not a burglar. He didn't wait for Gus to answer. He didn't even grab a glass of milk. He pounded up the back stairs, snatched clean clothes from his stay-over bedroom, and dashed for the hall bath.

By five after four, he was in Eddy's "office." It had been her playroom until she hit ten and inherited her granddad's rolltop desk. With that beast in one corner and a computer station in the tower bay, it did look official. Eddy was parked at the computer, Brutus the Hell Pug on her lap and chat window open. "About time," she said. "I was just going to try his ID."

Sean snagged the leather desk chair from the rolltop. Brutus hurled himself onto its seat, then dived for Sean's left flip-flop. Sean let him have it and plopped down before Brutus could realize he was losing the high ground.

Eddy had already typed *rorne* in the contact search bar. She scooted over so Sean could get at the keyboard. He settled his fingertips on the keys and stared down at the dirt still lodged under his nails. He hadn't taken time to scrub them, he'd been so frantic to be on time for the Reverend. Now, of course, he couldn't think of anything to write.

"Backing out?" Eddy said.

After sending that e-mail, he'd look like a major wuss if he didn't follow through and ace the joke. Besides, the Rev probably wasn't even online. "No way. What should I say, though?"

"Hello?"

As good an idea as any he had. Sean typed carefully, as if it were a real interview. *Hello Reverend, are you there?*

He was going to get a "not online" message. He knew it, but he knew wrong. A response popped onto the chat screen: *Good afternoon, Lord Grayfalcon. This is Redemption Orne.*

Eddy had pulled a couple iced teas from her mini-fridge. Good thing she hadn't taken a swig yet—she'd have hosed down the whole computer station. "Oh my God! Lord Grayfalcon."

"So I used my old account to mail him. Security."

Eddy mimed adjusting a headset mic. "Reverend Orne, will you accept a geek-to-geek call from Lord—"

Sean hip-checked her chair with his, gaining full possession of the keyboard zone. He typed: *Glad to meet you. You can call me Sean tho.*

"Security, hello?" Eddy said.

"He can't do anything with just my first name."

*I am very glad to meet you, Sean.*

*So what should I call you?*

*You may call me Reverend Orne, or simply Reverend.*

Brutus was sniffing Sean's right flip-flop. To get the pug away from his feet, Sean hauled him onto his lap. "He's not giving out his real name."

"His mom probably doesn't let him."

"Yeah, right. And she gets to call the shots, because he's living in her basement." Sean squinted at the chat screen, at a loss again. Finally, lamely, he typed: *Okay Reverend. So like I wrote, I found that clipping with your ad on it.*

*In* The Witch Panic in Arkham, *I imagine. At Horrocke's Bookstore.*

*Did you leave them there by accident? Because if you did, I can send them to you or something.*

*I left the book for you to find.*

*You mean for anybody to find?*

*No. I left the book for you in particular, Sean. No one else.*

Something crawled over his scalp, all cold, wispy feet, like the centipede in Joe-Jack's jeans. Eddy looked as weirded out as he felt. She sucked in air—was she going to scream? Instead she exploded into side-hugging laughter that caught him up, knocked the weirdness out of him, and made him explode, too.

"Oh my God," Eddy gasped. "Is this guy a freak or what?"

Sean, bending double, squashed Brutus. The pug did his impression of the fox that disemboweled the Spartan boy. Sean was no Spartan. He dumped Brutus and choked out, "I'll ask him. 'Are you a freak or just a nutcase?'"

"Do it."

He looked back at the chat screen. *I left the book for you in particular, Sean.* It had been a mistake to give the Reverend his real name. That gave the guy an advantage, let him pretend he *knew* Sean.

A new message appeared: *Are you still there?*

"Do it," Eddy urged.

"What?"

"Ask whether he's a freak or a nutcase."

Sean started typing the question. He erased it. "That's too snarky."

"Let me, then."

"If you won't be an asshole."

"Like I ever am. Move."

Sean yielded ground. As usual Eddy got right to work: *hey rev. i'm seans friend eddy. i'm kind of his agent.*

Jesus.

The Reverend wasn't fazed. *Good afternoon, Eddy. How can I help you?*

*we want to know how you did the ad. it really looks old.*

*The clipping is from 1895, as it says. I found it in the book when I purchased it. I changed one of the original advertisements to mine.*

"See," Sean said. "That makes sense."

*how did you change it?* Eddy typed.

The reply was instant: *Magic.*

So much for sense, but Eddy was already too into sparring with the Reverend to pounce on Sean. She leaned closer to the computer screen, like she could get in the Rev's face that way. *that's funny. seriously though.*

*I'm always serious about magic.*

*so you're a real wizard?*

*I am.*

Sean leaned forward, too. That tingle on his scalp had shifted to the back of his neck and morphed from creep-out to excitement. The Reverend was playing around, Sean knew that all right, but it looked like it could be a fun game. "Ask him if he's the Redemption Orne that's in my book."

"Why not? The more rope he takes, the higher we can hang him." Eddy typed: *so are you the same redemption dude that was around in the witch hunt days?*

*I am.*

"When was he born?" Sean said.

*when were you born then?*

No pause. *On the 28th day of February, in 1669.*

"That right?"

Where was his pack? There, on the rolltop desk. Sean propelled his chair over, pulled out *The Witch Panic,* and checked
the Orne bio in the appendix. "He's right."

"Doesn't prove crap. He's studied up on the guy. All his Internet IDs are Redemption Orne. I bet he *dresses* like Redemption
Orne. I bet he's got Redemption Orne *sheets* on his bed."

What would the sheets look like, black with little white Bi-
bles and little gold crosses? Sean jetted back to the computer
station, book in hand. "Let me back in."

"Go for it. Like I want to chat with a dead Puritan."

Sean reclaimed the keyboard, propped *The Witch Panic*
against the monitor for inspiration, and typed: *Hi Reverend.
This is Sean. I hope Eddy didn't piss you off.*

"Suck-up," Eddy said. She didn't want to talk to a dead Puritan, but she didn't mind craning over Sean's shoulder while
he did.

*Not at all,* the Reverend replied, which was nice of him.

*So you're how old?*

*337 years.*

*And you're still alive?*

*I couldn't talk to you otherwise.* ☺

"There!" Eddy said. "Like a three-hundred-and-thirty-seven-
year-old wizard would use a smiley."

Points off for the Rev or not? If a 337-year-old wizard could
use chat, why not emoticons? *Dumb question sorry. Only the book
said you probably died out in the woods?*

*No, I have never died.*

Sean's neck was tingling like crazy. *That's good. But how come
you've lived so long?*

*I once believed that it was only through the grace of the Chris-
tian god that man could live forever. I was mistaken. It is the communion of the Outer Gods that truly confers immortality.*

Eddy nudged Sean. "I'm reading about the Outer Gods in
that other book."

"Can they make you immortal?"

"Haven't gotten that far yet."

Sean typed: *What have you been doing all this time, Reverend?*

*I've traveled, in this world and in worlds beyond its frail co-coon. I've found teachers and I've taught. I've taken different names and identities—among mortals, one can't live too long and remain unquestioned, especially if one doesn't age.*

*You don't look old?*

*I look as I did when the Black Man made me immortal. I was twenty-three then.*

*So the Black Man is the same as the Devil?*

*There is no Devil. The Black Man is an avatar of Nyarlathotep.*

Nyarlathotep was a big-shot monster in Lovecraft's stories. That much Sean knew. Eddy supplied: "That's one of the Outer Gods."

Cool as hell. *But the Puritans thought the Black Man was a devil?*

*Sadly, yes. Few have ever dared to learn the truth of the worlds.*

Eddy blew a raspberry. "This guy could go on all day. Stop encouraging him."

What was wrong with encouraging him? The Reverend was way interesting. Still, Dad would come to pick him up soon. Sean was composing a see-you-later in his head when the Reverend sent another message: *We haven't discussed the apprenticeship, Sean. You wrote that you thought you'd make a good apprentice. What are your qualifications?*

That he'd played wizards in Dungeons & Dragons for years? That he'd read the Harry Potter books more times than Eddy? That Willow was his favorite *Buffy* character? Shit, his face felt like it was catching fire.

"Yeah, I'd like to know your qualifications, too," Eddy said.

"Shut up." But he did have to answer the Reverend. Should he make up a bunch of stuff? That would be fair, with all the stuff the Rev was making up. Only the Rev was supergood at it and

Sean wasn't coming up with any brilliant ideas. A crazy but compelling thought hit him: He should tell the absolute truth.

He typed: *I guess I was just screwing around. I don't have any qualifications.*

*You've never done magic?*

*For real?*

*Yes.*

*No. I mean, nobody can.*

*That's untrue. A few, a very few, are born to magical ability.*

*Not me I guess.*

*I believe you're wrong. The fact that you answered my advertisement proves to me that you have potential. Would you like to put it to the test?*

Man, the room was quiet. Brutus was asleep on a windowsill in the tower bay, and for once Eddy didn't come out with a smart crack. The computer hummed. Downstairs pans rattled. Sean might have magic potential. He could put it to the test. Bullshit, but why not answer *yes* if he felt like it? What could it hurt? Sean flexed his fingers, then typed: *Sure Reverend. That would be cool.*

"Feeding the troll, feeding the troll," Eddy murmured.

Sean shrugged.

*Very good,* the Reverend replied. *What type of magic would you like to attempt?*

Rabbit out of a hat was all he could think of, and he didn't even like rabbits. Magic from books wouldn't count, either, would it? Unless it came from nonfiction. Sean spotted *Infinity Unimaginable* in a corner, atop a teetering stack of books Eddy had labeled "TO READ," but he didn't have time to comb it for legitimate spells. He turned back to the monitor. *The Witch Panic* still leaned against it. What kind of magic had Patience Orne done? Healing stuff. Killing people stuff. He didn't have anyone to heal. Dad would definitely be against killing people. Getting a familiar—

All right.

Sean typed: *How about familiars? Like they said Patience summoned?*

This time the Reverend didn't respond at once. Maybe he was chewing over the idea. Maybe he was trying to come up with a good fake familiar spell. "I'm not kidding," Eddy began.

Sean waved her off as a new message popped up: *An interesting proposal, Sean. The familiar Patience summoned would be much too hazardous—you will have read of the havoc it wrought in Arkham. But there's another familiar that may be called with the same ritual, slightly altered. It is harmless and useful, and the ritual would be a rigorous test for you. Shall I send it?*

"Say no," Eddy said.

"Why?"

"Because, I don't know, this guy squicks me out."

"Or maybe you're just pissed that we were going to mess with his head, but he's messing the hell out of ours. We can't keep up."

*Sean?*

*Yes,* Sean typed. *That would be great Reverend, thanks.*

*You're most welcome. I'll send details of the ritual to your e-mail address. I look forward to seeing what you do with it. If you succeed, perhaps I can guide you further in magic.*

*Awesome.*

*But you must realize, the way is very difficult.*

*I bet. Like how they used to hang you guys.*

*That aside, Sean. When a young wizard begins the journey, he may have days of doubt and regret. But the days become hours, the hours minutes, the minutes mere seconds. Then, like the motes they have become, the young wizard sweeps even the seconds aside. He is free.*

The way Eddy started gagging ticked Sean off big-time. Bad enough her chin was practically on his shoulder, but the Reverend's last message was seriously deep, like something in a book you could read over and over. "Can it, will you? And if you don't like what the Rev writes, stop hanging all over me to read it."

Eddy fell back into her own chair. "What's with you?"

"Nothing! I'm just trying to read in peace, all right?"

"Read what? Dude's gone."

She was right. The Reverend had signed out of chat. "You scared him away," Sean said.

"How? I wasn't the one talking to him."

"Yeah, well, maybe he sensed how you were dissing him." But come on. How dumb-ass did that sound? Way dumb-ass, that was how dumb-ass. Sean kind of laughed. Then he all-out laughed. It was weird: Now that the Reverend was gone, Sean felt tension draining out of his muscles. It was like it had been a genuine job interview, after all.

"You're wacked," Eddy said. She was laughing, too, and Brutus started out of his nap into a barking fit. "I mean, you're as wacked as the Rev."

"Hell no. I'm not even half as wacked as he is. He thinks I'm wizard material, right?"

"Yeah, right. That's megawacked. You're still up there, though."

Sean arched his arm as if to shoot a basket from half-court. Brutus skittered around the office hunting for the imaginary ball. Taking advantage of the distraction, Eddy rammed Sean's chair broadside and retook the keyboard.

"Hey!"

"I've got to print this chat out for the Wacked Hall of Fame."

Sure, why not? "Eddy. You still think the Rev's some kid in Mom's basement?"

"Unless he's in a nuthouse."

"I'm serious. Didn't he seem kind of old?"

"What, like three hundred and thirty-seven?"

"No, regular old, like thirty?"

"Maybe. He could just be smart, though."

A knock sounded on the half-open office door. They both kind of jumped.

Rachel Rosenbaum had the life juices of a million strawberries on her industrial-strength apron. Funny how a math professor could be so into farmy stuff like pies and canning. Especially one who made everyone call her by her first name. Or maybe it wasn't funny. Understanding adults wasn't Sean's best subject. "I thought you'd be down for snacks," Rachel said. "The pies are out."

"Already?" Eddy said.

"It's after five."

No wonder Sean was so hungry, though he hadn't felt it before now. He hadn't even popped his iced tea, which stood in a puddle of condensation by the computer. "I guess I better call my dad."

"No, I called Jeremy and said you should stay for dinner. He'll pick you up around nine."

"Great, Rachel, thanks!" Sean hunted down his flip-flop; Brutus had jammed it under the radiator.

"Are we having anything besides strawberry pie?" Eddy groused.

"Thai takeout. Michael just got home with it."

Brutus was the first one out the door. Sean and Eddy lagged behind Rachel long enough for Sean to whisper, "I wonder if the Rev will send that ritual tonight."

"We'll check after dinner," Eddy whispered back.

# 4

The Reverend came through: When they got back to the office, the summoning ritual had arrived. Five single-spaced pages, it lay on Sean's Thai-and-pie-stuffed stomach, along with the printouts Eddy kept tossing over from the computer printer. Sean lolled farther back in his desk chair and stifled a belch.

"I can't believe I'm enabling you," Eddy said.

"You can't stop yourself. You're a research junkie."

"You're not going to try out this stupid thing. Remember, that's the deal."

"I just want to know what all this stuff means. Did you find out how to do an invoking pentagram?"

She swiveled toward him holding a fresh printout. After peering at the diagrams on it, she swept a star into the air with her pencil. "Only you'd use an athame, ideally."

"What's an athame?"

"A sacred Wiccan knife. But the important thing is the order you draw the lines in. Like, here's the *banishing* pentagram." She did some more pencil-sweeps.

To tell the truth, Sean didn't see the difference. "Okay. That's pentagrams. So, I get the part about summoning during the dark of the moon. But what about this Summer Triangle you're supposed to do it under?" *Summer Triangle* sounded like a Thai appetizer. His stomach groaned at the thought.

Eddy had resumed her Googlefest. A few minutes in, she said, "The Summer Triangle's an asterism. That's a star pattern that's not a constellation. Around here, you see it best in July and August. Wait, here's a cool part. 'The Summer Triangle seems to frame the star fields of the Milky Way, and the Great Rift crosses it.' The Rift's this huge dust cloud."

Sean leaned forward, bringing his flip-flops to the floor with a slap of rubber on oak. "Hey, Eddy. The Rev's e-mail says he found the ritual in the *Necronomicon* they've got at Miskatonic University. You think he did?"

"Total bull. You have to be some kind of kick-butt Mythos scholar to get at their copy. It says so right in *Infinity*."

"Okay, maybe he got it out of another magic book."

Eddy couldn't disprove that theory, so she attacked from another direction: "Why does the ritual have to be from any book? Occam's razor, the Rev made the whole thing up."

Occam's razor (or, according to Uncle Gus, "the simplest answer is likely right") was an idea Eddy had stolen from her mom. Sean itched to call it Rachel's razor, but he didn't need to get stomped. "It doesn't feel made up to me."

"You mean, like, it's giving you shivers?"

Not shivers, more like tiny cumulative jolts of excitement. "How'd he make up all these details?"

"He Googled them, like I'm doing."

"What about the incantations?"

"They're the fakest of all. If they were straight out of the *Necronomicon*, they'd be in Latin, not English."

Sean gave a last pathetic wriggle in the grip of Eddy's logic. "They're in English because the Rev translated them for us."

"Or because he made them up in English. Besides. What's he call the familiar you're supposed to summon?"

Sean flipped through the ritual printout. "An aether-newt."

"And it's a familiar that carries messages, right?"

"So?"

"Aether-newt, Ethernet. It's so fake, it's a pun."

"Coincidence."

"Pun, pun, pun. Fake-ass pun."

Was she right? It would suck, the way that would cheapen the ritual, even if the Reverend was only playing around with them, which Sean wasn't so sure he was. After reading the ritual, Sean was more willing to bet that the Rev really believed in magic than that he was a joker. Yeah, he could be one of those nutcases who seemed rational, apart from their one little nutty habit. Like Hannibal Lecter. Or maybe that wouldn't be a good comparison to share with Eddy. "Whatever. Look up that last thing, the powders you have to throw in the fire."

"All right, but that's it. I have to research some stuff for my summer project. You know what you're doing yet?"

"No." The worst thing about going to the Abraham Whipple School was how students had to do summer projects every year, starting in freaking kindergarten. Sean had been out of ideas since third grade. At least, ideas his teachers and dad would approve of. Sean tilted his desk chair into full recline and reread the section of the ritual with the aether-newt in it:

By these devices, you may summon two types of familiars or SERVITORS. The first is an ethereal—it has no material substance as most understand material. At its most visible, the AETHER-NEWT appears to be made of molten glass, but more often it is no more than a brightness enclosed in a soap-bubble skin. The clever wizard can even render it invisible to all but himself.

The aether-newt is harmless, though its ceaseless activity may make it an unnerving companion at first. Once it is bound to a master, it will patrol his home or go where he wishes and carry back intelligence. Material barriers are nothing to it—it passes through them as readily as through the void of space. Only strong magical wards can stop it.

The second Servitor is granted material form through the sacrifice of blood, and blood and flesh nourish it in our sphere. This is the sort that Patience summoned. Well-grown, the BLOOD-SPAWN can defend its master and destroy his foes. It must be strongly bound to the summoner's magical will, for though it may not harm the summoner whether bound or not, it will kill others for its food and sport. The blood-spawn is, in fact, one of the lesser minions of the Outer Gods themselves. Only a seasoned wizard should consider summoning it, and then only if he is favored by the Outer Gods, as they are jealous of their minions. (For these reasons, I don't include the specific incantation for calling the blood-spawn, only the one for the aether-newt.)

See, that was like really believing in magic, how the Rev worried that Sean couldn't handle a blood-spawn or the Outer Gods. Eddy had *Infinity Unimaginable* by the computer now. Sean popped up, snagged it, and reclined again. He opened the book to the introduction and savored the weirdness:

One might say it's a doomed enterprise to describe what cannot be imagined, especially when the unimaginable is infinity itself. However, this is the task students of the Cthulhu Mythos have always faced. The boldest of them was the medieval Arab Abdul Alhazred. In the *Necronomicon* (Book of Dead Names), he even dares to *name* infinity, and the name he gives it is Azathoth.

And what is Azathoth but Chaos, the primal mindless

force at the center of the universe? We moderns envision Azathoth as the singularity that has been expanding since the first moment of time; to use the popular term, the Big Bang. Cosmologists might even imagine it as a force from which multiple universes are spawned, like exploding buds from its "skin." Azathoth is the chief of the Outer Gods, and it is the Outer Gods and all they have wrought that the Cthulhu Mythos chronicle.

Cthulhu, ironically, is not an Outer God but the chief of a Greater Race which colonized Earth before the advent of man. Mighty as he is in the mythology that bears his name, his magic is no different in kind from other magicians', for all magic derives from the Outer Gods, who are its Masters. Azathoth is the Daemon Sultan, the ultimate source of energy. Nyarlathotep is Azathoth's Soul and Messenger. Yog-Sothoth is the Key and the Gate, keeper of knowledge. Shub-Niggurath is the She-Goat of a Thousand Young who turns force into matter. Thus, while the Christian mythos posits a Trinity, at the core of the Cthulhu Mythos is a Tetrad: the Father, the Mind, the Memory, and the Mother.

"All magic derives from the Outer Gods, who are its Masters." That line was a perfect fit with the Rev's ad: "Wanted, an apprentice in magic and in the service of its Masters." However much Eddy dissed him, the Reverend knew his stuff.

Sean stowed *Infinity* between his thigh and the chair arm. He went back to the beginning of the ritual and reread the whole thing. Those tiny jolts of excitement started again. There was stuff in the world you couldn't even dream about if you were a guy like Dad. Mom had been different. Crazy shit? Bring it—she'd always had as great a time with weirdness as Sean did, only, you know, being a mom, she'd known when to say "Enough, back to reality."

Directly over his face, the ceiling fan whirred at top speed, but it wasn't the tepid downdraft that was giving him goose bumps. Their prickle wasn't a bad feeling, like you'd get from a chill. It was more the aftermath of a great rush. Like you were rock climbing and got stuck under an overhang, then made a cat-scramble against gravity to the next safe spot, where you could rest and look at a bigger-than-ever view.

Sean tilted to his feet. He squeezed around Eddy's workstation into the tower bay; with its five windows, it was the perfect spot for surveillance. Left, he could look to the top of Keene Street. Right, he could look all the way down it. Straight ahead, across the street, he could spy on the house where the Partingtons had lived, empty now, FOR SALE. The dropping sun smeared fire across its curtainless windows. As the light faded off the glass, Sean thought he saw a ghost inside the house, gliding from window to window, but it was only the reflection of a guy skimming by on a bike.

Sean was still holding his printouts. He tossed them on the workstation and sat on the cool radiator. It came out of him then, not really surprising him, because he must have been thinking about it for a while. Subconsciously and all. "Hey, Eddy. Don't rip my head off, but I think I'm going to do the ritual."

Her eyebrows contracted dangerously.

"Just for fun," he added. "I'm not going to report back to the Reverend or anything."

"What could you even have to report? It's not going to work. Tell me you get that, at least."

"Duh. I said 'just for fun.'"

"What's so fun about fake magic from Internet weirdos?"

If she didn't feel it, there was no use trying to explain. Sean went over to check the calendar on her desk. "Maybe I can even do it this month. Little black circle's the dark of the moon, right? That's July 25."

"I so don't know you."

"My dad will be away that whole week doing consultations. It's perfect."

Eddy picked up her copy of the ritual and studied it with a funny frown pulling back her lips. After a couple of minutes, she said, "I told you I don't like this Reverend thing. He skeeved me out, how he wouldn't stop the bullshit about being Redemption Orne. And this skeeves me out, too." She waved the ritual, then dropped it back on the desk. It landed askew. "And I know that's stupid, so you don't have to tell me."

What bothered Sean was how Eddy didn't straighten up the ritual printout. Normally she'd knock the hell out of pages to get them in perfect alignment. "I'm not saying the guy isn't a freak, staying in character all the time. But Phil does that, too, and he's all right. Well, kind of. I mean, he's harmless."

Eddy snickered before she got all serious again, which was progress. "Yeah, but Phil's our friend. We know we can cut him some slack. The Reverend? Don't know him, no slack."

Sean made another concession: "The ritual *is* a little skeevy where you throw the human blood in the fire."

"Yeah, that's gross. Who's going to hang around while you siphon blood out of him?"

Sean moved to Eddy's side of the workstation. Since Eddy had hit thirteen, Rachel had made her leave doors half-open when she was hanging with guy friends. Kind of an insulting precaution when Sean was the guy. Come on, he'd hung out with Eddy since they were babies. Messing with her would be like messing with his sister, so all the open doors did was make it hard to talk about Not-Mom-Safe stuff like blood sacrifices. And if you couldn't talk about blood sacrifices with your BFF, who could you talk with about them? He lowered his voice to a whisper. "I'd use my own blood."

Eddy, too, went into whisper mode. "The Reverend says you can't. You're supposed to use the blood of an enemy."

"Well, anyhow, it doesn't matter. Blood's only in the ritual for a material familiar, and I can't do that one. The Rev left out the incantations for it."

"So you have to do the Ethernet thing?"

"Aether-*newt*. The powders are the only hard part of that ritual. You find out anything about them?"

"Powders of Zeph and Aghar, a big nothing. Rev made them up. Use salt and pepper."

"But he says where to get them." Sean pulled the relevant page from Eddy's discarded ritual. "'For the Powders of Zeph and Aghar, you may apply to Mr. Geldman of Geldman's Pharmacy in Arkham, an excellent compounder of complex materia.'"

"I Googled the place. Nothing."

"It could be too old-fashioned to advertise on the Internet."

"Or else it's a secret known only to witches." Eddy was back to normal—she started humming the *Twilight Zone* theme.

If any town would have a secret witch pharmacy, it would be Arkham. "Dad's going to take out Ms. Arkwright's windows pretty soon. I'll go along and look for Geldman's."

"Just don't ask the Rev for directions," Eddy said. "He finds out you're doing his crazy spell, he'll think you're his soul mate."

"I told you I wasn't talking to the Rev again. About anything."

Eddy shrugged. She dragged down her Favorites list and opened a site with pictures of quilts on it. "Whatever. I've got to work on my project. Which is what you should be doing, instead of playing wizard."

Sometimes Eddy sounded so much like Dad it was scary. Sean squinted up at the ceiling fan, and just like that, the Eternally Whirring Blades delivered the answer: "Hey! I'm going to do the ritual and write it up for my project!"

"Okay, you've officially cracked. The project's to try something from another culture."

"Right, and magic's from another culture. Lots of other cultures. I bet the Reverend stole crap from all kinds of real mythologies. Like the Outer Gods. They're real mythology."

This time Eddy shrugged all the way up to her ears. "It's your grade, not mine."

"I guess doing a ritual is as good as making Panda quilts."

"Pa *Ndau,* Cambodian story cloths. At least I'll have something to show. What'll you have, your familiar?"

"I'll paint Brutus green and tape a mop to his face. Or, since I'm doing the aether-newt and you can make them invisible, I'll just point up in the air and say, 'There it is.'"

"Shut up, I'm working. Anyway, there's a car outside. It's probably your dad."

Sean slid back into the tower bay. The Civic idled in front of Aunt Celeste's, and Dad stood on the sidewalk, talking to her and Gus. Sean grabbed his printouts. "Can I take the book?"

"I guess, since you need it for your totally legit project. And don't forget the pie Mom wants you to take home."

As if he could've forgotten it. Rachel waited at the front door with *two* pies. Good thing he'd tucked printouts and *Infinity Unimaginable* into his backpack, along with *The Witch Panic.* He had a lot of reading to do. And he had to start memorizing the ritual incantations.

A real sorcerer wouldn't carry a cheat sheet, would he?

# 5

**There** was no way Sean could avoid telling Dad about the summoning ritual, not if he wanted to practice it at home. When Dad looked at him cross-eyed (natch), Sean produced Eddy's stack of printouts to prove the ritual was serious schoolwork. That helped. So did saying he'd found the ritual in *Infinity Unimaginable,* a book by a bona fide professor, published by a bona fide university press. It was an outright lie, but admit some freak on the Internet had sent it to him? As a wizard-apprentice test?

Sometimes he had to keep Dad in the dark, the way they used to hood falcons to keep them calm.

"If I go along with this," Dad said, "will I have to torture you to get your project done?"

"Not a chance," Sean said, and that was the absolute truth. "I'd *want* to do it."

"That's what worries me. You promise not to blow anything up or cause widespread havoc?"

Sean promised. The Reverend would have mentioned it if the powders were explosive. As for widespread havoc, Sean would do the summoning in an isolated place, so any havoc would be strictly local.

The isolated place was easy: the closed-down Pawtuxet Industrial Park. It was a short bike ride from his house, and the parking lot by the river commanded a clear expanse of eastern sky, where the Summer Triangle would rise. As long as no cops or partiers showed up, he'd have privacy.

Site, check.

Figuring out site prep was the next step. The ritual called for a pentagram in a circle twelve feet across, and the day after getting Dad's permission on his project Sean tried to draw one on their driveway. His wobbly attempts brought Dad out to help. He hammered a nail into the blacktop and tied a six-foot string to it. On the other end of the string, he tied a piece of chalk. Then he walked around the nail, keeping the string taut as he dragged the chalk along the blacktop to make a perfect circle. Next Dad marked off five equal arcs on the circle and drove nails into the marks, which were where the points of the pentagram would go. By stretching a chalked line between two nails and snapping it from the center, he left a guideline on the blacktop. When he had all five guidelines, he chalked over them, and there: a pentagram.

Dad's opinion about any project: Make your work clean and accurate, like a good draftsman. Sean wasn't sure you had to be so fussy about neat circles and straight lines when you were doing magic; from all his reading, he was getting the impression that the thought behind the symbols mattered more than their execution. Still, he had to admit Dad's pentagram looked great. Check off the magical circle as doable.

For the next couple of weeks, Sean studied the more subtle parts of the ritual. His pentagram had to be "invoking" to call in energies. If you were drawing it in the air, you'd point your arm straight forward and sweep it from forehead to left foot. Left foot to right shoulder. Right shoulder to left shoulder. Left shoulder to right foot. Back to forehead. Pentagrams could also be either upright or inverted. Upright ones stood on the "legs" of the star, the two lower angles. Inverted ones balanced on the "head" of the star, the single apex angle. Some sources said the inverted pentagram was a symbol of black magic. *Infinity Unimaginable* said no, it was just a question of whether you wanted to attract or dispel energies. Since the Reverend's ritual had the summoner standing between the "leg" angles (called Earth and Fire), facing the "head" angle (called Spirit), Sean decided his pentagram must be an upright one. It all depended on your point of view, though. To Mrs. Ferreira next door, the pentagram had to look inverted. Pretty much every day he practiced, Sean heard her muttering in her yard about hex signs or glimpsed her peering through curtains and wagging her fingers to ward off curses.

Unlike Mrs. Ferreira, Zoe and Ethan from across the street thought the ritual was awesome. They especially liked it when Sean practiced throwing the Powders of Zeph and Aghar (salt and pepper for now) into the old tailgater grill he used for a brazier. But Zoe and Ethan were just little kids, and their approval couldn't outweigh the wrath of Mrs. Ferreira. Toward the end of the second week, when Sean had been shouting incantations for an hour, Mrs. Ferreira stalked up the driveway to Dad's studio. A few minutes later, she stalked back home, silent as death, with Dad on her heels. "I think you've done enough summoning," he told Sean.

"For today?"

"For permanently. Look at it this way: You can write in your project paper how a city neighborhood is no place for a wizard."

Sean would have flipped Mrs. Ferreira's bungalow the bird, except she was sure to be spying. Besides, he wasn't that pissed. He'd practiced enough. Now he needed to get over the last hurdle in the ritual. In the center of the pentagram, he had to draw something called the Elder Sign. Okay, but *which* Elder Sign?

There were two: the Star, which looked like a pentagram with a single flaming eye in the middle; and the Branch, which looked like a spruce twig sprouting five smaller twigs. The problem was, the Reverend hadn't specified which one to use.

Sean nagged Eddy into helping him research the Sign. She'd come to only one of his practice sessions, and that had been to bust on him for not driving to the beach the day before with her and Gina and Keiko and Marc. Oh, and for pulling a no-show on Saturday, when Sean was supposed to meet her and Phil at the movies. Sean had honestly forgotten about the movies, and he'd gone to the beach every other time the crowd went. Well, except for those two times the week before, but come on—for once he was throwing himself into a project, and all she could do was try to lure him away? He countered with that accusation, blah blah blah, guilt guilt guilt, until she gave in, not because he'd made her feel guilty (like that would ever happen) but just to shut him up. She scoured the Internet, then voted for the Branch Elder Sign, which most sources said governed limiting or confining magic. She reasoned that the Sign was only there to keep the familiar from escaping before Sean bound it as his servant. That kind of made sense, but on the other hand, the Star Elder Sign governed creation and calling magic. Summoning a Servitor was both of those, right? Besides, the Star looked way sharper than the Branch.

Behind Eddy's back, Sean wrote to the Reverend and asked about the Sign. Three times.

The Reverend didn't answer. And he didn't answer. And he didn't answer.

"He's probably been hauled off to the nuthouse," Eddy said after Sean confessed to the e-mails. She grabbed *Infinity* from him. "Besides, it doesn't matter which Elder Sign you use. Listen: 'The human mind requires symbolism to convert magical intention into magical action. Hence we associate abstract concepts of energy with the elements of Air, Fire, Water, Earth and Spirit. Then we create symbols like the pentagram to further concretize the abstract concepts.'"

"What's that have to do with anything?"

"You said it just the other day, when you were griping about your dad having to draw the pentagram perfectly. Symbols are props. So if you *think* you've got the right symbol, you've got the right symbol."

Yeah, Sean had read that part of the book a million times, and a million times he hadn't 100 percent gotten it. "Like I can use a smiley face for the ritual, as long as I believe in it? I don't think so."

Eddy slapped the book closed "You know what? You're obsessed."

"Bullshit."

"For one thing, you weren't going to contact the Rev again."

"Big deal. He's ignoring my e-mails."

"Talk about your dad having to do stuff just right. You keep practicing and practicing this ritual like it was actually possible to screw it up. Like your Ethernet thingie could get stuck half-way through the interdimensional whozit, ew, gross. It's a *joke,* okay?"

Funny. This was the first time he'd gotten excited about something without Eddy coming along for the ride and ending up at the steering wheel. He'd freak if he thought about it too much. The aroma of Rachel's latest batch of pies wafted into Eddy's office, still tart and sweet strawberry, like summer breathing. "It's not a joke," he said. "I'm doing my project on it."

"You think Mr. Boyd's going to know it if you pick the wrong Elder Sign?"

"He'll know it if I'm just screwing around. What about your Panda quilt?"

"Pa Ndau!"

"It's supposed to tell a Cambodian folk story, right? What if you took a story and goofed on it? It'd be like dissing Cambodians."

"You're worried about dissing wizards?"

"Not wizards. I don't know. Magic. Mythology and stuff."

Eddy rubbed her chin with *Infinity*'s spine. "All right," she finally said. "I guess you have to find out as much as you can." She rubbed some more. "You still going to Arkham tomorrow?"

"Yeah, Dad and Joe-Jack are taking out the Arkwright House windows. I'm going to look for that Geldman's Pharmacy afterwards, where the powders are supposed to be."

"Yeah, the powders, great. Well, Helen Arkwright works at the MU Library. I bet she knows the Marvell guy who wrote this." Eddy chucked him *Infinity Unimaginable*. "Maybe she knows about the Elder Sign. Couldn't hurt to ask."

This was why you wanted Eddy on your side—she always came up with a plan. It *could* hurt to ask Ms. Arkwright about the sign, if she laughed at Sean. But he'd risk it. Otherwise he might as well make a Panda quilt for his project, and no way he was doing that.

~~~~

**Jeremy** Wyndham was scheduled to return on July 21, rain or shine. He was getting the shine. By mid-morning, the garden thermometer had already swung its scrolled pointer past eighty-five; even in the usually airy library, Helen felt stifled. She stood in the center of the long room and looked up at *The Founding of Arkham*. It was her last chance to look before Jeremy took away the stained-glass windows for who knew how long. A couple months, he'd said, but renovating the rest of Uncle John's house had taught Helen that in contractor jargon *a couple* rarely meant two, more like five or six.

The center window showed five Puritans on a hilltop. Three soldiers in helmets and breastplates brandished muskets. A minister in austere black knelt and bowed his forehead to tented fingertips. Behind him, a more elaborately dressed gentleman seemed to scour the sky for the trumpeting angels the occasion merited. The angels hadn't shown up. In the background, with the softness of distance suggested by opalescent glass, was a curve of cliffs and spread of water: the mouth of the Miskatonic, as accurate as a photograph. Three ships floated in the river, sails furled.

The soldiers weren't as rapt as the minister and gentleman— they stared toward the right-hand window, in which Indians climbed the seaward slope. The Indians carried bows, but the leader had both hands raised, empty. Another Indian shouldered a slain buck, another strings of fish. They looked more interested in a barbecue than a massacre.

The left-hand window showed the landward slope, which was heavily wooded. At the forest's edge, a crow took wing against the pearly sky, cast off by a figure almost hidden in the trees. Helen stepped closer and studied him for the thousandth time. The figure didn't fit. Even as a little girl she'd known it. He was an allegorical figure in an otherwise historically accurate design, a man dressed in Pharaoh-chic, with skin the color of onyx and eyes all-over amber, no irises, no pupils. Uncle John had called him the Black Man, the Devil, a monster lurking in the wilderness, always ready to torment the righteous and to harvest unwary souls. The Black Man used to give her nightmares.

He still did. Well, not the Black Man per se, but the whole complex of gorgeous and precarious glass. Every morning of the three months since she'd inherited the house, she'd expected to come into the library and find the windows strewn across the floor. They were sagging, and some of the glass had cracked, and there was an ominous powdery corrosion on the lead cames. In many places, light oozed between lead and glass. Around the minister's head and the Black Man's upraised hand, it created accidental haloes that looked like clever design. But light leaks meant the putty had deteriorated, and where light could leak so could water, and water was the great destroyer. Another lesson she'd learned from ruined ceilings and rotted floor joists.

The windows had made it through one last night, which was all they had to do. Their savior was coming today to remove and restore, to reinforce and reinstall, all to the tune of thirty thousand dollars. Helen winced. The money would come out of her inheritance, and thirty thousand out of a million was, if not a drop from the bucket, no more than a ladleful. Even so, it was more than a year's earnings for many people, including her, this time last year.

She gave the tender flesh below her elbow crease a little chastising pinch. The library had been Uncle John's sanctum. It had been her own sanctuary even before she could read the books she hauled off its shelves. Of course she had to restore the windows: They were the library's heart. Wrong. They were its inward-looking eyes, and that was a perfect metaphor for her uncle's life, wasn't it? If not for her own.

The sun dashed gouts of color onto her sandaled feet. Her left looked jaundiced yellow, her right a necrotic green. She backed away from the chromatic contagion, toward the library doors. The Black Man watched her go, smiling his perpetual slight smile, evidently unworried about his approaching dissolution. No, he fully expected to be resurrected shinier than ever.

Helen bumped the doors open with her pack and traversed the hall as quickly as she could without knocking over stepladders or slipping on drop cloths. Plaster dust rose around her. She held her breath until she got outside. The house faced north, not good feng shui, but at this time of day, that meant the front steps were in the shade. She settled herself on cool stone, knees to chin, like the Helen who'd spent so much time here after school in the fall and winter and spring, after day camp in the summer, waiting for her father to leave work at the bank and come drive her home to their sensible ranch in the suburbs.

Uncle John's house had been a sort of remedy to the ranch, an echoing castle that went on forever when measured by her little-girl steps. In the castle library, John Arkwright had lived like a sorcerer surrounded by his grimoires, and scattered through the warren of rooms had been curios from all the impractical places he'd visited. Helen remembered lying in front of the library fireplace, devouring a folio of medieval woodcuts while snowy twilight drew in outside. She remembered climbing to the attic and wiping a spy-hole in a cobwebbed window so she could look out over the rooftops and the blurry lights of the city, all the way down to a wall of mist that made the harbor the edge of the world. The Arkwright House! When her parents and John had debated to whom he'd leave the place, nobody had voted to make it a bequest to the university. Though her father had always considered the house a white elephant, it had been in the family for too long to let it go. Besides, if John also left enough money to restore it, and Helen really loved it enough to take on the responsibility . . .

Helen had always loved the Arkwright House. God help her, she still loved it, but she'd assumed she wouldn't become the Arkwright in residence until she was, oh, a comfortable fortysomething with a comfortable forty-something husband and two or three kids old enough to know that lead-paint chips weren't a good snack choice. Instead she was twenty-five, with a master's degree in her pocket, but her archives and record management Ph.D. abandoned for the moment. There'd been no way she could have turned down the job she'd be starting in less than two months.

So, yes, to be honest with herself, it wasn't merely the geriatric ailments of the house that were making her cat-nervous. John had carried through on another vision of her future they'd concocted when she was a kid: that Helen would join the dynasty of Arkwright archivists at MU. He'd retired shortly before his death, leaving Theophilus Marvell head of the Arcane Studies Archives; and, on John's strong recommendation, Marvell had recruited Helen as his assistant. Her parents had recently moved to North Carolina; she'd been looking for opportunities closer to them, but even they had said the MU position was a plum she shouldn't refuse. She'd accepted, planning to stay with John until she found an apartment, during which time she'd pick his brain on the Archives. She had come and stayed, but John hadn't had the time or energy to pass on the torch of his scholarship. Typical of him, hater of fusses and long good-byes, he hadn't told the family about his diagnosis of pancreatic cancer until three weeks before it killed him.

She swallowed pain that still tasted raw and shrugged off her backpack. It bulged with books about the Cthulhu Mythos, handpicked by Marvell as her formal introduction to the treasures she'd help him guard, as Uncle John had guarded them, and Great-Grandfather Henry before him, right, that Arkwright dynasty. She had some basic knowledge of the Mythos from college courses in comparative mythology, but she'd worried Marvell would expect her to know a lot more, given it had been John's obsession. She'd worried for nothing. Their first meeting that spring, Marvell had said he knew John had never shared with her the details of his work. Mythos scholars were notoriously secretive and even—Marvell would admit it—a bit paranoid about the public learning the cosmic implications of their studies. He and Helen had shared a laugh, but now that she was deep into her Mythos books she couldn't pretend they were cozy reading. Fascinating, compelling, yes. Cozy, no, not at night in the vast old house, not at noon in her MU office, not now, in the open air of morning.

Helen looked down College Street. There was little traffic; July plus Friday meant a weekend exodus of summering staff and students. Through the gates opposite the house, she could see only one boy perched on the marble lip of the Pickman fountain. Beyond the fountain, a parrot-gaudy cluster of tourists crossed the University Green.

A van turned the corner: Clegg's Landscaping. Helen glanced at her watch. Nine twenty. Jeremy wasn't due until ten, but she had Marvell's latest letter to fill the time.

It was in the outer pocket of her backpack. Helen twitched the letter from its envelope and smoothed it on her knees, enjoying the roughness of the honey-colored sheets. They were lokta paper, handmade in Nepal. Buddhist texts had survived two thousand years on paper like this—talk about something an archivist could love. Marvell used it for all his correspondence.

> *Dear Helen:*
>
> *Write and tell me how hard you're working. I'm having too good a time here in London and need some guilt to keep me sober. Days in the bookshops, nights at the theater. Going to Scotland on the first of August—the enclosed card has my number there. But before I get lost in the mountains, I want to bring up something we'll need to discuss when I get back to Arkham. Lately I've been thinking about it, and I've decided to break the ice in writing.*

When she'd first read this paragraph, Helen had felt suddenly cold, catastrophizing: Now that they'd worked together for a couple months, Marvell was sorry he'd hired her. She couldn't blame him. He was fairly new to the Chief Archivist position himself, and he'd still be teaching—he didn't need an assistant barely out of graduate school. But firing her wasn't the ice he'd broken. Another van turned the corner, a florist this time. Helen blotted her upper lip with the back of her wrist. Then, fanning herself with the first sheet of the letter, she focused on the second.

*When your uncle John became ill, he asked me to safeguard some personal papers that you'd otherwise have found among his effects at the Arkwright House. At this point, John and I had agreed you'd be a good candidate for my assistant. Your uncle was eager for you to follow him at MU, but he was also concerned that you be properly prepared.*

*He turned to me not only because we were friends, but because I'm head of Arcane Studies. Your Latin and Greek would be powerful tools for tackling the Mythos, but still, you'd need help. I was to oversee your education in his place. I was also to decide when you should read John's papers.*

*Most are letters and journals written by himself and by Henry Arkwright, recounting experiences known only to a select circle of their associates. You need to know about these experiences and associates. But the papers are disturbing in a way that you'll understand now that you've started studying the Mythos.*

*I think you'll be able to do the papers justice by summer's end and so I want to pique your curiosity in advance. Curiosity is vital to anyone in our field, courage being the other essential. Your uncle believed you have plenty of both. I believe it, too, Helen.*

*Forgive me for not mentioning the papers sooner, and for writing now in this pulp-fiction manner. Don't worry about the papers, either. I'll help you with them. Study, but get some sun, too, and write back when you can.*

*Yours,*
*Theo Marvell*

Speaking of the sun, its white brilliance was rising like a tide up the steps. Helen bumped her butt up a couple to keep her toes in the shade. She folded the lokta sheets and returned them to the envelope. Soon she'd have the damn letter memorized. So the withheld papers described experiences known only to a select circle? About the experiences she was ignorant. About the circle she had a clue.

There had been rare days when she hadn't gone to her uncle's after school or camp because he was hosting his "club" in the library. The one time she'd been in the house during a meeting, John had warned her to stay in the front parlor. She obeyed, but she cracked the parlor door so she could peek at the arriving guests. Most looked like professors or librarians, no excitement there. One, though, was a woman in a police uniform; another, an Indian with a long black beard and orange turban. The last to come was a Native American man. He startled Helen by looking her in the eye she'd fixed on the hall. He looked, and he grinned, and he made a circling motion with his right hand, index and middle fingers extended toward her. The wind must have followed him into the house—she felt it gust against her cheek as the parlor door swung slowly inward and latched shut.

Later, when she dared to creep to the library doors, she heard someone say, angrily, that there had been "a manifestation, a verified manifestation." She felt sure the odd-cadenced voice that answered was that of the Native American, who said, "Yes, it's him, of course, Nyah-Tepp."

Nyah-Tepp was the name as she'd heard it then, meaningless. Only recently she'd realized the Native American had named Nyarlathotep, Soul and Messenger of the Outer Gods. Anyone who mentioned a god so casually had to be a member of a "select circle," didn't he?

As for what the withheld papers contained to make John think she needed protecting from them, she had a theory. In her new studies, Helen had read cases of scholars and cultists who'd suffered psychological repercussions from contact with Mythos documents and artifacts: crippling anxiety, obsessions, even delusions about the reality of the Mythos and its creatures. Was Marvell hinting that Uncle John and Great-Grandfather Henry had been deranged by their work? Well, as soon as Helen had learned the word *eccentric,* she'd applied it to her uncle. Had he been more than eccentric? What about Henry? There was that ridiculous Dunwich story Lovecraft had written, thinly disguising Henry Arkwright as "Dr. Armitage." In public Henry had insisted nothing supernatural had happened in Dunwich—bootleggers had haunted the village, not monsters from beyond. But had Henry been less skeptical in private, in his papers?

Great. Her new job and the crumbling house weren't enough to worry about. Let's add mysterious documents that might disclose a family weakness to crack and start believing in the craziest mythology on record. Be fair, though. Marvell hadn't said anything about a family weakness. Helen had concocted that herself. Which maybe supported the family weakness idea?

She needed a vacation, at least a mini-one. Today, instead of going straight to the library, she'd go to Tumblebee's Café and dive to the bottom of a large vanilla latte. She could sit outside to answer Marvell's letter, tell him she wasn't angry about the withheld papers, only confused. That was close enough to the truth. And to finish the mini-vacation, she could stop in the pharmacy across the street, the one with all the homemade nostrums and the old-fashioned soda fountain. One of Mr. Geldman's cherry colas would be just the thing to power her afternoon reading.

A Ford Econoline van pulled off West Street into College. Its battered white side bore the legend J-J REMODELING, but she could see Jeremy Wyndham in the passenger seat. Helen hoisted her backpack and went down the steps to meet him.

Jeremy introduced her to the driver, a compact man with grizzled ponytail and beard: Joe Jackman Douglass, carpenter. "Joe-Jack," the carpenter said, before throwing open the van doors and hauling out lumber.

"That's for frames to transport the windows in," Jeremy said.

"Sounds good." Would the day ever come when she wouldn't be standing on the curb planning her escape from a work crew? "You won't need me, will you?"

"No, not if you've left the doors open."

"They're open. You have my cell number?"

Jeremy checked his cell. "Right here."

A lanky boy, fifteen, sixteen, jumped out of the van at the rear end of a stack of plywood. He and Joe-Jack hustled the stack up to the entry porch. Then the boy bounded back down. He had sandy-brown hair, straight, even wispy, very unlike Jeremy's black waves. But their identical blue-gray eyes and long, straight noses were a giveaway.

"Ms. Arkwright," Jeremy said. "This is my son, Sean."

She took the boy's oversized hand. The calluses on his palm told her that this plywood hadn't been the first he'd wrangled. "Hello, Sean."

"Hey, Ms. Arkwright. Wow, you're in charge of the Archives at MU? You must be like a genius."

"Sean," Jeremy said sharply.

But the boy's tone was ingenuous, not insulting. Helen didn't even break into her usual blush. "Actually, I'm not in charge," she said. "I'm Assistant Archivist."

"That's still cool. I wish—"

A yell from Joe-Jack cut Sean short. He sprinted up the steps, his wish unconfided.

Jeremy watched him go, shaking his head. "Sorry about that."

"Nothing to be sorry about."

Joe-Jack now yelled for Jeremy, who paused only long enough to give her an absent smile before obeying the imperative call.

Helen headed for the university gates.

Halfway across the sunstruck green, she heard running footsteps behind her. Her pursuer was Sean Wyndham. Could something have gone wrong already?

Sean caught her up and skidded to a stop. "You walk fast," he gasped.

"And you run fast. What's up? Need something at the house?"

"No." Sean took a few seconds to recover his breath. "I just wondered if I could ask you a question."

Was he flushed with more than exertion? "Sure," Helen said. "About the windows?"

"No, about the Elder Sign."

She couldn't have heard him correctly. "What?"

"The Elder Sign. I thought you might know about it, working in the Archives and all."

Helen watched Sean's flush deepen, then realized she was staring as if he'd said something shocking. Well, *shocking* was a strong word, but he *had* surprised her. She mustered a smile, as if teenage boys asked her about the Elder Sign every day. "I've just started studying the Cthulhu Mythos myself," she said. "But I've read about the Sign."

Sean dashed wispy hair out of his eyes. "The thing is, which is the right one? The Star or the Branch?"

"Some authorities say only the Star is authentic. Some say only the Branch. A few say to use the Star in certain circumstances and the Branch in others, but then they don't agree on the circumstances."

"That sucks," Sean said. "That they don't agree, I mean. But maybe either one would work?"

As serious as Sean looked, Helen couldn't keep back a laugh. "Theoretically, I suppose. But then, it's all theory, isn't it?"

"You mean the Mythos? Oh yeah. It's not real. I mean, it's real like . . ." He seemed hung up on a word.

"Like any mythology is real, in a sociological sense?"

Sean considered this. After a moment he nodded. "I guess so."

"Why are you interested in the Sign?"

He shrugged. "Oh, you know. I read about it in stories. No big deal. Thanks, Ms. Arkwright."

With that he turned and ran back toward the gates.

No big deal. No, after centuries of contentious scholarship, the question of the Elder Sign's true form (if any) probably wasn't the hottest issue, particularly not in a teenager's life. Helen smiled, watching Sean's coltish lope. She'd have to mention him in her letter to Marvell, who often laughed about the twists pop culture gave the Mythos. Making a good joke of the encounter would prove she wasn't tying herself into such knots over Marvell's semi-disclosure that she'd lost her appreciation of everyday absurdities.

# 6

**Apart** from the windows Dad designed himself, the ones in the Arkwright House library were the coolest Sean had ever seen, especially the one with the Black Man. He'd have to snag some of Dad's documentation photos to show Eddy.

It was three o'clock before they had the windows in their transport frames. Dad and Joe-Jack wouldn't need Sean again until they carried the frames to the van, so he asked if he could run up to Horrocke's. From behind the handkerchief he was mopping his face with, Dad managed a muffled "yes."

Sean took off. He'd already snuck a look at Helen Arkwright's Yellow Pages and found Geldman's Pharmacy. It was on the corner of Gedney and Curwen, a couple blocks beyond the old railroad station. He found Gedney without a problem. It was a funky street. Half the shops were trendy, in restored buildings. The other half were ratty and run-down: a barber's, a newsstand, a Portuguese grocery with dried fish and hundred-year-old sausages hanging in its streaky window. That place would have made Mrs. Ferreira puke.

Geldman's, next to the grocery, across the street from a café, was obviously old but as shiny as the newest boutique. Its spring-green trim looked freshly painted. Its plate-glass windows were spotless. Even the yellow-glazed bricks of the building—the pharmacy occupied the whole first floor, an apartment the second—gleamed like someone had scrubbed them that morning. Suspended on chains in one window were two glass urns shaped like upside-down teardrops. You'd think they'd have ferns or spider plants in them; instead one held an emerald-green liquid, the other a ruby red. Freaky. Plus there was a scale outside the door that would give you your fortune with your weight. Sean didn't have time for that.

He pushed open the plate-glass door and stepped inside to the ringing of an invisible bell. The bell had to be electronic, which jarred the mood, but the anachronism of silent yet powerful air-conditioning was sweet after his run from the Arkwright House. Seeing no one in the pharmacy, Sean peeled his damp T-shirt from his belly and basked in the arctic breeze.

Apart from the electronic bell and the AC, the inside was as old-timey as the outside. To the right of the entrance, separating the shop from a private back area, was a wooden counter. Frosted-glass panels stretched from countertop to ceiling its whole length, so all Sean could see of the regions beyond was vague shadows. At the nearer end, the glass panel was framed to slide back, and the shadow behind it was unmistakable: an antique cash register. Like a priest taking confession, Geldman could open the panel to deal with customers. With Sean's luck, he'd be an old dude who hated kids.

Sean decided to look for the powders himself.

At the back of the shop was a soda fountain right out of a classic but colorized movie: Besides the rainbow of syrup bottles doubled in the backsplash mirror, its countertop was bubble-gum pink, its stools spearmint green.

In the middle of the shop, aisles of oak shelving were loaded down with bottles and boxes and tins, with paper sacks taped shut and cloth bags secured with drawstrings. Like in a regular drugstore, signs hung over the aisles, frosted glass like the counter panels—Geldman must have had a fetish for the stuff. But etched on them weren't the usual ANTACIDS or DEODORANTS or FEMININE PRODUCTS (stay away). Instead they read: LIVER, STOMACH, LUNGS, BOWELS, FEMALE PARTS (the "Feminine Products" after all).

Still fanning his belly with his shirt, Sean wandered down EYES/EARS/NOSE, then up FEET/BACK/JOINTS, which put him next to the window with the hanging urns. Could he dip right into the colored liquids, or was there wax over the surface, like on Rachel's homemade jam? He was reaching out to poke the nearer urn, the red one, when he heard a soft cough and about jumped out of his skin, or at least his T-shirt. Pulling the shirt down, he turned.

The man behind him was a couple inches shorter than Sean was but stood so straight so easily that Sean had the odd impression he was looking up at the guy. His hair was a bushy and glossy brown, kind of young-Einsteiny. Although his pale skin was otherwise unlined, he had crinkles at the corners of his eyes, which were as black as uncreamed coffee, and his smile exposed teeth as white as his lab coat, on which he wore a tag inscribed: "Solomon Geldman, Apothecary."

"How do you do?" Geldman said. He had a slight accent, German maybe, or Eastern European. "A hot day, isn't it?"

"Real hot, sir," Sean said. "Not in here, though."

"No. Excessive heat would be bad for the stock. Is there something I may help you find?"

Since there weren't any aisles labeled SORCERY SUPPLIES, asking Geldman for the powders looked like the only option. "I was looking for some stuff. This guy told me you'd have it."

"What might this stuff be?"

Though Geldman didn't sound sarcastic, "stuff" now struck Sean as a stupid thing to say. What was the word the Reverend had used? *Materia*. Lots more professional. "Materia," Sean said firmly, like he said it all the time. "The Powder of Zeph and the Powder of Aghar."

Geldman's eyes fixed on Sean as if they wanted to swallow him whole, but only in a nice way; they'd be sure to spit him out afterward as good as new. Sean took a step back, hitting bottles on the nearest shelf with his elbow. They rattled a protest.

Geldman took no visible notice. He smiled again. "Ah. I regret, young man, that your friend was mistaken. I couldn't supply you with those items. Something else, perhaps? A cooling drink? I recommend our sarsaparilla. Let me offer you a glass on the house, since I've had to disappoint you."

Sean watched the man head toward the fountain bar. After a second, he followed—what else could he do? Either the Reverend had put him on about Geldman's or, like Horrocke's, it kept the good stuff behind closed doors. *Whoever seeks, enter.*

Maybe Sean hadn't sought hard enough yet. Maybe he had to prove he was a legitimate customer. He sat on one of the spearmint stools and watched Geldman pour black syrup into a glass. He cleared his throat. "Mr. Geldman?"

Geldman began to jockey the lever of a brass spigot shaped like a horse with a curled-under fishtail for hind legs. It hissed soda water into the glass. "Yes, young man?"

"The guy who said I should come here? His name's Redemption Orne."

Geldman's only reaction was to pause in stirring the sarsaparilla. For a second, he stood absolutely still. Then, as gently as before, he plied his long-handled spoon, swirling tendrils of syrup through the fizzy water. "Reverend Orne sent you, did he?"

"Yeah, Reverend Orne."

Geldman set the glass on the pink countertop. "The sarsaparilla," he said, not smiling, not frowning. Neutral. "It will take me ten minutes to compound what you want. And how much of each?"

Once again, seeking had paid off. Sean had to stay business-like, though. "Like, three pinches?"

"A half ounce of Zeph and the same of Aghar should do. And am I to put them on Reverend Orne's account?"

The Reverend really *came* here? Came here a lot, too, because otherwise why would he have a private account?

"Young man?"

Geldman was waiting for an answer, and his steady gaze added to Sean's confusion. Okay, if Geldman wanted to put the powders on the Reverend's account, that meant Geldman assumed they were for the Reverend—Sean was just the delivery boy. If Sean told him the truth, would Geldman refuse to make the powders?

That would suck, so Sean blurted: "I guess you could put them on the account. If you think the Reverend wouldn't mind."

"If he sent you, I'm sure he'd wish it."

Geldman moved soundlessly to the counter. He opened a door Sean had overlooked, half wood, half glass panel, and vanished into the back. The door closed soundlessly behind him.

Sean took a nervous sip of the black drink Geldman had left him. It was like root beer, except more bitter and at the same time more sweet, and immediately after swallowing he did feel cooler. Sipping, he looked at the nearest bank of pharmaceuticals. STOMACH things, but no Alka-Seltzer or Pepto-Bismol in sight. Everything looked homemade, and there, practically in his face, were tall green bottles labeled "Patience Orne's, #6, for dyspepsia, one tablespoon at need, no contraindications." Patience was the real Redemption's wife, a witch. Geldman must have named a medicine after her because wannabe witches shopped at his pharmacy. Or did "Patience Orne's, #6" mean it was her own recipe?

Sean finished the sarsaparilla and roamed the aisles. There were more medicines labeled "Patience Orne's." Others were labeled "Dame Eliza's," "Hungry Tom's," "Dante Salvatore's,"

"Kokokoho's." Kokokoho was the Nipmuc shaman who'd been friends with the real Redemption. Cooler and cooler. The most common label was "SG's," which had to stand for "Solomon Geldman's"—since all the labels were hand-printed, he'd probably gotten sick of writing out his name. Another "Patience Orne's," this one for "general biliousness." The Reverend had to be kind of weird, didn't he, hanging out in a place like this? Maybe he was as big a nutcase as Eddy thought. It was one thing to have an alias on the Internet, where everyone used screen names, but apparently the Reverend used his alias with Geldman and even had an account as Redemption Orne. Or maybe Redemption Orne *was* the Reverend's name, because Mr. and Mrs. Sadistic Orne had decided to name their kid after some ancient preacher. If that was the case, the Rev could naturally get obsessed with his namesake.

Too bad Eddy hadn't come, so Sean could have impressed her with his Sherlock Holmes imitation. Another brilliant deduction hit him: To be a frequent flier at Geldman's, the Reverend had to live in or near Arkham. Could Sean wheedle his address out of Geldman? Better not try. If Geldman found out Sean didn't know where the Reverend lived, he might get mad and not give him the powders.

Speaking of mad. Wouldn't the Reverend get pissed if Sean charged the powders to his account? Geldman didn't know Sean's name. Still, the Reverend wasn't stupid. He'd figure out who had hit him up for Zeph and Aghar.

The glass panel over the counter slid back, and Geldman called: "Your order is ready, young man."

He'd just have to own up and hope for the best. Oh, and hope he had enough money with him, too. He'd gotten so confused when the account thing had come up he'd forgotten to ask the price.

Sean marched himself over to the counter. Geldman stood at the antique cash register holding a red-and-white-striped paper bag. Before he could hand the bag over, Sean said, "Look, Mr. Geldman. Reverend Orne didn't actually send me to get the powders. I mean, he told me to *come* here, but they're not for him; they're for me. So it wouldn't be right to charge them to his account. I'll pay for them."

Geldman's heavy eyelids fell to half-mast. "Very well," he said. "How much money do you have with you?"

"Twenty-six dollars."

"You may give me twenty."

That was a funny way to put it. "Um. That's what they cost?"

"Cost is relative, young man. Twenty will suffice in this case."

Who was Sean to argue? He fished out his cash and gave Geldman the two tens.

With a pull of the much-creased bills between his fingers, Geldman smoothed them to crisp newness. He depressed a key on the register. Its drawer popped open with a pleasant *ka-ching*, like in a cartoon, and Geldman deposited the tens within. "Now," he said, sliding the bag over the counter to Sean. "While these compounds aren't toxic, they can be irritating. Be careful not to touch your eyes or nose after handling them, and try not to breathe the dust."

Sean picked up the bag. Inside, glass tinkled against glass. "Yes, sir. I've got it."

"Keep the compounds dry and they'll last many years. Oh, and they're guaranteed to work. A full refund if you find otherwise."

Geldman's face was solemn, so Sean didn't crack a smile, either. "Right. Thanks, Mr. Geldman."

"You're welcome, young man."

That seemed to be it. Sean headed for the door. He'd opened it, to the ringing of its invisible bell, when Geldman called after him: "Oh, by the way."

Sean turned. Maybe since he hadn't been disappointed about the powders after all, Geldman wanted him to pay for the sarsaparilla.

However, Geldman only said, "Please tell Reverend Orne that I admire his eye. As always."

The Rev's eye? Sean nodded, though, and escaped. Geldman couldn't have meant an actual *eye*. Maybe the Rev's *taste* for something, like materia. But what about that guarantee? Should Sean come back after the summoning ritual failed and get the refund? Eddy would so crack up when he told her about this place.

A check of his cell phone told him it was after four, which meant Dad would be looking for him. Sean took a minute to pull open the stapled bag. Small as it was, its contents were lost in it: two clear glass tubes stoppered with corks and red sealing wax. The one labeled "Zeph" contained fine gray dust; "Aghar," fine yellow dust. He folded the bag into a compact square that fit inside his T-shirt pocket. Zeph gray, Aghar yellow, he chanted in his head as he ran down Gedney Street through the sticky heat of late afternoon, still sarsaparilla cool himself.

**7**

**Sean** had learned the ritual. He'd gotten the powders. Now Dad was going to blow the whole summoning project out of the water. "You've let me stay home by myself before," Sean protested.

"For one or two days," Dad said, not looking up from packing. "But I'll be down south for two weeks."

"There's a million reasons I should stay home."

Dad bore down on the lid of his suitcase. It was overstuffed—why didn't he just pack a bigger one? "Give me the top ten."

"I'm almost seventeen."

"You're seventeen in seven months. I wouldn't call that *almost.*"

"Aunt Cel's probably sick of me staying with her. And if I stay here, I can help your interns."

"Patrick and Farzin are on vacation. Sarah will only be working mornings. As for Cel and Gus being sick of you—"

Sean groaned. "Dad, I know they love me, but once in a while they might want to throw wild parties."

"Speaking of parties, you wouldn't be planning any?"

"With Mrs. Ferreira next door?"

After bouncing the suitcase half off the bed, Dad gave up trying to latch it. He dug out a couple pairs of jeans. "Thank God for Mrs. Ferreira."

"Dad, I don't want to have parties. I just want you to trust me."

"I do."

"Not much."

"Sean." Dad drew his name out, edgy-exasperated. "Two weeks is a long time."

A long time for Dad to be worrying about him. Sean knew that, he wished he could give in, but the ritual was too important. "After working all day, I'll be too tired at night to do anything but crash."

"Well. With the Arkwright windows here, I would like someone around to watch the studio."

"That's me, Dad."

"I'd leave my cell number with Mrs. Ferreira. With the Mandells, too."

Yes, he was so close now. "Cool, because nothing's going to happen."

Dad looked over at him. "I'd like to think you're smart enough to be on your own."

Sean was smart enough not to crack a smile. "I am."

The smile Dad worked up was weak, but he said, "All right. You can stay."

"Thanks, Dad!"

"You'll call me or Cel and Gus if there's any problem?"

"There won't be any problem, but yeah, sure."

So now he'd have the night of the twenty-fifth to himself, but he still didn't know which Elder Sign to use and Eddy would hardly talk about the ritual anymore. His account of the pharmacy hadn't cracked her up like he'd hoped. She said that Geldman sounded like the Reverend's chief competition for World's

Biggest Wack Job and that Sean was rising in the amateur ranks. "Come on. It's one thing to LARP or cosplay."

"Says somebody with twenty Éowyn costumes in her closet."

"So? Didn't I just say there's nothing wrong with it? But these guys take things way over the line. I think you're right, they're true believers. And that could get really weird. It could get dangerous."

Sean had to laugh at the face—rictus of terror—that she pulled. No way he'd ever admit it, but since he'd gone to Geldman's, thinking about the summoning ritual made him jittery, as if maybe, somehow, he could actually pull it off. "Lots of people must believe in magic," he countered. "The Rev can't be the only one who shops at Geldman's."

"Just because there are plenty of freaks in the world doesn't mean *you* have to buy into mumbo jumbo for dumbos."

That was harsh, but Eddy hadn't been to the pharmacy. She hadn't met Geldman. "I don't buy into it. It's just for my project. Look, you've got to come help me. You could tell Rachel my dad's back and stay over."

"Right. Then she'd find out from your aunt he's still gone and think we were at your house doing drugs and having sex. I'd be grounded until September."

It was crazy how some images could be "oh wow" and "totally gross" at the same time. Sean hoped the flush rising up his neck would at least stop at his jawline. "Tell her we're doing a pagan ritual," he said fast. "She'll want to come watch."

Wait, maybe that didn't sound right.

Luckily, Eddy just said, "You are so ignorant."

"But I want pictures of me doing the spell. It'll be a lot easier if you take them."

"Or maybe you're scared to do it alone?"

Sean was about to deny it, but why layer on the testosterone? This was Eddy. "Kind of," he said.

"Then don't do it. I won't tell anyone you backed out."

She wouldn't, either, but after all his practicing, after going to Geldman's, he had to perform the ritual on the right night, under the right stars.

Dad left the next day, Sunday, the twenty-third. Tuesday afternoon, Celeste came over with Gus's famous Polish lasagna. (It had kielbasa in it.) That his aunt didn't sense he was about to perform unhallowed rites amazed Sean—he felt as if he were glowing with the intention, like with the first fever bout of a flu. Not that he felt sick. He felt the opposite, eager, almost hyper.

That night, after she left, he tanked up on lasagna, then packed his sorcerer's gear.

⤙⤚

**Dad** had taken the Civic to the airport and was paying almost a hundred bucks for it to sit in a lot for two weeks. Overkill, since he'd taken both sets of keys with him. Maybe he thought Sean had made his own set on the sly (not a bad idea) or had learned how to hot-wire cars from his criminal friends (who, Phil?). The next best option was to borrow Dad's bike, which had a baggage rack to which Sean could bungee-cord his grill-brazier. It was a pain riding with the loaded grill at his butt. The charcoal kept shifting, and twice his backpack nearly knocked it off the bike. At the industrial park, he discovered that the parking lot by the river caught little light from streetlamps. Between the inadequate radius of his camp lantern and the unevenness of the worn blacktop, he had a hard time drawing his magical circle, but after smudging and rechalking, then fussing to light the charcoal, then fumbling with Dad's camera and tripod, he was almost ready. He squatted to draw the Elder Sign. Mosquitoes buzzed around him, kept from alighting by repellent. Even so, he seemed to feel their feet on his damp skin.

Feet? No, what he felt was the minute vibration of their buzzing. The air was charged; it gave substance to sound. The inner passages of his ears tingled to the shrilling of cicadas, and the passage of trucks on Old Post Road rumbled under his soles.

In the center of the pentagram, he drew the five-pointed Star with the eye in it—he'd finally picked that Elder Sign over the lame-looking Branch. Helen Arkwright had told him none of the experts knew which was right, so why not go with the sharpness factor? The smoldering grill went right on top of the Sign.

Next he set out the powders, Zeph inside the right "arm" of the pentagram (which represented Water), Aghar inside the left arm (Air). Lacking the recommended silver censers, he'd poured the powders into lidded bean pots. Zeph smelled bitter, metallic. Aghar smelled like rotten eggs. But he wasn't going to eat them, and he'd hooked some latex gloves from Dad's studio for when he handled the stuff.

Five minutes was all it took to photograph the magical circle. That brought him to eleven o'clock. Online, he'd looked up the transit of the Summer Triangle, the time when it would be highest in the sky, 11:08 tonight. When he switched off the lantern, Sean could see the Triangle clearly, Deneb and Altair and Vega glinting in the moonless sky. He couldn't make out the section of the Milky Way that crossed the Triangle—there was too much light pollution. Seen or unseen, it was there. That would have to be enough.

Sean walked around the pentagram, peering, listening. A breeze stirred the willows leaning over the black water of the Pawtuxet. In a house across the river, lights went out. Somehow that made him feel much more alone.

Wasn't alone exactly what he wanted to be? No bums, no partiers, no cops. He went to his backpack and pulled out his best approximation of a sacred Wiccan athame, which was the silver letter opener from Dad's desk. Any old stick would work, according to Marvell's book. A stick, a wand, a knife or sword, your own forefinger if that was all you had. All the athame did was symbolize the focused grasp of the soul as it channeled blind energy. Blind energy was everywhere in the universe, pouring out of Azathoth, the Source. It existed even in a parking lot behind a closed iron-casting factory.

Sean shut his eyes. Once you grabbed blind energy, you had to shape it or give it a direction, and the way you did that was through intention, through *meaning* for something to happen. He could handle an intention, if he concentrated. A dog barked across the river. He cringed like it was close enough to snap at him. Air lay heavy in his lungs. Maybe it really was charged, like air before a thunderstorm. Only there were no clouds and no forecast of rain.

He breathed deep, and the heavy air didn't smother him. The opposite: It invigorated him, as if it held more oxygen than usual. He moved. He had to start the ritual on time, 11:08.

Sean set Dad's camera to snap three photos after ten minutes, which was how long it should take to get to the climax of the ritual. He worked the latex gloves over his clammy palms. Then he walked to the magical circle and stepped between the pentagram's legs, the angles of Earth and Fire.

The storm that wasn't coming broke in that instant, not with external fireworks but with a blaze in his chest like lightning, a clap in his head like thunder. The electric jolt should have scared the crap out of him. It didn't. By stepping between Earth and Fire, he seemed to have stepped out of one Sean, sweaty and anxious, into another Sean, fearless. He paused, not even surprised, because the fearless Sean would have expected this: Of course, what else? If you plugged in a lamp that had been disconnected, it lit up, the circuit reestablished. Tilting back his head, he gazed at—addressed—the Summer Triangle. Now he could see what he had missed before, the creamy rim of the galaxy and the swath of utter blackness that cut through it: the Great Rift, gaping like a crude door between realities. It wasn't a door. It was a cloud of dust. Sean knew that, and he didn't know it, didn't *believe* it. The Rift was an aperture. It was a gateway.

He gathered the first pinches of Zeph and Aghar and threw them into the grill, his brazier. Mingled black and yellow smoke billowed from the charcoal, acrid and sulfurous. Mr. Geldman had warned him not to breathe in the powders. Sean hoped that breathing the smoke wasn't a no-no, because without a gas mask he couldn't help it. As he breathed it in he felt a tingling that started in his chest and spread outward to his head and limbs.

The ritual was working. He could go ahead.

Facing east, with the athame raised, he swept the invoking pentagram into the air. He didn't mumble the order of the lines to himself like he had when practicing; the motion came naturally to him now. Three more times, facing each quarter of the compass in turn, he swept out the pentagram. With each slash, his right arm grew heavier, as if more blood were pumping into it. But the weight didn't slow him. It seemed to give him added strength.

He faced east again, toward the pinnacle of the chalked pentagram, raised his arms, and began the first incantation: "To you, Lord Azathoth, springhead of all that is. To you, I offer obeisance, and to your Soul, Nyarlathotep. Here I stand, in Fire and Earth, before Air and Water. To Spirit I call!"

He repeated the incantation three times, thrice. His voice sounded far-off. That was because of the rushing in his ears, the torrent of wind or river, Air or Water, the ceaseless roar of Fire or the slow grinding of Earth upon itself. He tossed the second pinches of Zeph and Aghar. Sweet tiger smoke enveloped him as he straightened to chant the second incantation: "Send to me—"

Sean choked into silence. It wasn't the powders. Those drove his exhilaration higher. It was the figure condensing out of their smoke, clad in gold vestments, with gold eyes in a black face and black wings, scythe pointed like a falcon's: a vaporous angel that hovered between him and the Summer Triangle. It didn't speak, but the forefinger of its right hand inscribed the air with a spidery silver script, spelling out the words of the incantation that would summon an ethereal Servitor, the aether-newt.

"Send to me," Sean whispered. His voice failed again. Under the rushing in his ears, Eddy scoffed: Aether-newt, Ethernet. Proves it's all fake, doesn't it? Proves it's all bullshit.

How could an angel be bullshit?

As if it read his thought, the angel smiled. It was a gentle smile, reassuring. Its eyes, tilted ovals without pupils, should have scared him, but they were reassuring, too. It raised its right hand, and the silver script rose with it, to hang above its head. The air between them was a blank slate once more.

Speechless, Sean waited. Somehow he knew he had to.

With its left forefinger, the angel scratched red script into the night, words like lava welling through the cracked crust of a flow. *I give you blood to make a Servitor in the likeness of your own attendants,* the lava words began. It had to be the variant incantation, then, the one that the Reverend wouldn't write out, the one that would summon the blood-spawn. Sean didn't want that familiar. The Reverend had told him it was too dangerous. Sean wanted the other, the harmless one.

Aether-newt, Ethernet, lame lame lame.

The angel nodded as if it agreed. The Reverend didn't know Sean as the angel did. The angel appreciated Sean's ability and strength of will. To summon the aether-newt wouldn't be test enough.

There was sense in that. If you were going to do something, do it right.

The angel swept its right arm skyward. The silver script swirled away, thinned, vanished. Then the angel thrust its left arm earthward. The lava script descended until Sean could read it easily. Only how could he call a blood-spawn when he hadn't brought any blood?

Like the smoke that had birthed it, the angel expanded. Now Sean could see through its serpent-crowned head and falcon wings to the Summer Triangle. The Milky Way slashed the Triangle; the Great Rift slashed the Milky Way; a silver blade slashed them both. It was the blade of his athame, which he still held aloft.

He did have blood with him, after all. He could feel it pulsing under his skin.

He couldn't use his own blood, though. The Reverend had written it had to be the blood of an enemy.

But then, as the angel knew, the Reverend had underestimated Sean. Sean wasn't afraid. Inside the magical circle, he never could be.

He read the lava script, and he chanted: "I give you blood to make a Servitor in the likeness of your own attendants, substantial and potent. Send it to serve me in all things, and through me to serve you, Lord Azathoth, and your Soul, Nyarlathotep."

Sean chanted the incantation thrice. The last pinches of Zeph and Aghar went into the brazier and bathed him like incense. Pulling the blessing deep into his lungs, he watched fresh smoke waft the angel into treetops that shredded it until nothing was left but the gleam of its eyes, two gold stars within a leafy nebula. The lava script remained above the brazier, for his use.

He stripped off the stupid latex gloves and without hesitation drew the sharp edge of the athame across the palm of his left hand. There was pain, but it was unimportant. What mattered was the swift flow of blood. He clenched a fist over the brazier; he watched blood drip onto the charcoal, heard its hiss, smelled it burn. The more he squeezed out, the more intense grew a new exhilaration, a gut-deep physical excitement. In fact, he was getting a hard-on. It didn't seem perverted, though. It seemed the rightest thing that had ever happened to him.

The lava script was fading, but he only had to chant the close of the incantation once: "Blood speed my petition. Blood make the promise. Blood seal the bargain. By your wills, so be it!"

The "so be it!" burst out of him so loud that people sleeping in the houses across the river had to start awake, so loud that cops on Post Road had to roar into the industrial park to check it out. Sean didn't care. With the last words, he yearned and beat, not just his pounding heart, not just his aching root of a boner. His whole body shook. The lava script jittered in his vision until it had cooled to black crust. In the black of the treetops, the gold eye-stars still glowed.

Sean waited, ecstatic. The eyes waited.

Lightning flared. Real lightning. It forked through his rapture, making him stagger from the magical circle. A second flare hit him, a third, before he realized it was the flash of the camera going off as programmed. He'd been shaken awake at the best part of a dream, or at the worst part of a nightmare. Reaction shivers hit him fast, and that boner? Gone and come to nothing.

When he dropped his arms, the letter opener stabbed his thigh. He let it fall to the blacktop and looked at his left hand, which throbbed like a bitch now that he'd snapped out of— what? What had happened in the magical circle to let him slash his palm from the base of his forefinger to the crease of his wrist and barely feel it?

Sean smeared blood on his jeans getting a handkerchief out of his pocket. No great loss—his clothes already reeked of burned metal and sulfur. *He* reeked of it; the whole damn site reeked. The Powders of Zeph and Aghar, yeah, he'd be getting his money back on those. Before the camera flashes had driven him from the circle, he'd finished everything except the binding incantation, and, obviously, there was no familiar to bind. The magical circle was empty. The parking lot was empty. Not a stray cat. Not a mosquito. Not even a cicada singing, and they'd been going at it before.

Smoke still rose from the brazier, formless.

It had always been formless.

His disappointment was crazy, but so had been the way he'd

felt in the circle, and craziest of all had been that vision of an angel. Angel? More like the Devil in the Arkwright House windows, the Black Man. That was where Sean had seen it before. And the Reverend had said the Black Man was Nyarlathotep. So, when Sean called him, old Nyarlathotep had shown up, Pharaoh getup and all.

As Sean wrapped the handkerchief around his palm, he hiccoughed out a laugh that sounded more or less normal. Plain old psychology could explain everything that had happened. He'd gotten himself worked up preparing for the ritual. Geldman's Pharmacy had been gasoline on a banked fire, and tonight, boom! He'd exploded right into a hallucination. Damn, blood was already seeping through his makeshift bandage. He'd be lucky if he didn't need stitches.

Sean fumbled Dad's camera gear back into his pack. The time-delay photos would be a wash—they had to show him gaping like the world's biggest dork. He'd delete them before anyone got a look, even Eddy. The grill wouldn't be so easy to deal with, because the charcoal still burned high. Well, he'd have to leave the whole mess to cool. Maybe he'd come back for the grill, maybe not. It was half rusted out, and Dad never used it anymore.

Armed with the grill lid, Sean eased a foot back into the magical circle. No jolt, thank God. He clapped the lid over the stinking embers. Then his heel came down on something—the athame, the letter opener. The blood edging its blade made his stomach lurch, but he couldn't leave the opener behind; Dad *would* miss that. Mom had given it to him, after all.

And what would Mom have thought of how Sean had just used the opener? Crazy to wonder that now. He bent to pick it up, and that was when he heard the stealthy slither, like a snake gliding through dry leaves.

It came from inside the grill.

Slowly, he straightened. The slithering continued, augmented by a low rattle of lid against rim, as if the whole grill was vibrating. Earthquake? Idiot. The ground under his feet was quiet. A delayed chemical reaction of the powders? That made more sense.

What would make even more sense would be to get away before the grill blew up.

He stuck the letter opener through his belt and took a step backward. If he took a couple more, then a few more after that, he could grab his pack and get on the bike. Instead he stood still, eyes locked on the grill.

The rattling stopped, replaced by a sound like briquettes tossed aside, so that they pinged against the inner wall of the grill. The lid rose an inch, releasing a swath of smoky red light. The lid fell back.

Something was moving in the grill.

Which couldn't happen.

The lid rose, higher. Fell again.

It had to be snakes. Not live ones but those ash-snakes that grew out of tablets touched by a match, the kind they sold in fireworks stores. Ignited by the charcoal, the Powders of Zeph and Aghar were expanding into ash-cobras. Ash-pythons. Hell, ash-*anacondas*. Mystery solved. He could walk over, raise the lid, and the ash-snakes would crumble and blow away.

The lid rose and stayed up, a phenomenon to be expected under the ash-snake theory. Sean squatted to peer through the opening. He saw something white and writhing and grimaced at a new stench. Cute trick that Zeph and Aghar combined to make not only the ash-snakes but also a smell like the reptile house at the zoo. Fire-Serpents Deluxe, with Improved Olfactory Component! Maybe he wouldn't ask Geldman for a refund, after all.

Still squatting, holding his breath, Sean reached for the lid handle. It happened then, had waited to happen, the burgeoning outward of whiteness too solid to be ash, of whiteness split by maw and lit by two flat disks of fire.

Sean backpedaled so fast he propelled himself onto his butt. Before ass and blacktop had a chance to fully connect, he rolled onto his feet and ran, too busy sucking in air to scream when his one backward glance showed him the grill tipping over and something white flailing out of it in an avalanche of sparks. He had summoned it. Unless the Elder Sign confined it to the magical circle, it would come after him.

On the service road a few of the old streetlamps put out feeble light. Sean grabbed a post to break his momentum. He spun and collapsed against flaking metal. Behind him loomed the impenetrable shadow of the abandoned factory. Beyond that was the puddle of light cast by his camp lantern, with the overturned grill in its center.

There was nothing else. Nothing moved within his magical circle.

Sean pushed back from the post. If he'd really seen the white thing (with mouth and molten metal eyes), it had escaped. He'd used the wrong Elder Sign. Worse, he hadn't said the binding incantation. Whatever had answered the ritual was free. It might be crouching in the shadow of the factory, or it might be at shadow's edge, ready to hurl itself across the last few yards between them, and, if Sean was lucky, all he'd see would be a blur before it clambered up his body to his throat. His eyes felt bugged out to the stalks, trying to penetrate the blackness. His ears ached to catch the click of claws. Cicadas were what he heard, and mosquitoes whining close to his head. Across the river, the dog barked again.

The barking grounded him. Sean closed his eyes, listening to the ordinary night noises, dog and insects, cars, nearer now: hum and thud of tires on asphalt, fragmented bursts of rock and rap. He opened his eyes. The only movement was in the air in front of his face, where mosquitoes bobbed.

He batted at them with his right hand. His throbbing left hand he nursed against his chest. His head was starting to throb,

too, just when he most needed to think clearly. All right. He had
hallucinated the angelic Black Man. He must have hallucinated
the thing in the grill.

Why?

Psychology, because he had been overexcited. Or drugs.

The Powders of Zeph and Aghar.

What if they'd been laced with drugs? As soon as he'd
breathed their smoke, he'd felt superstrong, he'd seen things,
he'd cut himself without feeling it. Angel dust could do all that,
couldn't it? The white thing had been the last special effect of the
high, and now he had a wicked headache, the hangover.

Jesus, what was with Geldman, selling crap like that? Was it
a sick joke? Or a way to give customers the illusion they'd done
magic? Either way, it had to be illegal. And what about the Reverend, sending Sean to Geldman?

God, Dad would implode if he found out Sean had been stupid enough to contact the Reverend, then stupider enough to
buy drugs from a weird old dude who thought he was running a
wizard pharmacy. Yeah, the Rev and Geldman probably did
hang together, snorting Zeph and Aghar in their secret drug den
behind the frosted glass. That was why they were so fucked up.

What he had to do right now was dump the powders left in
his bean pots. He had to get rid of the pots, too. They were contaminated, and so were the tubes the powders had come in. To
get them, though, he'd have to return to the magical circle. Sean
looked up the service road to the line of modern streetlights that
marched along Old Post Road. Safe under their sodium glare, he
could walk home in half an hour. Come back tomorrow.

That wouldn't work. Someone might steal Dad's bike and
camera. Plus there were the spilled briquettes. If the wind picked
up, they could spit sparks and start a fire. As for the powders,
a bum could come along and try snorting them, and overdose,
and die, and his death would be on Sean's pounding head.

Big deal, going back for his stuff. He remembered now. Even

if a Servitor was unbound, it couldn't hurt the summoner. The Reverend had said so.

God, *the Reverend said so.* Sean was the crazy one if he took any comfort from that.

He made it safely to the grill, which lay on its side, its lid ten feet off. When he'd fallen on his butt, he must have kicked the grill over. Again, end of mystery. He scraped the scattered briquettes together. They stank with the new stink, the melding of Zeph and Aghar. He held his breath until he could smother the embers under the lid.

The bean pots he dumped into a plastic grocery bag that still held Geldman's glass tubes. He tied the bag shut with four hard-pulled knots. It would be safest to chuck it into the river, no matter how much Joe-Jack (Lord of the Pawtuxet Conservation Society) would kick if he could see. Sean had fished crap out of the water five annual cleanups in a row. He'd earned one supposedly nontoxic dump.

Reluctant to give up the light, he hung his camp lantern on the handlebars of Dad's bike and struggled into his backpack, so he'd be ready to move. Then he crept to the edge of the parking lot.

A narrow path led into the brush between lot and river. Sean sidled along it with the grace of a drunken elephant. His racket spooked something in the reeds, and it beat a rustling retreat. Coon, maybe. Skunk, possum. Just a plain old animal, but it could be rabid. Sean stopped, whirled the loaded grocery bag like a slingshot, and hurled it as far as he could.

It splashed down mid-river and sank. Sean didn't wait to say good-bye—the animal in the reeds was still rustling, and maybe it wasn't retreating. Maybe it was moving toward him.

Stumbling into the parking lot, Sean saw something gleam in the leafy shadows of the woods to the east. Was it stray starlight on an onyx forehead or a golden eye? Back by the river, had something just splashed into the water?

In three strides, he made it to the bike and jumped on. Though he could steer only with his right hand, he pedaled hard, out of the lot, onto the service road, toward the safety of sodium streetlights and the company of late-cruising cars.

# 8

**When** Joe-Jack arrived the next morning, he took one look at the bloody gauze wadded around Sean's hand and drove him straight to his aunt's. Sean told Celeste he'd cut himself slicing a bagel. East Side Ph.D.s were always butchering themselves that way, so she had no trouble believing her dumb-ass nephew had. She hustled him to her office, where her partner Dr. Goss sutured him up.

Celeste insisted he stay overnight at her house, which meant he couldn't clean up at the industrial park. No worries. Anyone was welcome to the stinking grill, and as for the magical circle, Gus said there were going to be afternoon thunderstorms. The rain would wash away Sean's pentagram, and that would be the end of the ritual.

Eddy came over in the afternoon. Sean told her the whole story, except for the hard-on part. She was cool and didn't say *I told you so*. Instead she tore into the Reverend and Geldman. "It's no joke, angel dust. You could have brain damage."

"I had a wicked headache, but I feel all right now."

"We should call the police."

Sean gave his bandaged palm a painful flex. "I threw the powders away. There's no evidence."

"We could place an anonymous tip."

"Eddy, we don't know it was drugs. Even before I burned any powder, I was feeling weird."

"You probably inhaled some getting ready. I mean, how else do you explain the hallucinations?"

He didn't want to say it, but he made himself: "Magic?"

"Real funny. You inhaled some when you poured the powders into the pots."

Last night he would have agreed. Now he'd had time to think about everything that had happened, and drugs wouldn't explain why he'd gone from jittery Sean to fearless Sean the very second he'd stepped into the magical circle. "I still don't want to report Geldman. Plus, I'd have to tell the police about the Reverend, too, right?"

Eddy paced, too indignant to sit down. "I've been thinking about the Rev. Know what I think? I bet he's really Mr. Horrocke."

Maybe Sean's brain *was* damaged, because it sure wasn't following Eddy there. "The old guy at the bookstore?"

"It makes total sense. Where'd you find the *Witch Panic* book? Horrocke's. Who's an expert on old books, probably knows all about forgeries, probably could make his own forged shit, like the ad? Horrocke."

"Jeez, take a breath."

If she did, it didn't slow her down. "Horrocke puts the book and ad out for bait, and you take it. Then he pretends he doesn't know anything about them and lets you have them for nothing. And—" Eddy suddenly turned and pointed at him, like she was the prosecutor and he was a crook on the stand. "And he tells you they're your destiny. Then what's the Rev tell you? He left the book and ad for you in particular. That's the destiny thing again."

Yeah, brain damage. His headache was even coming back. "I don't know."

"But it makes sense, right?"

"No, because why would Horrocke do all that?"

"All those books he's around. They've cracked him. He thinks he's a genuine wizard. He meets Geldman, who thinks *he's* a genuine wizard. They, what d'you call it, they reinforce each other. Or if they don't think they're wizards, they just like screwing around with kids. Maybe they're pedophiles."

That was a nice thought, not! "I'm not sure about Horrocke being the Reverend. It doesn't matter, though. I'm done with both of them."

Eddy finally let it go, though Sean could tell she was dying to spearhead a major police crackdown on magic pushers.

Over the next four days, while he was off work because of his bum hand, he worked on his project report. The pictures of his magical circle looked good, but as he'd expected, no amount of fiddling could save the three time-delay photos. He deleted them from Dad's camera. If only it was that easy to get the stink out of his clothes. After the third wash, he buried his jeans and T-shirt in a chest of old sweaters, hoping mothballs would conquer the lingering foulness.

"By their foulness shall ye know them." That was what the *Necronomicon* said about the Outer Gods and their minions. Too often now the line went through Sean's head, worse than a trapped song-fragment. He'd stopped reading Lovecraft, and he hadn't watched the movies he'd stockpiled for gorefests while Dad was away. The last thing Sean wanted to do these days was sit in the dark watching monsters kill teenagers.

Vague dread rode around in his chest. He hadn't said the final incantation, the one that would have bound the Servitor to him. The Rev claimed a Servitor would be "deferential" to its summoner even without binding. How deferential? It would only eat part of him? Crazy to worry about something that had never existed, but he couldn't shake a sense of being sought. *Infinity* mentioned that kind of feeling, also how performing rituals could cause euphoria, also how Nyarlathotep could appear in many forms, one of them a falcon-winged "angel." It all jibed with Sean's experience, though since he'd read the book before doing the ritual, those tidbits could have lodged in his brain as raw material for hallucinations.

Another thing. Zeph and Aghar were strong crap: He'd only "taken" them once, and yet he sometimes got a hankering for the high he'd felt, for the fearless Sean of the magical circle. Was he already hooked? Would he end up like the Reverend, with his own account at Geldman's?

It didn't help when Sean went back to work and Beowulf kept talking about a coyote pack roaming along the Pawtuxet River. "A lot of pets are missing," he said. "The Gagnons' poodle, and Alexa's cat, and Sweetie Pie."

"Who's Sweetie Pie?" Sean asked.

Hrothgar jammed his head between the front seats of the van and huffed, like, who the hell didn't know Sweetie Pie? "He's Trudy's dachshund," Beo said. "Oh, plus me and Dad found this dead raccoon near the baseball fields. Good thing a girl didn't find it. A girl would've freaked."

"Sexist generalization," Joe-Jack said severely.

"Well, maybe not Eddy," Beo conceded. "But its head was ripped right off."

Sean let Hrothgar scarf down his donut. The idea of animals getting killed along the river (near the industrial park) gave him a stomach-churning pang of guilt. Again, crazy. Hallucinations couldn't hurt anything.

"I'm not sure it's coyotes," Joe-Jack said. "Could be feral dogs. Or something rabid. I called Animal Control, but they probably won't do anything until some kid gets mauled. That's how government works."

"Right," Sean said, dutiful.

"Listen, Sean. You better not walk on the river trail until this gets straightened out. I'm not letting Beo go alone. Plus we're keeping Hrothgar on the leash, and we're keeping the gate shut, so he doesn't wander off. Right, Beo?"

Beo squirmed. "I never leave the gate open! Besides, know what I think it really is? I think somebody let loose a terrarium of giant Argentinian toads. Sean, you should've seen these humongous webbed prints near the coon."

"Swan tracks," Joe-Jack scoffed. "That's all those were. But you stay off the trail, Sean."

No worry—he hadn't been near the river since the ritual. "I'll stay off," he promised.

**Friday** the fourth of August, a week and three days post-ritual, Sean took the afternoon off and hung out at the Hope High tennis courts with Eddy and Phil. What with his still-sore left hand, Sean lost every set. He didn't care. Playing made him feel normal again.

Though he was really sleepy after dinner with Celeste and Gus, Sean didn't want to stay over at their house. Dad would be home Sunday, which left only Saturday for Sean to clean up. After Gus drove him to Edgewood, he took a shower and sat down to watch TV. Two hours later, he woke up and gimped to bed, where he fell asleep without any of his usual agonizing over the ritual, and the Reverend and Geldman, and web-footed coyotes by the Pawtuxet, and . . .

Eddy and Phil. In kayaks on the river, slamming a red tennis ball back and forth. They never miss a return: The ball is strung through a cord stretched tight from racket to racket. Slam. Sean can't play because he is *in* the water. His kayak has already gone over the falls by the Broad Street bridge. Any minute, he'll go over, too, because while the current flows upstream for Eddy and Phil, keeping them stationary, it sucks hungrily at Sean. He snatches at underwater weeds, but there are things in them that bite, and he has to let go. The foam of the falls catches him up. He yells for help. But Eddy and Phil just keep slamming that ball. *Slam.* Slam, *slam*—

With a choke, Sean jerked awake. Was he drowning? No, he couldn't drown in his own bed. He sat up, and he was dry, and breath rushed back into his lungs. Outside, the wind was slamming something around, probably one of the genuine working shutters Dad had installed on the carriage house. They worked, all right—worked at getting loose and banging themselves to death. Funny how the wind was ignoring the leaves of the maple outside Sean's window. They hung still in the humid air.

*Slam,* followed by the clink of metal falling, followed by a sound Sean had made often enough himself: the whack of the porch door flung open so hard it rebounded off the aluminum glider. Besides, there wasn't any wind—it wasn't just the leaves hanging limp, it was the gauze curtains in the open windows. All that slamming had been something pounding on the porch door, and at last the door had given way.

Instantly Sean's heart tripped into high gear. He checked the clock radio on the bureau, as if it mattered what time it was: Two fifteen in the morning, in the *night,* and that did matter. *Night* made it a million times worse to hear the intruder thumping around on the back porch. His first thought had to be right: It was a some*thing,* not a some*one.* A burglar would try to be quiet, unless he was a drug-crazed nut, like Geldman or the Rev. But they didn't know where Sean lived. Well, he didn't think they knew.

His cell phone was on the charger, on the bureau. He could call the police. That was the kind of advice he and Eddy always yelled at the TV when some idiot started down the stairs to the basement, at midnight, or 2:15.

Sean slid out of bed and padded to the bureau. What was he going to tell the police? An intruder. A trespasser. That was enough. He wasn't falling into any macho traps—let the police think he was a coward for not looking into the details for himself. And hell, he was still just a kid, right? Technically. Sort of.

Wait, it was quiet now. Though maybe that was scarier than the noise?

He stood in the blue glow of his flipped-open phone, listening. His heartbeat still pounded in his ears. Why should the thumping stop? The intruder was tired after breaking in? It was considering its next move? Or it had gone away again.

Gone away would be good. Maybe he'd better peek out and at least see whether the porch door had been busted open. What if he'd dreamed the racket? What if he'd had a drug flashback? What if he was going crazy?

Damn.

He tucked the phone into the waistband of his boxers. He stuck his feet into his flip-flops, then kicked them off. Bare feet were the ticket for sneaking around your house, checking out bumps in the night.

Sean took a long listen at the top of the stairs, another on the landing halfway down, shorter ones in the living room and dining room, a last long one at the swinging door to the kitchen. Slowly he pushed it inward. The blissful silence was broken—he heard the porch glider squeak. One squeak, as if something had knocked into it, not the cacophony you got by sitting on the thing. Another squeak. Then a scratching at the screen of the kitchen storm door, down low, where a cat or dog would scratch it.

He let out the breath he'd been holding. Okay. It was a stray cat, or a raccoon come after some sandwich scraps or pizza crusts he'd left on the porch. Coons were strong enough to push the door open if it wasn't on the latch. They'd done it before.

But he'd heard the latch break? A raccoon wasn't strong enough to do that.

He didn't *know* the latch was broken. He wasn't even sure

he'd latched the door. Yes, he had been latching it every night, and locking all the downstairs windows and doors. But tonight he'd been so tired, he could have forgotten. The coon was *there;* he heard it, stretching up to scratch the screens of the kitchen windows. Little bastard. It would tear the fabric. At least he hadn't called the cops, hadn't totally assumed it was a burglar, or a druggy perv, or, admit it now, what had been at the back of his mind and worming its way toward the front: his Servitor come home.

He slipped into the kitchen and fumbled through the utility closet for a broom. Weapon in hand, he snuck across the cool tiled floor to the light switch by the back door. Sometimes throwing on the porch light was enough to scare coons away. This one seemed bold, but unless it looked rabid, Sean would sweep it the hell off the porch.

He flipped the switch. The coon hissed and thudded into the glider, *squeak.* Sean reached to open the back door, but shadowy movement made him look left. The movement *was* a shadow, a hunched lumpy shadow thrown by the porch light onto the checked curtain of the nearer window. If it were the shadow of a coon, the coon was over five feet tall and its upflung paw, big as a man's hand, had tiger claws.

The next thing Sean was sure of was the solidity of his bedroom door at his back; the memory of his dash through the house was a quick-cut montage of furniture rearing up and bushes leering in at windows and stained glass bleeding red streaks down the landing wall. He still clutched the broom from the utility closet. That was proof he'd been to the kitchen.

He hadn't unlocked the kitchen door, had he? No. He hadn't had time before he'd seen the shadow. What about the other doors and windows downstairs? Had he missed locking any? He wasn't going back down to find out. He was going to lock the windows in his room, and then he was getting into bed, where he might even pull the covers over his head before calling the police. Or Celeste and Gus. Or Eddy to talk him through this flashback from Geldman's powders.

Oh God, though, his phone. It wasn't in his waistband. He clapped his boxers all over. No phone. His panicked run between kitchen and bedroom must have jarred it free. He'd have to go look for it, but first the windows. Sean shut and locked the one by his bed, then the nearer of the two that overlooked the front-porch roof. The third window stuck, its frame swollen with humidity. Sean shoved it up, trying to loosen it. Bad move. One of the sash cords went off track, leaving the window stuck open.

He needed a screwdriver to fix it. The flat-head driver in his Swiss Army knife would work.

His backpack. He'd stuck the knife in there, in case he needed it during the ritual, but he couldn't think about the ritual, he had to think about the pack, next to his desk.

Something dropped onto the porch roof from the overhanging maple. It sounded way heavier than a cat or raccoon. And it was white. Frozen at the open window, Sean saw that much from the corner of his eye. Then he made himself look straight at the intruder.

It was pallid, lumpish, around the size of a ten- or twelve-year-old kid. Moving with agonizing deliberateness, it climbed the mild pitch of the roof to crouch in front of the locked window. Dense-leafed boughs hung between it and the streetlights, mercifully shading out details, but Sean could see it reaching for the window. He heard scratching and a low whine. He smelled the stench of a neglected reptile house.

His heart had crawled into his throat, like it would be safer there than in the ribbed fortress of his chest. It cut off his breath, and he was going to pass out if he didn't get away. He was turning at the moment when, with intolerable speed, the thing scuttled from the closed window toward the open one—all he saw was a white blur and a spasming of tentacles around a needle-packed mouth.

He screamed seconds later, simultaneous with the slam of the bedroom door. He was in the hall, clinging to the knob, listening to screen fabric tear, and, God, he couldn't lock the bedroom door from the outside. The door opposite led to the third-floor guest room. Sean flung it open, flung himself inside, flung it closed. No lock. He tore up the stairs, tripped on the last one, and sprawled into dead darkness. Below he heard his bedroom door creak.

Still on his knees, he slammed the guest-room door and scrabbled at the lock tab until the dead bolt shot home. Claws clattered up the stairs. Sean ran. He barked his shins on an unseen coffee table and teetered over it. Flesh hit the door behind him; something hissed. Pinwheeling his arms, Sean stayed upright. He limped toward the faint light of the bathroom. Its door, like the guest-room door, was solid maple, original to the house. Joe-Jack had refinished the doors, because Dad didn't believe in flimsy modern crap. Thank God for Dad and Joe-Jack.

Sean locked the bathroom door behind him. There was one small gable window across from the toilet. He sank onto the lidded seat. The window was over the driveway. From it to the blacktop was a sheer drop and no trees nearby for things to climb.

If only he could call Dad, he'd spill every crazy damn thing he'd done since chatting with the Reverend. Too bad Sean's last crazy act had been to lose his phone somewhere below, in the part of the house the thing now ruled. Maybe if he yelled out the gable window, Mrs. Ferreira would hear. He would yell, too, if the thing got through the guest-room door.

It tried to get through for a while, scratching, thudding, rattling the knob. Sean huddled on the toilet and kind of whimpered. Finally, though, the claws clacked back down the stairs, and the house was still.

In the dark of the bathroom, Sean listened. He didn't dare turn on the light. It might attract the thing's attention and tell it exactly which window its prey was hiding behind. It couldn't get to the window, though, not unless it could fly.

He could only pray it had no wings, nor the ability to sprout some.

## 9

The rest of the night Sean listened for another assault on the guest-room door. He heard nothing until dawn, when a frantic yowl jolted him from dozing. It came from outside the house. It wasn't repeated. Soon after, the birds started singing, and presumably he was safe, because lumpish white things with needle-teeth couldn't stand the light of day—wasn't that a universal given?

His hope that the thing was a powders flashback dissolved as he opened the guest-room door. A reptilian smell hung heavy in the stairwell, and the varnish around the outside knob was gouged to the raw wood. In his bedroom, where the screen in the stuck window was rent top to bottom, he could barely breathe without puking. The stench came from his bed—congealing gray-green slime splotched his pillows as if something had drooled on them.

In the kitchen he found his dropped phone. On the back porch, the screen door hung open, and that metallic clink he'd tried to convince himself wasn't the latch breaking? The latch hook lay on the floor, wrenched right out of the door.

He'd have to fix the screen from his bedroom window and replace the latch. It was crucial to get things back to normal before Dad came home. No, even sooner: before night came again.

Sean hurried to his bedroom with a garbage bag and shoved his contaminated pillows inside. Then he wrestled the torn screen out of the window. He'd get Joe-Jack to help him with it, say he'd been air-guitaring and put his fist through the fabric. Air-guitaring to the Grateful Dead, yeah—that would get Joe-Jack's sympathy like Green Day never could.

Juggling the screen and garbage bag and trying to decide whether he'd been listening to "Truckin'" or "Friend of the Devil," Sean stepped off the back porch stairs onto the corpse of a cat, shredded and slime slippery.

The slaughtered cat did it. Sean couldn't stay in the house one second longer. He even put off calling Eddy until he was on the street. Her parents had taken the car to the farmers' market. She'd have to bike over to Edgewood. But if it was a three-alarm emergency—

It was a five-alarm.

She'd be there in an hour or so.

While he waited, Sean sat in the Broad Street Café, cutting untasted pancakes into smaller and smaller bits. The Saturday morning crowd chattered around him as if the world hadn't changed overnight. The Mandells were there, having a great old time, even after Ethan spilled grape juice on Zoe. Yet they had been *right across the street* from the house where the world had changed. If they had looked out their windows around two thirty in the morning, they would have seen the thing on the porch roof. Of course, they weren't the sort of people who'd look out windows in the dead of night. Good for them. They were sane, unlike Sean "Let's Summon Monsters" Wyndham.

At *best,* he was crazy. Maybe it showed: Mrs. Mandell

stopped at his table while Mr. Mandell herded Ethan and Zoe outside. "How are you doing, Sean?" she asked.

"I'm great, Mrs. Mandell."

"Zoe said you hurt your hand. Is it bothering you?"

"No. It's not one hundred percent, but it's okay."

"Isn't your father coming home tomorrow?"

"Yeah, he's supposed to."

"Well—"

Mr. Mandell knocked on the window. Mrs. Mandell gave Sean a quick smile and left the café. A couple minutes later, it was Eddy knocking on the window, still straddling her bike.

Sean gave her the evidence tour. She turned pale when she sniffed the bagged pillows and she didn't look at the mutilated cat any longer than she had to, but she stayed sharp enough to spot drops of dry blood on the flagstone walk. They followed the trail to the back fence. More blood smeared the gate that opened onto a shortcut to Roger Williams Park. A few yards down the path they found a puddle with webbed prints on its muddy margins. Some were coming, some going, and they were the size of Sean's hand, no swan tracks. Huge old yews bellied in on the path, casting midday twilight; after Eddy phone-snapped pictures, the two of them retreated from the claustrophobic green alley.

Back in the garden, they sat on the bench that had been Mom's favorite, the one surrounded by delphiniums, daylilies, and floribunda roses. Mom had told him the roses were named after fat bumblebee-winged fairies who tended them. Following the point of her finger, he'd seen leaves stir and flowers brighten, which meant the Flori Bundas were flitting among them. For days afterward, he'd combed the beds, trying to get a closer look at the fairies. Jesus, fairies. Still, if he'd stuck with them instead of moving up to Outer Gods, he'd be better off now.

"Okay," Eddy said. "The evidence is real. You're not crazy."

It was sad how sorry he was to hear that. He tried to make Eddy rethink his sanity: "Unless I zoned out and did it all myself."

"Like you were playing monster at the same time you were hiding from the monster? I doubt it."

"So? Was it a Servitor?"

Eddy stared at the sundial opposite the bench, as if it might shadow-point to the answer. "Let's not go there."

"Where else can we go?"

"To a hoax."

Hoax? The unexpected punch of the word rocked him. "What're you talking about?"

"A bitch-mean joke. The Reverend's scamming you."

"How? He doesn't even know where I live."

"But he knows your name."

"No, he doesn't. Well, just 'Sean.' I never told him the rest."

From a back pocket, Eddy produced folded paper. "It wasn't during the chat session. It was this."

Sean flapped open a printout of the e-mail he'd sent to the Reverend and blind-copied to Eddy. What was the problem? He'd used his Lord Grayfalcon account and signed it "Lord G." But—

The "From" line in the heading. It automatically gave his e-mail address *and* his real full name, "Sean Wyndham," because that was how he'd signed up for the account in the old days before he knew better. Idiot. No wonder Dad wanted to look over his shoulder whenever he got on the Internet.

"After you called, I looked over the Rev stuff," Eddy said. "I noticed how your name was on the e-mail. So I Googled it and got your Facebook account. Off that I got the link to your dad's Web site. *His* name's right in the phone book, with your address."

As easy as that, the Reverend could have tracked him down. "You think he's been spying on me, found out I was doing the ritual?"

"He didn't have to spy to know that. He knew it the minute you went to Geldman for the powders. And he knew that you'd think the ritual worked, because of the drugs Geldman put into them."

Okay, Eddy was the real damn Sherlock Holmes. From now on, he'd stick to playing Watson. "What else?"

"The Reverend counted on the hallucinations scaring you. He let you stew over them for a while. Then he put on a monster suit and broke onto your porch."

"It was a damn good monster suit. Like, movie quality."

"You said you barely saw the thing, you took off so fast. Body paint, a rubber mask, and monster hands. Easy to get."

"How about the slime and prints?"

"Geldman cooked up the slime. The Rev made the prints with, like, a giant rubber stamp. On a stick."

"Well, maybe. But in that case, Horrocke sure isn't the Reverend. He's too old to climb onto the porch roof and move that fast."

"Horrocke could have hired someone to play the monster."

"I guess." The costume and who might have been in it weren't the biggest problems, anyhow. Sean's empty stomach churned when he thought about the shredded cat, and Beo's decapitated raccoon, and all the pets missing along the Pawtuxet, Sweetie Pie, too, a little girl's dachshund. "But what about all the animals?"

"Which animals?"

"This cat and the animals by the river, that Joe-Jack thinks coyotes got."

The way Eddy frowned, Sean knew she hadn't factored the dead animals into her equation. She looked toward the porch. From their bench, they couldn't see the cat corpse, but they knew it was there. "The animals don't have to be connected with the hoax," she said.

"Beo saw webbed prints by the coon. I told you that. And the cat's covered with slime, same as on my pillows."

Eddy bent over, elbows on knees. "Killing people's pets is bad. I'm sorry. That's even worse than slipping you drugs."

"Hell, yes!"

"That makes the Reverend a sick bastard."

"And why's he coming after me? Like, what's his motive?"

"He's a crazy son of a bitch?" She chafed her forearms. "God, I've got goose bumps on me like hives."

She did, too. Sean's stomach churned harder: Eddy spooked meant the situation was serious. "Man, why can't I just be fucked up?"

"Because we're seeing the same things and *I'm* not fucked up." Eddy paused. Then she asked, "What are you going to do?"

He was supposed to know? That was why he'd called her!

"Somebody broke into your house. This time you've got to call the police."

"They'll talk to Dad, and he'll go ballistic."

"Then try to reach the Reverend. Tell him to lay off."

"Won't that just egg him on?"

"Call him or call the police. That's all I can think of, and I'm seriously recommending the cops."

"How about the Reverend first, then the cops if he starts giving me any crap?"

"If you don't mind wasting time, go for it."

Sean sent the Reverend an urgent message from the computer in the family room. Then Eddy got the rest of the Polish lasagna out of the freezer and nuked it. She looked like she was only eating to encourage Sean to choke something down, the way Dad used to when the hospice lady would bring them casseroles. Usually the trick had worked—Sean would start off picking and end up wolfing. Well, little kids didn't know enough to get the kind of gut-twist he felt now, waiting.

Sean was scraping his lasagna into the trash when Eddy yelled from the family room, "He's on!"

Sean dropped the half slab into the basket, plate and all, and ran for the computer. Eddy surrendered the chair at the keyboard without a fight. In the blankness of the chat window swam Redemption Orne's *Hello, Sean.* Okay. Should he rip the Reverend a new one right off? Or draw him out, see if he gave himself away? To buy time, Sean went with bland: *Hey Reverend. Thanks for getting on.*

*I was hoping I'd hear from you soon, Sean. I take it from your e-mails about the Elder Sign that you've been working on the ritual I sent.*

*Yeah but why didn't you answer?*

*I trusted you could solve the problem for yourself.*

Talk about trusting the wrong guy. *I think I screwed up,* Sean typed. *I used the Star instead of the Branch*

A pause. *So you have attempted the ritual?*

Damn, he was sweating. Eddy prodded his shoulder. "Go on. He already knows, so just cop to it."

*Yeah,* Sean typed.

*Did the Servitor come?*

Had Sean been hoping the Reverend would finally break character and start LOLing? Okay, so he'd been hoping. *I don't know. Some weird things have happened.*

*What things?*

*I got the powders from Geldman's. I did the pentagram and the first incantation. I thought I saw something come out of my brazier.*

*Did you bind the Servitor to you?*

*I panicked. I ran.*

*You didn't say the binding incantation?*

*No and when I came back nothing was there.*

Pause. *That's not surprising. It's the Branch that cages, not the Star.*

At last Eddy succumbed: "Told you."

Sean ignored her. *I couldn't find out, then it was the dark of the moon and I couldn't wait.*

"Okay," Eddy said. "So you've confessed, and he's playing along."

"Playing along?"

"Still pretending it's real. Don't let him. Tell him you know he's a fake."

The next message came up, more "playing along." *It's too bad you didn't manage to bind the Servitor. However, the summoning is much the harder part of the ritual. I'm impressed you pulled it off, Sean. Congratulations.*

*Congratulations?* The word hit him like a slap that wasn't playing around anymore, one that hurt like hell. He typed: *It's not funny. Giving me drugs.*

*Drugs?*

*The powders. Geldman put drugs in them to give me hallucinations right?*

*I don't understand.*

*He put angel dust or LSD in the powders so I'd see things. The thing in the brazier and that angel or devil guy the Black Man.*

*You saw the Black Man?*

*Because you drugged me. Thats serious ILLEGAL shit. So is breaking into my house. And killing pets.*

*Sean, I don't understand what you mean about your house and about animals being killed. The ethereal Servitor is harmless.*

Another slap. This one opened a wound that bled anger. *There isn't any Servitor. There's you and Geldman. You're hoaxing me.*

*You did summon the aether-newt, didn't you?*

God, Eddy had been so right about the Reverend. Sean pounded the keys until his sliced hand hurt again. *Will you stop messing with me? Or we'll call the police.*

*Sean, did you summon the AETHER-NEWT? It's very important.*

"He just won't give up," Eddy said.

*I guess you want us to call the police,* Sean typed. But he didn't send that message. The Reverend's last words drew his eyes: *It's very important.*

"Hit it," Eddy said.

Instead Sean erased his threat. He typed and sent: *Not the newt. The other kind.*

*The material Servitor, the blood-spawn?*

*Yes.*

*But I didn't give you the incantation for that one.*

*The Black Man wrote it out in the air like fire letters.*

A long pause. Then: *Whom did you bleed to make this Servitor?*

God, what he'd done seemed so gross now. The Reverend wasn't the only sick one. *Me.*

*You used your own blood?*

*Yes.*

Pause. Time stretched out. Sean stared at the empty screen space beneath his last *Yes.* Eddy leaned over his chair. "Why are you playing along with him again?"

A good question. *It's very important* grabbed his eyes. "I don't know."

"Well, you finally freaked *him* out, looks like."

Sean pushed back from the computer. "I don't think the Reverend's faking."

"What?"

"He thinks I summoned a Servitor."

"He's so psycho he's hoaxing himself, too?"

"Or else—" Sean felt like he was standing on a dock over black water. The posts holding it up were spindly, rotten. He could hear bugs inside the whitened wood, chewing it to pulp that wouldn't support the dock much longer. The words on the screen, the Reverend's words, *they* were the bugs.

"Back," Eddy said sharply.

The Reverend's new message raised the hairs on Sean's nape—it was as if the guy had overhead them just now. *Sean, do you believe I'm Redemption Orne, a wizard?*

"Say no," Eddy said. But Sean typed: *Sort of.* It was the truth. It was more the truth every minute.

*If you've seen the blood-spawn, you should believe it. Has it come to you?*

*Something broke into my house last night. I didn't see it real clear. Was it you screwing around?*

*Did it look like a man?*

The truth again: *No.*

*The Servitor will seek you. You're its summoner, though you didn't bind it. Also it was born from your blood, and it craves what first gave it substance in this world.*

*It wants to eat me?*

*It may not harm the summoner. But the drive to serve and the drive to devour will war in it. I wrote you that to summon the blood-spawn, you must use the blood of an enemy.*

*You didnt say WHY.*

*I didn't plan for you to summon the blood-spawn. I didn't give you the means to do it.*

Sean typed like a madman: *I just wanted the aether-newt but then the Black Man wrote out the incantation for the blood-spawn and I changed my mind and cut myself. I dont even know why. Theres drugs in the powders right? You can tell me. I wont get you in trouble.*

*During the summoning you were excited? Keener in your senses? Even aroused in body?*

*Yes,* he had to type, even though Eddy was breathing in his ear, reading. She must not have gotten what the Reverend meant by "aroused" because she didn't jump back from Sean's pervy self.

*There are no hallucinogens in Zeph and Aghar,* the Reverend sent. *What you felt came from you, from your own nature.*

Because Sean was a pervert? *What do you mean?*

*Yours was the response of a magician absorbing powerful magical energy. While you were doing the ritual, you felt as if the world was laid naked and passive before you, to be remade by your hand. You were strong enough. The stars were close above you. You knew something lay beyond them. It was not only wishing or faith. You KNEW, and the Lord Azathoth graced you by sending his Messenger.*

"Oh my freaking God," Eddy said. "There's no use talking to this guy. He keeps getting crazier."

"It's true," Sean whispered.

"What?"

He typed: *Yes it was like that.*

"Sean, Jesus!"

"I'm not going to lie."

*You have a powerful affinity for magic, Sean. You need to be taught.*

"I don't believe it," Eddy said. "He's still trying to recruit you."

Sean's fingers were shaking—he typed a mess of nonsense words, then deleted them and groped for the right keys: *All I want is you to leave me alone.*

*I can't do that now. You must dismiss the Servitor. It's too hazardous a familiar.*

The Reverend couldn't hypnotize him over the Internet, could he? Because Sean believed him, as simple as that.

He typed more gibberish, deleted, retyped: *How do I dismiss it?*

*There's another ritual for that.*

*Can you send it?*

*A moment. Don't sign off please.*

"Crap," Eddy said.

A dismissing ritual. Maybe you just called an interdimensional FedEx. Yeah, Sean could see it, the truck pulling up to the Center of All Being, and Nyarlathotep signing for a box with tentacles snaking out the airholes and slime dripping from the seams.

He let out a strangled laugh, which brought Eddy down on him. "What's funny? Why'd you ask him to send another ritual?"

The Reverend was taking a long time answering. Was that a good thing? Did it mean he was typing up the dismissing instructions on the spot? "It couldn't hurt."

"Yes, it could! Once he wouldn't own up to the hoax, you should've just said you were calling the cops."

"But he knew, Eddy. He knew exactly how I felt when I did the ritual."

"No, he knew exactly how Geldman's drugs would make you feel."

"He said there weren't any drugs."

"Oh, he can't lie? Come on, Sean."

"Leave me alone a minute, will you?"

"Fine. I'm getting a drink if we have to wait all day for this freak."

Eddy brought them cans of iced tea. Sean downed his in three gulps. Eddy took her usual baby sips, but even so, she had drained her can before the Reverend returned. His message was shockingly short: *I'm sorry, Sean. I can't give you the dismissing ritual.*

The hell? *Why not?*

*Another trial has been proposed. You must find the dismissing ritual yourself.*

"See?" Eddy said. "More bull crap."

Sean would give a million bucks if he could believe her. Instead he had to try talking the damned Reverend around. *I couldn't even find out which Elder Sign was right, where would I look?*

*About that, I'm allowed to give you one hint. The dismissing ritual, like the summoning, is in the* Necronomicon *at Miskatonic*

*University. But both summoning and dismissing are in a very dark place indeed.*

*Dark place, what does that*

The Reverend went off-line before Sean could finish typing. He gaped for a few seconds. Then he pushed the keyboard away. "I don't believe this!"

The keyboard hit the base of the monitor, which Eddy grabbed before it could topple over. "Let me sit down," she said.

"I don't believe it!"

"Sean, let me print out the conversation."

He got out of the chair, out of her way, but he didn't know where to go from there. Fear and frustration felt like bands around his chest, pressing in on his uselessly racing heart. "I can't believe he wouldn't send the dismissing ritual."

"The only thing we've got to dismiss is the Reverend. Right? Tell me he hasn't talked you into believing in Servitors."

Sean flung himself onto the window seat in the bay. The windows were up—Eddy must have opened them for air. Not that much was stirring, just enough of a breeze to carry in the cotton-candy scent of the butterfly bushes and the whoosh of the lawn sprinklers next door. If you didn't wander out into the backyard where the torn screen and dead cat were, you'd think everything was okay around the house. The garbage bag. That was out there, too, with the slimed pillows in it. Geldman could have made the slime, though. Why not? The metal and sulfur smells of the powders were part of its stink.

Eddy pulled paper out of the printer. "Done."

"What do we do now?"

"Same as we were going to do before. Call the police."

"Oh man. I don't want to. They'll think I'm a lunatic."

"Then wait for your dad to come home, and he can call them."

"Then I'd have to tell him about all the shit that's gone down since he left."

She slapped the printout on her palm, not looking any happier than he felt. "I think you've got to tell him. The Reverend and Geldman could be real trouble."

The Reverend and Geldman could be real-live wizards, too, but Sean was too worn-out to think that possibility through. It was hard enough to wrap his brain around telling Dad. "He'll kill me."

"He won't. Your dad's cool."

"Wrong. Besides, no dad is cool enough for this."

Eddy got up. "Here's what we'll do. You can't stay here alone."

"Hell, no."

"So bike back with me and stay at your aunt's. Go get ready."

Sean headed up to his bedroom to fix the jammed window. Next he locked up the whole house, checked the carriage house locks, and covered the dead cat with an overturned garbage can.

What got him was when Eddy suggested they put bricks on the can. "In case something wants to screw with the body," she said when he gave her a look.

Like the body could get more screwed up. "Let's just go, okay?"

They wheeled down the driveway while it was still bright afternoon, while Sean could still look back at his house without the dread he knew would find him once dark came, wherever he was.

**10**

**With** any luck, lost plane tickets or tornadoes would have stranded Dad in Georgia, but Sean's luck had gone to hell. Sunday afternoon, right on time, Dad called from the airport. He sounded surprised that Sean was at Celeste and Gus's. Surprised, then smug, as if he'd known all along Sean wouldn't like staying alone for two weeks.

If only Sean *had* been alone.

When he said he was going to wait out on the porch, Celeste smiled too brightly, and so he lurked, with his back to the wall, next to the screen door. Sure enough, as soon as the door finished its slow swing shut she hit the kitchen phone. Seconds later, she said, "Hey, Jere, how'd it go?"

Strike one, no Dad delay. Strike two, Celeste swinging into Concerned-Aunt mode.

"Three new commissions? That's fantastic. You'll have to have dinner soon and tell us about them. But I wanted to talk to you before you picked Sean up."

What did Eddy say whenever the Hell Pug chewed something to shit or pissed on the floor? *Et tu, Brute.* Exactly.

"No, the cut's healing fine. But he's been jumpy the last couple times we've seen him. Especially yesterday. I thought he came over to go out with Eddy and their gang, but they went and Sean just hung around with us." Pause. Laugh. "Right, we're big fun on a Saturday night. Listen, though. He kept getting up last night. I think he was checking the doors and windows downstairs. He's never done anything like that before. Maybe something happened at your house?"

All Sean could hear of Dad's response was a vocal rumble. It sounded low to him, but it kept cutting Celeste off: "What— No, we— I don't—" Finally she got in a complete sentence. "Okay, I just wanted to give you a heads-up." *Click.* End of call.

Sean slunk down to the bottom step. Eddy came over to keep him company. They didn't say much. It was kind of like a wake, or a pre-wake, since Sean wasn't dead yet.

The Civic pulled up ten minutes after Celeste's stealth call. Dad must have floored it on the highway. Normally Eddy would have chatted Dad up for a while, but today she only waved before running home. *Et tu, Brute,* again. Sean was on his own.

He considered getting into the backseat. No. With just the two of them in the car, that would be the same as admitting he had some reason to feel guilty, while riding shotgun would mean he had a clear conscience. Sean trotted around and slid into the passenger seat. "Hey, Dad!" he said. "What's up?"

Right off the bat, Dad scrutinized him, frowning. That was Celeste's fault. "Getting home is what's up. I'm exhausted. You look pretty worn-out, too."

"Yeah. Joe-Jack's really been working me."

Dad shifted his gaze to Sean's left hand. "How's that cut?"

Sean turned the hand over to show him a shiny pucker of new skin. Red dots marched along either side of the closed wound, suture holes. "Aunt Cel took out the stitches this morning. Ten of them."

"That's impressive for one crummy bagel."

Sean tried to sound proud. "Hell yeah. Did you get any of those praline things?"

"Three pounds," Dad said, but he didn't fall for the diversionary tactic. "Sean, did you really cut your hand slicing a bagel? Come on. You're an expert at that."

Sean sucked in his lower lip, which smarted. In goddamned August, it was winter chapped, he'd been gnawing on it so much. That was a little-kid trick, not anything he needed Dad to see. They'd started rolling. He looked out the side window in time to see Prospect Park go by.

"Sean?"

He kept his face to the park. "The bagel's what I told Aunt Cel. It's not what really happened."

"So what did?"

"I'll tell you, Dad. But can it wait until we get home?"

Dad didn't answer until after they'd swooped all the way to the bottom of College Hill: "All right. I guess it'll keep that long. Is there any food in the house?"

There couldn't be much, since Eddy had resorted to frozen Polish lasagna the day before. "Not a lot."

"Then we should stop at Shaw's before we go home."

"Sure, Dad. We could stop wherever you want."

Sean must have sounded too eager to scavenge an extra thirty minutes of grace, because Dad shook his head. "Why do I get this feeling I shouldn't have left you unsupervised?"

That should have been Sean's cue to get indignant. When he kept his mouth shut, Dad shook his head again.

The supermarket parking lot was packed, probably with people who'd decided to throw a last-minute barbecue and who'd come in search of burnable meat and the charcoal to burn it with. Dad had to park all the way down by the chain-link fence between the lot and the Pawtuxet River Trail. Joe-Jack's van was parked a couple spaces over. "Joe and Beo must be hiking," Dad said.

This late in the afternoon, when Joe-Jack was so worked up about the "coyotes" by the river? The dashboard clock read: 7:09. "It'll get dark soon."

"That never stopped Joe before."

It had better stop him now. What if the Reverend was hiding in the woods, waiting to kill more pets? What if something worse than the Reverend was there?

Shove that, Sean's inner Eddy commanded. As he and Dad trekked up to the supermarket, Sean tried to obey, but he only succeeded in squashing the fear when he spotted Joe-Jack leaning on a column by the entrance, cell phone to his ear. All right, then. Joe-Jack had just come for some veggie burgers to burn. Now he was just calling home to see if they needed soy milk, too. The world was in order, nothing to see here, move along, folks.

The one who moved along was a guy with a cartload of soda twelve-packs. As he labored past Joe-Jack into the parking lot, Sean saw that Beo was crouched behind his father, his back to the wall of the market, fists jammed into his mouth. Jesus, was he crying?

It was like a plug had been pulled at the base of Sean's skull, letting all the blood run out of his head. He stopped, dizzy. "They saw it," he said, because as the last drops drained he knew it was true. He knew it.

Joe-Jack closed his phone and turned toward them. His face had been scorched by too many summers outdoors to go white; it had gone gray instead. "They're coming," he said dully. "The police."

Dad had squatted next to Beo and put an arm around his jerking shoulders. "What for, Joe?" he asked.

"I didn't want to call them from the trail," Joe-Jack went on. He was looking at Sean. "In case the thing's still around."

"What is it?" Dad asked, raising his voice.

Beo choked.

"We were looking for Hrothgar," Joe-Jack said. "The gate was

open last night, and he ran off. He always comes back in the
morning; he gets hungry. Only not today. We walked the trail on
our side of the river. Then we drove over here to walk the rest.
He must've swum across, right? Stupid dog's always swimming
across, chasing the ducks."

Sean's heart constricted, forcing enough blood back into his
brain for him to speak: "You found him, he's hurt?"

Beo keened suddenly: "He's ripped up. I left . . . the gate
open . . . and he's ripped all apart—"

The sound of Beo keening pulled Joe-Jack to his son. People
drifted over to see what the crisis was. Sean shoved himself
between two orange-vested cart boys to escape the tightening
circle. He had to see what Joe-Jack and Beo had seen. It was the
last thing Sean wanted to do, but it was the first duty of his new
life. Because his life *was* new. As he started to run, he seemed to
feel under his feet the boundary that separated old normality
from sudden strange, and that boundary was a knife-edge pointing him straight into the woods beyond the parking lot.

"Sean!"

He hip-checked a line of carts snaking in from the lot, staggered, caught his balance, and ran on. He dodged a blatting
SUV, then skirted a refrigerator truck to strike the chain link
that shielded asphalt from thick August underbrush. A gate
opened on the river trail. He bolted through, into the shadows
under the trees.

"Sean, wait!"

Dad's voice was small, back in the old world. "Stay there!"
Sean shouted over his shoulder. After that he had to save his
breath. He pounded up the clearer sections of the path and
swerved and ducked through the stretches overgrown with
pokeweed and bull briars. A festoon of briar snagged his shirt,
and he got both hands bloody freeing himself to run on.

To his right, he began to glimpse crumbling brick buildings:
the old industrial park. That meant he was nearing his summon-

ing site. Sean stopped to breathe and listen. Cicadas, a sultry jungle sound high in the canopy. Otherwise silence.

Except for Dad's shout, nearer now: "Sean!"

Sean ran on. Cracked blacktop edged closer on his right; sun-dazzled river curved in on his left. There it was, the back of the iron-casting factory, but he didn't pause to see what might be left of his magical circle. He leaped a weedy culvert. The industrial park was behind him now. The trail veered toward the water, where the soil got sandier. One open patch looked particularly trampled. Sean stopped again. He easily read sneaker treads and the crepe-sole prints of work boots, Joe-Jack's, no doubt. Dog paw marks were all over the area, big ones. Other prints looked like a waterbird's, long, thin toes with webbing between them, but these prints seemed linked in places to impressions of a broad spurred heel. The complex prints were as big as the work boot prints.

Sean crossed the clearing. Purplish spots began to pepper the sand, mixed with splotches of a glistening gray-green. He didn't have to bend to identify the splotches—their stench shimmered in the air like heat waves. Here it reminded him of a rotting whale carcass he and Eddy had found on Second Beach one summer, but this was rotting whale mixed with metal tang and burning sulphur, the gray powder and the yellow, Zeph and Aghar.

"Sean!" And running footsteps, he could hear those, too.

Sean ran. Just before the clearing bottlenecked back into trail, he made a desperate broad jump over tufts of brown fur and a patchwork of purple-red and noxious green. The red had to be blood, soaked into the sand.

In the next clearing he saw the trunk of an ancient maple that had toppled across the trail during last winter's storms. Brown fur littered the sand around it. Brown fur and other remnants. That plug in his skull? Pulled again, blood racing down, making him light-headed. Sean leaned on the maple. For a few seconds, he closed his eyes and stood in spinning darkness. But he had come to see, to witness.

He opened his eyes.

The worst of it was the heap of fur and bone and viscera that lay not far from his feet. That was the greater part of Hrothgar, but tossed willy-nilly were flaps of hide, gnawed-through bones, the thick tail that had been so adept at sweeping bottles and knickknacks off low tables. The head lay on the verge of the river, one ear pricked, the other missing. Also missing were the eyes and, apparently, the tongue. At least, no tongue lolled through the screaming gape of mouth.

"Sean, where the hell are you?" From the first clearing, close.

He opened his mouth to answer. Bile rushed up his throat, but no words. Sean twisted over the maple trunk and vomited down its far side. Vomit, whale-metal-sulfur, ripe blood and waste, raw meat. He was going to drown in the rising stink—

"Sean." Dad's voice was harsh and tight, as if he were going to puke, too. Instead Sean heard him retreat from the slaughter yard. When he returned only seconds later, after no sound of retching, his voice was even: "Sean, do you hear me?"

He spit out bile. "Yeah, Dad."

"Let's go."

Go?

Dad took his shoulders and drew him up and around. It was all still there, the heap, the head. "Look at this shit," Sean said. "Oh man. Shit, *shit.*"

Dad ignored the litany of the forbidden word. "Come on," he said. "And stop looking."

The remnants were easier to face than Dad. Sean ducked his head. "What are we going to do?"

"We're going back to the car."

"No, about Hrothgar, about Joe-Jack and Beo."

"There's nothing we can do here, Sean. We'll figure it out later."

Sean pushed off the trunk, too violently. He stumbled, fell against Dad, then squirmed free and started down the trail on rubber-wobbly legs. He had to concentrate on his knees, so they wouldn't bend the wrong way. Dad followed a few steps behind.

They reached the back side of the industrial park. This time Sean looked into the lot where he'd set up his magical circle. The brazier-grill was still there, still overturned. Dad must have followed his gaze, because he said, "Some kids had a party, looks like." His voice was strained, trying too hard to sound casual. His footsteps became muffled, as if he'd left the trail.

He *had* left it. Sean turned to see Dad pushing through the underbrush to the lot. He froze, watched, silent. Dad kicked over the grill. Ashes. He lifted the grill cover. Dead briquettes. A halfhearted breeze carried the ghosts of Zeph and Aghar to Sean. Now Dad was scuffing a toe against the worn blacktop. From the trail Sean could just make out faded chalk, a sweep of circle, crisscrossed lines.

Dad straightened. His eyes met Sean's. He couldn't have forgotten all the practice sessions in the driveway and how he had taught Sean how to draw the pentagram.

Sean looked away first. He broke into a clumsy trot. It seemed to pump blood back into his legs; soon he was sprinting, and he sprinted the rest of the way to the supermarket lot and the Civic. Up by the entrance, Joe-Jack was talking to three policemen. Two cruisers idled in the fire lane. A police van, ANIMAL CONTROL, pulled up behind them.

Dad joined Sean half a minute later, panting. Sean waited until they'd both caught their breath before he asked, "Do I have to talk to the police?"

"Do you have something to tell them? Do you know what killed Hrothgar?"

Sean chewed his lower lip. "They wouldn't believe me," he said.

"Get in the car. We're going home."

Sean obeyed. Seven fifty on the dashboard, and the sun was balanced on the roof of the veterinary hospital across from Shaw's, about to sink out of sight. As Dad reached to jam his key into the ignition, Sean grabbed his arm. "We can't go to the house," he said.

"Sean, we've got to talk. Home's the best place."

It was scary to hear how thin Dad's patience had already been worn by this shitstorm Sean had landed them in. He couldn't back down, though. "No! It's not safe. Please, let's go back to Aunt Cel's. God, please, Dad."

Dad pulled his arm from Sean's grip and dropped his keys in the change tray. It wasn't so dark yet that Sean couldn't see that the glint in his narrowed eyes wasn't anger but fear, fear for Sean.

Seeing that was what touched off the explosion, the sobs. Sean managed to keep them almost soundless, but his shoulders heaved like he was puking again and the tears sheeting down his face were so hot he dabbed his fingers in them and checked to make sure they weren't blood. "What, Sean?" Dad demanded. "Why not home?"

Sean swallowed a few times and finally got the words out: "Because the thing that killed Hrothgar might be there." Yeah, all right. He said "the thing." He didn't say *some nutcase I met on the Internet,* because he couldn't believe in the Reverend in a monster suit, not anymore, not after seeing Hrothgar's scattered corpse.

The car keys rattled as Dad fumbled with them. At last one chunked into the ignition, and the Civic came to life with its usual mild cough. "Okay," Dad said. "Okay, Sean. We'll go to Cel's."

# 11

**Sean** slept through the night thanks to his aunt, who'd dosed him with Valium right after the supper he hadn't eaten. In the morning, still dopey, he lurched downstairs. By now, he hoped, Dad and Celeste and Gus would have decided what to do about the Reverend; the evening before, they'd done nothing but argue, well, Sean and Dad anyhow.

The kitchen was full of early sun and the smell of French roast coffee, empty of Dad and Gus. No Celeste, either, but she'd left Sean a note: "Gone to hospital. Jere and Gus gone to Edgewood house. Don't go out, your dad's orders."

Would Dad count Eddy's house as going out? Sean considered the question over cornflakes and still-piping coffee from the carafe on the table. The slap of flip-flops on the back porch made the question irrelevant. He opened the door before Eddy could reach it. Good thing: She was toting two pies and a newspaper. "You're finally up," she said.

Sean checked the clock. "It's, wow, eight eleven."

"I've been over twice already. Here, take these. Blueberry.

Mom said you guys might want pie for breakfast, like the Amish."

Why not? The Amish were sensible people who never got mixed up with Internet freaks. Sean cut himself a slice. "Want some?"

"God, no. Did you read the paper yet?"

"No."

Eddy plunked herself down across from him, and Sean saw that her eyes were rimmed with red. "There's an article about Hrothgar."

The pie, still warm, oozed purple juice. Sean ate a couple bites—he had to, now that he'd taken a piece. Eddy was tough, but dogs were like people to her. It killed him to see her bummed, like it had killed him to see Joe-Jack and Beowulf after their discovery in the woods. "You've got the article?"

"Yeah." She dropped the newspaper on the table. "I called Beo last night when I heard. He said you ran up the trail to look."

Sean was glad Rachel had moved on to blueberries—strawberry goosh would not have been easy eating this morning. "How'd you find out about Hrothgar?"

"Your uncle came over and told me. And he asked for the Redemption Orne stuff. You know, the chat records and the ritual."

"You gave them to him?"

"I figured if he knew to ask, you were talking. Weren't you?"

He nodded. Then, shunting aside cereal bowl and pie plate, he dragged the newspaper into range.

The story about Hrothgar was on the front page. The headline read: "Mystery Killer on the Pawtuxet: Man or Beast?" There were pictures on page 4, where the story continued. The biggest was of the clearing with the fallen maple, but all that remained of Hrothgar was some dark patches on the sandy bank. Otherwise, it looked like a travel brochure, the Pawtuxet at sunset, a place you wouldn't mind visiting.

The second picture Joe-Jack must have taken a while back: Beowulf hugging Hrothgar and getting his face tongue-washed. The third was of two police officers on the trail, one pointing at webbed footprints. Sean flipped back to the front page and started reading:

Yesterday afternoon Joseph Douglass and his son, Beowulf, were searching the Pawtuxet River Trail for their chocolate Labrador, Hrothgar. On the Warwick side, near the defunct Pawtuxet Industrial Park, they found the remains of their dog. He had been decapitated and dismembered. It appeared the attacker had also eaten part of the corpse.

The killing may be linked to recent animal disappearances in Pawtuxet Village. Several residents have reported missing dogs and cats, and last week Douglass found a mutilated raccoon corpse on the trail. Warwick Animal Control Officer Peter Annunziato was among the policemen who responded. "This was a big, strong dog," he told the *Journal*. "It took a powerful animal to kill him. There are coyotes along the river, but we haven't seen any attacks like this."

Annunziato knows of no bears or zoo escapees in the area. "Sometimes you get private individuals keeping dangerous exotics, but mostly in isolated places. Around here, it'd be hard to hide a big predator from the neighbors."

Annunziato did not comment on tracks found at the site. However, the *Journal* showed photographs to Dr. Angela Mercado, a wildlife biologist at the University of Rhode Island. "The triangular webbed marks are superficially like the footprint of an aquatic bird," Dr. Mercado said. "However, all birds have four toes, and these prints show five. Also, some of the prints are compound. They show the webbed toes, an arch, and a heel."

Asked to speculate, Dr. Mercado said, "My best guess is you have a hoaxer. The impressions resemble the print of a human foot in a shoe designed to make the webbed tracks. The wearer seems to be trying to walk on the balls of his feet, so only the webbed tracks appear, but sometimes his heels come down."

Footsteps on the porch jerked Sean out of the article. Dad and Gus came in, Gus looking sober enough, but Dad— Sean knew from experience how to read the muscle jumping in his jaw: He was down-to-the-bone pissed and trying to swallow it.

"Glad you're up, Sean," Gus said. And, "Hello, Eddy. Bearer of pies again?"

"Like always, Professor."

"Eddy," Dad said. "No offense, but we need to talk to Sean."

In other words, *beat it.* Eddy began to get up, but Gus told her, "Wait." He looked over at Dad. "Jere, Eddy's had the same contact with Redemption Orne as Sean. If he's a target, she may be, too."

It looked like Dad would argue. Then he shook his head and moved toward the counter. "Is there any coffee?"

"Over here, Dad."

"Grab a cup for me, Jere," Gus said.

Eddy gave Sean a furtive thumbs-up. "I brought Sean the paper, Professor Litinski. Did you see the article about Hrothgar?"

"We read it earlier. What do you think of it, Sean?"

He watched Dad carry two mugs to the table. "I didn't finish it yet. Did you see the stuff at the house?"

Dad took the fourth chair. "We saw the torn screen, dead cat, slimed pillows, fake footprints outside the gate."

Even though Eddy had already verified that the evidence was

real, Sean was relieved Dad and Gus had seen it, too. "Anything new?"

"I don't think so," Gus said. He poured coffee. "Why don't you finish the article? Then we can have a war council."

Dad took a slug of coffee like he really needed it. Probably he'd been up all night; Sean doubted Celeste could have forced any Valium down *his* throat.

Sean opened the newspaper.

> The Warwick Police Department has released no statement on the killing. An unofficial source remarked that human agency is being considered.
>
> Authorities warn residents along the Pawtuxet to stay away from the river trails. Residents should keep pets indoors and not allow young children to play outside unattended. They should report any suspicious animal or human activity to the police.
>
> Joseph Douglass spoke to this reporter last evening. "People better be careful," he said, looking over the fence that separates his yard from the river. "Anything that could kill Hrothgar could kill a man; don't even think about a kid. People better look out."

Sean refolded the newspaper. Had the others been watching him, trying to gauge his reactions? Good luck. He felt numb, and the only comment that came to him was, "The reporter didn't write about the smell."

"There was a smell?" Eddy asked.

"The same smell as on the cat and pillows."

"I bet the police told the paper not to mention it. So if someone calls claiming they know about the killing—"

"Exactly," Gus said. "If he doesn't mention the smell, no credibility."

Dad shifted in his chair, as if Gus and Eddy's CSI chatter

chafed his already-raw nerves. Sean cut in quickly. "What if Joe-Jack's right? What if the Servitor goes after a kid next?"

"Sean," Dad said. "There isn't any Servitor. No familiar, no monster. Someone's hoaxing us."

Two days ago, Eddy had nearly convinced Sean of that, but after Hrothgar he didn't dare bank on a hoax. "I don't think so, Dad."

"Sean, you've got to be reasonable."

"That's what I *am* being. We both saw Hrothgar—"

Dad shoved his mug away. It struck Sean's cereal bowl, which sloshed milk and sodden flakes onto the table. "The police saw Hrothgar, too. They think a man did it."

What was the line in the article? *"Human agency is being considered."* Sean said, "They're not sure."

"They will be when we tell them how someone broke into our house, our *house*, Sean. Some lunatic you met on the Internet, and you let him get your name, let him get drugs into you—"

This time Gus cut in. "We went through this last night, Jere. We said we'd start fresh in the morning."

Dad scraped his chair away from the table. He went to the counter and leaned on it with his back to them. Sean sucked in his lower lip. It cracked, and he tasted blood.

"The war council needs to proceed in an orderly fashion," Gus said. "Do we agree?"

"Agreed," Eddy piped up.

"Agreed," Dad said, turning around. "If we can keep it sensible."

"Contrary to popular opinion, I'm always sensible." Gus went into the dining room and came back hefting a folder. "The printouts Eddy lent us. Did she tell you, Sean?"

"Yeah."

"I've read through them. So have your father and Cel. So we're all familiar with the material."

Like she was in class, Eddy nodded. Dad nodded, too, but he didn't wait for the teacher to continue. "Sean, I can't believe you and Eddy talked to Orne. Talked to him twice. Couldn't you tell there was something wrong with him?"

Eddy's face went splotchy red—if there was one thing she couldn't handle, it was an adult she respected chewing her out. Sean was used to it, so he tried to draw Dad's fire: "Eddy didn't like how he wouldn't break character, but I thought he was just messing around."

"And you lied about the ritual, Sean. You told me you got it from a book. You promised you were done with it after Mrs. Ferreira complained."

"Jere—"

"Just a minute, Gus. Sean, what I want to know is why."

It hurt Sean to swallow, as if a shard of piecrust had lodged in his throat. "I don't know, Dad. I wanted to do the ritual; I really wanted to try and do it right."

Dad lowered his head, so all Sean could see was his rumpled hair and crooked part.

Gus took advantage of the silence and produced a sheet of notebook paper covered with his spiky handwriting. "Last night I worked out some theories. Here's Number One. Whatever's killing animals along the river is unrelated to what happened at your house Saturday night."

"Can't be," CSI Eddy said. "The MOs are the same. Shredded corpses, and the smell, and the prints."

Dad looked up.

"I agree," Gus said. "One's out." He slashed a pen across his notes. "So, Theory Two. It's an animal doing the killing, either on its own or under human supervision."

Eddy opened her mouth at the same time Dad cleared his throat. She deferred to him, and Dad said, "What would be strong enough to rip a Lab's head clean off? A bear, maybe a tiger?"

"Those are big, conspicuous animals," Gus said.

"Well, what about the human supervision? Orne. He's got a wild animal hidden, and he lets it run on the river trail at night. It starts killing pets. Orne thinks that when Sean finds out, he'll connect the killings with the spell he did. He'll get more and more scared, and then Orne will pull the big scare of coming to the house in his costume."

"The prints aren't from a bear or big cat."

"There's what the biologist said. Orne's wearing shoes that make a webbed print. He follows his animal and steps on any tracks it leaves."

"A lot of moving parts in that story. How would you control a bear or tiger? Even substitute a huge dog, like a mastiff. You could control the mastiff, but you'd still have to cover up hundreds of paw prints, in the dark. You're bound to miss some."

Dad scissor-rubbed his brow with a thumb and forefinger. "It's damn clumsy. But what else could it be?"

Gus tapped his notes. "Theory Three. No killer animals. A person's killing the pets and making it look like monster attacks. He's tiptoeing around in his webbed shoes. He's spreading his artificial slime. He's dressing up in that monster suit."

"Keep thinking for me, Gus," Dad said.

"Three A: The hoaxer is the person calling himself Redemption Orne."

"It has to be Orne," Eddy said. "He's the only one who knew Sean had the summoning ritual, so who else would put on a horror show about a Servitor?"

"And Three B: Geldman is Orne's accomplice. He gave Sean drugs to make him hallucinate."

Gus's Number Three was pretty much what Eddy had come up with earlier. There was something wrong with both their versions, though Sean couldn't put his finger on it. As for Dad, he was looking more convinced and more pissed by the minute. "I wish Sean had saved those damn powders. Now all we've got is the e-mail from Orne saying to buy them from Geldman."

"Yes," Gus said. "And Geldman could deny selling anything to Sean."

"But the e-mail makes a connection between Orne and him. We should give it to the police. Geldman could be selling this garbage to other kids."

What had been bothering Sean finally came clear. "No, see. Uncle Gus, Dad. Orne gave me the incantation to summon the *aether-newt,* not the blood-spawn. So why would he set up a blood-spawn hoax?"

The way Dad rolled his eyes, he didn't get it. Gus, on the other hand, nodded. So did Eddy.

"Here's another thing: The Reverend chats with me and Eddy once and decides to spend tons of time and money hoaxing us? Geldman takes a chance giving a kid drugs? I mean, couldn't he lose his license or even go to jail?"

"Sean," Dad moaned. "What's your point?"

"His point is the big question," Gus said. "What's Orne's motivation to terrorize a stranger?"

"Since when do lunatics need reasonable motivation?"

"Their motives have to make sense to them, at least."

"Let the police figure that out."

Dad said it like he was ready to grab the phone. But Sean couldn't give in. "Dad, there's a motive the police won't think of. What if Orne's really trying to see if I can do magic?"

"Theories Four and Five," Gus said. "Number Four. Redemption Orne believes he's a wizard. Geldman shares his belief, so they're not hoaxers in the usual sense. They're delusional, they're creating their own reality, and they're trying to drag Sean into it. Orne in particular, because part of his delusion is that he needs an apprentice."

Four was better than Three, but Sean still couldn't buy in.

"Uncle Gus, you think Orne and Geldman could fake all this stuff and not know they were faking it?"

Dad scowled. "Why not, if they're crazy enough? Besides, it doesn't matter what kind of lunatics they are. I want them stopped."

But it did matter what made Orne tick. The difference between a hoax and genuine magic was huge. It was a difference as big as the whole universe and its laws. Dad didn't understand that. Could Gus? "What about Number Five?" Sean asked.

"Five," Gus said. "Redemption Orne is a wizard. Magic works. Somehow Sean made a mistake with his summoning, and now a monster's loose."

Gus's bald statement launched a kick to Sean's psychic gut. Eddy gawped as if she'd gotten the same kick. It was one thing for Sean to spout cracked ideas, but for Gus to do it? He wasn't merely an adult; he was a philosophy professor and a former Navy pilot. Didn't he have to disbelieve in cracked ideas, kind of on principle?

To hell with kicks: Dad looked like he'd taken a sledgehammer to the head. For a few seconds, he stared at Gus. Then he blew up: "Come on! This is serious."

"I'm being serious."

"But you're talking fairy tales!"

Gus lifted his hand from his notes. "Not quite. The Cthulhu Mythos is as coherent a tradition as any religion. It's had followers since humans grew brains big enough to follow anything. It's got followers now. Orne could be one of them."

"Not just a wannabe, an actual wizard. That's what you're saying?"

"That's Theory Five."

Sean got his psychic breath back. "Dad, I know it sucks to think about monsters, but what if it's true? What if it's my fault all these animals got killed? What about Joe-Jack and Beo? They helped make the river trail; now how can they ever walk it again? And I can't even want them to, because they could get killed like Hrothgar, and it would be my fault."

Dad gripped the edge of the counter. "Sean, the only monster is Orne, and it isn't your fault he's playing a rotten game with you."

"If magic is real, it *is* my fault. It's my Servitor. I summoned it."

Either the counter was going to break or Dad's knuckles were.

Quietly (cautiously?), Gus cleared his throat. "Here's how I see it," he said. "We've ruled out Theories One and Two. Three and Four, the deliberate or delusional hoaxes, the police can handle without our help. We watch the news. If they announce the slime's synthetic, the prints are fakes, Hrothgar's wounds were man-made, we turn our information over to them."

"And if they don't find a hoax?" Dad said. "Do we go to them with Theory Five?"

"I'm not sure that would help," Gus said.

"It was a rhetorical question, Gus."

The frustration Dad packed into that last sentence was another kick in the gut. Man, if Sean could only go back a few weeks, skip doing the ritual, no, skip going into Horrocke's in the first place. But whatever his magical aptitude, he wasn't powerful enough to time travel. "I don't think regular weapons would stop it," he told his mutilated slice of pie—he couldn't look at Dad or Gus or even Eddy. "It's probably like the thing Patience Orne summoned. The Puritans tried shooting it and chopping it with axes, and that didn't even slow it down. It only went away when Patience died. They hanged her, and they heard it howling in the woods. Then they never saw it again."

"How do you know that, Sean?" Gus asked.

"It's in the *Witch Panic* book."

"Speaking of which, I liberated it from your backpack last night." Gus wrote some notes on the back of his theories sheet.

"We wanted to see the ad you found. I have to admit, I'm stumped how Orne managed to make the clipping look so old. I'd love to have an expert check it over."

"We already showed it to Mr. Horrocke," Eddy said. "He wouldn't say anything about it. Is that suspicious or what? I still bet he's the Reverend."

"That makes sense to me," Dad said. "Sean found the ad at his store."

It was no use arguing that Horrocke wasn't Orne. All Sean had to go on was his memory of the old guy looking into the stacks, then up at the ceiling, as if he could spot the true culprit that way. Too bad Horrocke hadn't wanted to talk about the clipping. *He* would have known if it was over a hundred years old. Who else would? Somebody at the MU Library?

The MU Library.

Ms. Arkwright.

Sean pushed back from the table. He risked a glance at Dad, whose face was unreadable except for the muscle spasm in his jaw.

Gus finished writing. He looked over at Dad and said, "I don't think we have enough evidence to accuse Horrocke of playing wizard. But we could talk to him before we go to Geldman's."

Geldman's? "You're going to the pharmacy?" Sean said.

"This morning," Dad said. "I want to know what was in the powders Geldman sold you. I want to know his friend Orne's real name and what his game is."

"We want you to come, too, Sean," Gus put in. "You can tell whether Geldman's being straight with us."

Sean expected Eddy to ask if she could tag along, but Dad's mood must have scared her off. All she said was, "Can I do anything here, Professor Litinski?"

"You can do a lot. Go online and research Redemption Orne, Solomon Geldman, Geldman's Pharmacy, Servitors, familiars. A location for Orne would be great. Any forums or blogs he might be involved in. Just don't contact Orne himself."

"I'm all over it."

Sean half-wished he could stay with Eddy, but at the same time he felt a queasy excitement over returning to Geldman's Pharmacy. Once they'd seen the place, Gus and Dad would understand how Sean had gotten sucked into doing the ritual. And while they were in Arkham— "Could we go see Ms. Arkwright?"

Dad had come back to the table to fortify himself with coffee and the remains of Sean's breakfast. "What are you talking about?"

"Ms. Arkwright. She's an expert on old documents, right? We could show her the clipping." But even as Dad gave him the evil eye, Sean realized how much more important Helen Arkwright could be. He turned to Gus. "Plus, she works at Miskatonic, with all the Mythos books, and Orne said we had to get the dismissing ritual out of the *Necronomicon* there."

Around a mouthful of pie, Dad said, "Helen Arkwright doesn't have anything to do with this." He swallowed. "And she's hired me for a very expensive restoration. The last thing I need is for her to think I'm a madman."

"But she could get us in to look at the *Necronomicon,* and then we could look for the dismissing ritual."

Eddy widened her eyes at Sean and mouthed, *Chill.* "Sean," Gus said. "We don't know we have anything to dismiss."

"But the *Necronomicon*—"

"You don't need any more crazy books," Dad said.

"But if it turns out we *need* the *Necronomicon*—"

"Let's play it by ear," Gus said. "Horrocke, then Geldman, then proceed from there."

"To the police," Dad said. He shook his head at Sean before heading to the bathroom.

At least Theory Five was still on the list—when Gus folded his notes, Sean saw that only Numbers One and Two had been crossed off. Wizards and monsters weren't on the top, but they were still in the game.

**Dad** called his interns and told them to stay away from the studio until further notice. Termites, toxic pesticides, he said. That was a decent lie for Dad.

They were on the front porch, heading out to Arkham, when a Providence police cruiser pulled up to the curb behind Gus's Volvo. Sean stopped on the bottom step, an instant horror movie running through his head. *The Cranston police have called Providence to arrest Sean, because back in Edgewood Mrs. Mandell is sprawled on her kitchen floor; bloody webbed prints trail up the stairs to Ethan's and Zoe's rooms; Mr. Mandell, in shock, still clutches the phone on which he's called 911.* A cop in plain clothes got out of the cruiser, tall and buff, with carrot-red hair. When he gave the three of them a cheerful wave, Sean's mind movie snapped. Who'd arrive to announce a massacre with a wave like that?

Shading his eyes, the cop looked over Sean's shoulder and said, "Mr. Wyndham?"

Dad was a couple steps above Sean. He squeezed past him, and Gus took his place at Sean's back. "I'm Jeremy Wyndham."

The cop met Dad halfway up the brick path from sidewalk to house, badge wallet open. "Thomas O'Conaghan," he said. "Good morning, sir."

The badge was just a glint in the sun to Sean. Dad peered at it. "*Detective* O'Conaghan," he said.

Detective. Sean got off the bottom step onto solid ground, only it didn't feel all that solid. Gus followed close, like he knew he might have to catch Sean when the truth came out and he dived.

"That's right," O'Conaghan said, still smiling. "I'm not here on official business, though. I'm interested in the animal killings in Pawtuxet Village. I understand you and your son were at the scene of one?"

"How do you understand that, Detective?" Dad sounded put out, which couldn't be a good way to sound around cops.

"I talked to Joseph Douglass," O'Conaghan said. "He mentioned meeting you and Sean after he found his dog. He said Sean went to see the body and you followed."

That was the trouble with Joe-Jack. If you got him talking, he'd spill every last detail, like a shook-up beer can spewing foam.

"Joe's our friend," Dad said. "Sean went to the breeder's with him and his son when they picked out Hrothgar. It was a shock to Sean, how the dog was killed."

"I'm sure it was, sir. Is that Sean?"

Dad looked around, as if he weren't sure. "Yes. And my brother-in-law, Gus Litinski. We're getting ready to go on a trip."

Like, *leave us the hell alone.* Again, O'Conaghan wasn't fazed. He walked right up to Sean and Gus. "Professor Litinski, is it?" he said.

"That's me, Detective."

"Mr. Douglass said Sean might be at your house."

"Yes, he often stays here."

O'Conaghan turned to Sean. He'd lost the smile, and his eyes, bright blue ones, were serious. "I'm sorry you had to see Hrothgar."

"Yeah." Surprise, Sean didn't croak. "He was kind of my dog, too. He always rode with us in the van and hung out while we were working. He was cool."

"I believe you," O'Conaghan said.

"Look." That was Dad, coming up, more put out than before. "I don't get what you're doing here, Detective. The animal killings must come under the Cranston and Warwick jurisdictions."

"As I said, I'm not here in any official capacity. It's a strange case. I'm curious about it."

"I don't think your curiosity's appropriate. Sean's been upset enough. Besides, we don't know anything more than we've read in the paper."

O'Conaghan nodded. But then he looked again at Sean, and Sean thought of Dad's eyes, of the concentration that got into them when he was doing a difficult glass cut. Not really a *sharp* look, because *sharp* could get mean and cut. *Focused* was a better word. "Sean, did you know there've also been animal killings near your house, in Roger Williams Park?"

He wasn't surprised to hear it, but he could truthfully say, "No, sir."

"Skunks, coons, feral cats, torn up like Hrothgar. And I heard from Providence Mounted Command that the horses in the park stables have been agitated the last couple of nights. I had a look around the stables this morning, and I found webbed prints like the ones by the river."

Great, the Servitor was thinking about expanding its menu to include major livestock. "That's crazy."

"Worrying," O'Conaghan said.

Someone put a hand on Sean's shoulder. It was Gus, who said, "The paper mentioned a possible hoax. Do you think that holds water, Detective?"

"It might, and it might connect up with an odd thing I noticed in the old industrial park. Looks like somebody's been playing around with pagan rituals there, drawing pentagrams and lighting fires."

Sean felt his jaw slacken, but he managed to keep his mouth shut. All he had to do was go on looking O'Conaghan in the eye like any innocent person would. Gus had taken over the talking: "The killings could be animal sacrifices, you're thinking?"

"I don't know what to think," O'Conaghan said, looking straight at Sean.

"Me, neither, sir," Sean got out.

"Which is what I told you a few minutes ago, Detective," Dad said. He was trying to sound all cool, like Gus, but Gus did it a lot better. "I'm sorry, we can't help you."

For another couple seconds, O'Conaghan's stare fixed Sean. Then O'Conaghan turned back to Dad. "I'm sorry I've held you up, Mr. Wyndham. If you remember any odd detail about what you saw yesterday, I'd appreciate a call." He handed Dad a business card. "Again, sorry for inconveniencing you. Have a good trip."

That was it. O'Conaghan returned to the cruiser. After it pulled away, Dad flung the business card like a Frisbee and it spun into the barberry bushes by the porch steps. "What was all that crap? And Joe—why'd he have to drag Sean into this?"

"The detective probably thinks it's weird how I ran to look at Hrothgar," Sean said. "He must think I know something."

"Bull."

Gus retrieved the business card. "His curiosity *is* curious. So is his mention of the pentagram."

"Yeah." Sean couldn't shake the idea that O'Conaghan had read his guilt in his face, but he also remembered, he realized now, that there'd been a spark of real sympathy in O'Conaghan's eyes. A cop wouldn't feel sorry for a perp, would he? Even a sort of accidental one.

"He can think what he wants," Dad said. "It's probably illegal for him to come snooping around us. What do you want that card for, Gus?"

Gus was tucking it into his wallet. "If we need to talk to the police, we might want to call Detective O'Conaghan first. At least he's already shown an interest in our problem."

Dad just shook his head as he headed for the Volvo. When he was out of earshot, Sean whispered to Gus, "Good idea, saving the card."

Gus tipped him a wink and nodded after Dad. "Father Hen," he said.

Shouldn't Gus say *Father Rooster*? No time to ask, because

Dad was yelling for them from the passenger seat. Sean and Gus hustled into the car. If Dad had been driving, they'd probably have peeled off, zero to sixty in five seconds.

Good thing Gus was driving.

# 12

**Their** stop at Horrocke's Bookstore was a wash. Horrocke offered them espresso, then blinked in mild astonishment when Dad turned it down and launched into a curt interrogation. All he got out of the old guy was, dear no, Horrocke had no idea where the book and clipping had come from. He had no idea who Redemption Orne could be, apart from the historical figure. Solomon Geldman? The gentleman must mean the famous alchemist, author of *The Keys to Eternity*. Horrocke had a copy of the Prague edition, if they cared to see it, 1705, in excellent condition, and quite a bargain at $7,500.

They didn't care to see the book. Out on the sidewalk, Gus persuaded Dad to let him have first crack at Geldman. As it turned out, Gus could have saved his breath.

*Unbelievable* was exactly the right word: Sean could not believe it. Fire hadn't crisped the pharmacy. Bombs hadn't leveled it. Those were catastrophes his brain could have handled. Instead, in the two weeks since he'd bought the powders time had beaten Geldman's to a pulp. Corrosion pocked the yellow bricks and the formerly spring-green trim. Plywood covered most of the second-floor windows. The shop windows had survived, but behind a thick coat of grime they displayed only dust and the two teardrop urns. One urn dangled by a single chain. From both the ruby and emerald liquids had evaporated, and spiders now spun webs inside the streaky glass. On the rusted canopy frames, shreds of canvas hung like mummy-flesh from bones; on the cornice, the gilt legend GELDMAN'S PHARMACY had faded to illegibility.

Sean couldn't blame Gus for asking, "Are you sure this is the right place?"

They were on the corner of Curwen and Gedney. Next door was the Portuguese grocery. Across the street was Tumblebee's Café. "It was here," Sean said. "Dad, the day we came to take out the windows."

Dad's voice grated with fresh frustration. "Sean, this place hasn't been 'here' for decades."

Sean rubbed a porthole through the grime on the nearest window. He peered in at a floor littered with smashed bottles, dented tins, and drawstring bags gnawed open. The scale that had stood outside lay near the entrance, a pink ticket tongue protruding from the fortune slot.

"Let's go," Dad said.

"Wait a minute, Jere."

Gus crossed the street to the café, where a woman in a bee-striped apron was delivering drinks to the sidewalk tables. "Excuse me," Gus said. "How long has that shop over there been closed?"

The woman frowned at Geldman's. "We opened eight years ago, and it's been like that the whole time."

"You'd think someone would put in a new business."

"I wish," the woman said. "I looked into it at City Hall. Some foreign company owns the place. They pay the taxes on time, so the city claims it can't do anything."

She went back into the café. A student-type guy at one of the sidewalk tables volunteered, "I think it's haunted."

Sean stepped away from the window.

"Oh?" Gus said.

"The Portuguese are weird about it. When they go by, they cross themselves. The old Poles do, too. Maybe it's where Evil Eye hangs."

"Who?"

Another student-type guy laughed. "There's an urban legend, some dude who goes around the North End at night. If he looks at you, he can suck your soul right out through your eyeballs."

"Pleasant," Gus said. "Did you ever see anyone go inside the pharmacy?"

"No. Who would?"

"Oh, kids."

"Yeah, maybe. But they'd have to go at night, and then Evil Eye would get them."

Gus laughed along with the two guys, then headed back to Sean and Dad. "That was productive," Dad said sourly.

"Possibly. We could go to City Hall ourselves and find out who owns the property."

"Why? Sean—" Dad cut himself off. He shook his head abruptly, like a wasp had landed on it. "Sean made a mistake. He bought the powders somewhere else."

Heat rose up Sean's neck. "Dad, if you think I'm a nutcase, go ahead and say it. I remember where I went."

The way Dad flinched, Sean might as well have swung at him. He recovered snake fast, grabbed Sean's elbow, and turned him toward Geldman's like he was a little kid who needed to acknowledge some mess he'd made. "Didn't you hear what that woman said?"

"It was open; it was totally different!"

"I can't deal with this, Sean! Either you *are* crazy, or you're lying to me again. Don't keep saying you got the powders here. It's impossible. You know what *impossible* means, right?"

Gus shoved between them, breaking Dad's grip. "Okay, Jeremy."

"The hell it's okay. Sean, if you've been buying drugs from somebody—"

Sean ducked away from them both. Across the street, the student types goggled at this new development. He went back to his porthole and dropped his forehead on the gritty glass. Had he ever been inside Geldman's? It was a memory no different in quality from every other memory in his head, from the yellow dump truck Mom had let him pick out all by himself when he was three right up to the taste of Rachel's blueberry pie that morning. But maybe Dad had asked the right question. Did Sean know what was impossible anymore?

Behind him, Dad and Gus conferred in whispers. Inside the pharmacy, across the frosted panels over the counter, two shadows wavered, one man-sized, one slender and childlike.

They were gone before Sean could call Dad and Gus.

"Sean," Dad said. No grating, no rage. Plain weariness.

Sean looked into his eyes. "I'm not lying, Dad. Maybe I *am* crazy—"

"No, I shouldn't have said that."

Luckily, before the apologies could get too intense, Gus said, "Both of you need to stop throwing around the *c* word. It'd be a better use of our time to get in touch with Helen Arkwright."

Dad didn't even blink, so getting in touch with Ms. Arkwright must have been what he and Gus had been whisper-debating just now. "To get the dismissing ritual?"

Gus shrugged. "Orne claims he took both rituals from the MU *Necronomicon*. If that's true, he had to fill out paperwork to see the book, and Ms. Arkwright might spot likely suspects in her records."

"We'll ask her to check the records," Dad said. "We'll tell her about Orne, the ritual, the killings. But we won't mention this Geldman's craziness."

The *c* word again, but Sean didn't call Dad on it. Seeing Helen Arkwright was at least a step toward the ritual, and to prove he could be sensible Sean resisted taking one last look through his porthole, to try to catch shadows behind the ruined counter.

~◆~

**From** her office on the third floor of the library, Helen could look down the MU common from end to end. It appeared normal, hypernormal, in fact, the epitome of a New England college green. Her visitors, on the other hand, were not what she'd expected a Monday afternoon to bring her way. Jeremy Wyndham, so down-to-earth when he'd evaluated her windows, had shown up with a story about would-be wizards and hoaxes. Telling it obviously embarrassed him; he turned often to his brother-in-law, the professor from Brown. Gus Litinski was a good advocate, adding cogent details to Jeremy's strange account. Sean, its principal actor, said nothing. From the way he fidgeted, Helen suspected he'd been warned to keep quiet.

When Jeremy finished, Helen lifted the plastic bag that contained Sean's clipping. "Given the content of the circled ad, I don't see how this can be anything but a fake. As for Nathanial Horrocke, he has an untarnished reputation with the library as a rare-book dealer. I doubt he'd be involved in a hoax like this."

Sean glanced at his father. "I don't think Mr. Horrocke made the clipping, either. And I don't think it's a hoax."

Jeremy coughed. Litinski spoke: "A hoax is our working theory, but before we go to the police, we wanted to find out if there's any special significance to Orne's summoning ritual."

"Professor Marvell's the one who would know. I'm afraid he's out of the country right now."

"Is there some way we could contact him?"

Helen had Marvell's number in her wallet, but would he want her to give it out? "I'm not sure that's possible."

Sean leaned toward her desk. "Please, Ms. Arkwright. I bet Professor Marvell would want to help. I bought his *Infinity* book. He seems like he'd get into the mystery and all."

The urgency in Sean's voice made her uncomfortable. Actually, the whole situation was uncomfortable; it was like a pop quiz in Mythos management, and as hard as she'd been studying, she wasn't sure she was ready. "He might, Sean, but maybe there's something I could do in his place?"

"Well, see, Uncle Gus thought you could check the Archives' records. Because if Orne got the ritual out of the MU *Necronomicon* he had to fill out forms, right?"

"Definitely, and meet criteria for access."

"He couldn't just be screwing around."

"No, he'd need to show he was a serious scholar. I can tell you that no 'Redemption Orne' has requested the *Necronomicon* since I came. I wouldn't forget a name like that. Besides, don't you think it's an alias?"

"Very likely," Litinski said. "There might be other clues, though, inconsistencies that would make you think an applicant wasn't legitimate."

That kind of record review would be time-consuming. It could also be interesting, a little detective work to break up her reading. Besides, Jeremy suspected the hoaxer of killing pets and breaking into his house. If so, the hoax had gone beyond a joke. Helen pulled over a notebook. "Do you know any other names Orne might use?"

"Reverend Orne," Sean said. "He wanted us to call him that, anyway."

Helen wrote down "Reverend O.—actual minister?"

"You could look for another name in your access records," Litinski said. "Someone who might be Orne's accomplice, a Solomon Geldman."

She had written down the name before recognition hit her. "Geldman?"

Again Sean glanced at his father before he spoke. "The ritual called for Powders of Zeph and Aghar. Orne wrote I could get them in Arkham, at Geldman's Pharmacy."

"The pharmacy across from Tumblebee's?"

Sean's reaction startled the hell out of her—he sprang halfway up, fell back, then anchored himself to his chair with both hands. "You've been there?"

"Sean," Jeremy snapped.

But why shouldn't Sean ask her that? "Sure. I go by it every morning when I get my coffee. Mr. Geldman seems like a very nice man. Hardly accomplice material."

Sean's eyes widened with shock or excitement or a potent mixture of both. "You've met him?"

Helen hesitated. What kind of reaction would a *yes* elicit? "I have," she said.

Litinski leaned around Jeremy to put a restraining hand on Sean's arm. "Ms. Arkwright, could you describe the pharmacy?"

"You haven't been there?"

"Please. Could you describe it?"

The request was as odd as Sean's outbursts, but she'd played along this far. "Let's see. Very quaint, I guess you'd say. A scale that tells your fortune, a soda fountain, and no regular drugs, just herbal remedies. Oh, and this is a funny thing. The window has two vases hanging from chains. One has red water in it and the other green."

This time Sean shot all the way to his feet. He wheeled on Jeremy. "That's it, Dad! That's just how I saw it the first time."

"Hold on," Litinski said, but excitement had crept into his voice, too. "What does Mr. Geldman look like?"

Helen hoped she didn't look as sideswiped by the uproar as Jeremy did. "I guess he's forty or forty-five, around my height. Brown bushy hair. He always wears a white lab coat. I see him outside on nice days, washing the windows or polishing the scale, and he says 'Hello, beautiful weather,' small talk, but he does it well. He has a bit of an accent, Czech or Hungarian, I'm not sure which."

Sean pointed at Jeremy like a preacher exhorting a congregation. "See? It's *him*. I'm not crazy."

"Sean, sit down," Jeremy said, standing up as if ready to enforce the order.

Sean reanchored himself to the chair, but he kept talking: "We went to Geldman's before we came here. Only the pharmacy was boarded up."

Helen glanced at Jeremy, who gave a shrug, and Litinski, who said, "Sean's telling the truth."

Marvell had warned her that the Mythos attracted crackpots. He hadn't yet taught her how to dislodge them from her office. "Look, Professor Litinski. I walked by Geldman's this morning. It was open. Mr. Geldman was loading fortunes into the scale. He gave me one. In fact—" Helen flipped to the back of her notebook and plucked out a slip of crisp pink paper. "I kept it, for luck."

"May I?" Litinski said.

She handed the slip over, as much to shake her sudden reluctance to part with it as to oblige Litinski.

" 'The extraordinary is coming your way,' " Litinski read. " 'Meet it with open eyes and mind.' "

Helen took back the fortune. "It doesn't mean anything, of course."

"Ms. Arkwright, an hour ago I saw the pharmacy boarded up, and the café owner said it's been like that for years."

Jeremy spoke slowly, as if reluctant to support Litinski's claim but unable to deny it. "It's closed," he said. "I saw it, too."

Three people with an identical delusion—that merited a case study. Helen tried to recall any conversation she'd had with Jess at Tumblebee's, any reference to that charming Solomon Geldman across the street. Wasn't it queer that neither of them had ever mentioned the pharmacy?

With her visitors united against her, to whom should she appeal? Litinski seemed the least agitated. "Professor, I know what I've seen."

"You've seen the pharmacy up and running. Jeremy and I and the people at Tumblebee's have seen it closed. Sean's seen it both ways. The place seems to have multiple realities. That shouldn't be, but it is."

Helen didn't feel like arguing the nature of existence with a philosopher, sane or otherwise. "No," she said. "Let's try the obvious first. I'll call Mr. Geldman."

"Where?" Sean asked.

"At the pharmacy." She hauled the Arkham-Kingsport Yellow Pages out of her credenza and turned to the pharmacy listings.

She found the Gs, but Gleasonville Drugstore followed Gargery's Drugs with no Geldman's in between. None of the picture ads were for Geldman's, either.

"Something wrong?" Litinski said.

"Maybe with my eyesight."

Sean came to the desk. "It's got to be listed. I looked it up in the Yellow Pages at your house. There. It was right there. I remember. It had this fancy border and a drawing of the pharmacy."

Helen looked at the blank yellow square under Sean's fingertip. An ad-sized vacancy in a packed book? "I know this is the same edition, the latest one."

Sean rubbed the blank square as if friction might activate

invisible ink. Then, for the third time, he bolted upright. "It's only open when Mr. Geldman wants it to be!"

"What?"

"The pharmacy. And even then, only certain people can see it's open."

Litinski beamed at Sean's insight. Jeremy looked baffled. As for Helen, it was true the library always kept the AC cranked, but she shouldn't have felt an icy finger trace her spine from nape to tailbone. "That's ridiculous," she heard herself protest.

"No, it's magic," Sean said.

"Wrong. Magic makes sense; it's self-consistent." Ah, she was echoing Marvell—he'd told her that right in this office, leaning backlit against the window, his hair a dark halo around his head.

Jeremy's hair was too unruly to appear angelic, and he was making it worse by shoving his fingers through it. "Look," he said. "All I want at this point is for *something* to make sense."

"I concur," Litinski said. "I propose we start by going to Geldman's together, the four of us."

*The extraordinary is coming your way.* Helen drew her hand from the fortune on her desk. She had books to read, notes to organize. But did she really think that after this meeting she'd be able to concentrate? "What if I find it open?"

"You might," Sean said. "It might always be open for you."

And what on earth, or elsewhere, would that mean? "All right." Helen sighed. "Whatever state the pharmacy's in, I could use an iced latte."

⤙⤚

**Geldman's** wasn't open. From the damage time and neglect had wrought, it hadn't been open for years, could never have been open for her.

Litinski and the Wyndhams sat at a table outside Tumblebee's. Helen sat inside, in the dim corner booth, as far from Jess's concerned looks as she could get. In front of her was Marvell's card, and it was 2:30 in the afternoon here, so five hours ahead in Scotland he'd still be up, still be able to talk her back into the real world.

Helen clasped her cell phone to her ear; it was cool, a comfort. Four rings in, a woman with a heavy burr answered: "Mc-Grigor residence."

"Hello," Helen said. Her mouth felt numb. "I'm calling from Miskatonic University for Professor Marvell?"

"Ah, Theo. And would you be Helen Arkwright?"

"Yes. Yes, I am."

"I'm Leezy McGrigor, Robert's wife. Theo's told us we're beholden to you for his visit. He couldn't have managed it, he says, if he hadn't gotten such a good assistant."

The tingle of a blush drove off some of Helen's numbness. "Perhaps he told you I might call if anything came up at the library?"

"He did. I hope there's nothing wrong, dear."

"No, no emergency. Could I talk to him?"

"It's a pity you didn't call yesterday. Theo and Robert have gone Munro bagging."

The hell? "Munro bagging?"

Leezy McGrigor gave a hearty laugh. "Munros are mountains more'n three thousand feet. Foolish people go about climbing them, just to say they've bagged the lot. Robert and Theo are tenting out on Beinn Dearg. And they don't even have phones with them! It's their little game, pretending to be Hillary on Everest. If they should topple themselves, I won't know of it until someone finds the bones."

Helen managed a chuckle. "I see. When will they be back?"

"A week. But they may ring me up before, if the weather's wet and they stop at an inn. Shall I tell Theo to ring you back?"

"Please, Mrs. McGrigor. Thank you."

"My pleasure. Take care, dear."

Helen flipped shut her phone. Yesterday it would have been a pleasure to dwell on Leezy McGrigor's friendly familiarity and the confidence Marvell had expressed in Helen. Today the conversation brought nothing but disappointment. Marvell couldn't help her.

As soon as she sat down at the table on the sidewalk, Sean asked, "Did you talk to him, Ms. Arkwright?"

"I'm afraid not. He's gone mountain climbing."

"Great," Jeremy said.

Litinski pushed a drink toward her, the iced vanilla latte she'd ordered. Condensation ran down the cup in milky beads; she was loath to touch it. Without looking, she tilted her head toward Geldman's. "All right. First leap taken."

"I'm sorry," Litinski said. "We've shoved you into a pit, haven't we? Or pulled you in after us."

Maybe she would have ended up in the same pit, Sean or no Sean. Marvell was going to give her Uncle John's papers. Would they prove, not that John's work had cracked him, but that it had shown him things like Geldman's?

Sean capped and uncapped his bottle of Coke. "I'm sorry, too. I'm screwing everybody up."

Jeremy's jumbo black coffee seemed to have done him good—some of his former wryness was back: "With Orne and Geldman around, don't be so quick to take all the credit. The important thing is, what do we do next?"

"We admit magic's real," Sean said without hesitation. "Geldman's proves it, right?"

Litinski responded first. "I can say this much: Geldman's makes me readier to believe."

"That doesn't follow for me," Jeremy said.

Sean spun the Coke cap tight, and his voice rose. "Dad, we can't just believe what we want. The Servitor won't go away."

An elderly couple two tables down turned to stare.

Sean dropped some decibels. "It could go after some kid. Or, I guess, it could come after me again."

In the sunshine Sean looked paler than he had in Helen's office. Whatever the truth was, he was scared straight through. Silence settled over them, broken only by the jittering of Jeremy's cup on the aluminum tabletop. He, too, was frightened. Nothing strange there. His son was in trouble. Nothing strange, either, in Litinski's involvement. He was family. What about Helen, though? Did she have to yield to the whirlpool suction of their problem?

On her back, like the radiation of an alien star, she felt the scrutiny of the pharmacy. Blurred as they were by sooty cataracts, its windows watched her, or something behind them did. She cleared her throat. "Maybe you know something about my great-grandfather Henry Arkwright?"

"He was Dr. Armitage," Sean said. "In Lovecraft, 'The Dunwich Horror.'"

"That's what Uncle John told me. I remember it upset my father when I brought it up. He didn't like John's jokes about our family history of monster hunting. Now I've got to wonder if they were jokes, what John actually believed. He said he accepted Henry's conclusions about Dunwich: The Whateleys had terrorized their neighbors, killed cattle, faked evidence, committed arson, all to validate their delusions that they were wizards favored by the Outer Gods. But one detail in Lovecraft's story is true: Henry Arkwright did consult the *Necronomicon* to understand what the Whateleys *thought* they had summoned."

Hope sparked in Jeremy's eyes. "Your great-grandfather used the book to uncover hoaxers?"

Again she thought of the private papers in Marvell's care. "According to the official records."

"Could you do the same? Find out what's going on with Sean?"

Litinski piled on. "If you'll come to Providence, Ms. Arkwright, you're more than welcome to stay with my wife and me."

"That would be awesome," Sean said.

The hope in his eyes was different from his father's. Sean didn't doubt the supernatural nature of his dilemma: Geldman's had clinched it for him. It had half-clinched it for Litinski. Jeremy was still struggling. And where did she fall on the spectrum? The ruined pharmacy refused to go away. Damn it, it *had* been open this morning! Geldman had been at his usual post outside, and he had given her the fortune, which had made her laugh, a laugh Geldman had shared, damn him, and now he was a ghost.

The extraordinary had come her way. She was supposed to meet it with open eyes and mind. Would it be reckless to obey the fortune and go to Providence? She barely knew Jeremy and Sean, had only today's encounter by which to judge Gus Litinski, but her gut said they weren't out to harm her and she already liked Litinski. He reminded her of John on his good days, when he'd shaken off whatever shadows dogged him.

If she turned her visitors down and tomorrow found the pharmacy restored, that wouldn't change the truth of today. Was it a truth she could ignore? Helen felt inside the hip pocket of her jeans. Geldman's fortune crinkled under her fingertips. "Professor Litinski, if you could promise your place isn't Hill House . . ."

"Nothing like it," Litinski said.

"Please come," Sean said. "And could you bring the *Necronomicon* with you? Not the real one. But I read on the library Web site you've got disks of it."

She had some rules to lay down if she was going to do this. "Most of the Mythos collection is on old microfilm, which we're scanning to new film and CD-ROMs. The *Necronomicon* was the first scan finished. I can bring disks, but they're going to be locked to my password. We consult them if I decide we need to, not before. Agreed?"

Sean answered at once: "Agreed."

"And the requests to view the *Necronomicon*?" Litinski said. "Can those travel?"

"The last three years I can access online. When should I come, then?"

As if the answer were self-evident, Sean said, "Today."

"Short notice." All right, so her feet were already getting a little cold, but she did have a solid excuse. "My car's in the shop until Wednesday."

Sean was undeterred. "You can ride with us. Can't she, Uncle Gus?"

Litinski snuck Helen an apologetic look. "Certainly you could, Ms. Arkwright. But I understand if you want your own transportation. Would Thursday be all right?"

She didn't get a chance to reply. "That's three days," Sean groaned. "Lots could happen."

"Or not," Jeremy said.

But he didn't sound too sure of that. Open eyes, open mind. If she was going to jump— "It's fine," Helen said. "I won't feel comfortable until I figure Geldman's out. If it's linked to your situation in Rhode Island, the sooner we look into that, the better."

"You'll come today?" Sean asked.

Again, the hope in his eyes. She had to at least try to live up to it. "I'll need to pack some clothes and go back to the library for the disks."

Sean bit his sore-looking lip. "Thanks, Ms. Arkwright. Really, thanks a lot."

When the others started for Litinski's car, Helen hung behind. She'd finally gotten up the nerve to face Geldman's. Beyond the urns a shadow more man-like than the rest receded before she was sure she'd seen it. In one of the unboarded windows upstairs, something white moved, like the whisk of a skirt. Moved and was gone.

She'd better not start this little field investigation by imagining things. Helen walked after the others, her steps keeping time with the swift heartbeat in her ears.

# 13

As Gus eased into the driveway, Sean spotted Eddy on her porch, waving a folder like a manila pennant. She vaulted over the railing, stuck the landing, and would probably have gone into a one-armed cartwheel if Helen—she'd told Sean to call her that during the ride—hadn't gotten out of the car and impressed Eddy into civilized behavior. Celeste was home, so they had an immediate war council in the study.

Searches on the major engines had yielded references to the historical Orne, but nothing Eddy could hang on their modern Reverend, no Web site, no networking accounts. From his e-mails, she had tracked down his Internet provider address. "Rwandatel," she said. "In Africa."

"He can't be in Africa," Sean said. "Not if he hangs around with Geldman."

"Sure he can. They could do business by mail. Or Orne could be hiding his real location. Remember the report Phil did on zombie computers? A hacker can take over PCs anywhere in the world and make them do stuff for him, like send e-mails."

"Zombie computers," Helen said. "How appropriate."

Everybody laughed except Dad, who said, "What else did you find, Eddy?"

"That's the only solid thing so far, but I'm still looking. I'm about to start on Geldman."

"Good work, Eddy," Helen said. She'd been scribbling in what looked like a mystical language, but Gus whispered to Sean that it was standard shorthand. "Your Orne's very secretive. Does that strike anyone else as suspicious?"

"It does me," Dad said. "But it's after seven. If we're going to show you the evidence in Edgewood, we'd better move."

Even after Geldman's, Dad clung to the hoax angle. A pharmacy spotless one minute, junked the next. Pinning that mystery on drugs or optical illusion was wishful thinking. At least Gus had the sense to pack his Colt .45, which he said was just like the one he'd used in the Navy. The pistol made Celeste nervous, but Gus had won sharpshooter awards, and he still went to a range to practice. If anyone could drop a Servitor with a bullet, it would be Gus.

After the investigators left, Sean ate cold cuts and potato salad with Celeste. As soon as he'd helped load the dishwasher, he climbed the back stairs to his room. Its two windows were wide open. He considered closing them, but there was no porch roof underneath and this wasn't Edgewood, a quick crawl from the Pawtuxet. Besides, the evening remained sticky hot.

Sean stripped to his boxers and crashed on top of the sheets. He thought about snagging his ragged copy of *The Lord of the Rings* off the nightstand, but that would have taken an effort, plus . . .

Geldman is waving him across the street to the shiny pharmacy. Inside witches and wizards load up shopping carts. They look like regular people, but Sean can tell they're magical by their aether-newts, which float over their heads like translucent neon salamanders, pink and yellow, turquoise and orange, lime green.

*You should have this,* Geldman says. He reaches over to the scale and pulls the tongue from its toothy mouth. *It was written for you especially.*

Sean opens the doubled square of cardboard. The baby-blue fortune inside is folded tight and he keeps on unfolding and smoothing, but there are always more folds and he can't get to the fortune, even though he can glimpse handwritten words through the thin paper.

*Well?* Geldman says.

*I can't read it.*

*You'll have to, you know. It's your future.*

*Can't you unfold it for me?*

Geldman shakes his head regretfully and opens the pharmacy door, and that's when Sean smells reptile-musk-sulfur. Some of the witches and wizards have blood-spawn Servitors as well as the aether-newts. Under the light of frosted-glass fixtures, the Servitors look strangely like Brutus the Hell Pug, if you were to swell Brutus double and flay him to the dead white flesh. The smell keeps Sean from following Geldman. Strange, though. The smell grows stronger now that the pharmacy door has swung shut, and the longer Sean struggles with the infinitely folded fortune the more his eyes sting in the noxious bloom . . .

He woke in thick dark, but he was safe in his bedroom at Celeste's house, not home alone like that other night. Geldman, the unreadable fortune, the magicians and familiars, they were neatly confined by the principal law of dreaming, that things in dreams had to stay in dreams. How, then, had the Servitor stink chased him out of sleep? No denying it had: It weighed down the already-heavy air, sinking into his nostrils and throat, where it burned like unclean bleach.

The smell paralyzed him. He rolled his eyes to the right. Nothing loomed in either window, and the screens were intact. Could the Servitor be on the ground below?

He rolled his eyes to the left, where a line of light marked the crack between door and jamb. Had he left the door ajar? He didn't think so, but someone could have opened it, maybe Dad, to check on him. Dad was back in the house—Sean heard his voice downstairs, along with Gus's and Helen's, then Celeste's. Helen was laughing.

That was the answer to the smell. She'd gone to collect specimens of Servitor glop for analysis. Still, why would she have put the specimens in Sean's room?

He moved to sit up. His left hand came down in sticky warmth.

Sean snatched back his hand and scrabbled to the other side of the bed. Enough streetlight filtered through the windows to show him gleaming wet on his fingers. It was the gleaming wet that stank.

With heart and gorge fighting to be first up his throat, he swiped his hand on the sheets. His feet hit the floor the next second. The thing had been here, drooling on his bed. He had to warn the others—

Only the thing hadn't left. As Sean rounded the foot of his bed, he saw it, a pale lump sort of like a man and sort of like a toad, crouched in the armchair by the door. Long taloned paws twitched on its drawn-up knees. Its head hung between them, bald dome, beard of wormy tentacles; above the worms, like flattened embers, two disks burned sullen red.

On the porch roof, the Servitor had been the size of a ten- or twelve-year-old kid. It was now at least as big as Sean, and it was guarding the door.

Sean grabbed the nearer post of the footboard. He was screaming, mouth sprung wide, only nothing was coming out except an almost soundless "uh-uh-uh." The bedpost in his hand existed. The thing in the chair was a nightmare. He could walk out the door if he wanted to.

He took a step.

As the Servitor mewled at him, its facial tentacles flared to either side of a toad-maw full of needles. The needles dripped stink.

He froze, nose and mouth scorched by the gust of its breath. Okay. Okay. He couldn't yell, but he could still move, and he had to move, because he would die if the Servitor came any closer. The smell alone would kill him. Already it seemed to have penetrated to the back of his nasal passages and burned through skull bone into his brain.

One backward step at a time, that was the way. There was a closet on the window side of the room. All he had to do was get to that and put solid wood between himself and the Servitor. Solid wood had worked that other night, and though Sean couldn't lock the closet from inside, he could damn well grab the knob and hold the door shut. One backward step every dozen heartbeats, until the bed was between him and the creature and he could sprint for the closet.

The Servitor's mewl turned to a guttural moaning. Was that some kind of language? Sean couldn't make out syllables or words, just the continual rumble of complaint or anger or appetite.

He turned to run too soon. His sudden move made the Servitor explode off the armchair. It leaped through ten feet of air and landed on the bed, mouth agape.

Jesus. God. Jesus.

Sean froze again. The thing could leap on him whichever door he headed for. Okay okay okay, it was inching closer across the rumpled sheets, but he was still alive. He would only die if it actually *touched* him. And remember: It couldn't attack him. Even though he hadn't bound it, he was the summoner, the master.

The flat ember eyes had no pupils. Sean could see that now. Instead they had vertical striations of a more intense fire, white, pulsating. The webbed netherpaws were even more heavily clawed than the forepaws. They could rake downed prey wide open, disemboweling it, like Hrothgar had been disemboweled.

It couldn't attack him. Orne had said so. Orne had to know.

Sean stayed motionless. To close his eyes was an act of courage beyond him, so he had to watch the way the Servitor's flesh was never still. It bloated and shrank; it melted and ran and resolidified under its shuddering skin. In some places the skin thinned until it split and oozed. In other places it puckered thick. The Servitor stretched a forepaw toward him, talons flexing to display a mottled palm. No. Yes. The thick puckered skin there opened. It was a mouth. It was a tiny mouth, with tiny needles of its own, and the tiny mouth moaned like the great one, only shriller.

The tiny mouth was hungry.

Sean couldn't close his eyes, but he couldn't look at the mouth in the outthrust palm. The Servitor's eyes were better to look at than that. Really, once you got used to them, they were amazing. If the vertical striations were pupils and there were three of them, did that mean it could see in three directions at once? Or did each striation pick up a different kind of radiation? One visible light, one infrared . . .

This kind of thinking was insane. It was splitting him in two, into a body that yearned for the safety of the closet and a brain that pretended the thing in front of him was an innocuous new species, nothing worse than a beetle. . . .

As the striations widened, they emitted light, the white glow of the superheated lava within the eyes. He could actually watch that interior lava heave and swirl, and something in him, something behind his own eyes, was drawn to the molten maelstrom, could yield to its grinding embrace. If he let it, if he surrendered. There'd be a few seconds of liquefying muscle before he was burned to the bone, but when his bones fell away in ash he'd turn phoenix. Would he spring back into life with falcon wings, like the ones on the Angel of the Summoning?

Points, points of claws, touched the center of his chest. As if it was as mutable as the Servitor's, Sean's flesh shrank. He stumbled back. His throat worked. His throat was smarter than his brain; it was determined to rip through its own clenched terror to get out a saving sound.

Downstairs, in the kitchen, Helen called: "Sean?"

His eyes pulled away from the suction of the ember-disks. He looked over the Servitor's heaving shoulder at the hall door.

Someone stepped onto the back stairs. One step, uncertain.

"Sean?"

Something else touched his chest, over the heart, and it was wet and pricking, and when Sean looked down he saw a many-forked tongue lapping his skin, a tongue from the mouth in the Servitor's palm, and seeing that broke the dam in his throat, all right, and he got off a scream like every wail from every horror movie he'd ever seen, stored up in his gut all these years for this one big nonfiction moment.

# 14

**Edgewood** turned out to be a neighborhood of Victorian houses on a more human scale than the grand behemoths around MU. The pedestrians, too, were more varied: older people, young couples with strollers, kids on bikes, teenagers in self-conscious packs. Down side streets to the left, Helen spotted Narragansett Bay, a blue expanse dotted with sails and crisscrossed by motorboat wakes. Land hugged the water on both sides; it looked approachable, without the implicit threat of open ocean that confronted Arkham.

The Wyndham house was a russet-shingled Craftsman. All business, Jeremy led Helen and Gus to the back porch, where they inspected a broken door latch and scratched screens. The screen from Sean's bedroom leaned against an overturned garbage can. No dainty scratches here—something had rent the screen wide open. Under the garbage can was a black plastic bag; and under the bag, the dead cat. Helen bent for a closer look. The corpse was eviscerated, gnawed, nearly decapitated. Worse, it reeked a loathsome combination of skunk and rotten eggs. She backed off, holding her hand to her mouth. Inside the black bag were Sean's pillows. The nastiness on their cases stank exactly like the cat.

Jeremy got plastic knives and sandwich bags from the kitchen. Somehow he was able to hunker over the cat and pillows long enough to collect samples. Sean had called the gummy stuff ichor, but according to the ancient Greeks, ichor was a venous fluid, the blood of the gods. This substance was more analogous to saliva. That or it was a hoaxer's concoction.

While Jeremy and Gus bagged the cat, Helen retreated into the cleaner air of the backyard. In the failing light, delphiniums and hollyhocks stood impressively tall. She made out a vegetable plot, a circle of roses and daylilies centered on a sundial, two rows of raised rectangular beds like a monastic herb garden. One of the beds featured prostrate rosemary burgeoning from a terra-cotta urn; she stole a sprig and rolled it between her hands, releasing astringent perfume.

Jeremy jogged down the flagstone path between the rows. "Gus is going to look over the house. I'm taking the garage and studio. We'd better stick together."

She glanced at the dense shade under a grape arbor, where much could hide. Sticking together sounded good.

The garage took up the first floor of a carriage house at the end of the lot. Nothing assaulted them there except the comparatively wholesome odors of gasoline and dried manure. Jeremy's studio was on the second floor. While he peered under tables, Helen took in a ceiling open to the ridgepole; four huge skylights, and clerestory windows running like a silvery ribbon around the exterior walls. On corkboards under the windows were pinned dozens of sketches. The three largest were same-size drawings of her library windows, with every bit of glass numbered and notes clustered thick around the margins.

"Everything seems fine," Jeremy said.

"Fine over here, too."

He straightened from flashlight-probing the space behind cabinets. "Oh, the cartoons of the Founding."

"Is that what you call them? They make me realize how complex the windows are."

Jeremy joined her. "While I was down south, my intern took the windows apart. Like to see?"

"Please."

Three long tables held trays of glass shards, each with a wax-penciled number that corresponded to the numbers on the cartoons. Some trays held already-cleaned glass, as brilliant as flattened gems. Others held glass in a cleaning solution. "I shouldn't have to do much repainting," Jeremy said. "All in all, we're looking good."

"I know the windows will be beautiful."

"That's the point," Jeremy said in a matter-of-fact tone that made her smile. "We better get going."

They returned to the room in which the staircase rose. Now that the lights were on, Helen saw that it, too, was a studio, with glass-faced cabinets, drafting tables, and easels. Jeremy's space had an exhilarating air of controlled chaos. This one was too dustless and polished and orderly to be in use. The one open easel supported a canvas that had turned its neatly stapled backside to the room. Propped against the canvas was a palette on which the paints had dried into a clumpy abstract of yellows surrounded by greens: *Egg Yolks in the Meadow Grass.* But the other thing she'd missed on her way in, the thing that made her stare, was a stained-glass triptych set high in the south wall. Though the sun had set, these windows glowed like noon, apparently backlit by spotlights under the carriage house eaves.

The left window showed a knight on a parapet, battling a Saracen. The right showed the same knight, armor exchanged for a simple robe, bending over the bed of a sick woman. Both were astonishing, but the central window fascinated Helen. It had a medallion centered on a background at once entirely wrong and undeniably right: a mesh of virulent yellow glass streaked with red and flecked with black—violent, unsettling. The medallion itself was ethereal blues, greens, and violets. It featured a woman with sandy hair, the sick woman from the right window, now flushed with health. Like a young Madonna not yet encumbered by a halo and queenly robes, she wore a white gown with a pale-blue girdle and sat in a walled garden, an easel before her, a paintbrush poised in her right hand. In her left, she held a spike of royal-blue delphinium, which she regarded with serene intensity.

Oddly, it was the delphinium that wore haloes of a sort, globular auras of spectral blue that surrounded each floret. Wait, and the bristle-end of the brush had a similar aura, a subtle golden luminescence that you saw more clearly when you looked away from it slightly. Any last doubt she'd had that Jeremy would do justice to the Founding windows evaporated, gone for good.

Helen stepped closer and saw that the plants in the glass garden were minutely rendered: apothecary rose, angelica, sage, foxglove, valerian, and elder. Plantains and violas studded the turf between beds. She looked for Jeremy and found him at her elbow. "What does it mean?"

Jeremy stood silent so long Helen was afraid the question had offended him. But when he turned toward her, there was an unprecedented openness in his eyes. "It's about the Knights Hospitallers. During the Crusades, they built a hospice at Rhodes." He pointed at the medallion. "That's my wife, Kate. She was a painter. This was her studio. She died about nine years ago. Ovarian cancer. Hospice helped us, me and Sean, so she could stay at home."

What could Helen say, beyond the standard *Oh, I'm so sorry,* and that too many years late? Helen didn't want to go on automatic now, so she kept her mouth shut and thought of Sean's sandy hair, of the profusion of delphiniums in the garden outside, of the rosemary in the urn, which like all the plants in the medallion was an herb of healing. She could still smell it on her fingers.

Jeremy cleared his throat. "It was very hard. Sean was so close to Kate. I tried to protect him from her dying, but he wouldn't put up with that. He stuck right by her the whole time. He didn't seem scared of how sick she was, all the medical bullshit. He was only scared when she was out of his sight. I think he was stronger than me at the time, really. Now I wish I could make up for it, if that makes sense."

"It does," Helen said.

"Sean thinks he's tough enough to deal with anything—I guess that's how he got into this mess with Orne. He *is* tough, in some ways. But he's not hard; he's not nearly as savvy as he pretends. If he'd come to me right off—"

"Would you have blown up?"

"Probably." He shook his head, his smile a rueful twist. "But even if you can't hold their hands, these kids, you've got to try."

Gus called from the bottom of the stairs: "You two all right?"

Jeremy shot her a guilty look, like they were conspirators caught in a dangerous conversation. "Fine," he called back. To Helen, he said, all action again, "I'll get the lights. You go."

Though sorry to lose sight of the windows, Helen trotted down the stairs and out of the carriage house. Gus stood by his Volvo, passenger door open for her. She slid into the car fast. It was full dark, and full dark went darker still after the carriage house lights went out, including the spots under the eaves that had illuminated Jeremy's triptych.

～✎

At the Litinskis' house, Celeste had laid out a small feast: rye and French bread, cold cuts and potato salad, a bowl of peaches, a pitcher of iced tea. "Dinner's ready," Gus said. "And I am ready for it."

Helen seconded that sentiment. Between the excitement of

Geldman's and coming to Providence, she'd missed lunch. "It looks delicious," she told Celeste.

"Please, dig in."

"Where's Sean?" Jeremy said.

"Oh, he went to bed right after we ate."

"Went, or you sent him?"

"Went."

Gus, Helen saw, had pulled out a chair for her. "Thanks," she said. "But I'd like to wash up first."

"Of course," Celeste said. "The bathroom's off the kitchen."

Helen scrubbed her hands, then her face, then her hands again. A faint whiff of Servitor (everyone's least favorite cologne) still clung to her. She sniffed her fingers and smelled only rose-scented soap. Was it on her *clothes*, then? If so, why hadn't she noticed it during the car ride back?

As she stepped out of the bathroom, the smell grew stronger. Jeremy must have brought in his samples to show Celeste. She looked around for the sandwich bags. What caught her eye instead, with a vengeance, was the back-door screen. It sagged open from eye level down. That couldn't be a natural dilapidation in a house as neat as this one, and it suggested other torn screens. . . .

Heart thudding, Helen walked to the door. The screen had been slit and forced inward. The smell came from grayish green slime beaded into the mesh, and from drops on the floor that formed a broken line to the stairway.

Sean had gone to bed. Bed was likely up those stairs.

The first thing she should do was go tell Jeremy and the Litinskis. The last thing she should do, the insane thing, was go upstairs alone. Nevertheless, her legs carried her along the broken line to the bottom step, where she peered up into darkness. "Sean?" she called softly.

No answer, no sound. "Sean?" She put a foot on the bottom step, where her sneaker slipped in a puddle of putative drool.

Enough. She backed toward the dining room. Before she could reach it to sound the alarm, she was spared the trouble by the scream that exploded down the stairwell.

Jeremy ran through the dining room door. "I think someone got in," was all Helen had time to say before he was pelting up the stairs. Gus was next in the kitchen, but he froze, and Helen's heart froze with him, at the sound of another scream, Jeremy's, a thud, a third scream, Sean again.

Think. "Your gun, Gus."

"Still locked in the car." He tore outside.

Celeste was in the kitchen now, beside Helen. Upstairs Sean babbled, "Leave him alone! Come on. Drink."

No sound from Jeremy. Celeste grabbed one of the kitchen chairs. Holding it in front of her like she was a lion tamer, she started up the stairs. "Helen," she whispered. "Come hit the light."

Helen ran over and flipped a switch inside the stairwell. The stairs went bright, a straight flight between cheerful yellow-and-blue-papered walls. The risers of the stairs were painted yellow, the rungs blue, a nice touch. It would be impossibly gauche for anyone to bleed on stairs like these, and so it had to be safe to climb them.

Helen sidled after Celeste. In the hall above, there was a hiss and a slurred whine. Sean again: "Jesus. Shit."

They would never reach the top of the stairs. Even so, Helen kept moving, dogging Celeste, and at last they made a landing where the blackness of the second-floor hall loomed, a new impassible barrier. Below, Gus banged through the ripped screen door. "Tell him go up the front stairs," Celeste whispered. She stepped off the landing, and the dark swallowed her in one gulp. As Gus peered up from the kitchen, Helen clambered down a few steps to rewhisper the message. He vanished. Helen was alone, caught between floors. She clambered back to the landing. What now, hit the lights again? She groped along the hall walls on either side of the door, and the seconds before she found another switch had hours of dread compressed into them, plenty of time to hear an ugly sucking noise, Celeste's quick breathing, distant steps, cautious, Gus. Helen's fingers struck a plastic lever. Light flooded the hall. She rushed into it, found Celeste's back.

To their left, there. Jeremy lay crumpled against the wall. Sean crouched nearby with one arm in the grip of an enormous toad. Toad? That was what it was most like, one that had lived in a cave so long its skin had bleached pallid. Nothing human, no hoaxer. It had fingerling tentacles along its spine and more tentacles around a mouth that split the bald ovoid of a head in two. Long icicles of teeth protruded, and when the thing reared, here swelling and there thinning, it flexed horny scimitars of raptor claws.

Too suddenly it sprang and in the one spring was on Celeste. She swung her chair. It countered with both forelimbs; the chair flew; Celeste slammed into the doorjamb and teetered on the edge of balance. The thing lunged; Celeste dived into the stairwell. Helen glimpsed her grab at the railing, catch it one-handed, spread-eagle into the wall. Then Celeste might as well have been on another planet, because the thing changed targets and hurtled at Helen, and there *she* was, there was the chair she snatched up, there *it* was, colliding with the legs of the chair, thrusting her backward, panting the stench of hell into her face. Her throat tore with the force of her own shriek. It was all animal, that shriek, but it was still her own, like it was her own knees buckling when the thing herded her into a corner and wrenched the chair from her nerve-dead hands.

She saw its eyes, flat and luminous, fire streaked white. She clamped forearms and elbows before her face and throat, thighs up over her belly, inadequate protections—

There was a sharp crack and a world-shattering bellow. Thunder on steps. Hands on her, fingers, not claws, Gus. "I hit it," he gasped. "I'm going after it."

He was gone again.

It was gone?

Helen dropped her arms. She saw Celeste and Sean helping Jeremy sit. He was conscious, moving weakly. Blood streaked the front of his shirt, but the blood was Sean's: His left wrist streamed red, where the thing must have bitten him.

Its smell surrounded Helen so thickly that it dripped to pool at her side. She looked up and saw lumpy pink gouts on the wainscoting at her back. That was what dripped. That was what stank more abominably than the gray-green slobber and what drove her to shaking legs and away from the corner.

Sean, his bleeding wrist clamped in an armpit, also wavered to his feet. His face had a fragile calm Helen doubted her own could match. "You saw it, right?"

She nodded.

"It knocked Dad down. It was going for him. But Orne told me what it would like better."

Sean's blood, the blood that had made it. It was only that afternoon, during the car ride from Arkham, that she had read Orne's e-mail and the chat records. Only a few hours ago. Helen nodded again, stupidly.

Celeste had come through the thing's attack with no visible harm apart from bruises on her temple and cheekbone. "Your dad will be all right, Sean," she said. "A lump on the head, that's it."

"Sean," Jeremy mumbled.

"Be quiet, Jere. Sit still so I can take care of him."

Right. Sean was the one bleeding. Helen watched Celeste lead him to a love seat at the front of the hall. "Helen, bring me some towels. The bathroom, there."

Celeste pointed, and Helen would have obeyed, except that something was charging up the back stairs. She shrank to a door beyond which more steps rose, but the Servitor hadn't come back, not yet. The charger was Eddy, armed with an aluminum baseball bat. "I saw it!" she said. Then she started to take in the situation. "Oh. Oh man."

"Eddy," Celeste said tersely. "Get me some towels from the bathroom."

Weren't the towels Helen's job? Before she could let go of the door to the third floor, Eddy had carried an armload of blue terry cloth to the love seat.

Helen pushed the door wide open and sank onto the lowest step. She had to sit, the way her knees were knocking. Jeremy sat on the floor, rubbing the back of his head. Water. She should get him some water, and some ice to bring down the swelling. She could do that much. Ice from the kitchen.

But what if the Servitor had come back, was down there?

Helen rose, stiff legged. A few feet away, the pink gouts smoked. Yes, smoked. They were eating into the paint on the wainscoting and the varnish on the floorboards. Gus had hit the thing. Shot it. The pink gouts were true ichor, the fluid flowing in the veins of the gods. Had the Greeks known the same stuff flowed in the veins of demons?

At the other end of the hall, Celeste was saying she needed to take Sean and Jeremy to her office. Fine. Helen would help. She had to help, had to stop her damned useless shivering. First the ice. Slow and careful, planting her feet well away from the globs of ichor on the stairs, Helen willed herself toward the kitchen, where unless the invasion of a Servitor had changed the fundamental nature of their little universe, there would be a refrigerator and ice trays.

**15**

**Back** when he was a kid and Mom was sick, Sean had heard a hospice lady say that lots of people died at three in the morning. Four in the morning was worse, though. That was when, if he'd fallen asleep, he'd wake up afraid Mom had died an hour before and he'd missed the chance to save her, to grab her hand and not let her go.

This four in the morning he woke up in one of the third-floor bedrooms at Celeste's house. It took him a few minutes to remember why he wasn't in his own room downstairs: His own room smelled like Servitor. Maybe it always would now. Besides, this room had an air conditioner, so the windows could stay closed and the door locked. It also had twin beds, the one Sean lay in and the one on which Dad was curled, tight as an armadillo. That was how he'd slept on the couch in the family room, next to Mom's hospital bed. Every night Sean would peer around the banister to make sure Dad was safely asleep before he'd tiptoe over to Mom. Awake, Dad would make him go back upstairs. Mom would let Sean sit on the hospital bed next to her. Sometimes he'd read to her in a careful whisper. Sometimes he'd just sit. She would call him Kit, and he'd let her, even though it was his long-discarded baby name. Kit didn't mean a kitten. It meant a fox cub, and she'd named him that back when he was a wild, tumbling, troublemaking ball of a baby, according to her, always doing dumb-ass shit like wedging his head under the sofa or pulling a whole bowl of spaghetti down on himself. Funny, Dad hadn't called him Kit much until after Mom had died. Then, after a couple weeks of hearing the name from his mouth, Sean had pitched such a fit Dad had never called him Kit again. And so, what with Mom dead, nobody had.

Sean shook the random memory from his head. Even with the AC on, he was sweating, and the new stitches Celeste had put in his wrist stung like bitches. He kicked off the sheet and sat up. The window beside his bed faced the backyard, dead black space. That was the problem with 4:00 A.M.—night was old, but dawn wasn't even a tease yet, and in the airless space between realities he couldn't fend off the memory of Dad silhouetted in the bedroom doorway, of the rubbery twist of the Servitor toward him, then its leap, so powerful that the kickback had shoved the mattress into Sean's nuts, doubling him over for precious seconds. It could have killed Dad. It would have killed Helen if Gus hadn't shot its ass—it had been right on top of her, too pissed off by the intrusion to care that Sean was bleeding for it. Or maybe it had already sucked enough blood. For the moment.

The only good thing was, they had all seen the Servitor, even Eddy. They were on the same page now, and maybe by this time tomorrow it would be a page in the *Necronomicon,* with the dismissing ritual on it. When Celeste had brought Sean and Dad back from her office, Helen had already been working on the disks.

*But the Servitor had almost killed Dad.* It had smashed him into the wall, then stretched toward him, as expandable as a slug, its jaws gaping. If Sean had taken a couple seconds longer to get over his slammed nuts, if he hadn't been able to grapple it away (like grappling a greased sack of snakes), if he hadn't thought to give it what it wanted more than Dad—

He shut his eyes so tight the lids hurt. Then he groped on the nightstand for his water glass and the two pills Celeste had left for him to take if he couldn't sleep. He had to sleep, and no dreams. He had to be ready to learn the dismissing ritual. The Servitor was his. His blood had made it. Whatever it did, he was at least partly responsible. Yet he hadn't meant for any of this to happen, had he? Like Mom hadn't meant to get cancer. It had been a cellular accident, nobody could blame her for it, and the summoning spell had been a *magical* accident, kind of.

Sean swallowed the pills and lay down. Twisting around to get comfortable, he ended up with his chin practically between his knees. That made him an armadillo like Dad, and what did armadillos do when they were in the middle of a road and a truck was bearing down on them? They curled up and lay there all smug, like their scaly hides were thick enough to take the crush. Trucks. He imagined one with tentacles sprouting from its grill. The armadillo that was going to survive that had better roll its butt out of the road, but before Sean could roll, or run, or grow titanium scales he sank down into sleep.

***

**Light** leaked under Roman blinds and over the chaise longue on which Helen sprawled, one sneakered foot up, one bare foot down. That arrangement made no sense. Neither did the sunlight. At around two, she'd lain down to rest—had she slept through the night, leaving Gus to struggle with the *Necronomicon* alone? A tasseled cord hung within reach. Helen tugged on it until the blinds were all the way up. Gus wasn't in the study, but through the French doors to the living room came a low rasp of snoring.

Stifling groans, Helen sat up. Her arms throbbed like they'd been wrenched out of the shoulder sockets, and her midriff ached where the Servitor had rammed the kitchen chair into her. The broad, ugly bruise under her sternum was the worst of her injuries. Celeste, too, had gotten off with bruises, but Jeremy was lucky to be alive. Sean had saved him by offering the Servitor the blood it craved most: its summoner's. The utter madness of the memory made Helen feel light-headed.

Coffee. A thermos carafe stood on the study table. She limped over and poured lukewarm dregs into her dirty mug. Disgusting, but caffeine was caffeine. After a few gulps, she was able to sift through the jumble of the last day: Sean's story, the deserted pharmacy, the Servitor. Gus returning from the unsuccessful chase and Eddy describing how she'd heard a gunshot and seen the fleeing monster on her way over. Good thing her parents had been out, or they'd have called the cops for sure.

Once he'd escorted Eddy home, Gus had advised Helen to go to bed. Bless him for understanding how futile that would have been. Ironically, she hadn't stopped shaking until they'd double-teamed the *Necronomicon*; the mental effort had focused her, and Gus's commiserating grin had let her laugh off the scare whenever a beetle or moth had tapped on the windows behind them.

From the table, Helen could make out Gus on the living-room couch. He slept with both feet sanely bare, and even his snore had a comfortable sound to it. Yet he'd seen the Servitor, too. He'd chased it. Helen couldn't have done that after the first shock. Right, who was she fooling? She could never do it, not if Servitors got as common as houseflies.

She slipped into the chair in front of her laptop. Since she'd meant to nap for just five minutes (ha!), she'd left the computer on. Auto-locked by her long absence, the *Necronomicon* lurked under an innocuous screensaver, pastel waves like wildflower meadows on speed, one swift summer after another.

*After summer is winter, after winter summer. The Old Ones wait patient and potent, for here shall They reign again.*

That was a prime bit of *Necronomicon*. Darkness under light, the book waited. Alone and hungry, Helen couldn't face it. She reached under the table for her backpack and slipped a hand inside. Her fingers grazed the cool plastic of a stack of jewel cases: disks of the Redemption Orne journals that she'd requisitioned on impulse along with the *Necronomicon*. The journals might come in handy, but right now she wanted the letter stashed under them. She didn't take it out. She just touched the lokta paper envelope, deriving flimsy comfort from the connection to Marvell, who believed she could do the job Henry and John Arkwright had done, who believed in her courage.

Well, Marvell hadn't heard her shriek. He hadn't seen her cowering under the Servitor or, afterward, unable to pull herself together enough to bring Celeste some towels.

Outside, a cardinal whistled two plaintive notes over and over. Helen walked to the bay windows. The song came from a huge beech tree in the yard next door, Eddy's yard, and there was Eddy herself, lithely climbing the fence. She saw Helen and pointed toward the back of the house.

Helen went to unlock the kitchen door. She heard footsteps on the stairs: Celeste coming down. A mighty yawn in the living room: Gus stirring.

Morning had arrived, and their forces were gathering.

A queasy stomach and throbbing wrist greeted Sean when he woke up, but to make Dad happy he forced down a bagel and some OJ. Gus showed him an article in the *Journal,* two paragraphs in the local section: no new pet killings along the Pawtuxet, police still investigating, residents should continue to exercise caution. Except the residents of Pawtuxet Village would be all right, now that Sean had moved to the East Side. "It followed me here," he said.

Gus nodded. "Helen and I are trying to find out how it managed that. You like to join us?"

Sean went into the study, where Helen was so intent on her laptop screen she didn't notice him until he pulled a chair back from the table, and then she jumped. "Sorry to scare you," he said.

Helen gave a weak laugh. "I've drunk so much coffee, kittens in pink and blue bows would scare me."

"Hell, I'm terrified of kittens, even bowless," Gus said. He sat at his PC. Dad came in from the kitchen and took the chair beside Sean's.

Helen got right to business. "I finally collected some of the creature's blood without melting the bag. The corrosives in it must go inert when the stuff dries. But what do we do with our samples? Find a confidential lab to analyze them?"

"Why bother with that?" Dad said. "We know the thing's real now."

Sean winced. Poor Dad, overnight winner of *Radical Mental Makeover*.

"Good point," Helen said. Like Eddy déjà vu, she pulled printouts from under her laptop. "Gus and I have been reading the *Necronomicon*. There are references to Servitors and summoning spells scattered through the text. Abdul Alhazred wasn't big on organization."

"He was crazy, right?" Sean said.

Gus shrugged. "So they say. If so, I just wish he'd had more method to his madness."

Another good thing was how great Gus and Helen were getting along. She smiled at his joke before reading from her top printout. "'It is neither fitting nor wise for a wizard to consult daemons of great power, unless after long service to the Outer Gods.

A wizard young in craft should call only the lesser daemons, which are still dangerous. Yet some may be useful servants when the wizard has mastered their speech, which is not of the spoken word but of the mind.'"

*Speech of the mind* had to be telepathy. Monsters weren't likely to speak English, or Arabic or Latin, either. For one thing, all their tongues would get in the way.

Helen read on: "'The major division in familiars lies between those which are of the aether and those which are of the flesh. Those of the aether can do no bodily harm in our sphere, and thus we recommend them to the young practitioner. The commonest is called by the ancients the wind-salamander—'"

"That must be the aether-newt," Sean said.

"In fact, that's a better translation." Helen corrected her printout. "'—aether-newt, an excellent spy. However, for the seasoned wizard, the choicest familiar is the f'tragn-agl, which signifies a blood-spawn. It resembles those Servitors which surround the throne of Azathoth, though smaller. Nevertheless, it has the strength of a man when summoned, and should it grow to man-sized or beyond, its strength will be that of many men. Neither fire nor steel may destroy the f'tragn-agl; dismembered, it will flow together like the sundered wave. When properly bound it is well suited to be a guard or assassin. Unbound, it will raven on its own.'"

Helen paused. "This next part repeats Orne's warning: 'The wizard must heed the blood-spawn's name. Blood secures it to the bubble of our world, and its lust for that incarnating blood is beyond all the lusts of men. Therefore, the wizard must never use his own blood to make it, for though the f'tragn-agl may not harm its summoner, yet it will desire his blood and grow the more fierce in deprivation.'"

Sean avoided Dad's gaze. It came back too clear, how slashing his palm for blood during the ritual hadn't hurt at all. In fact, his boner had only gotten harder, like he was some kind of

S/M sicko. Who could blame Dad for looking like he wanted to puke?

Helen's voice brought Sean back to the study: "The most important thing I get from these passages is that the Servitor can't hurt Sean."

"It *bit* him," Dad said.

"Sean gave it explicit permission to bite, to drink. So, physically, he's safe."

Sean couldn't stand that. "But the rest of you aren't."

"We're all right," Dad said. "And it won't surprise us again."

Gus shook his head. "It surprised me plenty when I shot it and it flowed 'together like the sundered wave.'"

"Maybe we need bigger weapons," Dad said. "An assault rifle or grenades. Splatter it into so many pieces it can't put itself together again."

"Or we could just call in the National Guard," Gus said dryly.

"Well, maybe we *should* call someone. What about that detective who came over? He seemed all right."

Dad hadn't thought O'Conaghan was all right at the time.

"I have his card," Gus said. "I saved it in case you changed your mind."

"I don't know, Gus."

Dad's nervous hair-habit was to grab at it like it was a possum he was trying to rip off his head. Helen was less violent. She worried one auburn lock, smoothing it straight, then curling it around two fingers. "None of us know exactly what to do," she said. "But I don't think we should involve anyone else if we can help it. It wouldn't be fair."

Dad and even Gus looked confused. Sean got her, though. "It's like UFOs, and how people think the government's covering them up because they'd cause a panic. But real UFOs would be minor-league compared to real Servitors."

Helen nodded at him. "Right, because UFOs wouldn't force you to accept the existence of something like the Outer Gods.

Since yesterday, I'm starting to appreciate why the Archives are set up to keep people *out*."

"If you measured a paradigm shift like an earthquake, this one would be off the Richter scale?" Gus suggested.

"Exactly."

"All right," Dad conceded. "I'm not dying to invite anyone into our club. But what's our next move?"

"We've got a magical problem, we look for a magical solution," Helen said. "Let's assume Orne *did* get his rituals from the MU *Necronomicon*. We keep searching it for a summoning spell that matches Sean's. The dismissing spell should be with the summoning one, Down paired with Up, as Alhazred puts it."

Gus rose. "I wish I could help, but I have new grad students coming in for orientation."

"That's okay," Sean said. "I'll help Helen." Wait, not that she'd asked. "I can, can't I?"

She looked at Dad, passing the question to him. Dad hesitated, which was like worrying whether he should let Sean read the theory of explosives after he'd already blown up the house. Finally, though, he nodded.

"All right, Sean," Helen said. "I'll translate; you take notes."

He took the pad and pen she handed him. Dad followed Gus outside.

Sean had wanted a look at the *Necronomicon* ever since he'd heard of it, and now the Tome of tomes was right in front of him. Okay, not the actual book, but still, a digital facsimile. The crabbed print and rusty discoloration made him squint, and the Latin owned him. Helen didn't have a problem. She scrolled along as fast as if she were reading English in clean modern print, now and then telling him a page number and translating a few lines.

Dad returned and paced around until he had to be getting on Helen's nerves. Instead of telling him to chill, which would have done zero good, she asked him to draw the Servitor as he remembered it. Smart move. He immediately hunted out Celeste's easel and watercolor box, and after a few minutes he wore a scowl of concentration that told Sean he was as happy as he could be under the circumstances.

Sean looked back at the laptop screen. "I thought I did pretty good in Latin last year, but I can't make out two words together of this stuff."

"It's a very idiosyncratic Medieval Latin," Helen said. "Took me a while to get used to it, too."

"I couldn't ever find the dismissing spell on my own. Kind of smacks me upside the head. I was thinking I might go to MU for college, take the Arcane Studies course."

"Why shouldn't you, if you still want to?"

"You mean, if the Servitor doesn't put me off it?" Sean caught himself scribbling spirals and quickly turned to a clean page. "Will it put you off working in the Archives?"

Helen punished that one lock of hair before answering. "If you'd asked me yesterday, I'd have said, 'No way.' It's a great position for someone my age." She grinned. "You won't believe it, but I'm only, what, nine years older than you."

"I believe it," Sean said, and not just to be nice. When she smiled like that, Helen looked like she could still be an undergrad, easy. "But maybe the Archives don't look so great now that you know magic's real?"

"I know some of it is real. That makes things different, but I can't try to deal with the big picture yet. My plan's to focus on finding the dismissing ritual. That sound good enough?"

"Real good enough." Sean meant it, but he glanced at the mantel clock, 10:30. Five or six more hours and the sun would hit its peak and start heading down. "Do you think we'll find the dismissal before dark?"

Helen glanced out at the bright morning. "Could be. But here's your first lesson in old-text scholarship—it's slow-lane travel."

Worrying about every approaching night hadn't helped him yet. He had to learn to concentrate, like Helen and like Dad at the easel. Sean lifted his pen before it could swirl out another spiral. "I'm ready," he said.

# 16

**At** Jeremy's insistence, Helen took a nap after lunch. She felt much better when she returned to the study around three. Sean, though, was on the chaise longue, with Jeremy hovering, thermometer in hand. "Over a hundred," he said.

Given the flush on Sean's face, Helen wasn't surprised. Nor was she surprised to see Sean bat his father's hand off his forehead. "I'm okay, Dad. God. It's the pain pills. They kick your butt."

"I already called Celeste," Jeremy said. "The wound might be inflamed. She might have to start him on antibiotics."

Very broad-spectrum antibiotics to kill Servitor bugs, Helen assumed. She went to the easel. She and Sean had described what they'd seen of the Servitor, and Jeremy had combined their impressions with his, only too effectively—the creature he sketched was coming alive. She went back to her laptop. "Rest some more," she told Sean. "I can—"

The kitchen door banged open. Sean swung his legs off the chaise. Jeremy grabbed a fireplace poker from the window seat where he must have laid it for emergency use.

And Eddy ran into the study.

Helen sank into her chair. Jeremy tossed the poker back onto the window seat. "Edna. Can you knock next time?"

Edna? Ah, the way Eddy winced indicated that Jeremy had lashed her with a hated real name. "Sorry, Mr. Wyndham," she said, plopping on the end of Sean's chaise. "What's with you crashing again?"

"Hey, I helped all morning."

"I hope you don't get sick from that bite. The Servitor left gunk all over our patio. Dad thinks a rabid skunk did it, and he's hosing everything down, right? Then Mom says he might aerosolize the virus and breathe it in. Bang, rabies, you're dead."

"Viruses," Jeremy said. "Thank you, Eddy."

"I'm *okay*," Sean snapped. "So how'd your research go?"

"Same as yesterday. Nothing about a Geldman's Pharmacy in Arkham, and I still can't find our Orne."

Helen put in: "Last night I checked requests to view the *Necronomicon* as far back as they go online. No one who looked like he might be our Redemption Orne."

Sean collapsed. "So we're screwed."

"No way," Eddy said. "I think I've figured Orne out."

Whatever Eddy had, she sounded close to bursting. "Let's hear it," Helen said.

"Say you come up with a screen name that's really cool. You'll use it everywhere. That'll be *you* on the Internet."

"With you so far."

"The guy messing with us doesn't use 'Redemption Orne' that way. Probably he's got other screen names we don't know about. But when he talked to Sean and me, he *did* use 'Redemption Orne.' Maybe because it's his *real* name."

"Hold on," Jeremy said. "If Redemption Orne was his real name, there'd be real-world records for him and some would show up on the Internet."

"There *are* real-world records. Like how he was born in 1669, how he was a minister at the Third Congregational Church, how he disappeared in 1692. See?"

Helen looked at Sean, who was nodding with atypical gravity. Eddy looked equally earnest. "You mean modern Orne and historical Orne are the same person?"

"Right," Eddy said. "Like the Rev always claimed he was."

Jeremy shook his head and kept shaking it, as if he couldn't find words strong enough to refute Eddy's insight. Helen's impulse had also been to object. But if you admitted—*had* to admit— the existence of monstrous familiars . . .

She cleared her throat. "Why not, though? How are immortal wizards more fantastic than Servitors?"

"They're not," Sean said.

"Immortality?" Again Jeremy seemed to find no other words, but he loaded a ton of disbelief into that one.

"We don't have to be talking immortality," Helen said. "Just extended life. That's always been one of the main goals of magic."

Jeremy walked to the easel and stared at his sketches. Drawing the Servitor, reducing it to two dimensions, seemed to have made it comprehensible to him. How could he draw Orne's three hundred plus years of life or understand how they had led Orne to Sean? "Say we go with our Orne being the Puritan Orne," Jeremy said at last. "How's that help us?"

Helen dug the rubber-banded stack of jewel cases from her backpack. "It could make these useful. They're facsimiles of Orne's journals."

"That's right!" Sean said. His pain pills might be kicking his butt, but he made it to the table ahead of Eddy. "I read in the *Witch Panic* book how MU had them."

"The library put them on film and CDs not long ago. What with your hoaxer calling himself Redemption Orne, I brought the disks along."

"Wicked!" Eddy said. "Maybe there's clues about the dismissing ritual."

"If you've got time, Eddy, why don't you start looking?"

It was Sean who took the cases from her. "Eddy," he said. "Go get your laptop so we can split these up."

Eddy took off like a gazelle, if gazelles were inveterate slammers; this time, she banged out the front door.

Jeremy shrugged at Helen. "If you light the fuses on these kids, expect big explosions. Sean, you sure you're up to reading?"

Sean had disappeared behind Gus's PC monitor. "Yeah, Dad. I'm *fine*. What should we read first, Helen?"

"Start with the two labeled 'Secret Journals.' The story is Orne kept them in a hidden cabinet because of the occult references in them. But I'm afraid there's no index yet and you can't search the facsimile text."

"That's okay. We'll just read straight through."

Eddy bounded back into the study. Soon she and Sean were leaning into their screens, their faces bleached by the electronic glow. It didn't look like the healthiest activity for a summer day, and Helen started to worry that she'd stepped on Jeremy's parental toes. There were Eddy's parents, too, who hadn't signed a Consent for Minor to Peruse Wizard's Private Papers form. Not that the Archives had such a form, at least not that Helen knew about.

And that was the rub, the fact that there was so little she did know, compared to the looming bulk of what she did not. She glanced at Jeremy, who'd started to apply watercolor to his sketches and who was as rapt as the kids. He'd shifted his easel to the windows facing the street, chasing the best light. Light, sun, the movement of it, the brightening and fading. It made time real.

Too real. Helen inserted another disk into her laptop and grimaced at the fresh pair of pages. Content aside, the *Necronomicon* was a horror to read, with a typeface so tortured the printers might have devised it to keep all but the most determined from studying the book. On the other hand, the illustrations were painfully exact. Here she had a series of woodcuts showing how to remove a heart. A beating heart, from a living (for an excruciating moment) human.

She scrolled to the next pair of pages, which were mercifully devoid of illustrations.

For a while the clink of Jeremy's brushes against the side of his water jar was the only sound, that and the occasional murmur between Eddy and Sean. Then Jeremy went into the kitchen. Refrigerator and cabinet doors opening and closing, chopping. Soon the smells of browning beef and garlic, simmering tomatoes and basil. As Jeremy returned to the study, the aroma wafted before him, tantalizing. "Dinner?" Helen said.

He took the chair beside hers. "In an hour or so. Linguine and Bolognese sauce."

"Great. I'm hungry enough to eat the whole city of Bologna."

Sunlight had deserted the study windows, and Jeremy didn't return to his painting. Instead he watched Sean and Eddy, who'd hardly come up for air since they'd dived into the Orne journals. Then, redirecting his gaze to Helen's screen, he asked, "How are you coming?"

"Moving along. Nothing specific about the rituals yet."

"Same here," Eddy said. "But the journals are awesome. Patience and Enoch Bishop and the Nipmucs were totally witches. All kinds of weird stuff was happening around Dunwich, and Orne must've known his own wife and father-in-law were in the middle of it, except you can tell he's in denial."

Sean was silent, but his mouse clicked as steady as a metronome.

Jeremy kept watching Helen's screen. After a few pages, he said, "What's that about?"

He was pointing at a broad bar of black in the outer margin of the text, too neat to be accidental, too ragged to be computer generated. "From what I understand, that's one of the big mysteries for Mythos scholars. An earlier owner of this *Necronomicon* wrote extensive notes in the book, marginalia. Then he or

someone else blotted them all out. The Archives have tried everything to uncover the notes. No luck."

"So that black stuff is ink?"

Before Helen could answer, the study table jolted toward her.
Poltergeist? No, Sean, whose excitement had catapulted him out
of his chair, just like in her office the day before. "Can I see them?"
he said, voice cracking.

"What, Sean?"

"Those things, the margin-whaties." Sean came around the
table. His face was definitely more flushed, and as he craned over
her Helen felt the pulse of fever-heat. "That's it, the black column?"

"That's one of the blotted marginalia."

Eddy looked over her laptop screen. "What's the big deal?"

"It's in the Orne journal I'm reading. Helen, you know who
owned that *Necronomicon* just before MU?"

"The Enoch Bishop Eddy just mentioned, I think. The
witchcraft court confiscated his books and gave them to the
university."

Sean went back to the PC. For a few seconds he mouse-clicked
frantically. "Here's what Orne writes: 'Today in Dunwich Village,
Mr. B. showed me the book of the Arab, which is called the Book
of Dead Names. I read little, for I found it more ungodly than
anything he has shown me before. The book is the more curious
because Mr. B. has writ in the margins many annotations, and
yet these cannot be read, for he has hidden them under a veil of
ink so devised that none without the key can penetrate it.'"

That was an explanation of the marginalia that Helen hadn't
heard before. She hurried around the table. "Are there any more
journal passages that mention Bishop's *Necronomicon*?"

"I had one," Eddy said. She'd caught Sean's agitation—her
ponytail bounced as she jittered in her chair. "I read it before you
talked about the marginalia, so I didn't know it was important.
Wait. Okay. 'Last night I found P. in the attic among her father's
effects. Beneath her was that vile book of the Arab, upon which

she'd fallen in a swoon. This morning she lies in bed with the windows close-shuttered, for any light strikes a great pain into her eyes. She confessed she was trying to read Mr. B.'s annotations and so had brushed onto the blots a solvent meant to make the words clear for a time. However, its smell had overcome her before she could read what appeared. The solvent is all gone, she says—and I did find an empty vial beside her—so she will not be able to try the feat again. I brought her to promise she would leave the book—all her father's books—untouched from now on. It seemed to relieve her to give her word.'"

The marginalia. Patience trying to peer through their veil. What was the connection to their situation? Sean's excitement argued there was one, but the insubstantial logic of sorcery had packed Helen's brain in black cotton. Blots. Enchanted ink. Something Orne had written in his second chat with Sean—

She met Sean's eyes. "Dark places?"

He nodded. "The *very dark* places in the *Necronomicon*. That was Orne's clue to where the dismissing spell is. Man, I'm stupid. I should have figured it out this morning, when I saw those blots." He punched his thigh. "Stupid!"

"Stop it, Sean!" Jeremy cut in, his own hands fisted. "If anyone's stupid, it's me, because I still don't know what you're talking about."

"We've been looking for the dismissing spell in the wrong place, Dad. Well, kind of. I mean, it's in the *Necronomicon* from MU, like Orne said, only not in the part Alhazred wrote. See, why'd it have to be exactly that *Necronomicon*? Because that's the one Bishop made his notes in and the spell's somewhere in his notes, under the ink."

Under the veil, which even the latest digital imaging had failed to pierce. The sickness that boiled up Helen's throat left a bitter slick on the back of her tongue. A mini-drama played out on Jeremy's face, first blankness, then understanding, then a red wash of anger that made Sean's flush look pale. "The bastard," Jeremy said, too flatly. "He's playing games with us. He's playing god-damned games."

Helen let go of the back of Sean's chair and returned to Jeremy. "Sean. Eddy. You keep reading."

"Okay," Eddy said, but for once she sounded uncertain.

"What good will that do?" Jeremy said. "We're screwed, like Orne knew we would be. Finding the dismissing spell is a test? What kind of test is it where you're bound to fail?"

Sean lifted a scared face, and his eyes begged Helen for the answer. She didn't have one, which had to be her karmic payback for all those classrooms where the answers had come too easily. She knew one thing: Her fear and Jeremy's anger would burn the air from the room, suffocate them, suffocate Sean and Eddy. They had to get out.

"Let's walk, Jeremy," she said. "We've been cooped up all day."

He looked from her to Sean. Whatever the boy's eyes begged of him dropped his gaze to Helen's laptop. "I don't like leaving the kids."

"They'll be all right. Eddy, will you watch the stove and lock up behind us?"

"Sure."

Helen touched Jeremy's shoulder. Knots of muscle, tight. To her relief, he let her urge him toward the door. "Where's that park we passed yesterday?" she asked.

He didn't speak. He walked. Helen followed, to the top of Celeste and Gus's street, over a couple of blocks, down a steep decline. At the bottom was an expanse of grass and trees that ended in an iron-railed embankment. Beyond the embankment was a cityscape of steeples and domes and skyscrapers. Tourists reveled in the photo op. Students lolled on blankets. At one of the benches by the overlook, a woman jounced a toddler in a stroller. Jeremy stopped, looking at the stroller. "Sean wouldn't ever stay in one of those."

That was easy to believe. Helen imagined a two-year-old Sean at the railing that guarded the brink, clutching iron pickets in grubby fists, staring at the insect people in the streets below, then tilting back his tufted head to gaze over the steeples and the domes and the skyscrapers, out to the hilly blue rim of Providence.

If Sean were here now, he'd be in the middle of that crowd that hung over the railing to watch rock climbers scale the embankment. Skirting the spectators, Jeremy steered Helen to a bench. Beside it, a stone figure in stylized Puritan garb stretched a giant's hand over the city. Redemption Orne? Right, Helen. The plaque on the statue's base read: ROGER WILLIAMS, FOUNDER OF PROVIDENCE. But was Williams stretching out his hand to confer a blessing, or was he warding off backsliders, like Orne?

Jeremy dragged in some of that air they were both supposed to be getting. "Thanks for herding me out of there," he said. "Sean and Eddy didn't need to hear it."

"I don't blame you for being mad. If the dismissing ritual's hidden in the marginalia, it's a rotten trick."

The woman with the stroller walked by. Jeremy watched her out of sight before he spoke again. "An ancient wizard, you'd think he'd have something better to do than screw around with teenagers."

"Orne doesn't strike me as a practical joker."

"How about a psychopath? He gave Sean a spell he knew could hurt him."

"That's the thing, though; he didn't." Helen hooked her arms around the back of the bench, trying to stretch the tension out of her own shoulders. "I reread the chats and e-mails this morning. Sean's right. Orne only sent the incantation for an aether-newt."

"So the Black Man actually appeared to Sean and gave him the blood-spawn incantation?"

Her stretches weren't working. Helen let her arms drop back to her sides. "That's the hell of this. Everything that's happened should be impossible, so how do you rule anything out? Even the Black Man."

"Satan."

"No, wrong mythology. Not Satan, Nyarlathotep." Soul and Messenger of the Outer Gods, yeah, and He of the Three-Lobed Burning Eye, check, Haunter of the Dark and Master of Magic. Master of Magic? Didn't that also make him Master of Magicians? Another connection hovered almost in her grasp. That critical juncture in the second chat, when Orne had seemed shocked to learn what Sean had summoned, when he'd seemed about to give Sean the dismissing ritual, then fallen silent for several minutes. What had he been doing during the pause? Why had he refused to give the ritual after all? There was a subtle message in his actual words. Too bad she didn't have the printouts with her, but she remembered the gist of the refusal. *I can't give the ritual.* Not *I won't give it.* And *Another test has been proposed.* Not *I propose another test.*

In the hot August afternoon, she went January cold. *After summer, winter.* "I believe in the Black Man," she said.

"The one in your windows?"

"No, a real god, as far as we're concerned. He's called the Master of Magic, so he's probably Redemption Orne's master. I don't know. I'm thinking aloud."

Jeremy shifted sideways to face her. "Go on."

"It started with the ad, Orne wanting an apprentice. Horrocke hinted it wasn't an accident that Sean found the clipping. Orne said right out he meant the clipping for Sean. Just Sean. Sean's special."

"Special how?"

"Well, from what I've learned so far—" That was, what she'd learned thinking she studied the particular magical system of a particular mythology, ergo a culturally relevant fantasy, but fantasy nevertheless. "What the books say is that not everyone can do magic. In fact, magic-capable people are very rare, with an innate ability to capture and control mystical energy. Supposedly, the ability's inherited."

"If it's inherited, where did Sean get it? I don't know of any witches on either side of his family tree, and I sure as hell can't do magic. Neither could Kate." But Jeremy paused. "That is, she was different, but it wasn't magic."

"What do you mean by 'different'?"

Jeremy stared into the dense foliage of the oak overhanging their seat. "She had a talent. Genius, I'd call it, and I don't think I'm being prejudiced. If you'd seen any of Kate's paintings when we were at my house, you'd know what I mean. We didn't go inside, though."

"No." And the only painting in Kate's studio had hidden its face from the world.

"Cel has a couple of her oils in her bedroom."

"I haven't gone in there."

"No, I guess you wouldn't have any reason to." His head still tilted back, Jeremy closed his eyes. "It's like, it's how Kate saw things with this crazy intensity. Color, movement, details. And she could get it all down on the paper or canvas, no disconnect between what was in her head and what she made out of it. That's huge for an artist. That's why her paintings breathe. Weird thing. When Sean was a little kid, he used to insist his mom's paintings were like our damn refrigerator."

"Refrigerator?"

"He said they vibrated. You know how a fridge does, not so much that you feel it through the floor, but if you press your hand against it. I'd humor him by saying, 'Oh, right,' but I never felt it. For me, it was just this feeling her work was more alive than anyone else's I'd seen."

Helen remembered the Madonna of the Paintbrush. "In your window of Kate, is that why you put auras around her brush and the flowers she's holding? Because that was how she painted?"

Jeremy opened his eyes and looked at her. "I guess so, but Kate's painting wasn't out-and-out surreal; it was a hell of a lot more subtle. I can't match her. Still, that's not magic. Sean doing the summoning spell, that's magic."

Who was Helen to point out that magic might have many forms and gradations? More important, who was she to suggest to Jeremy that his dead wife might have been a witch of sorts, carrier of magician-making genes? Nobody, a novice, that was who Helen was. She caught herself twining a curl of her hair around her forefinger, which was a nervous tic she'd thought she'd vanquished. She whipped her hand back down. "Well, I know I'm supposed to be the expert in this spook party, but I don't know the specifics of magic transmission. What probably matters more now is the idea that magicians are able to sense each other. Somehow Orne found Sean. After that, the Black Man could have noticed Orne's interest. He could have gotten interested enough himself to give Sean the blood-spawn incantation during the ritual, as a harder test. Then, as a second test, maybe he stopped Orne from handing over the dismissing ritual. There are hints in the chat record. Orne wrote he *can't* give the dismissing. He wrote another test's *proposed*. So you have to ask, proposed by whom?"

Jeremy frowned. "You're saying Orne wasn't trying to hurt Sean."

"I don't know that anyone's trying to *hurt* him. Test him, yes."

"Screw that. Where do they get the right? And are we supposed to deal with some damn monster-god on top of an immortal wizard? It's too damn much, especially if they cheat, making us look for an answer we can't even get at."

She understood every bit of Jeremy's outrage because every bit of it was her own. "I know," she said. "The thing is—"

Cheers from the crowd at the railing cut her off. A climber had reached the top of the embankment. Visibly wrung out but grinning, he hoisted himself to safety. He'd made it, one step after another, fingers locked into crevices, toes jammed between rocks. One step after another, fine, but he'd had the solid and tangible to deal with. She had words. Magic spells.

Words, a magic spell, had made the Servitor. It was solid

enough to kill animals, attack people. The words under Enoch Bishop's enchanted ink could put it down again, and only other words would lead her to what Bishop had hidden. "There's got to be a way to read through the blots. Orne says so in his journal, a solvent of some kind like the one Patience used. Plus I don't think he—or Nyarlathotep—would have made his only clue to the dismissing spell one that Sean couldn't crack. So here's what we do next. We find the way through the ink. The answer could be in the *Necronomicon* itself. It could be in Orne's journals. I'm going to keep looking in both places."

Jeremy had turned toward the overlook and the successful climber detaching his safety ropes from the railing. When he turned to Helen again, she noticed that his eyes weren't exactly the same blue-gray as Sean's. Sean's were paler, more rain than cloud, but after all, where did rain come from? "I know you're right about keeping at the books," Jeremy said. "So even if I act like an idiot sometimes, remember I trust you."

Whether or not she deserved his trust, Helen nodded to accept it. Wasn't audience confidence a huge part of the magic game? "I guess we better head back."

Jeremy pushed himself to his feet and gave her a hand up. As they started out of the park, another climber made it to the top of the embankment, to renewed applause.

# 17

**So** what if deciphering Orne's handwriting had kicked Sean's headache up a notch. So what if he'd flopped on the study chaise again—Dad didn't have to talk about hustling him to the emergency room. Good thing Celeste came home right after Dad and Helen. "I'm not surprised he's down," she said. "His temp's a hundred and two."

"An infection?" Helen said.

Celeste unwound Sean's bandage. Except for the yellow of the antiseptic she'd painted on the night before, it was clean. "The bite's not inflamed. Does it hurt, Sean?"

"It did this morning. Now it's just itchy."

Celeste began applying a lighter dressing. "That's a good sign."

Dad watched her work, like Celeste was going to screw up. "A fever that high can't be good. If it's not the bite, what's the problem?"

"It could be a systemic infection or an allergic reaction."

"Which could be dangerous, right?"

"I'll keep an eye on him tonight, Jere. If he gets worse, I'll take him to Al Goss."

That would be all right. Dr. Goss was cool. He had a replica of Aragorn's sword in his office. Andúril, Flame of the West. He even had the One Ring. Sean had snuck it out of its display case once and tried it on. It hadn't made him invisible, though. Maybe he was like Tom Bombadil, the only one immune to the Ring's power.

To keep Dad calm, Sean joined everybody in the dining room, where they were eating Dad's linguine. Sean ate a few bites, but once the heap of pasta on his plate started looking like an acceptable pillow he said, "I think I'll crash now."

"That's probably the best thing you can do," Celeste said.

No, it was the only thing. Sean made it to the third floor, out of his clothes, and onto his bed. Dad had tagged along—Sean was dimly aware of him turning on the air conditioner. "Thanks," Sean murmured. "You go help. With the reading."

"I'm not much good at that. I'm going to get some sleep myself."

Only Dad didn't lie down. He stood over Sean's bed. You don't have to babysit, Sean said. Or thought. He wasn't sure which. He saw a last ray of sunlight streak the wall, then closed his eyes and saw the last sunlight shimmer on the surface of the water that blanketed him. . . .

But it's strange. The darkness of the water seems light, and the sunlight seems dark. He's in the bright water, many feet under, which means he should be drowning. Or has he already drowned? He's not breathing. He lies naked in soft, cool mulm. Tentacles mingle with the weeds that wave around him; fish pluck at them curiously, and colors radiate from fish and weeds and tentacles alike, colors he can't name. The fish pluck, and he feels it. The tentacles are part of himself. They seize a fish and taste its alien salt and sweetness. The fish wriggles in his throat as he swallows.

He lies quiet again, unbreathing but alive, until the darkness above grows light. Then, with one fierce kick, he rises to the

202 Anne M. Pillsworth

surface and breathes. Breathing draws air through his tentacles, which tingle and smart with a thousand new scents. Most he's never noticed before, secret smells of river and earth, yet one scent is more compelling than the rest. It's the scent of men, of Sean himself, asleep in his bed. Yet he, Sean, is also in the twilight river, swimming toward the paleness of rising land.

He has *become* the Servitor. Somehow that's not scary. In fact, it's reassuring. As long as *he* is *it,* it can't do any harm.

What's more, he knows where he is. Glaring white, a road dives down a steep bluff to the shore of the river. A wall made of boulders dives parallel to it: the wall that separates Swan Point Cemetery from St. Joseph's Cemetery, as if the two populations of the dead have to be kept apart. That means the river is the Seekonk, and so he's still on the East Side of Providence, not far from Celeste and Gus's, where his primary body sleeps and dreams him into this one.

He crawls onto a muddy path that leads to the receiving tomb sunk into the bluff. On its marble steps, he waits for nightfall, flicking out tongues even more sensitive than his tentacles. Sounds bounce off the taut drumheads in the sides and back of his head. There is another sensation he doesn't understand, a not-quite sound as if water is rushing under his thoughts.

What he does recognize, no problem, is hunger. He clicks long talons over the tongues that flicker from his palm-mouths. As his emptiness grows, he shambles away from the tomb, easily finding his way to the trail that climbs the bluff. Night hides nothing from him. Is it something other than light that his Servitor-eyes perceive, some obscure atomic vibration that light waves actually mask? What are the unnamed colors that pulse around plants and insects, around himself? Rocks, water, and earth don't pulse. Do the colors only come from what's alive?

Beyond the crest of the bluff is the cemetery. He gallops past monuments, ducks under the canopies of weeping cedars where the shadow-brilliance makes it like hiding inside the shade of a lamp. Westward is the electric gloom of the city; westward, too, the human scent sings stronger in the olfactory clamor.

It occurs to him then that he's headed to Celeste's, to feed on himself. Definitely not a good idea. He'd better go back into the river and eat fish.

However, he gallops in the wrong direction, up the avenue of pin oaks, ginkgos, and hollies that leads to the gates. Lights (darks?) are on in the cemetery offices. A security van mutters outside. Sean skirts the building and van, running north to the boulder wall, then following the wall into the brushy wood that separates this quarter of Swan Point from Blackstone Boulevard.

Still unable to turn back toward the river, he hurtles onward. On this warm evening, under a nearly full moon, people will be out on the boulevard. He'll be able to watch them unseen, because the cemetery stands six feet above the street, buttressed by another boulder wall. He halts behind a rhododendron thicket. Through the screen of leathery leaves, he sees the grassy path nearest the wall, and the northbound lane of the boulevard, and the central parkway. Path and parkway swarm with walkers.

Under cover though he is, the black glare of the streetlights bothers him. The shafts from headlights are worse, and the thumping of car stereos makes him hunch pulpy shoulders over his drumhead ears. A pack of girls cruises close to the cemetery wall. It's gross how slime drips from his mouths at the smell of them. His emptiness expands. No, not *his* emptiness. He, Sean, wants to run back to the river. It, the Servitor, refuses to move from its ambush. It's the one making the decisions, which means Sean hasn't possessed its body after all; he's just riding around in its skull, a parasite plugged into its senses. That watery rush beneath his thoughts? That must be the Servitor's thoughts.

He—*it*—squats motionless. Mosquitoes don't trouble it— what runs in its veins doesn't interest them. An owl flies by, another silent piece of the night. Crickets and cicadas, which hushed at the Servitor's intrusion, sing again, and a fox pads close enough to peer at it through the spindly trunks of the maple saplings. The immediate scent of human blood fades—pedestrians are getting scarce.

Good. Let it go back to the river. *Go back.*

The blood-scent fades, then sharpens again. The Servitor's tentacles twitch. A man with a dog, a mini schnauzer, crosses the boulevard to walk beside the cemetery wall. He passes the clump of rhododendrons. He'll soon be safely away. Except the man stops, lifts the schnauzer onto the wall, and clambers up after her. Is he nuts? Sure, people walk dogs in the cemetery woods. But at night?

Not twenty feet from man and dog, the Servitor sinks to all fours. Saliva spills from its mouths.

The schnauzer has been frisking around the man's feet. Now she growls, snout pointed at the thicket. The man jerks her, bristling, onto one of the paths that ramble through the trees.

In the concealing brightness of the thicket, which must be pitch-black to the man, the Servitor is a shapeless shadow. Besides, the man's busy dragging the dog, who sees with her nose and bursts into maddened barks. "Christ, you'll wake the dead," the man says, and laughs at his own lame joke.

The Servitor eases onto the path the man follows. Hunger is a universe of void inside it. The man and dog are a few leaps away, hidden from the slowing life of the street by the trees. No one will help them. One talon-slash will end the frantic barking. Another will cut short any scream from the man.

He, Sean Wyndham, is asleep at his aunt Cel's house on Keene Street.

He, Sean Wyndham, moves with the Servitor in dream, and in dream he will feed with it.

*No. Stop.*

"What the fuck's that smell?" the man mutters.

It—Sean, *they*—crouches to spring.

*No. Back off!*

The Servitor doesn't spring. Instead the rushing stream of its consciousness rises toward the parasite-Sean. He shrinks from its frigid touch, but if he wants to speak to the Servitor, he has to endure the probing cold. He knows that as sure as he knows his name, which is Sean, Sean. *Back off. I'm the one that summoned you, so do what I say.*

The Servitor listens. It also takes a step after the man and dog. The schnauzer yelps and rips the leash from the man's hand. She runs deeper into the woods, with the man in cursing pursuit.

Dropping low, the Servitor gives insectile chase.

*I gave you my blood. I'll give you more. Mine!*

It pauses. It listens again. Its mindstream is inarticulate, but it coils around parasite Sean like a python of ice and constricts until thought is pressed to thought in such crushing intimacy that Sean knows the Servitor's intention. *If he promises the blood, it will come to him.*

*No! Go back into the river. Stay there until I come.*

*It is hungry.*

*I'll come. Wait in the river. Just wait there.*

Back at Celeste and Gus's, Sean is asleep, but sleep shreds, and the bright night wavers. The Servitor moves, but where? After the man and dog? No, God, please. No, it's away; it's galloping down another path—

"Sean."

Cool smoothness under his hands. Wood, a window frame. Sean stared out into a night that was dark, not light. Arms were locked around his chest. Dad, holding him.

Sean squirmed free. Helen stood in the open door of his room, Gus and Celeste behind her.

"It's all right," Dad said. "I think he was sleepwalking."

Celeste led Sean to his bed. He was shaking like crazy, and he felt sticky cold all over. The pillow under his hand was damp. With river water?

Celeste palmed his forehead. "The fever's broken. I guess you sweated it out, Sean."

Sweat, that was all right. He had never really been in the river. He, it, they.

"How do you feel?"

He rubbed his belly (his own belly). "My head doesn't hurt. I'm hungry." Hungry? That was an understatement. He was empty. Not like the dream-Servitor was empty, though. He'd have to starve for weeks to get as savagely famished as it was.

"That's good," Dad said. "Come on. We can both get something to eat."

Helen squatted in front of Sean. "We can make it a mass refrigerator raid. But, Sean, were you dreaming just now?"

It was no casual question—her gaze was uncomfortably intense. "Well, yeah."

"What about?"

He didn't want to tell her. But that couldn't be right. She was here to help him. "It was about the Servitor."

"Big surprise," Dad said.

Helen shook her head. "It might not be that simple. What was the dream like?"

"It was freaky, superreal, but not normal real. It was real like things would be for the Servitor, you know? Dark things looked light, and I could smell and taste things people can't."

"You mean you experienced things as if you *were* the Servitor?"

He had to tell the truth. "I was, like, a part of it, out there in the river and the cemetery. I stopped it from killing this guy. I'm scared—what if I was really in its head, not just dreaming?"

Nobody spoke. Dad scuffed his bare feet on the carpet. Then Helen said, "I was afraid this might happen."

# 18

Five A.M. came minus the rosy fingers of dawn. Outside in the persistent dark, wind strafed the porch screens with rain, and the gusts made restless music under the eaves. To be moving, doing, Helen started clearing the debris from Sean's midnight feast. He'd put away two plates of linguine, then bedded down on the living-room couch. Jeremy stood beside the kitchen door, an ear obviously cocked for sleepwalking. At the table Gus and Celeste pored over Helen's latest translations.

"I'm not sure I understand this," Celeste said.

Gus riffled through the pages he held. "It's a little clearer here: 'If the sorcerer desires communion with his daemon-familiar, he must put its ichor or saliva into his own veins. Such inoculation will weave a soul-thread between the two, so the sorcerer may, even at great distance, know the familiar's mind, see through its eyes and command it. Inoculation is simplest with those familiars made from the blood or bones of men, the f'tragn-agl or the hlaast.'"

Helen scraped strands of linguine from the plate she held, red and white, blood and bone. The plate shook in her hand.

Celeste sighed. "The way that thing mangled Sean's wrist, we can assume he was inoculated."

"I'm assuming the same thing," Helen said. She scraped another plate. It shook like the first and made a telltale clatter as she slotted it into the dishwasher. "He had the symptoms Alhazred describes: fever, headache, tiredness."

"And this says the psychic connection starts with dreams," Gus said. "Then progresses to a waking connection, telepathy, I guess."

"That's when the shit hits the fan, right?" Jeremy said, sudden and sharp. Helen dropped a fork. Good timing: a little more noise to ramp up the tension.

Celeste, at least, was unrattled. "Jere, let's not wake Sean up. What else, Gus?"

Helen slotted the offending fork, more cutlery, glasses. She heard paper rustle. Then Gus read: "'It is perilous for a sorcerer to maintain the soul-thread indefinitely. Unless his mind is as adamantine and cold as the daemon's, such union must end in his madness.'"

"So how does a sorcerer switch off the modem?" Jeremy said.

Gus shrugged. Celeste excused herself to get ready for work. Passing the sink, she gave Helen's arm a light squeeze. Celeste meant to reassure, but she might as well have squeezed Helen's throat, the way it tightened. She hadn't come to Providence to wash dishes or to translate ominous passages and then run away from them. Her place was at the table, however useless she felt there.

Helen closed the dishwasher. She didn't make it to the table, but she did turn to face Jeremy. "Alhazred writes that to break the connection, a sorcerer 'sunders the soul-thread and holds both ends in his hands, to knot together again when he pleases.' How he does that I don't know yet. The only other way to break the psychic connection is to dismiss the familiar."

"Which puts us back to square one. Worse. The connection

could start driving Sean crazy. And, if what Sean dreamed was real, the thing could start killing people."

Helen nodded.

"Sean ordered the Servitor off that dog walker," Gus said. "The connection turned out to be a good thing there."

He was offering her a baton. Helen took it and tried to run. "Right. Sean seems to have some control over the Servitor, even though he didn't bind it."

"Sean called it off by promising it his blood," Jeremy said. "Same way he called it off me. It'll come to collect before long— am I the only one that feels like we've got a clock ticking?"

Jeremy didn't wait for Helen's response. He disappeared into the living room. An armchair creaked as he sat, probably the one by the couch, next to Sean. Gus looked after him, shaking his head. Then he began collating the printouts.

Should she help? Pretend to be accomplishing something? Helen felt her throat squeeze closed again. She turned to the window over the sink. Night had paled to an aqueous gray—this dawn was all water, dank wind, barrages of rain, the prickling at the corners of her eyes. It was hard to remember the sun-drenched park where she and Jeremy had sat the day before.

One step up the embankment at a time, but at the moment she couldn't see any cracks into which to cram her fingers and toes. Uncle John would have had the answers. Probably he'd written them down in the papers he'd entrusted to Marvell. But with Marvell out of touch, John might as well have taken the papers to his grave.

Helen told the window, "I want to call Scotland again."

"Please, use our phone," Gus said.

The kitchen phone was a step away. Helen pulled out Marvell's card and put in the call. Leezy McGrigor answered. "Helen, is it? How nice to hear from you again."

"Thank you, Mrs. McGrigor. Have you heard from Professor Marvell?"

"Ah, no. The weather's been so fine, I imagine he and Robert have been tenting out instead of running into town. Good luck for them, but not for you, I'm afraid?"

"No. I need to reach him if it's at all possible."

"Well then, here's what we'll do. I'll send my Forrest, my son, you know, up toward Beinn Dearg. I reckon he'll find our rogues."

"I hate to be so much trouble—"

"Not a bit, my dear. Theo would never forgive me if I didn't do my best by you."

She gave Leezy McGrigor both her cell number and the number at the Litinski house. Turning from the phone, she saw that Jeremy had returned to the kitchen door. "Mrs. McGrigor's going to send her son after Marvell."

"And meanwhile?" Gus said. "We keep at the disks?"

"That, and figure out who else to call for advice." Someone at MU, at the library? Marvell couldn't be the only one who knew magic was real. Another believer. Still better, a practitioner, like Redemption Orne—

The thunderclap of realization must have shown on her face: Jeremy and Gus were staring at her. "Gus, if you could go on with the *Necronomicon*?"

"No appointments today. I can keep right at it."

"Okay. I need a shower and breakfast. Then, Jeremy, can you drive me back to Arkham?"

"If Gus will stay with Sean. Why?"

"I want to try him again, alone," Helen said. "Mr. Geldman, at the pharmacy."

~⚶~

**Lulled** by the rhythmic scrape of the windshield wipers, Helen fell asleep before Jeremy made I-95. She didn't wake up until they were in Arkham, rumbling over the iron bed of the Peabody

Avenue Bridge. The dashboard clock read: 10:31. "That was quick," she muttered.

"Two hours. Couldn't break any records in this storm."

She smoothed her T-shirt, peering out the rain-bleared side window. "Wait. Don't turn here. Go straight up to Curwen Street."

"Why?"

"We've got to park a couple blocks from the pharmacy, out of sight. I'm going there by myself, remember?"

"I've been rethinking that plan. I'm going with you."

"I wish you could. Stop, Jeremy! Go straight."

He went straight, but he said, "I'm going."

"You can't. The pharmacy was always open for me until the other day, when I went there with you. What if it doesn't want you to see it and you jinx it for me again? Wasted trip."

Jeremy's lips tightened out of existence. God, don't let him go stubborn on her now. "He could be dangerous, Helen. We don't know what he's up to."

"I'm not afraid of Solomon Geldman."

"You don't know him."

"In a way I do. Every time I've seen him, I've felt—" What? Could she explain it? "Protected," she said, and it sounded right.

"What the hell does that mean?"

"Safe, watched over, I don't know. But I've got to go with the feeling."

Even though Jeremy offered no further argument, Helen wasn't sure he'd given in until they turned onto Curwen and he pulled the Civic to the curb two blocks from Gedney. "This do?"

"Looks fine," Helen said. "Do you have an umbrella?"

Jeremy got out and rummaged in the trunk. What he unfurled over her as she stepped into the rain was a cheerful yellow monstrosity on which someone had drawn black skulls and crossbones. "Sorry about this," he said, handing her the umbrella. "Sean's sense of humor again."

"I like it. The *Flying Dutchman* look." Though if she remembered her Wagner, that opera hadn't ended too well for the girl. "Wait here five minutes. If I don't get into the pharmacy, I'll be in Tumblebee's."

"And if you do get in, how long should I wait outside?"

"Thirty minutes? Sixty. Let's say an hour."

"Then?"

"Call my cell. If you can't reach me, try to get in. There's a gangway next to the pharmacy. Maybe you could find an inconspicuous window."

"Breaking and entering. I'm already set for that." Jeremy opened his windbreaker to reveal a flashlight and cat's-paw crowbar stowed in the inner pockets.

Should she laugh or be grateful for his forethought? Why not both, so she did laugh, and she said, "Thanks, but I don't think you'll have to use those. Five minutes."

"Five. Not one more." And he meant it; she'd better not dawdle.

Helen trotted off under the pirate parasol. Thunder grumbled out at sea. Raindrops exploded on the bricks under her feet. As she neared the corner of Gedney and Curwen, she dipped Sean's umbrella in front of her face, but even as she shielded herself from disappointment she knew she didn't have to. Geldman's had been open for her before. It would be open for her again. She passed the side windows of Tumblebee's, then halted by its steps and peeked under the rim of the umbrella.

Geldman's Pharmacy was alive and well. The display windows radiated warm interior light. The green awnings offered shelter to the storm drenched. In one of the lace-curtained windows of the second-floor apartment, a black cat washed its face.

The door opened, and Solomon Geldman wheeled out the fortune-telling scale. He looked up as Helen forded the flooded street. "Good morning, Ms. Arkwright. Wet but good, like all mornings."

Jeremy's paranoia had infected her, after all—she was reluctant to step under the awning and into Geldman's sphere of influence. "I've been thankful for mornings lately."

His brows lifted. "Then you've found the nights long?"

"Very. I was hoping we could talk."

"Of course. Let's get out of this wind."

Furling her umbrella, Helen braved the awning. As far as she could tell, it shot no mesmerizing rays through the top of her skull. She followed Geldman inside and trod immaculate tiles to the counter, where he took the umbrella and deposited it in a stand. "Have you come for yourself or a friend?" he asked.

"A friend, Sean Wyndham. He bought the Powders of Zeph and Aghar here."

"I remember the transaction. Shall we go in back? I could offer you tea."

During the short walk between sidewalk and counter, she had regained her conviction that she'd be safe wherever Geldman was. Even so, she gave the entrance (escape route) one last look. Though she'd heard no splash of approaching footsteps, Jeremy stood pressed to the pharmacy door. Obviously he could see the place as she did, because his eyes met hers wide with astonishment. He tried the door. It didn't budge. He knocked, then pounded on the spotless plate glass. The slam of his fist made no more sound than the fall of snowflakes on the other side of the world.

"You won't let him in?" Helen said.

"No. He doesn't belong here. However, it wouldn't be polite to leave him unacknowledged." Geldman closed his eyes.

On the other side of the glass, of the world, Jeremy spun toward the scale. It poked an insolent pink tongue from the brass slot under its face, out-in-out, until he grabbed the proffered fortune. As Jeremy read it, Geldman recited: "Mr. Wyndham. Please don't worry. I mean Ms. Arkwright no harm. May I suggest you have coffee at the establishment opposite? The house blend is very good, and it's best not to loiter around abandoned buildings."

Abandoned? Yes. Where Helen and Geldman stood, the pharmacy remained alive and well. Beyond them, it had gone dark, because the windows were opaque with grime and the door was boarded over with warped plywood. The scale now lay inside, face smashed, one more piece of garbage on the dust-furred tiles.

"Mr. Wyndham has gone for his coffee," Geldman said. "Shall we?"

He had opened a half door in the counter. Helen turned from the abrupt wreckage and passed through it. She stepped aside to let Geldman take the lead. He walked down a corridor with closed doors to either side and a closed door at its end.

Geldman opened the end door.

# 19

**From** the stutter of overhead fluorescents, Helen walked into a parlor lit by candles in sconces, candles in chandeliers, candles in silver and crystal sticks. The army of tapers redoubled their flames in a dozen ormolu mirrors. Two armchairs and a tea table stood before a hearth ablaze with votives. Flocked red paper covered the walls, red velvet curtains a pair of windows that had to overlook the gangway. Convenient for Jeremy, if he needed to stage a rescue. He wouldn't. Helen stood on the mild wilderness of a carpet like a woven forest, at ease, almost at home. To her left, next to an ebony secretary laden with books, was a stairwell. To her right, behind one of the armchairs, was a brass perch on which bobbed a raven-like bird, all glossy black except for its white bib.

Geldman took the armchair over which the bird presided. Helen sank into the other, and the cushions plumped and gave, molding themselves to her particular curves.

To the bird, Geldman said, "Please tell Cybele we'd like tea."

It flapped up the stairwell. *"Corvus albus,"* Geldman said. "The African pied crow. This one's my familiar."

Well, if frankness was to be the order of the day. "So you *are* a magician, Mr. Geldman?"

"Or a wizard, sorcerer, witch. I'm not fussy about the label, although you'll find that many are. *Wizard* is my preference, since it derives from *wise*. Like yourself, Ms. Arkwright, I aspire to wisdom."

"You seem to know a lot about me."

"I know what I've seen in you."

"Is it what you see in someone that decides whether this place is open for him?"

Geldman smiled. "It depends on both the person and the situation."

"Why did you hide it from me the other day?"

"Sean's father and uncle were there. Also, you needed to learn more about Sean's dilemma before we spoke."

"You know what's happening to him?"

"I know he's summoned a blood-spawn."

Even here, in the sanctuary of the parlor, anger sparked in her. Geldman knew how much trouble Sean was in, he was partly responsible for the trouble, and yet he'd stayed in hiding to await further developments?

She opened her mouth. Geldman raised a hand. "One moment, please."

Like a herald, the crow flew out of the stairwell, croaking, "Tea! Tea! Tea!" By the time it had resettled itself, a girl of ten or so appeared at the bend of the stairs, carrying a silver tray. She looked at Helen with open curiosity; Helen looked back equally unabashed, struck by the porcelain delicacy of the girl's face, the flax blonde of her hip-length hair, and the flax-flower blue of her eyes. She wore a sleeveless white shift. Her feet were bare and so white they glowed.

Geldman went to take the tray. "Thank you, Cybele."

The girl continued to gaze at Helen.

Geldman touched Cybele's forearm with his elbow. "Go up. You haven't finished your reading."

Cybele retreated around the bend. Helen heard the swift patter of her feet up the steps.

Geldman put the tray on the table between them. It was arranged as daintily as a photo in a decorating magazine: white tea service, white linen napkins, silver spoons, and a plate of tiny white-iced scones embellished with candied violets. As Geldman poured, laughter boiled up Helen's throat. There was no bile in it, but it wasn't clean laughter, either—it had too much reaction in it, reaction to her interrupted anger, reaction to the terror of the last two days, reaction even to the wonder of parlor and familiar and angelic young food stylist. And the candles. Though they'd been burning at least since Helen had entered the room, none was diminished, none showed a drop of wax run down its side.

The laughter came up shrill. Helen stifled it behind her hand.

Geldman placed a cup of tea before her. She pressed her hand harder against her mouth while Geldman presented the crow with a scone. It dropped the scone into the perch seed cup and pecked with a connoisseur's air. "Excuse me," she whispered at last.

"There's nothing to excuse."

She steadied her cup on the saucer. The tea was summer fragrant; the smell alone calmed her, so that she didn't get hysterical again at her genteel remark of "Cybele's an unusual name. A goddess, wasn't she?"

"From the Neolithic Anatolians to the Roman worshipers of Magna Mater and beyond."

Helen sipped tea: lavender, rosemary, thyme, other sweet and bitter herbs her taste buds couldn't identify. It was like a liquid distillation of the physic garden in Jeremy's window, or of

the garden Kate had actually planted in their yard. "Is she your
daughter?"

"After a fashion."

Geldman's smile didn't alter, but heavy lids hooded his eyes.
There were questions he wouldn't answer, which was just as well.
If Helen hared after everything that beckoned in this new world,
she'd forget her business. Sean, Jeremy, the Litinskis, they couldn't
afford that. She couldn't afford it. "How did you find out what's
going on with Sean?"

"A colleague of mine has been testing him. It's his affair,
really."

Geldman poured himself tea with such graceful nonchalance
that Helen's fingers tightened on the fragile rim of her saucer. As
if in response, the cup exhaled fresh fragrance, which enticed
her to drink and be soothed. "I suppose your 'colleague' is Redemption Orne."

"Reverend Orne, yes."

"Tell me about him."

"That would be a long story, Ms. Arkwright."

"Then tell me what I need to know."

Geldman set down the teapot. "First, let me assure you he's
no impostor. He's the same man who came to Arkham in
1690."

"How has he lived so long?"

"Wizards have many ways to extend their lives. To discuss
Orne's method would be a professional indiscretion. Suffice it to
say, he's made excellent use of his time. He's a master among
masters."

"Is he your master, Mr. Geldman?"

The crow cawed at her. Geldman laughed. "Be still, Boaz. No,
Orne isn't my master. Nor am I his. But our paths have often in-
tersected, even when they've had different goals."

"Are you suggesting Orne is a dark wizard?"

"Are you suggesting I'm a light one?"

Was she? "I'm not afraid of you."

Geldman bowed. "The dichotomy of dark and light is simplistic, but in the way of magic I follow doing harm diminishes one's power. Reverend Orne labors under no such restriction. He's done harm, even murder. Still, I know he'd prefer to avoid violence."

The mollifying tea didn't bar reasonable doubt from her mind. "Orne's a murderer, but you're not his enemy?"

"No."

"I don't understand."

"Why should you?" Geldman's voice was fond, a favorite uncle's. "You've just come among us. But I assure you Orne doesn't want to hurt Sean. Quite the opposite. He wants to foster the boy."

"So it's true he wanted Sean, not just anyone interested enough in magic to be looking through the books in Horrocke's back room."

"Sean, no other."

"How did he know Sean would ever go to that bookstore? How did he know exactly where to put the book and clipping, so Sean would find them?"

Geldman eyed the ceiling or, perhaps, the tip of Boaz's beak, for the crow hung head down, jabbering in a language full of gutturals and sibilants. When it had finished and returned to its sconce, Geldman said, "Orne has been watching Sean for many years, mostly through a familiar like the one he meant Sean to summon."

"An aether-newt? One Orne's made invisible?"

"Just so. And once Sean reached apprentice age, Orne had only to create the lure—the clipping—and have his newt topple it into the boy's hand at some convenient moment. If Sean didn't take the lure, he wasn't ready for the test. But if he did take it—"

"Which he did."

"Then Orne would propose the test."

Questions jostled pell-mell in her head. "But—how did Orne find Sean in the first place?"

Geldman finished his tea before asking a question of his own: "Before you returned to Arkham to work in the library, you hadn't studied magic?"

"Not at all. Assume I'm ignorant."

"I'll assume you're an intelligent young woman and that you've already wondered about the part genetics plays in magical aptitude. Inheritance is crucial, but full expression of aptitude depends on complex gene interactions and environmental stimuli. Also, there may be bursts of magicians in families, two or three in as many generations. Then the trait may go dormant for so long that the birth of a new magician seems like a singular occurrence. However, we magicians do track the known bloodlines. Reverend Orne's been following the line that comes to Sean through his mother. He tells me this bloodline's produced several apt individuals over the centuries, Sean being the most promising yet."

So Kate Wyndham *was* the source of Sean's ability. How would Jeremy react to that news? Helen shook her head.

"Ms. Arkwright?"

"It makes sense, but it's so new."

"Perhaps I shouldn't burden you with more."

No backing off now. "What more? I need to know, Mr. Geldman."

"Sean isn't Orne's only object. Your inheritance interests him as well."

Helen put down her cup and saucer too quickly, and they rang in musical protest. The last of her tea put forth its alluring bouquet, but she resisted the urge to drink the edge off her alarm. "*My* inheritance?"

"You've inherited more than the Arkwright House, you see. You've also inherited your uncle's aptitude, and your great-grandfather's. It was Henry Arkwright who restored your line's reputation for paramagic. John, too, was a capable paramagician. However, Orne has even higher hopes for you."

Geldman paused. Helen couldn't speak. He added: "I concur with the Reverend's opinion."

*Paramagician* was a term she'd seen in her reading, something to do with receptivity to magical energy without the ability to shape and use it on one's own—all she'd really grasped was that paramagicians could assist magicians and deploy magical items prepared for them. It hadn't sounded like a glamorous profession. "You've got to be wrong," Helen said.

"I'm not. I've sensed your aptitude myself, which is why I've allowed you to see the pharmacy as it is, whole. Reverend Orne's assessment of you is another proof, and finally, you've become a curator of the Arcane Studies Archives. Since Henry's time, the curators have always been magicians or paramagicians. The Order requires it."

Helen raised her hands in surrender. "Order?"

"The Order of Alhazred."

"I've never heard of it, Mr. Geldman!"

Boaz croaked: "Abdul's! Abdul's Irregulars! Go to, liar, go to, go to!"

With an abstracted wave of his hand, Geldman silenced the crow. "Ah, I see. Professor Marvell hasn't told you about the Order yet."

"You know Professor Marvell."

"Of course."

"He's a wizard, too?"

"Oh no. A profound scholar of magic, but in practice only paramagical."

That was a relief—she knew one person who wasn't a full-fledged sorcerer. Though apparently he *was* a member of a secret society. "What is this Order?"

"I shouldn't have mentioned it. I wouldn't have, if I'd known you were entirely uninitiated. You must ask Marvell."

"He's off in the mountains in Scotland. I can't get hold of him, and I need help now. Sean needs help."

Geldman leaned forward and spoke with quiet emphasis: "I'll do whatever I may, Ms. Arkwright. Believe me."

All right, focus. Let this Order of Alhazred go, and magical genetics, and even her own supposed aptitude. Sean first. "Tell me how to dismiss the Servitor."

"That's one of the things I may not do. Orne has set Sean the task of dismissing it, and Sean has turned to you. I think Orne may have intended that as well."

After his promise to help, Geldman's refusal bit deep. "I don't care what Orne's set us to do! And why should you care? You said he wasn't your master."

"He isn't. But I won't interfere in his business."

In the candlelit parlor, Helen sat in the park with Jeremy; that's how strongly the memory took her. She saw sun on the roofs and spires and domes of Providence. She heard her own voice saying that it wasn't Orne who gave Sean the incantation for the blood-spawn, it was the Black Man. "Are you afraid of Orne?" she said. "Or are you afraid of his master? Of Nyarlathotep?"

Geldman didn't draw back or blanch, but his heavy lids drooped farther, like gates closing over his eyes. "I'd be afraid of Orne if I crossed him. As for his master, I have nothing to do with him."

At the sound of a footstep on the stairs, Helen twisted to her left. It had to be Orne (or even the Black Man) coming down right on cue. Instead it was Cybele, standing at the turn. A harsh moan made Helen twist back toward Geldman, but it was Boaz who moaned, swaying on his perch. "He's a lion; be vigilant," the crow said. "He's walking about. He's hungry, so he walks, and walking makes him hungrier."

"True enough, Boaz," Geldman said. "Luckily, the Reverend

doesn't mean to devour Sean. If you can't reach Marvell, Ms. Arkwright, you'd better talk directly to Orne."

The crow's eerie litany had sounded familiar, and Geldman's use of the word *devour* fixed the reference for her. In the Bible, it was the Devil who walked about, seeking whom he might devour. "How do I get to him?"

"I have the means." Geldman rose. "If you'll step over here."

From the direction of the stairwell and Cybele, a warm breeze fanned Helen's hair while leaving the multitude of candle flames unperturbed. She looked toward Cybele, who nodded, the slightest fall and rise of her chin, but that was enough to make Helen trail Geldman to the secretary. He folded back ivory-inlaid doors that had hidden a deep desk well. In it was a manual typewriter, an ancient Royal as glossy black as Boaz. Beveled glass windows in the sides displayed the internal mechanisms. Silver typefingers and tape reels sat exposed on top.

"Unlike the Reverend, I don't take to every new device," Geldman said. "I bought this in 1914, the first year it was made, and I've never had to buy another."

"You want me to type a letter to Orne?"

"No. A moment."

He opened a drawer and took out a sheet of white bond, which he wound into the typewriter. Then he brought together the top and bottom edges of the sheet and ran a forefinger along the seam. Helen blinked. The edges had fused: The sheet was now a cylinder that would continuously feed. "What about when this one gets full?" she said.

"It won't. Type: 'Hello, Reverend Orne.' He should answer shortly."

Answer? But Helen typed. The keys were unexpectedly responsive. The type-fingers flew, clacking crisply against the paper, and Hello, Rev. Orne appeared, rich black on the virgin white field.

The keys under her fingers plunged. Helen started back. Her greeting vanished from the paper and, all on its own, the Royal clacked out: Hello, Helen. I'm glad to meet you at last.

The Royal fell still. Gingerly, Helen positioned her fingers over the keys and typed: I'm glad to reach you, Reverend.

As soon as she lifted her fingers, the typewriter clacked away. Her typing faded as Orne's response appeared: I hoped you'd consult our friend, Mr. Geldman, and that he'd bring us together.

When the keys stilled, she typed. Before long the rhythm of typing and lifting her hands became automatic. Mr. Geldman says you're interested in Sean because he has magical potential. Is that right?

Yes, and he's already proven how great his potential is. I look forward to you doing the same.

As a paramagician?

Exactly. Do you remember why you decided to consult Jeremy Wyndham about your library windows?

My uncle. He left some notes about restoring them. Jeremy's name was first on his list of possible consultants.

I wanted to establish a connection between you and the Wyndhams. So I left you those notes, in your uncle's hand.

A forgery? Delivered by one of your familiars?

I confess it.

Why not? It was the least of Orne's sins. Your point was?

To make it easier for Sean to appeal to someone at Miskatonic University if he needed access to the Archives. I hoped he might appeal to you and so you'd be drawn into the test. If you were worth testing.

She had lived up to Orne's expectations. Did he expect her to feel proud, instead of manipulated? Maybe it was her turn to play games. You knew all along you weren't going to give Sean the dismissing ritual?

A brief pause. Then: I intended him to learn how to dismiss the aether-newt himself or else to learn how to make it a useful companion. Then he told me he'd summoned the blood-spawn, which I never intended. There had been interference with my plan

Helen experimented, dropping her fingers onto the keys. Yes, that stopped Orne's communication, and she was able to type: Your MASTER interfered. Nyarlathotep. He came to Sean during the ritual as the Black Man.

She hoped that Orne's longer pause meant he was squirming. Your deduction is correct, Helen. Sometimes the Master of Magic does respond in person to calls for his intervention. Sometimes he doesn't intervene as one might hope.

He gave Sean the blood-spawn incantation. Why?

He thought that the Servitor would provide a more rigorous test for Sean. The choice itself—blood-spawn or aether-newt—was a test. That Sean had the pluck to try the blood-spawn was impressive. In a way, I'm pleased with him.

Then why won't you help him? He's in danger. So are the people around him.

I know there's danger, and I feel it as acutely as you do. When I first heard of the blood-spawn, I was going to give Sean the dismissing ritual at once.

During the second chat you had with him?

Yes.

Your master interfered again?

Yes. Pause. The Black Man said I must hold to my original plan and let Sean manage the Servitor he'd summoned. Pause. Don't think that you lash me, Helen, when you call Nyarlathotep my master. To earn allegiance to him is a matter of pride, not shame. Pause. Besides, the original plan has worked this far: Sean came to you. You have consulted the Necronomicon, perhaps my old journals as well?

Damn, and she'd been about to needle Orne about how his secrets had fallen into enemy hands. He'd anticipated that circumstance. Intended it, probably. We've read them, she typed. Leave it at that.

You don't disappoint me, Helen. So, the one misstep is that Sean substantiated the Servitor with his own blood, then failed to bind it properly. But it still can't harm him or take his blood against his will.

Did she have some news for Orne after all? But Sean's given it his blood to save others. He'll give it his blood again if he has to.

Geldman, who'd been reading over her shoulder, let out a gust of the guttural-sibilant language Boaz had used earlier. It sounded like a curse. As her last words faded, the typewriter stayed still. Helen turned to Geldman. "What is it?"

He was frowning, clearly troubled. As if in sympathy, Boaz flew in tight circles around the room. Cybele sat and rocked on the stairs, knees cradled in the thin circle of her arms.

"What?" Helen demanded. "Is it very bad, him letting the Servitor take his blood?" Then she remembered. It wasn't what the Servitor had taken but what it had given. "I read a little about inoculation and soul-threads. Is that it?"

"You didn't tell me Sean had been inoculated, Ms. Arkwright."

"I thought you and Orne must know. You said Orne's been watching Sean."

"Orne didn't tell me this. I can't believe he knew of it, or he'd have taken some action."

"He's known everything else." But had he? "Wait," Helen said. "You could be right. If Orne *was* able to watch Sean all the time, wouldn't he have watched him do the ritual?"

"I would imagine so."

"But he couldn't have watched the ritual, because when Sean

told him he'd summoned the blood-spawn instead of the aether-newt Orne was surprised."

Geldman's frown deepened. "Someone must be keeping Orne's spies away from Sean. That would require placing a powerful ward around the boy and his immediate surroundings, which is a task beyond most magicians."

"But not beyond the Master of Magic?"

"No. Not beyond him."

The typewriter rattled back to life. Helen swiveled to it. How did the Servitor take Sean's blood? Orne had typed.

It bit his wrist and drank.

Then he's been inoculated. Tell me how it happened.

Fingers shaking, typos multiplying, Helen banged out the story. Geldman drew closer to read. "Sean has great courage," he said. "To step between the Servitor and his father."

*Clatter.* She read Orne's response: Sean hasn't been trained to endure a psychic bond with the Servitor. There will be complications. Has he been ill?

He was yesterday. Last night the fever broke, he seemed better.

He's passed the first danger. The greater danger remains, how his growing bond with the Servitor will affect him mentally. Has he dreamed that he was in its mind?

Last night.

Awake, has he a sense of connection to it?

He didn't this morning.

That connection will come and progress until it fills his waking mind. Then psychological trauma may occur.

Oh God. What sort of trauma?

Psychiatrists would call it psychosis, schizophrenia. A distortion of the senses, thoughts, and emotions. A warping of the self from what's native to what's alien. If the mind is overwhelmed by these changes, catatonia may result.

Psychosis, schizophrenia, catatonia. Would complications persist after dismissal?

If the trauma was severe enough. And there's a third stage, the most dangerous, when the Servitor begins to see through the summoner, as the summoner has been seeing through it. Even the most powerful wizard avoids such intimacy, lest the daemon possess him.

And if possession occurred?

Normally the daemon would destroy the summoner. Alhazred himself was torn to shreds by possessing daemons. Once the summoner dies, the daemon returns to its own plane. Self-dismissed, you might say.

"You bastard," Helen said. She typed: That's not a solution I'll accept.

Nor I, believe me. I told Sean to seek the dismissal in a very dark place in the Necronomicon. What do you make of the riddle?

The dismissal's not in the text of the book, it's in Enoch Bishop's blotted-out marginalia. The blotting ink's magical. You can see through it with the right counter magic. Some kind of solvent, like your wife used?

Patience lied to me about the solvent. It's another magic that defeats the ink. You needn't try the Voorish Sign or any other simple measure. And you needn't look further in my journals. They contain no magic. I wasn't a wizard when I wrote them.

Damn it, they didn't have time for sparring. If we dismiss the Servitor soon, will Sean recover?

The sooner you dismiss it, the better the prognosis.

How long do we have?

Since he's learned no defenses, as little as a few hours. It depends on his strength of will.

Helen was suddenly tired to dropping. What was real in this mess she'd stumbled into? Why was she the one who had to save

Sean, without even Marvell to consult? Who'd given her the as-
signment? Not Fate or Chance. Not God, unless you counted Nyarlathotep. Redemption Orne was the one who'd set her up for the
job, and what did he want from her, even if she *was* paramagical?

Something touched her forearm. It wasn't Geldman's hand:
too slim and soft. Helen lifted her tons-heavy head. Cybele. The
girl had come down the stairs to her side.

Helen didn't push the small hand from her. It was a cool point
of sanity. Sanity? Yes, looking into Cybele's eyes, Helen was sure
of the word. Sanity, *sanitas*. Health, cleanliness. She had never
seen anything as clean as those flax-flower eyes.

Cybele lifted her hand. She pressed her palm to Helen's forehead: Coolness bloomed from it, penetrating skin and bone and
brain, but gently, like balm. Time dissolved, or at least Helen's
sense of it. A second or an hour could have passed before Geldman drew Cybele away. As the girl moved, Helen breathed the
air that had passed over her, and it held the scent of rain on flowering grass.

Geldman's tea had calmed her. This cool blooming was different. It left her no longer afraid of her fear or angry at her
anger. The emotions weren't blunted, though. In fact, they were
sharper, but sharp like tools, or weapons.

She put her fingers back on the typewriter keys. We've worked
out your riddle, Reverend. Tell me how to see through Bishop's
ink.

Orne responded at once: If Sean hadn't been inoculated, I
might have let you search further. Now his danger's too great
for delay. Ask Mr. Geldman for Bishop's #5. It's very dear, but
he may charge it to my account.

Is it a drug?

It's a vision-enhancing potion. Its effects are not altogether pleasant. But if you come through, you'll have proven
yourself as a paramagician.

To hell with that. But Helen typed: What do I do?

You must access the true Necronomicon, not your digital copy. When you've got the book ready, drink the potion.

And I'll be able to see the dismissal?

Let my word be a lamp unto thy feet, and a light unto thy path. Don't delay, Helen.

The typewriter platen whirled the cylinder of paper through the machine, leaving it blank. Helen turned to Geldman and Cybele. "I guess that's the end of the conversation?"

"Yes, Ms. Arkwright," Geldman said. "I'll go prepare Bishop's Number Five for you."

After sending Cybele back upstairs, he left the parlor. Helen returned to her armchair and ate the tiny scones. Chatting with wizards was hungry work, and besides, it probably wasn't a good idea to take potions on an empty stomach.

Geldman called her out into the pharmacy, which had gone whole and bright again, at least for them. Beside the cash register were two bottles with waxed corks and hand-lettered labels. Bishop's #5 was tiny, like a single-injection vial, brown glass, pentagonal. "A few minutes after you've drunk the Seeing Draught, your vision will begin to change," Geldman said. "You'll see more things than what's under Bishop's ink. Don't be alarmed. What didn't harm you when invisible won't harm you when it's no longer so."

Helen didn't like the sound of that, but she tucked Bishop's #5 into her shirt pocket.

Geldman continued. "The gross effects will wear off in an hour. You'll have a headache and light sensitivity afterwards; that's expected. But tell Mr. Wyndham that if your eyes bleed or you experience blindness he must bring you back here at once. No physicians or emergency rooms. They won't know how to treat you."

Better and better. She nodded.

Geldman handed her the other bottle, cobalt glass, flat and

long necked. "This is a gift, Ms. Arkwright. It's the best assistance I can give Sean."

She read the label: "Patience Orne's Number 11. For the strengthening of the will." She looked up at Geldman.

"The Reverend's wife, yes," Geldman said.

"I should trust something of hers?"

"I dispense many of her compounds. This one will help Sean withstand possession. Give it by the teaspoonful, as often as needed."

"Thank you. Thank you very much, Mr. Geldman." Helen slipped the cobalt bottle into a candy-striped bag he gave her. She pushed open the counter door but hesitated to step through. Whatever other new worlds waited for her, she doubted they'd be as cozy as the one that Geldman ruled.

He handed her an odd umbrella, yellow with black skulls and crossbones. Oh, right, Sean's. "Thank you," she said again.

Geldman took her elbow and led her to the street door. "You'd better go. Time moves fast outside, and Sean's caught in it."

Taking a deep breath, Helen stepped out of the pharmacy. She left the shelter of the awning and unfurled Sean's umbrella. Inside, Geldman walked away over shining tiles. In a second-floor window, Cybele stood stroking the arched back of a cat as sooty dark as she was pale.

Jeremy's shout spun Helen around. He pelted toward her from Tumblebee's, windbreaker half-off, coffee sloshing from the cup he clutched. "What happened?" he said. "Did he kick you out?"

"No, why?"

"He couldn't have said much."

She asked the question of herself, as well as of Jeremy: "How long was I in there?"

"Not even fifteen minutes. I came like you said, five minutes after you. I saw you with Geldman in the pharmacy. Then the place . . . died. Like now."

She looked. In the few moments her attention had been broken, the pharmacy had turned deserted, decayed, and in the second-floor window the curtains hung in dirty shreds over the yellowed skull of a cat.

Only Cybele remained, one white palm pressed to the glass. Then, like mist, she shimmered, attenuated, and was gone.

# 20

It was a dirty trick, Dad and Helen sneaking off to Arkham while Sean was asleep—as poster boy for the whole Servitor mess, he should have gone with them. Besides, Gus and Eddy were the ones hunkered down over the *Necronomicon* and Orne's journals. Sean couldn't sit still long enough to help.

He prowled the house, rereading Helen's translations. The new ones were about psychic links between summoners and familiars. He'd messed up big-time, letting the Servitor drink straight from the vein. Yeah, he should have cut his wrist, bled into a paper cup, and handed the Servitor that, avoiding inoculation. But with no knife or cup on hand and no idea of the risk he was taking, he'd done the best he could. Dad was alive. They were all alive.

All alive, but now Sean had a "soul-thread" linking him to the Servitor. Alhazred wrote: "A sorcerer sunders the soul-thread and holds both ends in his hands, to knot them together when he pleases." What good was poetic crap like that? Sean needed plain instructions, *Soul-Thread Maintenance for Dummies*.

Gus looked up as Sean circled through the study. "I'm ready for lunch," he said. "What about you, Eddy?"

"Sure, Professor Litinski. How about omelets?"

"Sounds good. Sean?"

He put a hand on his food-distended belly. "I've kind of been eating all morning."

"No kidding," Eddy said. "Every time you go through the kitchen, I hear the toaster pop."

He'd had two bagels, three corn muffins, and a piece of Rachel's blueberry pie. On top of breakfast. His stomach groaned with the overload, but he was still hungry. Nerves? Whatever, he'd better lay off before he hurled.

"You guys go," he said. "I'll read where you left off, Eddy."

"Top of the screen. I was just getting to a good part."

Sean sat in front of her laptop. Orne's handwriting was funky, with those Ss that looked like Fs, but he'd gotten used to it yesterday. He started with an entry dated "29th October 1690."

On Saturday last, Peter Kokokoho and I walked in Cold Spring Glen, where there is ever a rushing air, and so the Nipmucks have named their village Noden, "it is windy" in their tongue.

Peter asked if I could hear voices in the air. I told him I heard what might be voices, but I could not make out what they said. He said the voices speak in the language of the old ones, who were gods before my God was born, and principal among these gods is Hobbamock, though that is not the name he gives himself, which Peter said is Nyarlatotepp. This name I have seen in Mr. B.'s book. I suppose he taught it to poor Peter. It is a shame Mr. B. confounds the Nipmucks with his dubious learning. Patience maintains that he does no harm, but he is her father, and she cannot speak ill of him.

Nyarlatotepp is Hobbamock, Peter said, and Hobbamock is the Black Man of the woods, whom we call the
Devil. Men may speak to the Black Man in the Glen or on
the hilltops, for the Black Man walks in these places at certain times. But Peter will not speak to him, or so he assures
me, and, indeed, I hope he would not relapse so.

Oh sure, Peter knew all about the Black Man, but he'd never
talked to him. Orne was doing some wishful thinking there,
like Dad trying to believe in the hoax theory long after it had
stopped making sense. Wishful thinking was a kind of hope.
It was a bitch when you lost it. Maybe that was why Orne had
given up on religion and become a wizard. A minister could
preach his head off, but his people would still go out and sin. He
could pray himself blue, but bad things would still happen. At
least when you knew the right spells, your magic worked. You
got results.

Sean pushed back from the table. The dismissing ritual was
under the marginal blots in the *Necronomicon*, so unless Geldman told Helen how to read through them they were screwed.
It was a waste of time to keep reading, and so it was crazy for
Eddy to be laughing in the kitchen, like things could still go
right. Jesus, from the smell of it, she was putting kielbasa in her
omelet.

*Nausea* wasn't even the word for the way Sean's stomach
turned. He made a stumbling dash to the second-floor bathroom, where the morning's foodfest rocketed out of him.

Even as he heaved dry, he was hungry again. God, for what?
Kielbasa omelet? Sean flushed the toilet and got up to rinse his
mouth. A wave of dizziness forced him to sit on the edge of the
tub. Was he getting sick again? His forehead felt damp but cool.
He'd sit for a couple minutes, then go down and read even
though it was useless. Dad and Helen were going to Geldman's,

and Geldman wasn't a bad guy. He'd help. Sean closed his eyes. Weird, what the Nipmucs called their village. Noden, it is windy. . . .

*The deep water around the Servitor runs bright; it stares up through the brightness at the blazing black of day and the surface-paddler that's blackest of all.*

Black equaled white. Sean knew the paddler was a swan, though the Servitor couldn't name it—

He jerked but not awake, because he hadn't been asleep. Sean goggled at the actually white tiles on the floor and walls. Actually white, too, were the curtains at the window, and actually blue the wedge of sky he saw when the curtains fluttered apart.

He stood and looked into the mirror over the sink. His face was white (actually white, scared). After a few seconds, he closed his eyes again.

*The black paddler is right above. The Servitor can swim up and grab the webbed feet, drag the paddler under, and devour it, as it has devoured other paddlers since it found the abundance of this greater river. But its hunger is not for paddler flesh.*

Sean opened his eyes. He must have been developing a waking connection to the Servitor all morning, and he'd been too stupid to realize it. He'd been starving because the Servitor was starving, and bagels and muffins were like swans, not the right food for their hunger.

For *its* hunger. *He* was Sean in the bathroom. He was not the thing in the river. Keep that straight and he'd be okay. The connection could even help. The Servitor was his camera and microphone, while he was the spy, following everything from a secure location.

He closed his eyes.

*Other paddlers float by. These are not alive. They are vessels used by humans to traverse the water; humans dip in false feet to propel themselves along. There are long vessels with many feet.*

*There are short vessels with two feet, like the one that approaches. A false foot dips in on one side. It rises, and a false foot dips in on the other side.*

*There's flesh enough inside such small vessels to satisfy it until the summoner comes—*

A kayaker-eating spy camera was not cool. Sean opened his eyes wide and was back in front of the bathroom mirror. Okay, but what good did that do? The camera was still running, still thinking about having a snack, even though the cameraman wasn't looking through the lenses. Sean squeezed his eyes shut tight, was in the river, flung out thought. *Leave the boats alone. Stay down on the bottom.*

*The Servitor writhes, roiling the riverbed on which it lies. A sparkling cloud of silt rises around it. If the summoner won't let it hunt, when will he come and feed it?*

Feed it, like he'd promised in his dream. *I'm not sure.*

*Maybe the summoner doesn't mean to come.*

*No! I'll come soon. Wait.*

*The summoner must come to the river, to the stone building where there were bones, though only dust remains. If the summoner will give his blood, it will tell him secrets.*

*I will. Stay there until I do.*

*Its hunger burns. It twitches among the water weeds, still watching the floating vessels.*

In the mirror Sean saw beads of sweat on his forehead and upper lip. He wiped his face with a hand towel. Hungry? He was hungry now like when Mom had died, when people had brought food to the house, but it had been the wrong food. Nobody brought the salad with red lettuce and green peppers, like Mom liked, and the lasagna had sausages, which Mom hated, and none of the cakes was chocolate with vanilla frosting, which was what she had on her birthday. It would be bad to eat what Mom didn't like now that she was dead. It would be mean, like she didn't matter anymore.

Grandpa Stewie and Uncle Joe, when Sean told them how mean it would be, they made a lasagna with spinach and mushrooms, and the red and green salad, and the chocolate cake with vanilla frosting. Then Sean ate, and Dad ate, too. Dad cried, sitting at the table, eating. They ate because they were so hungry and finally there were the right things to eat.

"I'm going crazy." Confirmation: Sean said it out loud to his reflection, which was sweating again. Soon he'd stink like a pig, but he wasn't taking another shower. The water running over him would be like lying in the river with the thing that had decided it would rather not feed itself, either, unless it got exactly what it wanted. Plus, he'd have to close his eyes and closing his eyes was no longer a great idea. Coffee. Lots of coffee.

The phone rang. He was halfway downstairs when Gus yelled, "Sean! Your father."

He ran the rest of the way to the kitchen and snagged the phone. "Dad, are you guys okay?"

"Fine. What about you?"

How much of the truth should he tell? It depended on what they'd been able to do in Arkham. So he tried a neutral answer: "Not bad. You guys get into Geldman's?"

"Helen did. She talked to him and to Orne, too, over a magical typewriter. I guess you had to be there."

Dad sounded up for the first time in days. Sean gripped the receiver. He put his other hand over his stomach, which was unsure whether to growl at the proximity of Eddy's omelet or to clench into upchuck mode. "What did they say?"

"Orne told Helen how to read the blotted passages. They've got to be read in the real book, so we're going to the library."

Relief, sudden and draining, made Sean close his eyes. Instantly he was in the river. He popped his eyes open. "That's great! Can we do the spell tonight?"

"I guess so. You stay in the house until we come, understand?"

"Right. I will, Dad."

"Wait a second."

A pause while the phone switched hands, because now Helen spoke. "Sean, how are you feeling?"

He knew what she was really asking, but what good would the truth do? She and Dad were already doing as much as they could. "I'm okay," Sean said. "Eating like a pig."

"Did you read the printouts I left?"

"Yeah."

"Have you had any feeling, awake, that you're connected to the Servitor?"

Again, when it came down to it, he couldn't lie to her. "A little, I guess."

"What's that mean?"

"Well, if I close my eyes, I can get into its head. But that's good. I can tell it's just lying around in the river. I can tell it to stay there."

There was a long silence on the line. Had Helen covered her mouthpiece to relay the news to Dad?

"Sean."

Helen's voice, in his ear. He almost jumped. "Yeah?"

"Mr. Geldman gave me a drug—a potion—that should help you. He says it'll strengthen your mind against the Servitor."

"That's good. If you trust him."

"I do. So hang tight. We should be back before dark."

The line went dead before Sean could thank her—they were in a hurry. Good. He handed the receiver back to Gus, who was studying him, maybe to make sure sympathetic tentacles weren't sprouting from his chin. Eddy was staring, too.

Sean summarized the call for them.

"Ms. Arkwright rules," Eddy said.

"Yeah. Is there any coffee?"

"I'm going to make some," Gus said.

"I'll do it."

Like Joe-Jack, Gus indulged in fresh-roasted beans from the Coffee Exchange. Sean picked the seriously caffeinated Kid from Brooklyn blend, and he leaned over the grinder, trying to breathe in some jolt from the fumes. One way or another, he was going to stay bug-eyed awake until Dad and Helen got home.

# 21

On the sunniest day, the stained-glass windows in Special Collections drowned the reading room in submarine gloom; today, under storm clouds, the principal illumination came from the tabletop lamps under which patrons hunched, so many divers after doubtful pearls. "You could wait out here," Helen whispered to Jeremy. "Come up with a plan to make these damn windows less dreary."

Jeremy didn't even glance at them. "Forget it. This time I'm tagging along."

Part of her was annoyed by his persistence, but a bigger part was relieved. "I'll have to sign you in."

"Sign away."

Luckily, Matt Bridgeman was on duty rather than Mrs. Wolff, who deplored the admission of "tourists" into the Archives. When Helen said Jeremy was a visiting scholar, Matt didn't eye his jeans and demand credentials. He simply countersigned the guest log and buzzed them through the door behind the desk.

They entered a vaulted room the size of a gymnasium. It had open stacks in the middle and conservation labs and special security rooms around the perimeter. The Arcane Studies Archives were in the east corner, behind a steel door with both a dead bolt and an electronic lock. Helen had always smiled at the extra safeguard, new technology to protect dusty lore. Now, as she punched the entry code and slotted her key, she wondered why the safeguards weren't stronger.

Even with air filtration and dehumidifiers, the Archives smelled of decomposition only tenuously arrested. There were no windows, and the overhead lights were dim, leaving much of the long room in shadow. Metal shelving held the newer books, closed cabinets the older and more fragile. A single table occupied the no-man's-land between the two storage camps, low-UV lamps on its stainless-steel top and aluminum chairs around it. A glass door opposite the entry led to the microfilm and digital media room. They wouldn't need to go in there. Today they were after the genuine article.

"I expected a stuffed crocodile at least," Jeremy said.

"A stuffed croc would reek pollutants. We're state-of-the-art conservation here. Very expensive, but Arcane Studies has gotten a lot of private funding over the years."

"From whom?"

"Most of the donors are anonymous, which I used to think was odd. Not anymore. Grab a seat."

Going through her book-handling routine soothed Helen, and she omitted no detail. First she spread a blotter on the table and centered on it a Plexiglas book cradle. Beside the cradle went book weights and notepaper and pencils. A microspatula for turning pages. Acid-free bookmarks. Finally, cotton gloves for them both.

"You should put those on now," she told Jeremy. "In case you have to handle the book."

He obeyed without comment. Notwithstanding his joke about the crocodile, he understood fragility. Old glass, old paper, both brittle, as fleeting as life but precious enough for immortality.

Fleeting as life, that was a comforting thought. Evidently it didn't apply to people like Orne.

But, as Geldman had implied, it could apply only too aptly to Sean.

Helen went to the largest of the metal cabinets. Like the entry, it had both a keyed lock and an electronic one. She opened them and hefted out the archival box that contained the *Necronomicon*. It settled heavily against her breastbone. Funny, this was the first time she'd touched the greatest treasure under her care. That couldn't bode well for her paramagical aptitude—shouldn't the thing have *drawn* her? Or, if she was a good little parawitch, shouldn't it repulse her now? Instead its bulk was just a weight she was relieved to shift onto the table.

"That's the infamous tome?" Jeremy said. He sounded unimpressed.

Helen lifted the lid of the archive box. There was no burst of noxious green light, no ectoplasmic hand darting for her throat. Just cracked and gnawed leather. The binding of the *Necronomicon* was calfskin, not human hide; analysis had proven that. Still, she didn't like the give of the leather when she removed the book to the cradle. It felt like there was flesh beneath it. And blood: The *Necronomicon* fell open, releasing a tang of damp iron.

"Nice," Jeremy said, wrinkling his nose.

"It's in good condition, actually, given its age." The text block was intact, though the book looked much perused. Helen stripped off her gloves. "I'm going out to take the potion."

"You're sure about this?"

"As sure as I'm going to be."

Jeremy stepped between her and the door. "All the warnings Geldman gave you. Eyes bleeding, going blind. You shouldn't have to be the one to risk that."

She couldn't deal with another wrangle like the one they'd had on the way to the library. "Jeremy, I'm the paramagician."

"Maybe you are, maybe not. I'm Sean's father. That's fact. I should take the potion."

"Geldman gave it to me. I'm taking it."

"Helen."

She ducked around him, into the neighboring washroom. Even the brief delay at the door had planted dread in her gut, where it instantly took fresh root. Damn Jeremy for making sense when sense was what she had to give up.

Helen fished the tiny brown vial out of her breast pocket and twisted its cork to break the seal. "Bishop's #5" sounded like the name of a perfume, but the only perfume it smelled like was one that had sat on milady's vanity for too many years after her demise, rotting with her. Acrid vapor stung Helen's nostrils as she lifted the bottle. Quickly, before she could chicken out, she poured thick liquid into her mouth. It was the nastiest thing she'd ever tasted, tongue-scaldingly bitter. Somehow she swallowed and somehow withstood the urge to retch. Though not retching might be a mistake. What if the "potion" was poison, a way for Orne and Geldman to get rid of her? Good job, Helen, realizing that now.

Bishop's #5 burned all the way to her stomach.

She grabbed a paper cup from the dispenser, filled it to slopping over, and drank. Would the water dilute the potion? Who knew, but washing the taste out of her mouth was not optional.

"Helen?" Jeremy, outside the washroom.

She straightened from the sink, coughing. "God, that was filthy stuff."

"Can I—"

"Wait."

After pocketing the empty vial (in case the coroner wanted to analyze the dregs), she came out. Jeremy blatantly scrutinized her face. "Better now?" he asked.

"I think so. Let's get to it."

By the time they were seated at the library table, Helen actually did feel better. The sting in her mouth had changed to a pleasant tingle, like the aftertaste of a strong liquor, and, speaking of liquor, she was two drinks buzzed, or three.

"Is anything happening?"

She put on her gloves, picked up the microspatula, and started turning pages in the *Necronomicon*. The most extensive of the blotted marginalia were toward the middle of the book, on two pages facing each other. "I'm feeling tipsy."

"Is your vision sharper?"

Pages 548 and 549: The outer margins were solid columns of black. Helen adjusted a table lamp over the book. "Not yet. Did you ever see this old horror movie with Ray Milland?"

"*The Man with X-ray Eyes*?"

"Right. He saw so much he gouged his eyes out, didn't he?"

Jeremy laughed, but he moved his chair beside hers and he took charge of the pencils.

"I was kidding," Helen said.

"I know. But if you find something, you can dictate. Save time."

Fine. She didn't mind him sitting closer. That made it easier for her to study the fabric of his T-shirt. She hadn't noticed how complex its color was, blue and yellow, both fully present despite their simultaneous merging into green. There were even more colors in the skin of his forearm, tans and browns, creams and reds and venous blues. As for his gloves, and hers, they were rainbows. Naturally. White light contained all the wavelengths.

"I think the potion's working," she said. "It's not like X-ray. More like I can see a wider range of light." The *Necronomicon*, too. Its pages vibrated with colors separating and shimmering back together, not only the rainbow spectrum but what she supposed were the normally invisible wavelengths, ultraviolet, infrared. The blotted Bishop marginalia stayed black, but there was a subsurface pulse to them, as if beetles were tunneling up through the smothering obscurity.

She bent closer to the musty pages. The pulsing points were

paler than the ink, as if they were not so much bugs as goldfish rising to the surface of dark water. The points were in groups. The groups looked like words, sentences, paragraphs. Helen laughed. "Yeah. It's definitely doing something."

"I'm ready," Jeremy said. His voice sounded the same, so the potion must be affecting only her eyes. Helen fixed them on the marginalia.

That the words floated upward was an illusion. Instead her vision grew more piercing, like a double-pointed stake that penetrated both the marginal ink and her own head. She felt pressure at temples and brow, above both ears, at the back and the top of her skull. So that made the penetrating sensation less like one stake and more like she was wearing a cap lined with many dull spikes. The cap slowly shrank, and every time it contracted, the spikes sank a little deeper into her skin.

She had to ignore the discomfort. Words in an archaic hand wavered white in the first blot, and yes, she could read them. *About the airy and the fleshly Servitors, I have took Counsell with the Blacke Man, who has given me words in plaine English better than any of the Arab. For Summoning, it were best to wait until the Triangle of August is high and the Moone is darke. Prepare then the Powders of Zeph and Agaar. . . .*

"I've got the summoning ritual."

"Great job! What about the dismissing?"

"I'm hoping Bishop wrote them together." She skimmed onward; her still-sharpening vision made it easy, and the constriction of the spiked cap didn't deter her. *To You, Lord Azathoth, Springheade of All that is. To You I offer Obeisance, and to your Soule, Nyarlathotep.* Yes! That was the incantation Sean had used.

She skipped to the next block of lucid black: *To dismiss Servitors, it can be done under any Starres, but beste to return to the same Summoning Ground.*

She put a gloved fingertip under the words. Her hand was

shaking, but she wasn't afraid. The tremor came from excitement. "Here," she said.

"Okay, I'm ready. Dictate away."

Helen read the start of the dismissing ritual. Then she paused, flush with her new perceptions. The world radiated a perfect, a crystalline reality. Jeremy's right hand moved as he wrote, yet the movement was as gradual as the turning of a plant toward light. Was she seeing *quicker* than he could move? When he told her to continue, his lips formed the words much more slowly than she heard them. Her own hand, reaching toward the microspatula, *looked* like it reached forever even though she *felt* the cool handle in her fingers seconds later.

"I've got that, Helen. Keep going."

She read on while Jeremy wrote with vegetable lethargy. "'Make the pentacle, but now the banishing one, so that Spirit points to the wizard. Then let him send the Servitor to the center, to be constrained by the Elder Sign as before.'"

She paused again. The cap of spikes grew too tight—the dull points dug into her scalp, breaking her concentration. Her eyes roamed the gaudy-glorious room. Was she getting dizzy? Was that why the crystalline world began flaking away in places? The air distorted, distended, cracked into rifts in which vigorous life stirred. And there, not three feet from the table, an air-rift gave birth to a lean translucence with dozens of appendages, some of which seemed to be limbs, because it crawled on them up the air, then down the air, then onto the table. On the more bulbous end that seemed to be its head, feathery stalks behaved like antennae, stretching toward her with avid curiosity.

"What's next?" Jeremy said.

The creature on the table wasn't the only one in the room. More wriggled out of rifts to coil in the air. More crawled over the ceiling and floor, the cabinets and shelves. Had they all burst into her dimension at once, or worse, had they always come and gone, unseen?

"Helen?"

Oh holy God, one was on her back—she glimpsed the filmy substance of its feelers over her shoulder. Helen jumped out of her chair, which fell in slow motion until, immediately, she heard it crash. Gossamer creatures scuttled out from under it. She backed away from the table, which receded at a glacial pace. Jeremy, too, moved like a glacier, though his hand was on her arm before her yell trailed into silence.

A wall was at her back. She ground into it, to crush the gossamer. But it didn't crush. Instead it oozed whole through her chest and relaunched itself unharmed.

It had been inside her! In sick horror, she clutched at the spiky pain in her temples. In addition to the gossamer-bleeding rifts, other openings began to trouble the air, irregular patches of an ethereal fabric that separated the room from some very other place.

"Helen, what's going on?"

The ethereal fabric stretched. Behind it were entities much larger than the gossamers that passed freely from plane to plane. Through a patch that thinned alarmingly, she caught the gelatinous heave of an enormous haunch and then the glint of clustered eyes.

She covered her face. "Jeremy. I'm seeing creatures. All over the room. I don't know what they are."

"I don't see anything."

"You can't. I can."

"Can they hurt you?"

"I don't know!" Helen pressed her palms against her closed eyelids. It didn't help—she saw through both lids and hands. A gossamer drifted through Jeremy's shoulder. It brushed intangibly across her face. "I'm sorry," she moaned. "I don't know what to do."

"It's all right. I'll help you. I'm here."

His arm was around her shoulders, his palm on her forehead,

warm through the glove. Warm. Cybele's palm had been cool when it had pressed a calmer fear into Helen, fear that didn't fear itself. She remembered the scent of flowering grasses. She remembered Geldman saying that what didn't hurt her when it was invisible couldn't hurt her when she saw it.

"Helen, can you finish reading the spell?"

Fear that didn't fear itself. "I've got to," she said. "Get me back to the table."

Interminably, quickly, he led her through the swarming gossamers. Had they sensed her awareness and flocked to it? Their long, limber bodies slid over the pages of the *Necronomicon.* Their appendages clung to her hands. But she could see right through them, to Bishop's pale script lolling in the ink.

The ethereal patches, strained from within, she didn't look at. "Where did I stop?"

Jeremy fumbled paper. "'To be constrained by the Elder Sign as before.'"

Helen clamped her hands to her temples. She read more instructions, an incantation. They weren't long, thank God, and she finished before her swelling bladder of a head burst. It didn't matter then that she slipped sideways from her chair. It didn't matter that she dropped; the gossamers cushioned her fall like a mattress of strange life, like the thick thatch of flowering grass that she smelled again for one unending instant.

**22**

**Celeste** called around four. Sean told her he had no fever, no headache, no problem. That was two-thirds true. As the Servitor's hunger grew, Sean's stomach threatened to implode with empathic emptiness. He crashed on the chaise, where he didn't sleep; aside from the rumbling in his gut, he'd never felt more awake.

Now, whether he opened or closed his eyes, he lay both in Gus's study and in the cool brilliance of the Seekonk River. The soul-thread had started two-way transmission. When his eyes were open, Sean was the main "sensor" and the study had the greater solidity—the river bottom was a transparent overlay, a watery ghost come to haunt the house. When they were closed, Sean surrendered "sensorship"—the river bottom became the reality, the study a queer distortion like an infrared image the Servitor picked up right through Sean's eyelids. One big difference: The river overlay Sean received was constant, while the study image the Servitor received and then cycled back to Sean was sporadic, an occasional flash in the mesh of shared sensation. The best Sean could figure was that the Servitor only looked through his eyes when it felt like it. It seemed to have much more control of the soul-thread than he did. What if it got to the point where it could read his mind and found out he was going to dismiss the hell out of it?

The frigid stream of its consciousness had morphed since their dream-contact. It was now more like bubbles of alien intention percolating inside Sean's skull and putting out slow probing pseudopods. To battle the bubbles, he had to keep his eyes open and concentrate on the study. Trouble was, he also had to pay attention to the river, to make sure the Servitor stayed put. Maybe the Servitor could deal with simultaneous inputs, but Sean's mere human brain was boggled. To really watch it, he had to close his eyes and exchange river ghost for river reality.

And the Servitor needed watching. It was not happy.

Sean closed his eyes.

*Water muffles the sounds of the air-world, but the Servitor's hearing is keen. It listens to the purr of boats, the calls of birds, the high hum of airplanes. Nearer and louder is the growl of a motorcycle.*

Boats, birds, planes, the motorcycle. This morning the Servitor hadn't known that web-footed paddlers were swans and small human vessels were kayaks. This afternoon it knew the names of everything. How could it have learned them except through Sean? More proof it was getting deeper into his mind.

*The motorcycle roar stutters and stops. Staccato laughter replaces it. Humans. Very close. The Servitor rolls off its back and starts to swim up the shoreward slope.*

Sean arrowed thought at it: *No.*

In return, he felt the minute taps of bubble pseudopods. *It is starving, and the summoner hasn't come.*

*No. Stay put.*

*It will only look.*

*The water darkens as the Servitor strokes toward sunlight. In the gloom, fleeing minnows are streaks of life-radiance. Faint, fail-*

*ing radiance outlines the trunk of a tree fallen into the river. The still-leafy aerial boughs will conceal the Servitor when it looks at the humans. Just looks. It insinuates itself into the sunken branches, bunches small, stretches lean, until its head breaks the surface.*

*The reek of gasoline fumes and pot smoke burn the sensitive forks of its tongue, but they can't mask the odor of human blood in human flesh. On the steps of the tomb recessed into the bluff, twin auras pulse, a man and a woman, passing a joint. Their motorcycle is plastered with mud.*

They must have plowed through every bog on the riverside path instead of just taking the paved road down. Jesus, people were stupid to go off by themselves like this, first the guy with the schnauzer, now these bikers. They thought they were immune to muggers and pervs and psycho killers. Inhuman monsters didn't even cross their minds, because inhuman monsters weren't real.

Too bad this particular inhuman monster didn't know it couldn't exist. The Servitor began splashing and snapping twigs, getting clear of the fallen tree. If the bikers would stop blowing smoke at each other and cracking up over it, they'd hear. If they'd pay attention to the shadowy spots around them, like you had to in a world monsters could invade, they'd see.

*It drifts toward shore behind the tree trunk. It won't just look, after all. It needs to eat.*

Sure, monsters ate, and why not eat people? People weren't the monster's own kind, so it wasn't cannibalism, wasn't wrong for the monster. Sean, though, was human. Last night, in their dream-connection, he'd called the Servitor off so he wouldn't have to endure the nightmare of its attack. Today, in their waking connection, he knew what was about to happen was real, no nightmare, and so his obligation to stop the attack was that much greater. If he stopped fighting for control, he'd see the man and woman impaled on talons; he'd hear their screams, he'd smell their blood, taste it, feel the give of bone under needle-teeth. He'd become an accidental murderer.

*The Servitor's claws touch bottom. It sinks to its belly in the mud of the shallows. Overhanging trees cast bright shade around it. Soon it will be in the reeds at the water's edge, through which it can start its final stalk.*

An accidental murderer or worse. What if he wanted to let it happen, so he could fill the emptiness inside him, inside them?

*He will like the killing, because the Servitor likes killing and Sean is becoming it.*

He forced his eyes open. On the high ceiling of the study, the transparency of the riverside and the clueless bikers played like a washed-out movie. Okay. He could stand a movie massacre, and maybe distance would get him off the hook for complicity—

Eddy bent into view over him. The movie played on her face.

He closed his eyes. What would Eddy say if she knew he was letting people get slaughtered? What about Dad or Helen Arkwright, Celeste or Gus, Joe-Jack, Phil, and their other friends, Geldman even?

"Hey, Sean."

*The Servitor heaves itself into the reeds.*

*Go back.*

*It will not.*

"Sean, come on."

*I'll come now, if you do what I say.*

*It doesn't believe. It peers through the reeds at the bikers. The woman frowns.* "Something stink?" *she asks the man.*

"Tide must be going out."

"Sean, stop faking it. I know you're awake."

This time he hurled thought like a javelin: *I mean it. Wait in the river. I'm coming.*

*The Servitor rocks back on its haunches. It let its prey go last night because the summoner promised to come to the river and give it more blood. The summoner never came.*

*I swear, I'll come this minute. Let them go. Wait for me.*

*If he doesn't come, it will find other meat.*

*Coming.*

Eddy was shaking him. Sean kept his eyes clamped shut until *the Servitor eases back into the water. Life-radiant clouds of minnows scatter before it.*

She'd shake his damn teeth loose. He shouldered Eddy's hand away. "Lay off! What's wrong?"

"What's wrong with *you*? Your face was all screwed up. Were you dreaming?"

"I was *resting.*"

"You're sweating buckets, too, by the way."

He was. The study was hot, in spite of the river-ghost swaying over it. Sean stood up, on carpet, in riverweed. Gus wasn't in the room. "Where's my uncle?"

"Downstairs, on the treadmill. I've got to go. Mom's taking me to Pa Ndau class; then I'm supposed to go over to Keiko's."

Eddy gone, Gus in the basement gym. No one to stop Sean. "Right," he said. "No problem."

"You sure? I mean, were you in the Servitor's head just now?"

"Yeah, but nothing's going on. It's still in the river, down near the old receiving tomb."

"Because if you need me to stay, I'm here. The class is no big deal, and I can go to Keiko's another day. We were just going to hang out."

For Eddy to blow off a school project was, like, revolutionary. For a second, Sean felt like he was going to bawl. Then he said what he had to say to get her gone: "I'm okay. Except I smell like a pig. I'm going to take a shower."

"Make sure you call me later, about the dismissing ritual."

"Soon as I know."

Eddy gave him a last look so long Sean was afraid she wouldn't leave after all. Then she trotted into the kitchen, and he heard the back door slam.

What about Gus? Sean didn't have time to set up much, but he did turn on the shower in the hall bathroom. Gus would hear it running when he came upstairs and for a while, at least, he'd think Sean was still in the house.

Outside the front door Sean stopped. He was crazy to go, especially if Dad and Helen would be back soon. Could he break his new promise to the Servitor? When he was up in the bathroom arranging the shower trick, he'd closed his eyes and heard, river muffled, the retreating roar of the motorcycle. So the bikers were safe.

Yeah, but all the Servitor had to do to find people-snacks was take a jog up to the boulevard.

Through superimposed riverscape, he peered down Keene Street. No Civic, no Dad and Helen. Should he call them? If they did have the dismissing ritual, he could go to the Servitor with a big surprise, not just with the blood in his veins.

For one second, that was all, he closed his eyes. It was long enough for the bubbles of Servitor-thought to deal him pseudopoidal prods of impatience.

He opened his eyes. No Civic. No more time. On the steps to the sidewalk, he wobbled, light-headed from hunger or disoriented from navigating two surrounds at once. He stiffened his knees. Then he walked toward Hope Street, and beyond Hope, toward the cemetery and the river.

# 23

**The** first things Helen saw after her fall were black rectangles slashed with fiery pinstripes. The rectangles billowed and collapsed, billowed, collapsed, like membranous air-gates through which monsters struggled to birth themselves. She shrank away, then made out what the rectangles were: blinds drawn against afternoon sun, stirred to false life by the AC unit underneath them.

The blinds covered the windows of her own office at the MU Library. She lay on the couch. Someone had taken off her cap of spikes and wrapped her forehead in a damp cloth. When she touched the cloth, a hand towel, her fingers came away wet with water, not blood, so her swollen bladder of a head hadn't burst after all. That was a plus.

On the minus side, her intact head throbbed like an infected tooth. "Damn," she muttered.

The mutter incited movement beyond the arm of the couch on which her feet were propped. Helen peered between her sneakers, expecting to see gossamers. Not one. Only Jeremy, with a cell phone at his ear.

To the phone, he said, "Wait, Professor. She's waking up."

Professor? If it was Gus, why the formality? And why was Jeremy talking on *her* phone?

He knelt by her head. Too loudly, he said, "Helen? You hear me?"

She winced. "Like a megaphone."

"Sorry. You can see me?"

"I can see fine, I guess. How'd I get here?"

"After you passed out, that guy at the desk wanted to call nine-one-one, but I talked him into helping me get you over to your office. You've been unconscious for hours—it's after six. I was about to drag Geldman out of the pharmacy. But as long as your eyes are all right. I mean, I could tell they weren't bleeding, and your pulse and breathing seemed okay, but I couldn't tell if you were blind."

Bleeding, blind? Oh, Geldman's warning. "Is that him on the phone? Mr. Geldman?"

"No. It's Marvell."

The name made her sit up, which was a mistake—pain jolted from the top of her skull into her cervical vertebrae. She dropped back onto the unforgiving vinyl cushions.

"Whoa!" Jeremy said, gruff with alarm. "Lie still. He called about a quarter hour ago. I've already told him everything."

Jeremy put the phone in her hand, warm from his grip. Helen pressed it against her ear. "Professor?"

"Helen! Thank God. You're all right, aren't you?"

Her eyes watered at the vigor of his voice, buzzy as it was. "I guess so. I don't have the symptoms Geldman said would mean trouble. You know Geldman? He knows you."

"Oh yes, I know Solomon, and I'll be giving him hell for selling you a potion that could've blinded you."

"He had to. Didn't Jeremy explain?"

"The boy's father? Yes. Rotten mess, and you in the middle of it."

"Are you still in the mountains?"

"No, I'm in London. Leezy McGrigor said you were in trouble. Her son drove me into Inverness, and I was lucky enough to catch the last plane south. I'm flying to New York in an hour, then on to Rhode Island."

Helen's throat tightened. "I'm sorry to break up your vacation, but I can't tell you not to come. Talk about planes, I feel like I've been piloting one upside down while trying to read the flight manual."

Marvell laughed, then spoke with an equally comforting gravity: "I'm the one who should be sorry. The Order trusted me to watch you, and here I put myself out of reach for days. And I don't know how to apologize to Mr. Wyndham."

"You know Geldman. Do you know Redemption Orne, too?"

"Only his history. The Order heard rumors of his survival years ago, in Henry Arkwright's time. No one could confirm them."

The Order, twice now. "You're talking about the Order of Alhazred."

A couple beats of silence, followed by a sheepish, "Yes, Helen."

"Geldman was surprised I didn't know about it."

"I should have told you sooner. What you've already done, on your own, proves that."

Given the trouble Marvell was taking now, Helen couldn't let him berate himself. "No, you were right. I needed to do that background reading first."

"The Order of Alhazred, then. Well, briefly, it's an international group, magicians, paramagicians, ordinary people. They've got two things in common: They all know the truth behind the Cthulhu Mythos, and they all work to mitigate the dangers posed by its creatures and adherents. Henry Arkwright was one of its founders, after the Dunwich incident."

"Which Lovecraft wrote the truth about, whatever Uncle John used to say."

"Lovecraft was an Order member, though not a popular one, the way he told tales out of school. Obviously there's a huge amount more I have to tell you, but the important thing now is keeping you and the others safe. I've already contacted another member in Providence, Thomas O'Conaghan. I told Mr. Wyndham about him, and it turns out they've already met."

O'Conaghan, right. The detective who'd stopped by the Litinski house. "Can he help us with the dismissing ritual?"

"I'm afraid Tom hasn't witnessed a dismissal before. I have, so I want to be there when Sean tries it. Especially now that he's been inoculated—he could need someone to keep him on track."

"Even if he takes the Patience Orne potion?"

"That should help, but it's not a sure thing. For tonight Tom is going to take all of you to a hotel downtown. The Servitor won't want to expose itself to traffic and crowds. Tomorrow night, we'll get rid of it."

It seemed time to say good-bye, but Helen didn't want to give up the connection to Marvell, distant as it was. "This call must be costing a fortune."

"To hell with that. Look, Helen. I'm going to help you make sense of what's happened. I remember what it's like, to find out the impossible is real."

She cradled the cell phone closer. "Professor, I saw things after I took the Bishop potion. Creatures floating everywhere. And gates—I don't know, with some kind of veil over them and things inside trying to get out."

"The floating things are called ghost-efts. Their niche seems to be interdimensional rifts. They're always passing in and out of our plane—they're as common as dust mites, only less harmful; I've never heard of anyone who was allergic to them."

"The other things? In the gates?"

"They can't get to our plane without powerful intervention from our side."

"Like Sean's ritual?"

"No, something much more difficult. Don't worry. Sean won't be summoning any of those beasts."

Helen smiled.

"I do have to go now."

"All right. See you soon, Professor. Thank you."

The connection broke. For a few seconds, she kept the silent phone to her ear. Then she put it in her shirt pocket and swung her legs off the couch. Fresh pain jolted into her skull, not quite as horrific this time.

Jeremy was still there. He'd been there the whole time. "O'Conaghan's supposed to meet us at Cel's."

"And take us to a hotel. Sounds like a plan." Helen got to her feet and headed toward her desk, more or less steady. She had sunglasses somewhere. A scrabble through her drawers turned up everything but. A cell phone rang, Jeremy's. "Gus," she heard him say. "How's it going?"

Was O'Conaghan at the Litinski house already? Damn it. She'd probably left the sunglasses in her car, now at the garage.

"What? You've got to be kidding."

The sudden tension in Jeremy's voice made Helen almost slam her fingers in a drawer.

"Well, when did he go?" Jeremy demanded. "What? Okay, we're coming. Jesus." A pause. "No, you stay there. He might come back. And, Gus, remember that Providence detective? We've heard from Marvell. He says O'Conaghan knows about Servitors, but I can't go into it now. Ask O'Conaghan. He's coming over to your house to be our bodyguard until Marvell flies in. Helen found the spell we need. Right."

He pocketed the phone and turned to her. "Sean's gone. He left the shower upstairs running so Gus would think he was in it.

After half an hour, and the water still running, Gus checked. No Sean. No Sean anywhere in the house. Nobody over at Eddy's, either."

The shower-subterfuge ruled out an innocent walk, didn't it? Helen straightened. No sunglasses? Too bad. Instead she grabbed a visor from the coatrack and jammed it on. "Let's go, then," she said.

# 24

All the way to Blackstone Boulevard, Sean walked submerged streets. Cars hurtled through the ghost aquascape like massive catfish; people wavered past like the drowned undead. Too quickly now the superimposed river, the Servitor's input, was starting to obscure what was actually around him. Twice he bumbled into fireplugs. Once he stepped into traffic and an SUV catfish nearly splattered him across the weedy blacktop.

He dashed across the boulevard, last of the car-gauntlets, to the gates of Swan Point Cemetery. Instantly the Servitor rose from the river bottom. With two equal surrounds in motion, Sean's disorientation became unbearable. He sat on one of the boulders in the cemetery wall and closed his eyes, to see through the Servitor alone.

*It paddles to the shore. Draped in silver shadow, the riverbank is deserted, the smell of humans a distant titillation. Much closer now is the smell of the summoner. The Servitor must make a safe place on land, for the summoner can't live underwater.*

*It flops up the marble steps of the receiving tomb, tries the door, and finds it riveted shut. The leaded windows beside the*

*door are too narrow for the summoner to squeeze through. Low in*
*the façade are two iron grates a yard square, but these are too vis-*
*ible from the turnaround at the end of the road. Gnarled rhodo-*
*dendrons hug the curving tomb walls; the Servitor jostles through*
*them to the place where marble façade turns to brick. Where the*
*brick wall runs into the side of the bluff, the Servitor finds another*
*ventilation grate.*

*With a flex of its shoulders, it yanks the grate out of crumbling*
*mortar to expose a bright square of night, dankly cool and redo-*
*lent.*

Through the Servitor, Sean peered inside the receiving tomb.
How many times had he and Eddy speculated about its contents?
Good old practical Eddy had been right: The place was empty.
No skeletons, not a bone. No disintegrated coffins, either, al-
though there were three walls of coffin niches.

The Servitor squeezed into the tomb and squatted, waiting.

Now that the Servitor was still, its visual input stationary,
Sean could walk again, and he did walk, down the main road of
the cemetery. He passed gravestones and obelisks, flower beds
and trees. He also passed down an endless corridor of coffin
niches. Maybe this tomb overlay was too appropriate to cause
disorientation, because before long he was able to run, and he
did run, hunger driving him.

<hr />

The receiving tomb ran twenty feet into the hillside, twelve coffin niches left, twelve right, eight in the back wall. In the old
days, thirty-two corpses could have wintered in comfort, waiting for a spring thaw to break up their silent party. Though the
Servitor had hauled the grate back into place, leaving the slits in
the ventilation chimneys the only source of light, Sean saw the
tomb clearly. The thing was, eyes open or shut, he now saw only
through the Servitor—its sensory input had overpowered his
own. Dark was light. Heat had shape. The weird chromatics of

life-auras flared off fungi and mildew, ants and spiders, fat-bodied moths. To a nose made Servitor-sensitive, decay steamed off the dripping walls. The stench should have driven Sean from the coffin niche in which he sat, but it didn't bother him. Neither did the stench of the Servitor itself, or the way it crouched beside him, its beard of tentacles clutching his left arm.

The Servitor knew magic. It had slurred some kind of incantation over his arm, and a nipple—a witch's teat—had sprouted from the inner fold of his elbow. In approved familiar fashion, the Servitor suckled blood from the teat. It didn't seem to be taking a lot, but Sean's blood was rich as cream to it, and their joined hungers diminished.

As the Servitor fed on Sean, Sean fed on himself.

He closed his eyes and sank deeper into the coffin niche. A new change came, soft, the bloom of the Servitor's thought-bubbles into full amoebic life. They swarmed on Sean, engulfed him, dragged him from the surface of the Servitor's senses down into the deeps of its mind.

*Three black suns rise into a sky of poison green, the largest bulging above half the horizon. Buildings jut from a shoreline of algae-slimed rock, crazy big buildings with impossible angles and curves. Maybe they aren't buildings at all. Maybe they're crystals, alive. Aware. The sea that laps the shore is definitely alive, because it evolves stalked eyes and mouths out of its tarry viscosity.*

*It isn't a water-sea. It's a vast colony of shoggoths, a protoplasmic ocean. The buildings have a shoggoth-view, which must be a plus to a certain kind of real-estate investor, and why not? The permutations of the shoggoths are more varied than the roll and crash of waves, and the piping of temporary mouths is much more musical than gulls.*

*Are they singing?*

*A voice answers him from nowhere in particular, human, male, smooth and low: The shoggoths always sing.*

*What do they sing about?*

*About what they want. They always want. It never ceases with them.*

*Isn't that dangerous?*

*It can be. But it does keep them singing.*

*From far off over the sea of shoggoths comes the rasp of metal scraping across loose mortar. It's not part of the shoggoths' repertoire, because when Sean opens his eyes and drifts back into the receiving tomb the singing fades away and*

the grating persisted. A heavy thud followed, and a square of dark opened toward the front of the tomb, where the wall was nicheless. The Servitor released Sean and dropped to all fours. Its rage swamped him. Let it spring and he'd feed with it on blood and flesh not his own, on the one stupid enough to interrupt their communion.

"Sean?"

Eddy, calling from outside.

Sean lurched to his feet. Dizziness hit, and he had to lean against the lip of the niche above his seat.

"Sean! Are you in there?"

The Servitor inched forward. *No,* he willed.

*Yes.*

*No, she's my friend. You can't hurt her.*

"Sean!"

He rasped, "Eddy, don't come in."

Of course she came. The dark square flushed with her aura as she ducked through and pushed herself upright with the aluminum bat she carried.

The Servitor hissed but stayed beside Sean. He felt its rubbery hide under his palm—he'd put his hand on its head. Too bad it didn't have a dog collar he could hang on to. Not that a collar would help. If the Servitor went for Eddy, it would carry him along as if he were as light as a tick.

"Sean, I can't see for shit. It's in here, right? I can smell it."

Eddy's courage shocked him. She knew the Servitor was in

the tomb, and she'd still come inside. "It's next to me," he whispered. "But it's not hurting me."

She lifted the bat waist high, close to her body. "God, Sean, what are you doing with it?"

What did she think, they were making out? Let her—what they *were* doing was even more intimate. Sean flashed hot, then cold, like he might pass out. Had the Servitor taken that much blood?

He slumped back into the lowest coffin niche.

In what had to be total darkness to her, Eddy shuffled forward.

*Go back to the river.*

*It will not.*

*You have to.*

*He's not its master, for he never bound it.*

Eddy's form was dark, her aura brilliant, the penumbra of an eclipsed sun. She was taut with life, and to the Servitor's many-forked tongues her scent was sweet. This one was meat almost as rich as Sean's blood.

The Servitor tensed.

Almost as rich, though, only almost. So long as Sean had a drop of blood left, the Servitor would prefer it.

He thrust out his left arm to expose the seeping teat. At once the Servitor battened on to it and kneaded him like a kitten nursing. There was no pain, and it wasn't so bad to feel protoplasmic thought wind around him. He

*isn't afraid. Let him change*

"Sean! What are you *doing*?"

Her shout slapped him awake. Say he was stranded in a blizzard and had to keep alert, had to keep moving, or else he'd freeze to death. He'd want Eddy to keep slapping him, wouldn't he?

He stared at the not quite blue and almost violet of her full-body halo. "I've got to feed it, or it'll eat someone else."

Guided by his voice, Eddy shuffled toward him. "What do you mean?"

"It's drinking."

"Blood? Your blood?" Her foot struck Sean's. She shifted the bat under one arm and groped for him. He felt her hands on his face, on his shoulders. From his shoulders they slid down his arms, and she couldn't help but touch the Servitor, which reared back and shrilled a warning.

"Oh my God."

"Don't touch it. It'll bite." And it would bite with the shark-sized mouth in its head, because it stayed erect, rebattening on Sean with one of its palm-mouths.

Eddy shrank away. She clutched the bat again. "You can't stop it?"

"I don't know. No." His eyelids weighed a ton each. It hurt to keep them up, so he could look at Eddy instead of the things the Servitor wanted to show him. He had to fight the seductive tug of its mental pseudopods; yielding loosened his grip on one reality and sucked him into another, and that couldn't be right, could it? It would be easy. It would even be pleasant. But once you went fully under, would you ever resurface?

Eddy stuttered, which she hadn't done since, what, kindergarten? "S-s-sean. L-l-listen. Soon as me and Mom got back from class, your uncle came over. He was looking for you; he said you went off without telling anyone. I tried to text you; you didn't answer. You don't have your phone, do you?"

"No."

"I figured. Then I'm like, where would you go? You'd go to the *Servitor*, because it was taking over, it could force you to go, right? I wanted to tell your uncle my theory, but this guy pulled up in a black Camry, and it had to be that cop that came around the other day, because your uncle obviously knew him and called him 'Detective.' They went in the house, and Mom wouldn't let me go over, so I snuck out to look for you."

He let his eyelids fall; they were just too heavy. At once he drifted down to where the three black suns *rise. The shoggoths are singing, and their songs are beautiful. Why hasn't he known that before? He*

saw Eddy through the Servitor's eyes. It wanted her. What had that voice told him about the shoggoths, that they wanted without end? So did the Servitor; so

*do the things in the living crystal buildings. They are shadows barely glimpsed through the translucent walls, and they scream without sound but with a desire that tears him. He*

"Sean, we've got to get out of here."

"I can't."

"I'll call your dad."

"No, it'll hurt him if he comes. It'll hurt you if you try to get help. Just talk. Keep talking. Don't let me go."

Her voice rose to a stricken squeak. "God, talk about what?"

"It doesn't matter. Don't let me go."

Silence, but Eddy hunched down at his right side, opposite the Servitor, and she grabbed his hand. Hers was shaking bigtime. "Okay," she said. "Here's what it's about. My story cloth I'm making. There's this hunter in Cambodia. And he meets this tiger in the jungle. The tiger eats him and steals his clothes. I mean, obviously, it's a folklore tiger, not a real one. It dresses up and goes to the village, pretending it's the hunter. . . ."

Her voice

*spins out like spider-silk, which is crazy strong, really, strong enough to cling to, no problem that the meaning of her words comes and goes. So long as he can hear her above the insidious singing of the shoggoths, he can keep one foot in his own world and not leave her alone with the Servitor, not sink, not drown himself. . . .*

# 25

Jeremy sped through the traffic on Route 128 as if their mission would protect them from crashes and state troopers. Under her visor, Helen hid from both head-spearing sunlight and the sight of his stuntman maneuvers. She wasn't too sanguine about divine intervention—the God of her upbringing seemed to take no interest in human heroics, and the Outer Gods, which seemed far more interactive, didn't even pretend to be benevolent.

As he and Helen neared the exit to I-95, Jeremy's cell phone rang. He pulled it out of his windbreaker and handed it to her, thank God or gods. It was Celeste. "Where are you two?" she asked without preamble. "Is Jere all right?"

"About to get off One Twenty-eight. Jeremy's breaking all land-speed records; that's why I'm answering. A second." Helen tapped the phone to speaker mode and upped the volume, so Jeremy wouldn't kill them trying to overhear the conversation. "Has Sean come back?"

"Not yet. Eddy said he was still at our house around six, when she left for some class. He didn't say anything to her about going out, and now she's gone, too. Eddy, I mean. Rachel just called to ask if she was with us."

"You think Eddy's looking for Sean?"

"Maybe. And Detective O'Conaghan's been here. He and Gus are out looking for the kids now."

"We'll be there soon," Jeremy said.

"Take care, then."

Helen silently echoed Celeste's sentiment as the Civic cut off a pickup and swerved onto the exit ramp to honks of outrage. Before she could tuck the phone into her pocket, it rang again. No speaker this time, not while Jeremy played chicken with eighteen-wheelers, trying to get to the far lane of the packed interstate. Helen pressed the phone to her ear, and someone whispered into it, frantic, unintelligible. "Hello?" Helen said. "I didn't hear you."

"Ms. Arkwright?" The whisper grew marginally louder. "It's me, Eddy."

"Eddy?"

"We're in the tomb. Me and Sean."

"What—"

"It's right here, with us. The Servitor. It's possessed Sean, I don't know, it's drinking his blood, and I'm trying to talk him back, but you've got to come, I think he's losing it."

Tomb. "What tomb, Eddy?"

"I can't keep talking; it's getting mad. The one by the river, Swan Point. Where they used to keep bodies in the winter. Shit—"

Eddy cut off. The Civic jolted as Jeremy braked hard—listening to Helen's end of the latest call, he'd practically ridden up the ass of the car in front of them. "Tell me," he said, watching the road again, grim faced.

"Eddy says she's with Sean and the Servitor in some tomb. It's feeding on Sean's blood. It's trying to possess him, she thinks. Swan Point, that's what she said, a tomb where they kept bodies in the winter."

"The receiving tomb, I know it. Hit five."

"What?"

"Five, Gus's cell. Tell him to meet us at the entrance to Swan Point. And bring O'Conaghan with him."

Helen speed-dialed Gus and got through the call. The way Jeremy laid on the horn, floored the accelerator, jerked from lane to lane, she felt like she was on one of those obnoxious carnival rides that tried to make you lose your corndogs and cotton candy. "Gus will meet us at the cemetery. He'll call O'Conaghan—they're in separate cars. Damn. I'm even more scared for Eddy than I am for Sean. He's still got some protection as summoner, but her—"

"Yeah, what I was thinking."

Helen groped at her feet and found her backpack. She pulled it onto her lap and hugged it. The cobalt bottle was inside, Geldman's gift, and the dismissing spell. But if Sean was possessed already—

Shut the fuck up, Helen. She just held on, to the backpack, to the restraint strap across her chest. Maybe the Outer Gods *were* playing road angels for her and Jeremy. After all, the longer the good guys lived, the longer they could be toyed with.

~~✦~~

**Eddy's** tiger walks on two legs, dressed in stolen hunter's clothes. How it expects to pass for a man, with its striped face, its teeth and claws, Sean can't make out. And how did it put on the clothes in the first place, and what shifts of skeletal structure let it walk upright? Okay, so it's a folklore tiger, but Sean's walking the shore of the shoggoth-sea again, and though they're also folklore, the shoggoths look totally real. That means the tiger will have to be at least as convincing as they are to keep Sean from drowning in the Servitor's thought-stream.

Good old tiger. It sheds its disguise and drops to all fours. Now it's sleek and tawny, like Eddy, and like Eddy it clings to his right side, freaked straight through, yet holding its ground.

Together they pace the shoreline. Ahead is the largest of the living crystal buildings. Inside this palace the courtiers are dancing, giant shadows that weave past irregular apertures in its walls. It's not shoggoth-song they move to, but some interior riot of sound that sets crystal and air and earth vibrating.

The tiger presses against his thigh. It growls. Sean grasps it by the scruff of the neck.

The smooth, low voice speaks again. *She can't come with you.*

*But—*

*It's not possible. Let her go.*

He has to obey the voice, doesn't he? Sean breathes on the tiger, and his fingers sink through its hide as it thins to striped smoke. It cringes and coughs out a roar.

He blows lung-bottom breath at it, and the tiger-smoke shreds to nothing. Eddy is gone. He is alone.

*There will be reward.*

*Come*, the voice says. *I'm waiting.*

~~~~~~~~~~

**Outside** Swan Point, Gus told Helen and Jeremy that O'Conaghan was coming to meet them. Though Helen would have been glad to wait for him, she didn't blame Jeremy for insisting they move. Sean had been missing for more than two hours, Eddy for not much less.

The iron gates of the cemetery were locked, so they left the cars outside and hiked in through an adjacent patch of woods. Helen had worried that her hypersensitive eyes would cripple her, but while the deeper dusk under the trees slowed Jeremy and Gus, she threaded the narrow paths without hesitation. Bishop's #5 was still partially affecting her, minus the ghost-efts, which she didn't miss one bit.

When the woods gave way to a groomed necropolis, Jeremy took the lead. They struck a road that paralleled a stone-and-boulder wall. "The receiving tomb's this way," Jeremy said.

Headlights stabbed the darkness at their heels. They ducked into a dense clump of cedars. A white sedan marked SWAN POINT SECURITY cruised by and made Helen flash on teenage drinking excursions to the big new cemetery outside Arkham. The Old Burying Ground in the city proper would have been more atmospheric, and it had no patrols. But they'd never gone there, because fear would have turned the beer sour in their mouths.

That sour tang spread through her mouth as they broke cover and trotted deeper into a labyrinth of the new and ancient, the rational and grotesque. In her gut, hadn't she always known the world was like this place? Now, courtesy of Bishop's #5, she'd see the lurking monsters with no shadows to soften them, in terrible detail down to the tiniest scales. She noticed that Gus carried an unlit flashlight in his left hand. His right he kept tucked inside his jacket. A jacket in this heat? He had to be wearing it to hide his pistol, was probably resting his hand on the butt, in case the monsters came out to play.

Abruptly their road plunged to an expanse of moon-spangled water. Running no longer required energy, but braking did. Helen's backpack thumped on her spine. Her heart lurched as a winged figure rushed up on her left. An angel, but in stone, no help. She rocketed past it, onto the gravelly flat at the end of the road. Someone grabbed one of her pack straps—Jeremy—and kept her from pelting straight into the river. Gus pinwheeled to a halt beside them. They stood, panting, then froze into silence— Helen cutting a gasp in two—when a girl screamed nearby.

Or was it near? It seemed muffled. Helen stared back up the road, but a lance of moonlight struck white out of the shadows to her left; potion-keen, she made out the façade of a marble tomb under the hillside.

Another muffled scream. From inside the tomb.

"Eddy," Jeremy snarled.

He sprinted, Gus a stride behind. They'd reached marble steps before a third scream tore the open air. A slim figure burst out of rhododendrons clustered at the far side of the tomb: Eddy, for sure, trailing blond hair and running like a deer up the nearly vertical hill. A second form burst from the bushes, loping on all fours. It shot a flat, burning glare at Jeremy and Gus, but it didn't swerve from its pursuit.

Eddy leaped a tree trunk and crashed down in a brushy hollow. The Servitor took the obstacle like a steeplechaser. Jeremy was over next. Gone. Gus turned, waving frantically at Helen with his lit flash. "Look for Sean!" he yelled.

Then he climbed over the trunk and slid out of sight into the hollow.

Alone, she clutched the straps of her pack as if they were ropes keeping her from plummeting down the face of a cliff. Inching closer to the tomb, she picked out muddy footprints on the worn steps. Boots and sneakers had climbed this way, and the webbed paws of an enormous, Servitor-sized, toad.

The door of the tomb was bolted shut. But Eddy hadn't come out the door. She'd come out of the rhododendrons.

Helen crossed the porch and jumped back to earth. She sidled between clutching branches and curved wall until her foot hit a metal grate. It had been yanked from the wall of the tomb, leaving a jagged square.

The tomb exhaled rot like diseased breath, along with a slurred moaning. In his right mind, would Sean ever moan like that?

Remember, the trick was to not fear her fear. Geldman and Cybele had armed her with that realization, and Marvell was coming, and to her heightened vision the odorous blackness wasn't impenetrable. She bent and made out a niche-lined chamber and there, opposite the grate hole, the scuffed soles of Sean's sneakers, with Sean in them, whole.

Helen ducked into the tomb.

A whole Sean in body, yes, but he was slumped inside the lowest of three coffin niches, his eyes fixed like a blind man's.

His lips twisted with strange sounds, hisses and clicks and an eerie high whistle that raised every hair on her head. Did she hear words? If so, they were words in the mythical language of aliens so *not* mythical that the smell of this one choked her.

As she approached Sean, the stench grew. Servitor saliva gleamed on his arm like a network of slug trails. There were smears of blood, too, though she couldn't see any new wound.

"Sean," she whispered. "Can you hear me?"

In response, he hissed alien syllables and snapped at her, a rabid dog, or an infuriated Servitor.

Helen fell back from the boy. She didn't need Geldman or Marvell to diagnose Sean's condition; after all they'd been through, she and Jeremy had arrived too late. The Servitor had freed itself from Sean's imperfect control, and what she was hearing was its voice, mangled by his human tongue. Did that make the possession final?

If so, Eddy would die, Jeremy and Gus would die. Then the Servitor would return to feed on its summoner and on the idiot crouched in front of him, wringing the straps of her backpack until the buckles cut her palms.

Her pack.

Helen shrugged it off her shoulders and groped inside. Notes, pens, Marvell's letter. Where was Patience Orne's #11? She couldn't have lost it. She hadn't: Geldman's cobalt bottle had slipped between the pages of a notebook. She pulled it out of the pack and dug at the wax seal with a fingernail. Why hadn't she thought to pop the seal earlier, before she was standing in a tomb with an emergency on her shaking hands? She hadn't thought one damn thing through—

Her nail broke, but the wax yielded. She pulled the cork. Instantly the bracing smell of clean wind welled from the bottle. Wind? Did it even have a scent?

Remembering Geldman's tea, Helen held the mouth of the

bottle under her nose. She inhaled, and her hands steadied. Just like that. Patience or Cybele, clean wind or flowering grass. Her mind was clear. She knew what to do. Geldman had told her.

She took two long last steps toward Sean. As she pushed him upright in his niche, he growled and spit. She grabbed his jaw and forced his mouth open. With one hand left to administer the potion, she couldn't do anything about his flailing arms, so before he could bat the bottle to the floor she waved it under his nostrils. One, two, three times, and the clean wind did its job. Sean's arms dropped. He went limp, and she was able to pour potion into his mouth and lever shut his jaws, praying he wouldn't gag the stuff out. He didn't. He swallowed. Seconds later, a convulsive spasm went through him.

Helen scuttled back to cork the bottle and stow it in her pack. Sean's staring eyes had closed. He rocked out of the coffin niche and dropped to his hands and knees, head hanging. For a few seconds the words he muttered remained unintelligible; then plain English crept in: "Stop it, help them!"

Her eyes saw without light, but they couldn't pierce whatever darkness the Servitor had poured into Sean's mind. Nothing left for her to do but wait, and the waiting suffocated her more thoroughly than the tons-heavy air of the tomb.

# 26

*Sean's passage through the Servitor's mind is the drift of a leaf to ground. Back in the three-sunned world, himself leaf light, Sean drifts toward the palace of living crystal. It thrusts a terrace over the shoggoth-sea, and the Black Man appears on the precariously tilted surface to watch his approach. They will talk at last. Sean will begin to learn.*

*But wind rises in a torrent that sucks him up (no more than a leaf) and whirls him away from the palace. The Black Man spreads falcon wings and rides the wind after him. . . .*

His return to the Servitor's mind was no leaf dance but a terrible caesarean birth, as abrupt as the stroke of the surgeon's scalpel and torn by screams.

The screams were Eddy's.

She was out of the tomb. It—they, Servitor and Sean—was out, too, bounding after her up an oblique slash in the face of the bluff, a path treacherous with deadfalls and the slithering layers of last year's leaves. Yet Eddy in her blazing aura, aluminum bat gripped like a balance pole in front of her, was sure-footed prey and kept one leap ahead of it. Its own pursuers (Dad and Gus, from the shouts) were clumsier. One went down with a snapping of rotten boughs. The Servitor shot a rubber-necked glare at Dad, who didn't stop for the fallen Gus; instead, he pumped arms, pumped legs, as if he raced the nightmare memory of what he'd found after his last run through the woods.

The Servitor savored Sean's own memory of Hrothgar, along with its anticipation of shredding Eddy to similar bits.

Near the bluff top, the path flung itself into a steep incline. Eddy pelted up it, with the Servitor—with them both—still a leap behind. But Sean knew the Servitor *wanted* to trail, wanted the hunt to end a little farther on, in the hollow that cemetery landscapers had tricked out with slate steps and masses of rhododendron, azalea, and mountain laurel. It was beautiful in early summer, a place for visitors to take a break from thinking about death, but even in bare midwinter it shouldn't have witnessed Eddy screaming like that, as if death was exactly what she saw barreling at her.

*No no no!* But yelling his psychic throat raw did no good. Drunk with Eddy's scent, vast eardrums quivering to the pumping of her blood and heaving of her lungs, the Servitor ignored Sean.

In the center of the hollow, a natural arena, Eddy wheeled and brandished her bat like a broadsword. The Servitor circled her on claw tips, spider quick. Eddy pivoted to keep her face to it, gasping defiance: "Oh no. No fucking way. No you don't, asshole."

Eddy, the tiger. *I can't let us, you can't make me watch it—*

The Servitor could do whatever the hell it wanted. It sprang, to a burst of pain for both of them as Eddy swung the bat into its shoulder. No deterrent, though—even as she cocked the bat for another swing, the welt swelled outward, healing. The Servitor blocked her second blow. Eddy swung a third time, and it seized the bat and hurled it, Eddy still attached, halfway across the hollow. She landed on her back and sprawled, still. The Servitor crouched to spring again.

Something else sprang, heralded by a scent-blast of blood tantalizingly similar to Sean's. The something, the someone, Dad, crashed down on the Servitor's back and locked his arms around its neck. Like a sack of living jelly, it burgeoned against his choke hold. It bucked. It spun. At the kick Dad gave its hind legs, it heaved over backward—no collapse, though, because it meant to fall and to trap its attacker beneath it. Breath whooshed out of Dad, a gust of heat on the back of the Servitor's head. It ground sharp-knobbed vertebrae into his chest until his grip on its neck loosened, until it could squirm around, bringing them belly to belly.

Dad's aura flared with the terror that Sean should never have brought on him. But Sean had no limbs to grapple the Servitor. He had no mouth to scream. He was nothing but mind, imprisoned, impotent.

The Servitor's mouth gaped. Sean felt its stretch and the gnash of its needle-teeth. He felt Dad's hands grab its shoulders to hold it off. The Servitor churned its hind legs, shredding the mossy ground, trying to scrabble its raptor claws into play and slice Dad open. Like Hrothgar. One claw caught cloth, then skin, ripped downward. Dad yelled.

Pain again, not Dad's but the Servitor's. Eddy (yes, tiger) was back up and flailing her bat, sinking aluminum into the Servitor's gelatinous flesh. It keened with hatred and hunger, but Dad had clamped his legs around its hips to keep it out of evisceration mode, Dad would not let it have Eddy, and Eddy would not let it have Dad, and Sean yearned toward them both, still trapped.

Dad's arms started giving way to the Servitor's lunges. Where were Gus, Helen? Where were the goddamn security guards? They'd shown up quick enough that time Sean and Phil had snuck in to see what hung around Lovecraft's grave at night. No guards now, no Gus, no Helen, but even so, Sean wasn't alone. The Black Man had defied the gravity of the three-sunned world to slip with Sean into the Servitor's mind. He, too, was bodiless, yet Sean *knew* his chosen form, knew his falcon hover, his golden eyes, the tilt of his mouth corners into the mildest of smiles.

"Eddy!" Dad shouted. "Get out of here! Get *out!*"

Eddy stayed put. She sank the bat into the Servitor's back, inches deep, and it whipped its head, spraying ropes of drool into Dad's face. Sean watched his eyes close as the Servitor pressed closer to his throat. The forks of its tongue already lashed his skin, already tasted blood. Sean tasted it, too, God, he did, and the horror was so great that even bodiless, he thrashed.

Then fingers clutched his jaw, fingers with nails long enough to dig in. They levered his mouth open, so he had to take the in-thrust of cool glass, had to choke on bitter sweetness like the sarsaparilla from Geldman's but a thousand times more intense. . . .

The Servitor tasting Dad . . .

Fingers levering Sean's mouth shut, making him swallow . . .

Knees and palms, his own, coming down on a gritty concrete floor. He had slipped into his body again, but he couldn't stay there. He clamped his eyes shut and shot his mind back into the Servitor's. He came of his own will this time, no prisoner. That made a difference. It made the thing hear him and stop its gnashing the moment before its needles tore into Dad: *No you can't. Gave you my blood. You can't have his.*

*It would have it. The summoner's command wasn't enough to stop it this close to the kill.*

*No,* the Black Man agreed. *You're not its master yet.*

Sean *knew* the beat of his wings. *You stop it, then!*

Golden eyes narrowed. Mild smile remained the same.

*Stop it, help them! Want me to come to you? Help them.*

The Black Man spoke without haste, in syllables no human tongue could ever twist out of itself. They did the trick. The Servitor vaulted off Dad to land on the slate steps above the arena. Sean saw Eddy's last swing miss, saw Dad sit.

Then Sean saw nothing as heat scorched the Servitor like a branding iron stamped into its nape. As if uninterested in sharing their agony, the Black Man folded his falcon wings and stooped. In a second he was gone, probably a universe away. In another the Servitor spotted the wielder of the heat: a tall man on the lip of the hollow, casting black light from a thick wand-tube-rod in his hand. A fresh shaft lashed the Servitor's face. It howled—Sean howled with it—then plunged into a thicket of mountain laurels.

The rake and gouge of branches was nothing to the black light. The Servitor floundered through the bushes until it emerged on the path from the river, nearly plowing into a limping Gus. He jerked up his pistol, but the Servitor had already abandoned the path for the sheer slope of the bluff. It slid out of control. Sean slid with it, scrabbling. . . .

Scrabbling at the filthy floor of the receiving tomb, because that was where he ended up, that was where he was Sean and no one else, with only his own mind and senses. Between the natural mustiness of the tomb and the lingering reek of Servitor, smell was the sense working hardest for him. Or against him. Desperate for clean air, he crawled toward the only hint of it, a dim square of light.

"Sean."

It was Helen's voice this time, not Eddy's. He made it to the square and crawled through it. Helen crawled out after him and helped him to the marble porch facing the river. He sucked down air that tasted bitter and sweet, like the stuff someone had forced him to swallow. "It was you? You gave me something?"

"A potion," Helen said. "From Mr. Geldman."

The potion that would strengthen his will. Helen had told him she was bringing it back from Arkham.

She grabbed his arm. Why? Oh, he was kind of swaying. "Sean, listen. What's happening? Where's the Servitor?"

The potion had worked, and so well that his souped-up will

had popped him right out of the thing's mind. That was great. That was bad. "I don't know," he whispered. His throat was too dry to manage more volume than that. "We're not each other anymore. It possessed me, right, like it said in the *Necronomicon*?"

"I'm afraid so."

*Possession* wasn't that scary a word to him, because wasn't possession the ultimate excuse for bad behavior? *Hey, I didn't do anything—it was the monster wearing my skin.* Except in Sean's case, it was him kind of wearing the monster's skin while the monster was still inside it and in control. Either way, he couldn't dodge all the blame for the continuing shitstorm. The Black Man had suggested calling the blood-spawn, but he hadn't forced Sean to change incantations and squeeze his own blood into the fire, so that the Servitor could spin itself a material form in its new home. He closed his eyes. Though he didn't get even the faintest overlay of Servitor sight, Geldman's potion hadn't severed the soul-thread; after a few seconds, Sean felt it again, like a fish line hooked into his solar plexus, and when he concentrated on that sensation the line snapped taut. "It's coming," he said.

Seconds later, the Servitor galloped up the riverside path and crouched, a lashing shadow, at the foot of the steps. Helen drew close to Sean. Did she think he could protect her? Right, like he'd protected Eddy and Dad just now. The Servitor had learned that its summoner was weak and ignorant, that when Geldman's potion wore off it could own Sean again. Tentacles rearing, it probed his mind.

The fold of his left elbow oozed warmth from its new teat. Sick with disgust, Sean dashed a trickle of blood off his forearm. To get rid of the gummy residue of Servitor-saliva would take serious scrubbing, and Jesus, it stank. *He* stank. "Get away!"

Its tentacles reared and swayed like eyeless cobras. It was laughing at him, and when it slouched off into the river it went of its own accord.

Helen let out a ragged sigh. "Did you—"

"No. It wanted to go. It knows it can get me later."

"I have more potion. And the dismissing spell."

Someone was running down the bluff path. Helen shut up. After a few seconds, she shouted, "It's all right. He's all right!"

Her eyes were working better than his. Sean didn't see Dad until he heaved himself onto the tomb porch, panting. Drool stains blotched his face, and one leg of his jeans was slashed and black with blood. Man, if Sean could just curl up and croak, only him croaking wasn't the way to make things right for Dad, who was probably still crazy enough to want him around. What Dad needed was for Sean to be as all right as Helen had yelled he was.

"He's had some potion," Helen said. "Looks like it's working."

Dad didn't take his eyes off Sean. "Where's the thing?"

Again, it was Helen who spoke: "Back in the river. How about Gus and Eddy?"

"They're up there, with O'Conaghan. Gus sprained his ankle. Otherwise they're both okay. O'Conaghan showed up with some kind of magical flashlight. It scared the bastard away."

A flashlight, not a wand, dumb ass. That's what had cast the burning beam. Sean refound his voice: "He's that detective, right? Did Uncle Gus call him after all?"

Dad had started coughing. Helen said, "Professor Marvell finally called me back, Sean. He and O'Conaghan are in a group that deals with Mythos, ah, outbreaks. O'Conaghan's going to take care of us until Marvell flies in tomorrow."

So there were Mythos police. That explained why O'Conaghan had been interested in the animal killings and why he'd noticed stuff like the pentagram. Mythos cops. Beyond cool, but right now Sean couldn't think about anything but Dad and what to say after this last close call. The best he could come up with was flat-out lame: *I'm sorry for almost getting you killed, Dad. Again. Oh, and I'm glad I didn't get Eddy killed, or Uncle Gus, or Helen.* For things to be so majorly fucked up, so that he couldn't find words strong enough to apologize, he had to have done something terrible, hadn't he? Not just something stupid. Something evil.

Dad finally stopped coughing. "Sean," he said.

Sean swallowed the impulse to launch a preemptive strike of excuses, however lame.

"I told you not to leave the house," Dad went on.

That was the worst accusation he could manage? The absurdity of it smacked Sean upside his already-scrambled head, and he couldn't help grinning. The grin was a gateway expression to laughter. At first he fought it, but what the fuck. He laughed, laughed because Dad was alive to lecture him, and because he was alive to hear it, and for all he cared, Dad could go on lecturing forever.

Dad didn't go on. His brows knit. Then he bent over, hands on knees, and heaved staccato barks that sounded like they hurt him, but they were laughter, too, definitely laughter.

Helen was the toughest of them, because her voice merely hitched. "There's a car coming, Jeremy."

"Must be O'Conaghan's. Privileges of being a cop. Security let him in."

A black sedan with the red-haired detective at the wheel crunched into the gravel turnaround at the bottom of the road. Eddy hung out a window, mud caked but unmangled. Gus sat in the backseat.

"I'll tell them you guys are right behind me," Helen said. She hoisted her backpack and headed for the sedan.

She must have figured Dad wanted to be alone with Sean so he could get back to chewing him out. Slowly Dad recovered from his barking. He straightened, pawed back his hair, and then closed the gap between them.

Laughter cut and feet planted, Sean braced to say it again, the simple thing that might not help, but which was true. It was so true he ached with it. "Dad, I'm sorry."

"We're almost through this. Hang on with me, Sean, okay?"

The way Dad held out his hand made words gush from Sean, like spoiled food he couldn't, shouldn't, keep down: "While we were in the tomb, while it was drinking, the Servitor showed me this weird place, another planet, and I was getting all into it. The Black Man was there—he wanted to talk to me. I started running right to him, instead of staying here with Eddy, and that could've got her killed. Why'd I want to talk to the Black Man so bad?"

Dad's hand made it to Sean's shoulder. "Geldman told Helen some things. I don't understand it all yet. Hell, I don't understand any of it. But we'll worry about that after we've dismissed the Servitor. One job at a time, all right?"

One job at a time. That was what Sean had watched Dad learn to do in the bad times after Mom had died. At first Dad hadn't been able to do anything at all. Cel and Gus and Grandpa Stewie and Uncle Joe had seen to the funeral and the visitors. They had cleaned the house and kept food in the kitchen and looked after Sean. Dad had let them while he'd paced his studio or sat in Mom's among the drawings and canvases and paint tubes and brushes that lay exactly where she'd left them after she'd gotten too sick to work. But when they'd tried to pack up Mom's stuff and close her studio, Dad had freaked. Those jobs were too important. He was going to do them by himself. And he had done them, a closet one day, a dresser the next, then a bookcase. The night he'd started on Mom's studio, Sean had followed him and said he couldn't lock Mom's unfinished paintings away while they were still humming. Not that Dad could feel the hum—he'd never been able to. That night, though, he'd let Sean touch all the paintings, all the drawings, one at a time, and then he'd made it Sean's job to take care of them while they hummed and to put them away when they'd stopped.

The humming. Jesus. Oh Jesus. Sean hadn't thought about that for years, except as one of those nutcase things little kids make up and talk themselves into believing. Had it actually happened, then, a sign he had magical potential? In a way, it didn't matter if the humming had been real. Not believing, not understanding, Dad had let him treat Mom's paintings as if they were alive. He'd let that be Sean's duty, for as long as Sean had needed for it to be.

Helen had gotten into the backseat with Gus, and both of them had squeezed over to leave room for Sean and Dad. Eddy was waving at them from the passenger seat. What with his throat gone tight, Sean just cocked his head toward the car.

"Right," Dad said. His throat didn't sound all that loose, either. "We'd better go."

They walked toward the turnaround. Dad limped a little, and it was good, the way he leaned on Sean, that and the way Sean found he could carry the weight.

# 27

En route from the cemetery, Helen listened to Eddy spin the cover story she'd tell her parents. See, she'd suspected Sean was goofing around in Swan Point, so she'd gone after him, but he was all the way down by the river and she'd slipped in this gross puddle of sewer runoff. That would explain the mud and the Servitor-stink, wouldn't it? O'Conaghan approved Eddy's alibi, and Helen would have goggled at her sangfroid if Eddy's words hadn't tumbled out a little too fast, a little too shrill. The girl was holding up damn well, considering how close she'd just come to dying. The full horror of it would probably hit her later. Helen had better ask Marvell what they should do to help Eddy and, yes, what they should do to help Helen. Eighteen reasonably smooth years as a kid and adolescent, then seven years more or less cradled in academia, had left her mental armor of personal invulnerability little dinged. Since Monday, however, the Servitor-situation had corroded that armor to brittle lace.

Before Eddy dashed into her house, she bequeathed her bat to Helen. Charred and pitted at the business end, it remained a sturdy weapon. Helen shook her head.

Celeste, older than Helen, seemed as relatively resilient as Eddy and the bat. Maybe the hustle of triage kept her too busy to overthink. She parked Gus on the living room couch and packed his sprained ankle with ice. She bandaged Jeremy's leg. She even checked Helen's eyes, which had returned to near normal. It was Sean, unhurt, who baffled Celeste.

Helen looked over Celeste's shoulder at the bizarre growth in the fold of his elbow: an inch-long conical nipple, rosy with blood flow. The Servitor had drunk from it, Sean explained, meeting no one's eyes.

"Witch's teat," O'Conaghan confirmed. "I've seen them before. Familiars create them."

"Can somebody take it off me?"

"Nobody will have to. It'll shrink away after the dismissing."

Thank God and thank Marvell, they had a real Mythos expert now. "Are you a magician, Detective?" Helen said.

"No. I'm a paramagician. Well, studying to be one."

"I see."

"I'm afraid I don't," Celeste said. "Is that like a paramedic?"

"Pretty much. I can't do magic the way a magician can, but I can use magical tools."

"Like that flashlight of yours?" Jeremy asked.

"Exactly. It's a regular one modified to turn magical energy into wavelengths that repel things like the Servitor. Still, the light shouldn't have been enough to drive it off its—" O'Conaghan looked at Jeremy, then shrugged. "Its prey."

Jeremy snorted. "Actually, it had already given up on this prey before you came. Sean must have ordered it off."

"Did you, Sean?"

Sean pulled away from his aunt. "It was the Black Man. You know who he is, Detective?"

O'Conaghan's expression didn't change, and maybe Helen wouldn't have noticed him paling except for the way his freckles suddenly stood out like spattered brown paint. "He's an avatar. Of Nyarlathotep. You're saying *he* called off the Servitor?"

"The palace I went to in the Servitor's mind, the Black Man was there, and I was going to talk to him. Then the potion pulled me back so I was seeing out of the Servitor again, only the Black Man came with me. I tried yelling at the Servitor to leave Dad alone. It wouldn't listen. The Black Man said something to it, and it stopped right away."

Sean ran out of breath, and his forehead had sheened over with sweat. He staggered. Celeste, Jeremy, and O'Conaghan converged on him. O'Conaghan, the closest, broke Sean's fall and deftly maneuvered him into an armchair. While Celeste tucked Sean's head between his knees, O'Conaghan drew Jeremy to Gus's couch. He gestured for Helen to follow.

Conference time. Helen went to the couch. Screw her wobbly knees. Celeste could only handle one fainter at a time.

Low-voiced, O'Conaghan said, "I didn't know how deeply Nyarlathotep was involved in Sean's case."

"Isn't this Nyar-thing supposed to be a god?" Jeremy said, so tightly his teeth had to be clenched. "Why would a god pay attention to one kid, my kid?"

Gus said it without a trace of sarcasm: "He sees the fall of a sparrow."

"This god's not worried about sparrows," O'Conaghan said. "Magicians are what interest him. If he's after Sean before he's even someone's apprentice, Sean must be a serious adept."

"That's good, isn't it?" Helen said. "That Sean's adept, I mean."

O'Conaghan pulled his tie and collar loose, exposing more freckles. "Could be. But direct contact with any Outer God is incredibly dangerous, even for a master magician. We can't let Nyarlathotep get at Sean again. He's doing it through the Servitor, so we've got to dismiss it tonight."

"Professor Marvell said to wait for him."

"But when you talked to him, you didn't know the Servitor had already possessed Sean, so he didn't have all the facts."

"What about the hotel idea?"

"That would just keep the Servitor at a physical distance. Psychically, it could get to Sean wherever he is."

Sean had raised his head. Could he hear? Helen dropped her voice further. "As long as the Patience Orne potion is working, the connection seems broken."

"How much is left?"

She didn't even know. Helen took the cobalt bottle from her pack and held it to the light of the nearest lamp. It couldn't be, but it was: She'd already poured more than a quarter of the bottle's contents into Sean.

O'Conaghan came over to look. "Was it full to start?"

"Yes."

"It won't last the night."

She had pressed the bottle to her sternum as if it were a guardian amulet. "If you think Marvell would want us to go ahead—"

"Let's do it now," Sean said. His voice was calm, but Helen saw the white-knuckled grip he had on his left elbow. "When I close my eyes, I'm seeing through the Servitor again. The potion's wearing off."

"Helen," Jeremy said. "Give him more."

"No, Dad. She's got to save it for when I do the dismissing spell. It's going to be hard. The Servitor doesn't want to go. Like, it's still got a job to do."

Helen put the obvious question, seemed she was good at that: "What job, Sean?"

"Bringing me to the Black Man. Even if I'd bound the Servitor, I wouldn't be its real master. The Black Man is, in the end. In the beginning, too, I guess."

Alpha, omega, merged and twisted into lazy-eight infinity.

"Sean's right," O'Conaghan said. He touched Helen's pack. "You've got the ritual in there?"

With excruciating care, she stowed the cobalt bottle and withdrew the other treasure, Jeremy's penciled notes. "Here. Sean, are you ready to learn it?"

Unfolding himself from his chair, he nodded.

Helen trailed him into the study, which was impenetrably dark to her again normal eyes until Jeremy flicked on the chandelier. The light made her wince, but only for the first seconds of adjustment, and she was relieved to realize that her headache was subsiding. Before the night was over, though, she might wish she had more of Bishop's #5, so she could see what was hidden but, too certainly this time, not harmless.

⤳

**Helen** stayed awake and jittery during the study session. Maybe it was end-game adrenaline, maybe a communication of urgency from O'Conaghan. It wasn't the coffee Celeste brought in. Helen didn't dare touch that—why brandish a lit match at gasoline?

She, Jeremy, and O'Conaghan all memorized the incantations of the dismissing ritual along with Sean—if he stumbled, they had to be ready with prompts. It was a good thing that Enoch Bishop had been Puritan enough to prefer English to Latin pomp. Puritan wizards with their new and improved spells. Should she be worried that it was beginning to make sense to her? She fed Sean a couple teaspoons of Patience Orne's #11, but his eyes still furtively strayed to corners and ceiling. Around eleven, he shoved his chair back. "We've got to go," he said.

Gus's swollen ankle barred him from their party. Celeste insisted on taking his place, which was a relief. Given the Servitor's record, it was likely they'd need a field medic more than a sharpshooter. Helen shouldered her pack and Eddy's bat, Celeste her emergency bag and Gus's oak walking stick. O'Conaghan had his flashlight and service pistol. For pentagram drawing, Jeremy had pocketed pastel sticks. For his weapon, he turned down Gus's Colt, muttering that he'd probably shoot his own foot off with that. While the rest of them piled into the cars, he disappeared around the back of the house. He returned shouldering a pitchfork with a worn-smooth handle and a well-oiled iron head. "Granddad Wyndham's," he said. "Cel's got a garageful of his tools." A good choice, if the books Helen had been cramming all summer were right: Tradition conferred a certain magic of its own.

Celeste rode with O'Conaghan, whose Camry took the lead. Helen rode in the backseat of the Civic. In the front, beside Jeremy, Sean slumped silent. No wonder: What more could any of them have to say?

As they crossed from Providence into Edgewood, however, Sean groaned. "I'm seeing with it all the time now. Even if I open my eyes."

Helen scooted forward. "Can you tell where it is?"

"It's swum down the Seekonk. Now it's in the harbor, where the tankers dock. If it comes up the bay and around the neck by the Yacht Club, it'll get back into the Pawtuxet."

"All right. That's what we need it to do."

"But it knows we're going to dismiss it. It must think it can repossess me, no problem. It must think I can't stop it."

"You *can* stop it, Sean," Jeremy said. "You summoned it; you can get rid of it."

"I don't know, Dad. The Black Man doesn't want it back unless it brings me. I don't want to see him again. I don't want to talk to him."

The rise in Sean's voice was slight, but it started Helen's adrenaline flowing as effectively as a siren in the ear. She pulled out the cobalt bottle. "Take some more of this, Sean."

Sean didn't turn toward her. He shook his head. "Save it for the spell. So I can do it. Please."

Helen subsided and tucked away the bottle. Sean was right, and God knew, he was strong, but the steel in him was stretching, and steel could only stretch so far. When it had reached its limit, a light touch, even a touch of comfort, could snap it.

Did Jeremy sense the same thing? He pulled back the arm he'd stretched toward Sean and locked both hands on the steering wheel. O'Conaghan's Camry had stopped at a green light, waiting for them. Jeremy hit the gas, and both cars made it through before the red.

# 28

The Post Road entrance to the industrial park had an aluminum gate, chained and padlocked. Sean had been able to edge around it on his bike; a car trying that trick would slide into the drainage ditch. O'Conaghan got wire cutters out of his trunk and cut the lock. When their cars were through, he resecured the gate with a padlock of his own. They were lucky he'd brought the gear, or maybe it wasn't luck. Probably Order of Alhazred members were always prepared to break into cult hideouts and ancient crypts. Sean was too scared right now to appreciate the coolness of it, but maybe a year from now he'd think tonight had rocked. That was, if they all survived it.

They parked in the lot by the river, where faint smears of chalk still marked his summoning site. "That pentagram's what convinced me the animal killings might be Order business," O'Conaghan told Helen. "I heard about it from a friend on the Warwick force. His theory was some kids had gotten their heads messed up by heavy metal."

Which would have been a lot safer than a kid whose head was messed up by Redemption Orne. Sean stood at the broken apex of the pentagram and closed his eyes, so he could look through the Servitor's without distraction. It had scaled the falls at the mouth of the Pawtuxet and climbed into the undertrussing of the Broad Street bridge. There it hunkered down, as if content to wait while he prepared.

"Sean."

He opened his eyes. Helen stood next to him, holding out Patience Orne's #11. Dad had a handful of pastels, O'Conaghan a length of string. They were ready. His turn. He took the blue bottle and sucked down every bittersweet drop. In seconds, the ghostly overlay of Servitor-sight was gone. His mind was all his own, and he had to use it fast, before he lost it again.

The moon had been dark the night of the summoning. Tonight it was full. Its brilliance bleached out the Summer Triangle, but according to the hidden notes Helen had read, you didn't need a particular phase for the dismissing ritual. Besides, Sean welcomed the extra light. Between the moon and the head beams of O'Conaghan's Camry, Sean had no problem inscribing a new circle. The banishing pentagram was inverted, which meant the angles of Earth and Fire had to point east and the angle of Spirit west, where Sean would stand. He crab-scuttled, drawing. Dad walked alongside, handing him fresh pastel sticks as he needed them. They weren't as good for the job as sidewalk chalk—they broke easily, and the lines were thin. It wouldn't matter. The important thing was the excitement the pentagram triggered in him. O'Conaghan and Helen, Dad and Celeste—they wouldn't matter, either. He, Sean, would be alone with the gathering energy, the overflow from Azathoth the Source. He'd pull it in and then pour it out into the incantations Helen had taught him. He remembered every word: The Patience potion had made his mind clear to all horizons, north south east west, inside, out.

He straddled the downward point of Spirit and in the center of the pentagram drew the Elder Sign, a branch with five twigs,

Hand of the Elder Ones who had known enough magic to control monsters worse than the Servitor. A tingling current crept upward from his fingertips. This was the *right* Sign. The tingle proved it.

He stood up.

"All set?" Helen said.

Celeste had ducked into the Camry, where she toggled the headlights from low beam to high as if practicing, then doused the lights altogether. Only the moon was left to gleam on Helen's bat, the tines of Dad's pitchfork, and the silver cap on Gus's walking stick. O'Conaghan held the stick now, along with his flashlight.

Sean held nothing. The dismissing was much simpler than the summoning. No athame, no powders, just short incantations. As he brought his feet together in the angle of Spirit, lightning struck him again, without thunder, without pain, piercing him so that power could flow through him and from him, so that he knew he could do the ritual; of course he could—it was crazy he'd ever doubted it.

"All set," he said.

"Is the Servitor coming?"

Helen couldn't know. With the potion in him, could Sean?

He closed his eyes. Consciousness of the Servitor didn't rush at him. But inside his circle, now the fearless Sean, he understood how to mentally grip the soul-thread that joined him to his familiar. It was like a supple umbilicus, spun out from his solar plexus into the night. To restore the numbed connection, he simply had to squeeze it.

He squeezed.

*Black moon in the white sky and silver water rippling with black moonlight. The current tries to push the Servitor back over the falls, but the current is too weak to do that, too weak to slow its swim upstream.*

Head back, eyes keen, Sean looked at a spread of stars undimmed by the full moon, in which the Summer Triangle lorded it over all the rest. "It's coming up the river," he said.

A wisp of double vision clouded his eyes, white river over the stars. Was the potion already starting to wear off? Seemed like it, but that was no reason to panic. In the angle of Spirit, Sean could rely instead on the thrum of power at his core and the answering thrum that vibrated through the soles of his sneakers from the Elder Sign.

*The Servitor swims below the surface, only the ridged crown of its head cooled by air. It slithers over submerged branches.*

The branches had to belong to the downed maple in the clearing where the Servitor had torn Hrothgar apart. The clearing was near the riverside lot, so it was almost time to pay the son of a bitch back for Hrothgar and for what it had tried to do to Eddy and Dad. Anger braided new force into the energies swelling Sean. Anger was good. With it, he was going to kick the Servitor right out of the world.

Sean squeezed the soul-thread again.

*It is coming. It is here.*

Fearless Sean as he was inside his magical circle, his heart faltered when he looked toward the river and saw its lumpish, lashing form push through the reeds to the shore. Bloated with his blood, it had grown taller than any man. A ghost-movie of himself and the others, paralyzed, played over its approach. Sean closed his eyes and didn't open them again. The double vision was too confusing—better to see through the Servitor alone.

*It sees the fitful flare of human auras, smells human breath and sweat and blood. Through the air against skin and the earth under paw, it feels the pulses of its opponents accelerate. Why should it care about their weapons? They are the ones afraid, not it, and so the Servitor slouches toward them without hurry, clicking its claws on the blacktop. True, the summoner is stronger within the pentagram, but along the soul-thread their minds come together like magnets of opposing polarities, and which mind must be the stronger in that meeting?*

The meeting came on too fast. Sean fell back along the soul-thread, yielding even as he commanded: *Come here, into the center!*

*The Servitor walks straight into the circle and crouches, its haunches obscuring the Elder Sign. Let the summoner cage it in space—it can still reach into his deepest sanctuary.*

Eyes open, eyes closed, no difference. *Suddenly all is black, and in the blackness he and the Servitor are together as they were in the tomb, speeding through a void that either of them might shape, only Sean doesn't know how. . . .*

"Sean. Say it. Say the spell."

*That voice is far outside the void, which thickens and drowns the voice. The void is nothingness solidifying into nerve, coalescing into brain, the Servitor's mind reaching up to envelop his and drag it down until Sean drops into green light in a three-sunned sky, under which the shoggoth-sea sings and the Black Man walks in his palace of living crystal, waiting.*

# 29

In Eddy's aluminum bat, Helen had inherited a weapon proven against the Servitor; clutching it as if ready to swing for the fences, she joined the others around the pentagram. O'Conaghan stood, by choice or apt chance, at the angle of Earth, Stability. Ditto the aptness of Jeremy at Water, Emotion and Intuition. Of the two angles left for Helen, Air (Intelligence and Art) pointed toward the river, the direction from which the Servitor would come, and so she was forced to park at Fire, Courage and Daring. A good joke, when what would have suited her better was an angle of Fear and Trembling. Fire should have been Marvell's, but Marvell was still miles high over the Atlantic. As for Spirit, Sean's angle, the ritual prescribed it. Maybe that certainty of place comforted him, or maybe his composure had come from the empty bottle in her backpack.

No, it wasn't from the bottle. Sean had simply calmed down when he'd drunk the last of Patience Orne's #11. A qualitative change hadn't come until he'd formally entered his magical circle. In that one step, he'd gone from desperate determination to precocious assurance. The new Sean stood as poised as the statue of a Greek hero, his face bleached in the moonlight, his lips relaxed into a smile. The longer he stood like that, arrogantly unbudging, the more Helen wanted to shake him back to normal. From the way Jeremy shifted his American Gothic pitchfork, he shared her uneasiness concerning the new Sean.

The crickets singing in the woods fell silent, and the mosquitoes that had whined around her head disappeared. Something wicked their way came, but she felt the pricking of dread in her nape, not in her thumbs. Helen watched the black flow of the river, heard the plash of stealthy swimming, smelled a now-familiar stink.

The Servitor rose from the water a giant, grown a couple heads taller than O'Conaghan. A roaring charge would have been less unnerving than the way it ambled, nonchalant, toward its destruction. Could it be stupid enough to go willingly to the center of the pentagram, or was the new Sean so masterful it couldn't resist his mute command? Either, neither, the Servitor crossed the angle of Air and entered the trap. Atop the Elder Sign, it squatted, forepaws dangling from knees, furnace eyes banked as if to conserve their fire, as still as Sean, silent, another statue.

And now? There was only the incantation left to do, but the Sean-statue didn't stir or speak.

Prompt him—that was her job. "Sean," she said. "Say it. Say the spell."

In the space between two breaths, the first breath deep, the second a harsh gasp, precociously mature Sean turned kid again. His eyes widened as if he'd never seen the Servitor before, or as if he was seeing it one time too many. His hands opened and closed like panicked starfish. Then they fell to his sides, slack like his head, which lolled back so that his unblinking stare fixed the moon-faded stars.

"Sean," Helen whispered. Jeremy shouted it: "Sean! Do you remember what to say?"

No response, unless the flare of fire in the Servitor's eyes was one.

Helen watched horror lengthen Jeremy's face, grimness harden O'Conaghan's. She looked back at the miraculously upright rag doll that was neither old nor new Sean. Sean had vacated the premises, leaving no forwarding address, and, after the silence of their contest, the Servitor hissed its triumph.

"What the hell's going on?"

O'Conaghan answered Jeremy: "Sean's possessed again. We've got to disrupt the connection."

"How?"

O'Conaghan flicked on his flashlight and pointed it at the Camry and Celeste. A signal: The Camry's high beams lanced the magical circle, crossing the white spear of the flashlight. Caught in the dual thrusts, the Servitor hunched and snarled, but Sean didn't blink, or murmur, or twitch.

Helen dashed a wrist over her tearing eyes. "It's not enough!" she called to O'Conaghan.

He hefted Gus's walking stick. "So we give it all we've got, understand? Together, on three."

Attack it? The Servitor had put on a lot of bulk since it had effortlessly swatted aside her lion-tamer chair. Eddy's bat seemed to have bulked up, too. Helen doubted she could lift it, much less swing.

"Ready?"

Jeremy obviously was. Lips peeled back in a snarl to match the Servitor's, he aimed his pitchfork dead at its belly. He must have been longing for this chance since he'd realized his son's tormentor was a solid threat. Unfortunately, its solidity was fluid and its life beyond their reach, and there had to be something they could do besides wear themselves out on its protean flesh.

"One," O'Conaghan said.

There was nothing else *she* could do. She'd used up Geldman's gift and blown her scanty Mythos lore. Marvell had tried to prepare her. He was flying to them. But she wasn't ready, and he would come too late.

"Two."

Though Jeremy stepped toward the Servitor, he was no longer looking at it. He was staring at Sean, his snarl erased by a grimace of grief.

Yes, Helen had to hurl herself at the Servitor. But Jeremy—

"Three," O'Conaghan said, at the same moment Helen yelled, "Wait!"

The two men froze, their faces thrown into grotesque chiaroscuro by the glare of high beams and flash. "Jeremy," she said. "You've got to talk Sean back, like Eddy was trying to do."

"That didn't work!"

"You're his father. Call him back, and we—we'll go for the Servitor."

Before O'Conaghan could nod agreement, Jeremy had dropped the pitchfork and run to Sean.

Helen lifted the weighty bat. She from Fire, O'Conaghan from Earth, they moved in on the Servitor, which reared to full height to meet them.

~⚶~

The three black suns float over the palace, suffusing it with strange radiance. Fundamentally, it's a vast crystal pyramid budding off smaller crystals: blocks, and more pyramids, and weirder units like many-faced gamer dice, all of them skewed as if by extension into planes that Sean can't fully perceive. In the palace, in everything here, there are tantalizing hints of *more*.

He runs along the obsidian shore. Enormous shoggoth-waves arch over his head without breaking. Pseudopod wavelets lap his feet. He should be afraid, but he isn't. He should be fighting to burst the bubble of Servitor-will that keeps him in this alien place, but he can't remember why. To dismiss the Servitor? To be free of it and its Master? Now that his struggle's done, he realizes that the freedom to plod through a normal life is nothing compared to an invitation to the palace. The shoggoths are no threat. They're an honor guard—their song tells him so, direct to his nerves.

He reaches the steps to the projecting terrace, each a yard high, steps for titans. No problem—he has little weight here, and he bounds up, eager. The terrace shivers. Then, tenderly, it folds around his feet and legs, body and head, and delivers him to the palace through an inward-spiraling chute, like a reverse birth.

They have gone, the shadows that were dancing the first time Sean saw the palace. He's alone in their ballroom, an echoing emptiness with walls and ceiling too far off to see in the dim violet light seeping out of the floor. It's glass, the floor, or colorless crystal, or unmelting ice, he can't tell which. Through the smooth transparency, he can see what emits the light: spiky, prismatic spheres like diatoms puffed to the size of basketballs. The diatoms are aware of him, too. They swarm to the place where he stands until they pack themselves into an unbroken carpet of bioluminescence. Their concentrated glow is like a spotlight under his feet; Sean flinches, expecting a burn, but the glow carries no heat.

With the diatoms beneath him, the rest of the ballroom is impenetrable shadow. Far off, a foot falls on the glassy floor. Spotlighted for examination, encircled by the dark, Sean can only wait for whatever approaches, and that he can only wait is fair, right? The Black Man has waited a long time for him.

Diatoms stream from Sean to make a walkway for their Master. His sandaled feet are the first Sean sees of him. Next comes the white linen hem of his robe, next the fall of its pleats from an enameled harness, the swing of bare arms, the sheen of bare chest. Last to emerge from the shadows are the austere planes of a narrow face and the sleek gold of one of those tall Egyptian crowns.

The man isn't dark skinned like an African. He's the impossible gleaming black of onyx. He's the guy from Helen's window, for sure, and the falcon-winged Angel of the Summoning, and the golden-eyed pursuer who saved Dad and Eddy in the cemetery hollow.

The Black Man steps into the spotlight and speaks in the smooth, low, absolutely reasonable voice that Sean remembers from his first foray into the three-sunned world: *I know you, Sean. Do you know me?*

*I think so.*

*Name me.*

Though names have power, he has to say it: *Nyarlathotep.*

*That's one of my names. What do you want from me?*

The question throws Sean. He gives the first answer that comes to him, which should be true yet isn't: *Nothing. I don't even want what you've already sent.*

The Black Man's lips twist, wringing the softness from his smile. *You asked for the Servitor, Sean. You even gave your blood for it.*

*I didn't know any better.*

*You did know. In the magical circle, you believed, you desired, or I wouldn't have given.*

He wanted the Servitor. Is that the truth he's been running from? There may be a worse truth, though, and the worse truth is

*You want more, Sean.*

Under the Black Man's gentle-again smile, Sean realizes the ugly futility of lying to him. *Yes,* he says, and then he smiles, too.

⤚✦⤙

**Though** the Elder Sign confined the Servitor to the center of the pentagram, it didn't much hamper it. For one thing, Helen and O'Conaghan had to keep carrying the fight to it. For another, it remained elastically agile. O'Conaghan was agile, too, despite his height. He laid into the Servitor with walking stick and flashlight and parried its claws so skillfully Helen wondered whether the Providence police trained for staff fighting, and if she had time to wonder that, she wasn't doing her share of the fighting. Her climb up the back stairs had been a fluke, not courage but ignorance. Enlightened now, afraid of her fear, everything in her screamed, *Run.*

One thing kept her at the angle of Fire, and that was the way Jeremy stood rocking Sean's limp yet upright body, no hand-on-the-cradle rocking but a manic jerking that snapped the boy's head from side to side. Then Jeremy seemed to realize what he was doing. He pulled Sean tight against him and whispered into his ear. What? What could Jeremy possibly say to drag his son back to them? It was none of her business. Her business was to help O'Conaghan, any and all the gods, damn it.

Run then, but in!

Helen circled to the Servitor's back and made a dash at it. Before she could lift Eddy's bat, it wheeled. Raptor claws swung so close to her face that one nicked the tip of her nose. An inch closer and they'd have taken the whole nose off. That would have saved her from the sting of its heated stench, but she didn't give it another shot. She backpedaled fast, out of range. When the Servitor rounded on O'Conaghan, she ran in low and slashed at the backs of its knees. No Achilles weakness there, but its counter-swing did go over her this time.

Self-congratulations were premature. Before she could get away, it seized the back of her shirt and hoisted her into the air. Helen jammed the bat between its jaws and kicked at its midsection, but it didn't let go until O'Conaghan redoubled the ferocity of his attack. She dropped and rolled out of the pentagram. The bat! In her fall she'd lost it, and now the Servitor snatched it up and hurled it at the Camry, shattering the windshield. If Celeste screamed, the blat of the horn drowned her out. She had to be all right, though, because the strobing of the headlights continued.

The headlights and O'Conaghan's flash were a mixed blessing. They infuriated the Servitor. They also intermittently blinded
Helen. Nor was O'Conaghan immune to the confusion—finally
he dodged the wrong way. The Servitor struck the flashlight
from his grip, then seized the walking stick, snapped it in two,
and clubbed him with the pieces. O'Conaghan went down.

Suddenly Helen could hear Jeremy gabbling the incantation
he'd learned along with Sean. The Camry's horn had stilled,
the strobing stopped. Celeste was out of the car, bag in hand,
running into the pentagram. Already the Servitor reached
for her.

No thought. No time. Helen sprinted to the Servitor and
grabbed handfuls of the tentacles that sprouted from either side
of its spine. She gave them a vicious twist. It reared, yowling.
Hidden mouths opened in the wormy growths, spewing caustic
ooze at her, but Helen held on. Around the convulsed bulk of the
thing, she glimpsed Celeste dragging O'Conaghan to safety. As
the Servitor began spinning in trapped circles, Helen let go and
was herself flung out of the pentagram, where she landed atop
the doused flashlight, a gouge of pain in her hip. Her elbow barely
missed the tines of Jeremy's pitchfork.

Jeremy: "To you, Lord Azathoth, who has shown me favor."

"To you, Lord Azathoth."

The second voice, slow and slurred, was Sean's. Helen scram-
bled to a crouch and saw him writhing in Jeremy's arms, saw
him open his eyes, open his mouth. Released from the torment
of light and the swatting of human flies, the Servitor bent over
Sean. Sean's eyes rolled up. His body went limp again.

O'Conaghan-Earth was out of the contest. Sean-Spirit and
Jeremy-Water swayed beneath the Servitor. Only Fire was left,
with the flashlight under her. Helen wrenched it free. There were
no switches on the long black barrel. Well, did a wand have a
switch? The thing was magical, O'Conaghan had said, but he could
use it because he was a paramagician. Marvell was a paramagi-

cian. Uncle John had been one, and Great-Grandfather Henry, and she, Helen, could be one, too. Geldman believed it. Orne believed it. Forget Orne, but how—

She clutched the barrel in both hands and willed the flash to go on. It pulsed. She ground her teeth and willed harder, imagining the flood of light she wanted. A flicker played behind the thick lens. Another flicker. A beam! Helen shot it at the Servitor. It twisted toward her, but her beam was much weaker than the one O'Conaghan had produced, and when the Servitor saw that it gave a growl eloquent of contempt and turned back to Sean and Jeremy.

Her beam failed altogether. Helen dropped the flashlight. Eddy's bat was in the Camry, too far away. Gus's stick was broken. That left the pitchfork. Helen groped for it. She climbed its shaft to her feet, carried it into the pentagram, stepped between Sean and the Servitor. It bared its needle-teeth to the roots, ready for her. Was she afraid of her fear? No, her fear was pure now, her mind was clear, and so, bracing the shaft under her arm, Helen rammed the long iron tines into the monster's belly and herself into its sucking embrace.

❧

**What** *more do you want?* the Black Man asks.

The diatom light encloses them in a violet dome. Within the dome, Sean wants everything.

*Everything, to own for yourself?*

That isn't right. *Not to own, just to know.*

It's a good answer—the Black Man's nod approves it. *Then our mutual friend was right about you.*

*Mr. Geldman?*

*Geldman isn't my friend. But Redemption Orne is.*

*Did you send the Reverend after me?*

*No. In seeking you, he meant to serve himself. However, through him, I've come to know you, and that's all that matters.*

Something moves in the infinite blackness outside their light-dome, perhaps the air itself: a slide and whisper of disturbed molecules. *Why, though? What can I be to you?*

*You are one who wants to know everything. There's a lust in the wanting that grows upon itself, always more powerful and exquisite. I can set you on the path of knowing.*

The air-whisper grows louder. Violet light flares as the diatoms bunch tighter under the floor, under their feet. *What will you want in return?*

*Everything.*

That shouldn't sound like a good bargain, but here, within the dome, it makes perfect sense.

What doesn't make sense is how that air-whisper turns into Dad's voice, rippling the dome and making the Black Man waver like a reflection on water: *Come on. You've got to help me here.*

The voice doesn't touch the Black Man's serenity. *Accept me, Sean, and I'll give you what I've given Redemption Orne. Life without end or age, an infinite path to travel, and I will bless your apprenticeship with Orne, my servant.*

*Got to pull together, Kit. You remember being Kit, don't you? How your mom used to say it: "You're my brave little Kit." Remember? You've got to remember.*

Mom used to say? Mom's dead, or is she? Perhaps she lives a new life out there in the infinite dark—the Black Man can tell him the truth of it. Yet it's not Mom who calls him Kit right now; it's Dad, after a terrible long time. Dad is certainly alive, by the river with Helen Arkwright and Detective O'Conaghan and Aunt Cel. The Servitor's there, too. It must be fighting—

*Perhaps it will kill them,* the Black Man says.

*You can stop it. You stopped it before.*

The Black Man shrugs. Light courses along the gold links and enamel scales of his harness, a cascade of winks. *It served me to oblige you at that moment. I didn't want you distracted by the deaths of your friends.*

*So stop it again! You can do it no problem; the Servitor's yours.*

*No, it's yours, Sean. Besides, you're the one who cares.*

The diatoms bunch and vibrate under the glass floor; their agitation becomes Sean's, or his causes theirs, or perhaps the agitation's mutual. *You don't care?*

*About your father and friends? No. They'll rather oppose me than otherwise. However, you may care for them, if you still like. Go back to them. I won't stop you.*

If he still likes? If he still cares?

*To you, Lord Azathoth, who has shown me favor.* Dad's voice. The incantation.

The incantation. The dismissing spell.

*And to your Soul, Nyarlathotep.*

What kind of Soul doesn't care if people get hurt or killed? This one, gold eyed, crowned, only looking like a man because he wants to. No, because *it* wants to.

*Kit, come back.*

He reaches for the sliding air that is Dad's voice. The extension of his arm shatters the violet dome, and the sliding air rushes in upon the Black Man, who smiles as gently as ever, unperturbed by his own dissolution. *You'll remember me, Sean,* he says.

The dome is actually a bubble in the Servitor's mind, its prison for Sean, but now the bubble bursts, annihilating the palace, the shoggoth-sea, the black suns in the green sky. He

stood clutched against Dad's chest, with Dad's lips by his ear, muttering words Sean knew by heart, because he'd studied them once, long ago, tonight. He mouthed them after Dad, then said them aloud: "To you, Lord Azathoth—"

The Servitor loomed over them, blotting out the Triangled sky. Sean saw both it and, through its eyes, himself and Dad, insignificant. It tried to wrap him in another bubble of its mind. He saw his own eyes go blank. He felt the words clog in his throat.

Then he felt a terrific burst of pain, but it wasn't his, and it knocked him free. Helen had speared the Servitor with something, and now she struggled in its forelimbs as it molded itself around her, trying to swallow her whole into its body.

"Sean! Say it now!"

He broke out of Dad's arms and staggered. He couldn't get the right words out; there was no magic left in him—

The reason for that was the unmarked blacktop under his feet. Dad had dragged him out of the magical circle.

Sean croaked: "Put me where I was."

Dad hustled him forward. His feet entered the angle of Spirit, and it was like before but different, the lightning inrush of power but no fearless Sean, no cocky Sean who could do anything. If he could do this one thing—he would do this one thing!—it would be enough.

He spit the incantation out:

"To you, Lord Azathoth, who has shown me favor, and to your Soul, Nyarlathotep! Take back the creature of your sending. Let it serve you again, the masters of all."

The Servitor shrieked, swelled, thinned, like a cloud of gas escaping from compression. Helen hung suspended in its center.

"Blood made the promise! Blood sped my petition! Blood sealed the bargain! Now end it, return!"

In one instant, the Servitor-cloud burst outward, rolling over lot and river, swamping the casting factory, towering to the Summer Triangle at the zenith of the night sky. In the next instant, it collapsed on itself, solidifying again until what had been Servitor became Master, the Black Man stepping out of the center of the pentagram with Helen in his arms. He lowered her to the ground, and with the third instant came his silent explosion into sparkling powders, gray and yellow, acrid and sulfurous, Zeph and Aghar. They drifted toward the ground, where Helen coughed and gasped.

The magical circle was too bright. A car's headlights lit it. Outside the pentagram, Sean heard Celeste's voice, and Detective O'Conaghan's. So they were alive, too.

Sean stepped back out of the angle of Spirit, breaking the circuit of magical energy. Dad grabbed him as he keeled over, and Sean let his eyes close, to darkness, nothing else, alone again, one, himself.

# 30

**Like** the day in Arkham when it had all started, the Sunday after the dismissing ritual was perfect, the only clouds harmless white puffs on the horizon. Sean sat with Eddy on the front steps of Celeste's house and stealthily probed the crook of his left elbow. The witch's teat, withered to a bump smaller than a mosquito bite, was his personal souvenir from the Servitor. He'd been lucky. Gus was still hobbling around on his sprained ankle. O'Conaghan had needed twenty stitches in his scalp. But crushed against the impaled Servitor, drenched in its corrosive ichor, Helen Arkwright had gotten the worst of the fight: third-degree burns on her chest and abdomen, her arms and hands. Celeste had been about to take her to the ER when Professor Marvell had arrived, along with an Order of Alhazred first-aid kit. One thing in it was a pot of ointment labeled "Cybele's #1." Helen had nodded as if she knew who Cybele was, and a couple applications of the grass-scented ointment had improved her burns so much that Celeste had canceled the ER trip.

Marvell was going to drive Helen home after Gus's big celebration dinner. It bummed Sean to think of her leaving, but he stuck on a big smile when she came out on the porch with Marvell. "Hello, Eddy," Marvell said. "I hope you're coming to the dinner?"

"You bet, Professor."

"Excellent. Do you mind if we talk to Sean alone for a few minutes?"

Eddy got up to go without protest—she'd already had a private talk with Marvell and Helen, which she'd breezily labeled a half-debriefing and half-counseling session, but Sean had sensed she'd been grateful for their attention. Even so, thirty seconds after she'd run into her house Sean saw her spying from the bay window of her office. Too bad the conference convened under the porch roof, out of her sight. Helen and Marvell shared the swing. Dad came out and leaned against the railing. That left the wicker armchair for Sean. He took it, a little antsy. The armchair didn't look like a witness stand, but somehow it felt like one.

Marvell clapped his hands on his knees. That was the gavel. But in his polo and khakis, he didn't look like a judge. He looked like the kind of professor you'd want as your advisor, old enough for you to take him seriously, young enough to still be cool in a Dad-ish sort of way. Gray streaked his dark brown hair at the temples, which Eddy found weirdly hot, and she was a total fangirl about his voice: deep and precise, with a classy Boston accent Gus called Back Bay. "Sean," Marvell said. "You've shown enormous magical potential during this Servitor business. Have you thought about what you want to do with your talent?"

Sean waited for Dad to answer for him: Sean wanted to forget all about magic.

Amazingly, Dad kept his mouth shut. He looked at Sean, as neutral as Marvell and Helen, or trying to be. All right, so that muscle in his jaw twitched—he probably couldn't help that.

With Dad staying out of it, Sean said, "I'm not sure. I mean, I told the Black Man I wanted to know everything. Is it messed up, wondering about magic and other dimensions and stuff?"

"No, Sean," Marvell said. "I'd be the last one to tell you that."

"Plus when I did the summoning, I felt great. It was this huge buzz. But the buzz is what made me cocky enough to call the blood-spawn. I didn't mean to, not until the last minute."

Marvell nodded. "I believe you, Sean. And from what you've told us about the ritual, Nyarlathotep had a lot to do with you summoning the blood-spawn instead of the aether-newt. Like Orne said, he wanted to give you a more rigorous test. You see, Nyarlathotep's own power appears to be enhanced by any energy captured and used by allied magicians, as if it cycles back to him through their psychic connections. So it's to his benefit to find out who the most powerful magicians are, or might be, and to pursue them."

Sean caught himself fingering the teat bump. He pulled his hand away. "When he wants someone, does he always get him?"

"No," Helen said. She'd rested her bandaged arms on her thighs; now she leaned forward on them, gingerly. "Nyarlathotep must have wanted Solomon Geldman, and Geldman doesn't serve him. He won't give up on you after one try, though; that's what I'm afraid of. Orne hasn't given up, either. His e-mail this morning proves it."

The e-mail she meant was in Sean's back pocket, folded as small as Geldman's dream-fortune had been. He'd already gnawed its message into his memory: *Sean, I can't apologize enough for what's happened. I meant you and yours no harm. In time we'll meet face-to-face, and you'll know me better. Remember what you are—at least you can't doubt your nature now, or the nature of the worlds. R. Orne.*

And *You'll remember me,* the Black Man had said. Oh yeah. Like Sean could forget. The real question was, should he *pretend* to forget? If he scraped together a huge heap of "normal" stuff and shoved it in front of this new door that had opened for him, maybe he could make a barricade. How long the barricade would

SUMMONED 315

stand was another real question, and the third real question was whether the force that broke the barricade would come from outside the door or inside, from him. "I'm not sure what I want to do," he said again.

Marvell cleared his throat. "Whatever you decide, the Order will do its best to protect you and track down Orne. Detective O'Conaghan will keep an eye out here. And I've given your father my private number. If you have any questions, call."

Sean saw Dad pat a back pocket, so Dad had a paper talisman, too. "Thanks a lot, Professor."

"You can try to stay away from magic," Marvell went on. "That won't be easy now that you've had a taste. Or you can develop your talent, in which case you need teachers."

"Like the Reverend?"

Dad shifted on the railing—the loose section creaked.

"I guess we can say Orne's applied for the job," Marvell said dryly. "I wouldn't recommend him. But I could help you with the basics, set up a private tutorial while you're still in high school. Afterwards, there's a program at MU for training magicians and paramagicians."

"You can get a wizard degree?"

"Wizards don't need academic credentials. This program's under the auspices of Arcane Studies and the History Department, which confer the, ah, official degrees."

*You can't doubt your nature now.* Which was what, wanting to know everything? That wasn't such a fun feeling anymore. It was edgy, nervous, and yet that only made it stronger. Again Sean looked at Dad, who *had* to say no to wizard lessons. Only Dad stayed quiet, like he'd actually let Sean make a decision like this. No way. Was there?

He turned to Helen. "You've got talent, too. What are you going to do?"

She picked bits of lint from the gauze around her wrists, but when she raised her head she looked Sean straight in the eye. "I'm going to learn everything the Order can teach me. After the Servitor, I can't get caught again flying the plane upside down."

Marvell laughed like this was a private joke.

Dad cracked a smile, like he was in on it, too.

"Besides," Helen said. "I'm Professor Marvell's assistant at the Archives. Looks like magic's part of that job, even though it isn't in the *official* position description."

More laughter. Sean joined in. But then he had to ask Dad straight out, "Would you let me? Study magic?"

Dad's jaw spasmed. "I'm not sure, Sean. The professor and Helen make some good arguments for it. But after what we've just gone through, no one here can deny the dangers. You least of all. Right?"

"Right, for sure."

"Still. What you and I were talking about last night. How we both had this sense your mom was different. Saw differently. How you said you could feel her paintings vibrate."

It had been the longest talk they'd had in years, out on the back porch after everyone else had gone to bed. "They hummed," Sean said.

"Hummed, yeah. Well, I believe it now, that you *did* feel that. Mr. Geldman told Helen magic comes to you from your mom, and I think Helen reached that conclusion earlier, on her own." Dad looked at Helen, and after a moment she nodded. "So it makes sense you'd be the one to pick up on Kate's magic the strongest, since you're like her."

It was happening way too often these days, Sean's throat closing up on him. He shrugged, and luckily Dad went on without waiting for more: "And if Kate had magic, and it's part of what she gave you, it can't be a bad thing. Not by its nature, know what I mean?"

"We think magic is neutral," Marvell said quietly. "How the magician shapes it is what makes it good or bad, so to speak."

Dad gave his hair a brief savaging. "That makes sense, too. Anyway. I'll have to think about your offer, Professor, the tutorial thing. And Sean, you'll have to convince me and our new friends you could handle it. With school coming up, I guess the tutorial couldn't start until next summer?"

"Next summer would work," Marvell said.

Helen winked at Sean, but with Dad watching him he could only smile back.

"Sean," Dad said.

Sean looked up into a face dead serious but not the least bit pissed anymore. "Here's the thing," Dad said. "Whatever we decide about your magic, run away from it or take the next step, you've got to know I'm with you."

So Dad didn't say the baby nickname; he stopped himself at the last second, like he was embarrassed to use it, or thought Sean would be embarrassed. But Sean heard the name anyway: Kit. *I'm with you, Kit.*

He gave Dad this lame nod, then had a good fake coughing fit before he turned to Marvell. "So it's okay if we can't tell you what we want to do yet, Professor?"

"It's fine, Sean. Take your time."

"Speaking of time," Helen put in. "Dinner must be about ready."

They all got up, but the honk of a horn made them turn to the street. Joe-Jack's van pulled up, and Beowulf jumped out with a squirming chocolate Lab puppy in his arms. Sean ran down the steps to meet him. "Jesus, Beo! When'd you get him?"

"This morning. Only it's a her. Dad wants to call her Wealhtheow, but that totally sucks!"

Joe-Jack came up, grinning. "Hey, the only other female in Beowulf is Grendel's mother. Want to call her that?"

Sean didn't want to upend Joe-Jack's world, but come on. "Maybe you could pick a name from something else?"

"All right. How about Brunnhilde?"

"I want 'Lucy'," Beowulf said.

Having spied the new action from above, Eddy ran out to join the party, Brutus at her heels. While the pug distracted everyone by pouncing on their feet, Sean took the puppy and carried her onto the porch. Marvell had gone inside. Dad and Helen stood at the top of the steps. "What would you call her?" Sean asked Helen.

She stroked the puppy's soft ears and got licked all the way up to her elbow. "Lucy," she said. She looked up at Sean and smiled. "Nice and ordinary."

Dad yelled a dinner invite to Joe-Jack and Beowulf. Beowulf recaptured the puppy as everyone piled into the house. Sean ended up the last one on the porch, with Eddy.

"So?" she said. "What was your secret conference about?"

Like there might be more spies in the neighborhood than Eddy, Sean made a big deal of going to the railing and peering around. The roof of the house across the street caught his eye, for no other reason than the way the late-afternoon sun had turned it this crazy mellow red, with an achingly blue sky coming down to meet it.

"Give, Sean!"

"It wasn't much," Sean told her. "They just want me to become a wizard, that's all."

# Acknowledgments

The people behind this book are many. Way back in time, my father spun tales of Irish elements, while my more practical mother supplied the slate-blue Royal portable I lugged through my apprentice years.

My first auditors and the actors in so many dramatizations of my juvenilia were niece Amy and nephews Tom and John and Bob and David. Special thanks to niece Buffy and nephew Sean for badgering me into telling them the whooooole story of *The Lord of the Rings* every time they visited. It was an invaluable exercise in epic structure and characterization!

Gretchen Robinson led a great writing seminar at the Attleboro Public Library, which led to the creation of my writing group, Interstate Writers. Thanks to them all, especially Ken!

Jared Millet, whom I met during a National Novel Writing Month, was one of the first to critique *Summoned,* and thanks must go to his sensibility and eagle eye.

James Frenkel acquired *Summoned* for Tor and did a fantastic edit from the finest points of grammar to the subtlest of big-picture themes. His suggestions have greatly enriched the underlying themes of the series. My editor, Miriam Weinberg, has added many fresh insights, and her enthusiasm is a constant in-spiration.

Craig Tenney of Harold Ober Associates is simply my dream agent. He is also a telepath, because every time I needed encour-agement and a nudge, he sensed it and was there with a call or e-mail. I think I traded in most of my good-karma stamps when I found him, but it was a trade-in more than worth it!

And thanks far from least to Charles Arouth, my spiritual guide. He kept me going through many a down period with sage advice, such as "If you can think it, you can do it."

I could always think it. With the help and encouragement of all above, I've finally done it.

Breath taken. Let's do it again!